Praise for

The Map That Leads to You

"Will strike a chord with fans of Nicholas Sparks's sweeping and sentimental tales." —*Booklist*

"Readers who love romance novels with a bittersweet twist will cling to every word . . . Recommended for fans of Kristin Hannah and Nicholas Sparks." —*School Library Journal*

"An incredible story of friendship, romance, and secrets." —*Metropolitan Luxe*

"Monninger's writing spoke to the part of my soul that yearns to be a free spirit. I fell in love with this story again and again." —Jamie McGuire

"A beautiful novel about the joys of friendship, the risk of romantic love, and the power of a secret to unravel a future that appears to offer every possibility of happiness. This is a story about the people who make us who we are, what we keep and lose along the way, and who we decide to become when we design the map of our lives, leaving an open path for surprise and wonder." —Adriana Trigiani

The Map That Leads to You

J. P. Monninger

St. Martin's Griffin
New York

THE MAP THAT LEADS TO YOU. Copyright © 2017 by Temple Hill, LLC. All rights reserved. Printed in the United States of America. For information, address St. Martin's Press, 175 Fifth Avenue, New York, N.Y. 10010.

www.stmartins.com

Designed by Kathryn Parise

Map © Archive Photos/Getty Images

The Library of Congress has catalogd the hardcover edition as follows:

Names: Monninger, Joseph, author.
Title: The map that leads to you / J.P. Monninger.
Description: First edition. | New York : St. Martin's Press, 2017.
Identifiers: LCCN 2017002671 | ISBN 9781250060761 (hardcover) | ISBN 9781250153166 (international edition, sold outside the U.S., subject to rights availability) | ISBN 9781466866560 (ebook)
Subjects: LCSH: Man-woman relationships—Fiction. | Young women—Fiction. | BISAC: FICTION / Contemporary Women. | FICTION / Coming of Age. | GSAFD: Love stories.
Classification: LCC PS3563.O526 M35 2017 | DDC 813/.54—dc23
LC record available at https://lccn.loc.gov/2017002671

ISBN 978-1-250-06077-8 (trade paperback)

Our books may be purchased in bulk for promotional, educational, or business use. Please contact your local bookseller or the Macmillan Corporate and Premium Sales Department at 1-800-221-7945, extension 5442, or by email at MacmillanSpecialMarkets@macmillan.com.

First St. Martin's Griffin Edition: June 2018

10 9 8 7 6 5 4 3 2 1

For Andrea and Christina

Acknowledgments

....

The *Map That Leads to You* has benefited from the kindness and work of many people, and no appreciation I outline here can adequately thank all those who had a hand in its eventual publication and in its journey to its readers. As always, my agents, Andrea Cirillo and Christina Hogrebe, encouraged me and supported me throughout the long composition of this novel. Andrea and Christina changed my life for the better from the day I met them. The team at the Jane Rotrosen Agency works with quiet grace in every aspect of my writing life, and I send out my thanks and my sincere appreciation to everyone there.

Thanks and gratitude to Jennifer Enderlin, publisher at St. Martin's Press, and to all her wonderful staff. Thanks, also, to Marty Bowen and Peter Harris and Annalie Gernert at Temple Hill. Peter Harris advised me and read pages and made suggestions and kept me laughing. He has a keen eye for fiction and dramatic construction and this novel benefited more than I can say from his contribution.

To anyone involved in this publication I haven't yet met or have inadvertently forgotten, forgive me and accept my gratitude. More than any other novel I've written, this was a collaborative process. I also want to thank Plymouth State University, our lovely little college in the White Mountains of New Hampshire, for giving me the freedom to write the books I need to write. Plymouth State University has been my teaching home for more than a quarter century, and I am grateful to the administration and students for allowing me time to pursue a writing life.

Finally, thanks to my family and friends and to my old, old faithful dog, who waits patiently for her afternoon walk while I fiddle with pages she will never understand. I have biscuits in my pockets, I promise.

I should like to bury something precious in every place where I've been happy and then, when I was old and ugly and miserable, I could come back and dig it up and remember.

—Evelyn Waugh, *Brideshead Revisited*

Prologue

....

Commencement Day

It's your mom, of all people, who gets the perfect photograph of
you and your two best friends the day you graduate from Amherst College in Massachusetts. Your mom is famously lousy with
a camera and hates to be called on to snap a picture, but, channel-
ing some final mommy voodoo before full adulthood sweeps you
away forever, your mother comes through when all the vast lightning storm of flash shots falls short. Remarkably, it's not one of the
thousand shots that the parents demand, not one on the way to
the stage, not one of you, all three—young, the world ahead, the
gowns lifting in a soft New England breeze, the green Amherst
oaks aching into the sun, your fake diplomas raised above your
head—that are a must at commencements everywhere. None of
those. Not the one with your parents, or the one with your friend
Constance's little girl cousins who are dressed sweetly in sundresses.
Not the degree-conferral shot, not the staged handshake with the
college president, not the final moment when people chuck their

stupid mortarboards into the air and almost blind people with their whirling square Frisbees.

It's something both smaller and bigger. It's a profile shot, all three of you sitting in folding chairs, your faces tilted up slightly to hear the speakers, the sun making you squint the tiniest bit. People pretend to be unaware of a photographer, of an about-to-be-snapped photo, but in this instance it is real. Your mother got the shot like a ninja, you still don't know how, but it captures Constance first. She is blond and hopeful, her expression so kind, so innocent, that you feel a swell in your throat every time you look at it. Then Amy, dark and broody, but the center of everything, the fun, the joke, the loud talk and the wild energy, the screw-yous, and the up-yours, and the sweet, always-kindness that rests behind her eyes. Yes, she is looking up, too.

And then you. You look at that girl, your image, a dozen times, a hundred times, to see what it is that lives in that face. Who is this girl, this economics major, this two-time summer intern, the girl with a fancy, lucrative job as an investment banker waiting for her at the end of summer? You hardly recognize her; she had changed over these last four years, grown deeper, perhaps wiser, a woman in place of a girl. In the same instant, it is unbearable to look at her, because you see her vulnerability, her shortcomings, her struggles. You are the third in a line of three friends, the one who gets things done, the one who is a bit obsessive about control, the one who will always be sent to herd Amy to wherever she needs to be corralled, to lend substance to Constance's ethereal drive for beauty. Your color is halfway between Constance's blondness and Amy's wolf hair, the final ingredient in whatever combination you three form. You are bone to their cartilage, gravity to their flight.

One moment in four years. It captures everything. In a matter of weeks, you will all be in Europe for what used to be called the grand tour; you will be traveling and kicking ass all across the old countries, but for now, in this instant, you are on the verge of everything. And your mother saw it, and caught it, and you cannot glance even once at that picture without knowing your three hearts are linked together and that in a crazy world each of you has two things—two pure and limitless things—that she can count on for today and every day forward.

It is the last great minute before he walks into your life, but you don't know that, can't know. Later, though, you will try to imagine where he was in this exact instant, when he had turned and started to travel toward you, you to him, and how the world around both of you took no notice. Your life would not be the same, but that was all waiting, all up in the air, all fate and chance and inevitability. Jack, your Jack, your one great love.

Part One

Amsterdam

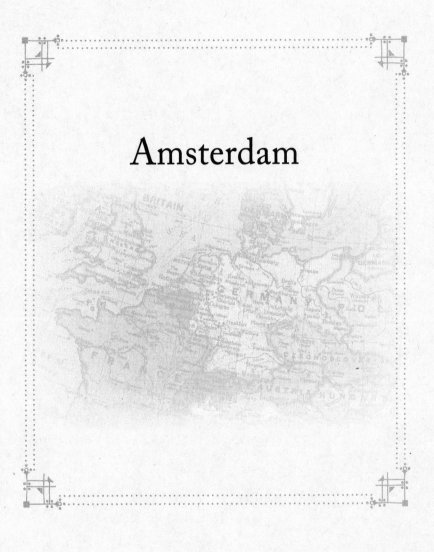

1

....

Here's the thing: the rest of it wouldn't have happened if the train to Amsterdam hadn't been crowded. It was that kind of obnoxious crowded, with everyone greedy for space, everyone annoyed that the train was overbooked and jammed, so I kept my head down once I had a seat, and I tried not to look up. I was reading *The Sun Also Rises*, which is a cliché, of course—recent college grad reading Hemingway on her first trip to Europe with her two friends—but I didn't care. I had already made Constance and Amy drink coffee and cognac at Les Deux Magots, and I had walked the Left Bank in Paris and sat with the pigeons alone in the Jardin du Luxembourg. I didn't want to leave Paris. I didn't want to leave its wide boulevards, the men playing boules in the Tuileries, the cafés, the harsh swallows of strong coffee, the funny little horns on the scooters, the paintings and museums and the rich crêpes. I didn't want to leave the early mornings when the café workers swept the cobblestones and rinsed down their areas with black hoses and silver water, or the evenings, either, when sometimes you smelled smoke, or chestnuts, and the old men with the long fishing poles sat on their three-legged stools and threw their lines baited with maggots into the Seine. I didn't want to leave the booksellers along the river, the moldy stalls lined with old, yellowed books, the landscape painters who came and spread their oils across stretched canvas, attempting to capture what could never be captured but only hinted at, turned into a ghost of what the city held. I didn't want to leave Shakespeare & Co., the English bookstore, the echo, the long, long echo of Hemingway and Fitzgerald, of nights splashing in the Ritz fountain, or squinty-eyed Joyce nibbling through his prose like a mouse hungry for print. I didn't want to leave the gargoyles, either, the surprising, watchful stone eyes staring down from cathedrals, from Notre Dame and a hundred other churches, their white faces sometimes streaked with mysterious black, as if stone could hold tears and release them over centuries.

They say you can never leave Paris; that it must leave you if it chooses to go.

I tried to take Paris with me. In Paris, I had read *A Moveable Feast*, and *A Farewell to Arms*, and *Death in the Afternoon*. I had them all on my iPad, a mini-Hemingway portable library, and although I was traveling with Constance and Amy, I was also traveling with Hemingway.

So I read. It was late. I was in Europe and had been for two and a half weeks. I was on my way to Amsterdam. Constance fell asleep next to me—she was reading *The Lives of the Saints* and was on her own spiritual journey to read and see everything she could about saints, and to see every statue or representation of saints, which fed her special passion and the subject of her senior thesis, hagiography—and Amy stuck her head over the seat behind me and began chatting up a Polish guy named Victor. Victor smelled like sardines and wore a fatigue jacket, but Amy kept elbowing me a little when he said something she thought was cute, and her voice got that singsongy flirtatiousness that meant she was roping a guy and tying him up. Victor was good looking and charming, with a voice that made him sound vaguely like Dracula, and Amy, I saw, had hopes.

That's where everything stood when Jack appeared.

"Could you hold this?" he asked.

I didn't look up. I didn't understand he meant me.

"Miss?" he asked.

Then he pushed a backpack against my shoulder.

I looked up. I saw Jack for the first time.

Our eyes met and didn't let go.

"What?" I asked, aware one of us should have looked away by now.

He was gorgeous. He was actually more than gorgeous. He was big, for one thing, maybe six foot three and well built. He wore an olive fleece and blue jeans, and the way they hung on him made the combination look like the most interesting outfit anyone had ever thought to wear. Someone or something had broken his nose a long time ago, and it had healed in an apostrophe shape. He had good teeth and a smile that started in dimples just an instant before he knew it was going to start. His hair was black and curly, but not 'Fro-ish, just Dead Poet-y. I noticed his hands, too; they were large and heavy, as though he wasn't afraid to work with them, and he reminded me—just a little bit, just a bit, because it sounded silly to say it even to myself—of Hugh Jackman, the freaking Wolverine. This fellow looked insouciant—a stretch of a word but accurate nonetheless—a man who lived behind a wink that indicated he got the joke, was in on it, didn't take it seriously, but expected you to go along with it. What that joke might be or how it counted in your life wasn't quite clear, but it made the corners of my mouth rise a little in the ghost of a smile. I hated that he drew a smile out of me, even the reflex of a smile, and I tried to look down, but his eyes wouldn't permit it. He dog stared me, humor just on the other side of his look, and I couldn't resist hearing what he wanted next.

"Could you please hold this while I climb up?" he asked, extending the backpack again. His eyes stayed on mine.

"Climb up where?"

"Up here. In the baggage rack. You'll see."

He plunked his backpack on my lap. And I thought, *You could have put it in the aisle, Wolverine boy*. But then I watched him roll out his sleeping bag in a space he had cleared on the baggage rack across from me, and I had to admire his skill. I also had to admire his hindquarters, and the V of his back, and when he reached for his backpack, I looked down out of shyness and guilt.

"Thanks," he said.

"No problem."

"Jack," he said.

"Heather," I said.

He smiled. He put the backpack into the baggage rack as a pillow, then climbed up. He appeared too big to fit, but he wedged himself in and then took out a bungee cord and roped it around the supports so that he wouldn't fall out if the train went around a bend.

He looked at me. Our eyes met again and held.

"Good night," he whispered.

"Good night," I said.

2

It sounds crazy, but you can tell a lot by the way a person looks when he or she sleeps. It's a little bit of a study with me. Sometimes I take pictures of sleeping people, and Constance calls it my nightscape series. In any case, I watched Jack in small glimpses, like a movie, because the train sped along and the lights from outside came in every once in a while and illuminated his face. You can tell if someone is a worrier or not, a frightened or brave person, a clownish type or a serious person by his or her sleep expressions.

Jack slept peacefully, flat on his back, his eyelashes thick—he had good eyelashes, caterpillar eyelashes—and now and then I saw his eyes flicker in REM cycle under his lids. His lips parted slightly so that I could see glimpses of his teeth, and his arms stayed folded on his chest. He was a beautiful man, and twice I stood to stretch my back and snuck looks at him, the flashing lights turning him into a black-and-white film, something out of a Fellini movie.

I was still watching him when my phone rang. It was the Mom-a-saurus.

"Where's my adventure girl now?" Mom asked, her voice coated with morning coffee. I pictured her in our kitchen in New Jersey, her outfit for the day waiting on a hanger upstairs while she had her coffee and non-carb breakfast on a tiny plate in the kitchen.

"On the train to Amsterdam, Mom."

"Oh, how exciting. You've left Paris. How are the girls?"

"They're fine, Mom. Where are you?"

"Home. Just having my coffee. Daddy's gone for a couple of days to Denver on business. He asked me to give you a call, because there are tons of letters here for you from Bank of America. They look like human resources things—you know, insurance, health plans, but I guess some of them need your attention."

"I'll get to them, Mom. I've already been on the phone to the HR people."

"Listen, I'm just the go-between. Daddy has his ways, as you know. He likes things covered, and you're going to work for his friend."

"I know, Mom," I said, "but they wouldn't have hired me if they didn't think I could handle the job. I graduated with a 3.9 from Amherst, and I was offered three positions besides this one. I speak French and a little Japanese, and I write pretty well, and I come across in an interview when I need to, and—"

"Of course," Mom interrupted because she knew this stuff, knew everything, and I was being defensively dogmatic. "Of course, darling. I didn't mean to imply anything different."

I took a deep breath. I tried to be calm when I spoke again.

"I know there's probably paperwork, but I'll leave time before I have to start in September. Tell Daddy not to worry. It's all going to be fine. I have it all under control. You know I'm the type to get those things done. He doesn't need to worry. If anything, I'm a tad obsessive about details."

"I know, honey. I guess he's a little divided, that's all. He wants you to explore Europe, but he also knows this job is pretty big. Investment banking, sweetheart, it's—"

"Got it, Mom," I said, seeing her with her *T. rex* head, slowly lifting me from the ground in her mouth, my legs wiggling. I changed the subject and asked about my cat. "How's Mr. Periwinkle?"

"I haven't seen him this morning, but he's around here someplace. He's very stiff, and he has lumps, but he's still eating."

"Will you give him a kiss for me?"

"How about if I pet him for you? He's filthy, sweetheart. Just filthy, and I worry about what's on his skin."

"Mom, he's been in our family for fifteen years."

"You think I don't know that? I'm the one who has fed him and taken him to vet visits, you know?"

"I know, Mom."

I turned my iPad over. I didn't like seeing my face reflected in the glass as I talked into the phone. Was I really getting annoyed with my mother over my cat while sitting on a train on the way to Amsterdam? That felt a little bit insane. Luckily, Amy came to my rescue by standing and slipping past me. She wiggled her eyebrows in a little signal. Victor, I saw, followed her down the aisle toward Lord knows what. Poland was about to be conquered.

"Listen, Mom, we're getting ready to pull in to Amsterdam," I fibbed. "I need to get my stuff together. Tell Daddy I will get to the paperwork the instant I get home. I promise. Tell him not to worry. I've e-mailed with people at the office, and I'm all set to start in September. It's all good. They actually seem happy to have me, and they're glad I'm taking this trip. They encouraged it, remember, because they know I'm going to be working flat out when I start."

"All right, sweetheart. You're the boss. You stay safe now, okay? You promise? I love you. Give a kiss and a hug to the girls."

"All right, Mom, I will. Love you."

The connection closed. The Mom-a-saurus lumbered off into the Jurassic Age, her feet making indentations into solid rock as she walked. I closed my eyes and tried to sleep.

3

What are you reading?"

It was late. I couldn't sleep after all. Amy hadn't returned. Constance seemed to sleep well enough for all of us. I was carried away to Spain with Hemingway, drinking too much and watching the bulls. Fiesta. The mountain trout streams. I was so involved in it that I didn't notice when Jack climbed into the seat next to me.

"Excuse me?" I said, and I turned the iPad against my chest.

"My legs went numb sleeping up there. Not right away but after a while. At least I got a little sleep. Do you want to try it? I'd boost you up."

"I could climb up if I wanted to."

"It was an offer, not an insult."

"You'll have to move if my friend comes back. The seat is taken."

He smiled. I wondered why I was being bitchy. It was likely a defense mechanism. He was so good looking—and so knew it—

that I couldn't help wanting to puncture his confidence. My neck
flushed. It's my one tell. My neck always flushes when I'm nervous, excited, or under pressure. When I took exams at Amherst,
I looked like a ring-necked pheasant. I used to wear turtlenecks to
cover it, though the heat of the collars only made it worse.

"You were reading, right?" he asked. "I saw the way your hand
flipped the pages. Do you like these e-books? I'm not a big fan
myself."

"I can carry a lot of books in one small device."

"Hooray," he said, his tone mocking but flirty.

"Traveling, they make sense."

"A book is a companion, though. You can read it in a special
place, like on a train to Amsterdam, then you carry it home and
you chuck it on a shelf, and then years later you remember that
feeling you had on the train when you were young. It's like a little
island in time. If you love the book, you can give it to someone
else. And you can discover it over and over, and it's like seeing an
old friend. Can't do that with a digital file."

"I guess you're purer than I am. You can also throw a book on
a shelf, then pack it the next time you move, then unpack it, then
pack it again. And so on. An iPad holds more than any bookshelf
in any apartment I'm likely to get."

"I mistrust devices. Seems like a gimmick to me."

But saying that, he grabbed the iPad and turned it over. It
happened so quickly that I didn't have time to prevent it. I was
conscious of the train-ness of the whole experience: cute guy, train
moving, lights, scents of food from back in the bar cars, foreign
languages, adventure. Also, he smiled. He had a killer smile, a
conspiratorial smile, a smile that said mischief wasn't far off, come
along, we're going to have a better time than you're having alone.

"Hemingway?" he asked, reading a page. "*The Sun Also Rises*. Wow, you've got it bad."

"Got what bad?"

"Oh, you know, the whole Hemmy thing. Paris, kissing the old women in the slaughterhouses, wine, impressionists, all that. The usual romance of the ex-patriate experience in Europe. Maybe even the I-want-to-be-a-writer-and-live-in-a-garret thing. You might even have it that bad. I thought women didn't like Hemingway anymore."

"I like the sadness."

He looked at me. He hadn't expected that, I could tell. He even bent back a little to see me more fully. It was a look of appraisal.

"East Coast," he said tentatively, like a man caught between choices of ice cream flavors. "Jersey, maybe Connecticut. Dad works in New York. It could be Cleveland, maybe the Heights, I could be off that much, but I don't think so. How close am I?"

"Where are you from?"

"Vermont. But you didn't tell me if I was right or wrong."

"Keep going. I want you to tell me my whole profile."

He looked at me again. He put his hand softly on my chin. It struck me as a pretty good pickup tactic regardless of how accurate he might be. He turned my face gently from side to side, looking seriously at me. He had wonderful eyes. My neck glowed like red flannel. I glanced quickly to see if maybe Constance had stirred at our voices, but she still slept. She could sleep through a hurricane, I knew.

"You graduated recently. You're in Europe with your buddies now . . . sorority sisters? No, probably not sorority sisters. You're too clever for that. Maybe you worked on the college newspaper together. Good college, too, am I right? East Coast, so, maybe Sarah Lawrence, Smith, something like that."

"Amherst," I said.

"Oooooo, so smart, too. Tough to get into Amherst these days. Or well connected, which is it? How smart? Hmm? That remains to be seen. But you're reading Hemingway in Europe, so that's either very impressive or terribly clichéd."

"You're being a jerk, you know? A condescending jerk. That's the worst kind."

"I'm doing a male display in order to meet you. The thing is, I like you. I liked you right off. If I had tail feathers, I would spread them out and dance around you to demonstrate my interest. But how am I doing so far? Is it working at all? Feel any pitter-pat in your heart?"

"You were better before you opened your mouth. Much better, actually."

"Okay, touché. Let's see. Mom involved in charities, volunteer work. Dad has made it big. Corporate big, not entrepreneurial big. But that's just a guess. Lots of dough either way. You're reading Hemingway, so you have artistic feelings, but you don't trust them because, well, because they aren't practical. Hemingway is part of the well-read résumé, right?"

I took a deep breath, nodded to accept what he said, then slowly began to speak.

"And you are a pretend back-to-earther green Vermonter jackass who talks a lot, probably reads—I'll give you that—who has one of those quiet little trust funds that allows you to wander around the world, picking up girls and dazzling them with your wit and wisdom and erudition. The thing is, you're not about the sex that might come along with that package, although you don't mind it. You're about getting the girls to fall for you, to marvel at your wonderfulness, because that's your particular pathology. And so you can riff on the whole Hemmy thing as if you two are old drinking buddies, but Hemingway did this all for real—he was *after* something you'll never understand—and you, you're just playing at it, and you should leave now because Amy should be back soon."

He smiled. If I hurt him, his eyes didn't give him away. Then he winced playfully.

"Just take the knife out of me before I go."

"I'm sorry, Jack," I said, and I couldn't help laying on the name a bit and mocking him with it. "Did anyone ever mention that you look like a bad version of Hugh Jackman?"

"The Wolverine?"

I nodded.

"I give. You win. Mercy."

He started to stand, then he grabbed for my calendar that I had beneath the iPad.

"Tell me that's not a Smythson. Smythson of Bond Street? Oh, good gracious, the most expensive, tony Day Runner anyone ever saw? Tell me you don't actually own one of those."

"It was a graduation present. And it wasn't full price, believe me. It was a deal thing, and it was pretty much for free."

"I'm trying to imagine what kind of person needs a pretentious calendar to remind her that she's doing okay."

"Punctual people. People who want to remember appointments. People who are trying to accomplish something in this world."

"Oh, and you're one of those?"

"Trying to be."

"How much do those things cost, anyway?"

"Not your business. Go bother somebody else, would you?"

"Oh, good Lord," he said, dropping the Smythson back in my lap. "Do you really think if you get every gold star the teacher hands out there is a huge refrigerator in the sky where you get to hang your special papers? That some supermommy somewhere will put refrigerator magnets on your accomplishments and everyone will stand back and applaud?"

I wanted to punch him. I nearly did.

"Do you really think, Jack, that roaming around Europe and trying to be a lost, romantic soul will turn you into anything other than a cynical drunk sitting in a bar somewhere and boring everyone around you?"

"Wow," he said. "Are you just traveling for your résumé? So you can say at a cocktail party someday that you've been to Paris? Why did you bother coming over here if you see travel that way?"

"I don't see it any one way, Jack. But little hipster dudes who are, like, a hundred years late to the party, to Paris, and all that between wartime romance, well, they're pitiful. Some of us believe in doing things. In making things. So, yes, sometimes we get calendars from Bond Street that help us organize our day. That's called human progress. We have cars and planes and, yes, iPads and iPhones. Deal with it, Vermont boy."

He grinned. I almost grinned back. I had to admit he was fun to spar with. I didn't think he took much of what we said seriously. The only thing he seemed to take seriously was the way our eyes kept catching and holding.

"Well played. I admit it, well played. I like your passion. It doesn't take much to get your tongue sharpened, does it?"

"Is that the best you can do? Are you calling me a sharp-tongued shrew, Jack? I'll know most of the references you throw at me. I'm well educated and wicked smart. Drift away, Jack Vermont. Go back to contemplating the great significance of your life, or maybe plot out the next novel you will never write. Go find a café where you can sit and have pretend conversations of pretend importance with other pretend expats who like to believe they see a little more deeply into the human experience than we poor, benighted businesspeople. That will make you feel terrifically superior. You can look down from your lofty heights and throw your thunderbolts."

"Pretend expats?" he said, grinning again. He grinned to get me to grin, and I had to fight not to give in to him.

"Should I go on? Or do you get the idea?"

"I do," he said, and he slowly stood. "I think this went very well. How about you?"

"It was great."

He made a show out of creeping past me out to the aisle—and he did have a great body—and then he swung up into the sleeping rack again. When he settled back, he waited until I looked at him. He stuck his tongue out. I stuck mine back at him.

4

·····························

That's where it stood for a while. My neck burned red, and I had trouble controlling my breathing. For a ten count, I sat with my face in my hands, trying to get control of myself. I didn't like thinking I was so easily pegged, because I *was* from New Jersey, and my dad *was* a corporate suit, and my mom *was* a Junior Leaguer. I hated thinking I was a convenient type, a person some-one like Jack could identify in the first minutes of meeting me. I also didn't like the venom that came out when I turned it on him. Then again, he had crossed a line. I watched him while the lights continued to flicker and flash from outside. I had been in the no-man zone for months, ever since I'd broken up with Brian, my major college crush. I still couldn't bring myself to think about the fact that I had brought Brian home, even decorated the family Christmas tree with him, only to discover he had screwed a girl on a dare the week before. He had been drunk, and the girl had been a local bartender with a wide bra strap and a head full of blond-tinted hair, and he'd been put up to it by his friends. *Bar dare, bar dare, bar dare, ha ha ha, funny, funny, funny, another round*, they chanted. So he had gone off into her car, or his car, or to an alleyway, for all I knew, to have his rendezvous. And it didn't mean anything, that was for sure, the world agreed on that, but all I could remember was looking up at Brian's cordovan corduroys as he stood on the stepladder and took ornaments from my hand, while my dad made drinks in the dry bar off the living room and my mom, the *T. rex*, lumbered around the house with a wispy sweater over her shoulders like a cape and $300 trousers from Eileen Fisher hiked up to the bottom knobs of her ribs. Bing Fucking Crosby played on Pandora. I confess: I felt the dreamy romance of the entire thing—Christmas in the country, snow falling, *Holiday Inn* and all that rot—until his friend Ronnie Evers Facebooked a picture of Brian with his hand down the back of Brenda the bartender's skinny jeans, his tongue stuck out like an acid-band lead guitarist, while she ground her buffalo legs against his thigh and leaned back cowgirl-style.

What followed, when I twigged it all out from Twitter and Facebook and a few tagged photos, was a quiet little scene between Brian and me down in the old rumpus room, our tight, controlled voices hissing like old radiators.

How could you? Her? You did her?

It was a joke. A bet! I was drunk!

Oh, jeez, Brian. For fuck's sake.

Everything's okay. Jeez, lighten up, Heather. We're not engaged, you know?

Fuck you, Brian.

But we had tumbled out of our particular little Eden. We split up the next day, his bag thumping into the trunk of his old Volvo sedan before he pulled out, Christmas lights leading him away.

When I turned back to the house, I spotted Mr. Periwinkle, our ancient cat, watching from the upstairs window.

So Jack. Constance was still asleep. Amy was still gone. The train car had settled into that kind of restless calm that comes to things in motion when people are trying to sleep, but keep waking up. I smelled coffee from the bar car behind us. Now and then, right out of a noir movie, we got the train sound that comes when you go through a stop or past a siding: duhhhhh-de-de-de-de deallllllllh-hhhhhhh. A Doppler effect, I knew from first-year physics.

I decided on coffee. And decided halfway thumbs-up on Jack the Wolverine, so that when I passed him I took a little snapshot of him with my iPhone. He didn't wake. But then I felt guilty about what I had said to him, how harsh I had been, so when I ordered my own latte, I ordered one for him, too, figuring someone would drink it if he didn't want it. While the porter made the coffee, I looked at the picture. Jack was drop-dead gorgeous but slept deeply—zombie sleep, really—and I wondered what that was about. Brian had always slept halfheartedly, an insomniac itching for the world to start again. Jack sank way, way down when he slept.

I carried the order back, one in each hand, which proved harder to do than you might think. I stopped next to his head and stared at him for a second, figuring eyes always woke people up. It did. Maybe he detected the presence of someone, I don't know, but he looked over at me and smiled, and it was a sweet, innocent smile, one he might have given his mom on his tenth birthday.

"I got you a coffee," I said. "It was the least I could do given your pitiful life."

"Let me get up."

I stood and waited. He slowly slid down. It was my first time standing next to him, and I liked the way he seemed to curl around me. Big shoulders, big muscles, a riot shield of a man.

"We could drink these out between the cars," he said, arranging his bag so he could leave it. "I could use some air, miserable, trust-fund, lame-ass Vermont boy that I am."

I nodded.

"You are," I agreed. "Sad but true."

He finished with his bag and grabbed his coffee. I wondered, as I followed him out to the space between the two cars, if what I had done could be called a pickup.

5

....

Sorry if I was being a jerk earlier," he said. "I sometimes over-sell."

"To women?"

"I guess."

"Are you a show-off in general?"

"Only around women as beautiful as you."

"How old is that line?"

"Not so old. Maybe I mean it. Maybe I think you're beautiful. How tall are you, anyway?"

"Five six."

"That's the perfect height, you know? Trapeze artists are all five feet six inches or under. So are human cannonballs. The people who get shot out of cannons . . . they're five six."

"You're making that up."

"It's a known fact. An accepted fact everywhere. It's the first question if you go for a job at a carnival. Even lion tamers are five six or under."

"Have you worked in a circus?"

"Of course."

"But you're taller than five six."

"The women have to be five six. The men can be any height at all if they work behind the scenes. That's what I did. Mostly I talked people into throwing softballs at a stack of bottles. I was a barker."

"I don't believe a thing you say."

"And a lion bit me once. You probably won't believe that, either. Right on the thigh. Right in the meaty part of the thigh. I was asleep and suddenly there she was, a female named Sugar. She was known to have a bad character, but I never had a problem with Sugar. She looked at me as she bit down as if to say she was sorry, but it was her nature, after all. I was just a midnight snack."

"You are so full of it, but I could almost listen to you for a while."

He shrugged and sipped his latte. We stood between the two cars, facing each other, our backs against the walls on each side. The track seemed to fly underneath us. You could smell things obscurely—hayfields, and cinders, rain maybe, an electric scent that came from a motor—but mostly it dissolved into simple movement.

"I've often wondered why Sugar let go. It haunts me, really."

"Maybe you taste bad. Was this in Vermont?"

"It was in Istanbul. It's a long story. I'm sorry. I get nervous, and then I talk too much. Or try too hard. That's what I did with you earlier. A fatal flaw, I guess."

"I wouldn't call it a fatal flaw. Just a flaw."

"I was hoping you would find me Byronic."

"I think if you need to hope someone finds you Byronic, then you aren't Byronic. Ipso facto."

He looked at me and sipped his coffee. The coffee wasn't very good.

"Ipso facto?" he asked. "Latin for 'pretentious'?"

"*By that very fact.* The enemy of my enemy is ipso facto my friend."

"You are such an A student, aren't you?"

"And the problem with that is . . . ?"

"Just that you're an apple polisher. That's why you have a Smythson calendar. What's the worst grade you ever got? Outside of gym class, I mean."

"You think I wouldn't get an A in gym?"

"I think you were probably picked right away in dodgeball, then everyone on the other team tried to peg you in the head because you are such an A student. Ipso facto."

"Did you always know everything about everyone instantly? Or is it just about me?"

"Oh, I know you. You're the class-president type. The hang-the-crepe-paper-at-the-big-dance type. The girl on the ladder. The girl with tape."

"And you're the slacker cool boy lurking around in his own myth."

"I like that phrase. 'Lurking around in his own myth.' See? You have potential."

"Oh, thank goodness. I'd shrivel without your approval."

He looked at me and smiled over his coffee.

"What's your flaw," he asked, "fatal or otherwise?"

"Why should I tell you?"

"Because we're on a train going to Amsterdam, and we have to talk about something. And you're wildly attracted to me, so it's a way of flirting that you secretly desire but are reluctant to admit."

"You don't suffer from a lack of confidence, do you?"

"I assume because I am attracted to you, you are probably attracted to me. Plus, when our eyes meet, they lock. Do you know what I mean? You know what I mean, Heather of the North Woods."

I shook my head. He was correct about everything. The fact that he knew he was right about everything made me nervous.

"Your flaw, remember?" he asked. "I'll keep asking. That's another flaw. I am sometimes overly persistent."

"My flaw is hard to put into words."

"Try me."

I took a deep breath, wondering why we are sometimes willing to tell secrets to strangers on trains that we would never tell to anyone else. I went ahead, anyway.

"Whenever I look up at a plane, I always hope it falls out of the sky. Right then. I don't know if I really want it to, or just have a perverse impulse, but it's what I hope. I have a fantasy of running out into a meadow and finding a downed plane and saving people."

"That's not a flaw. That's a psychosis. You need help. You need extensive psychological assistance."

I took a sip of coffee. The train clattered loudly over some sort of trestle.

"And when a bride comes down the aisle," I continued, "I always want her to trip. My mother won't let me sit on the aisle if I'm at a wedding for fear I'll stick my foot out."

"Have you ever done it?"

I shook my head.

"Not yet, but I will. It can be any formal occasion, actually. Anything that has everyone all dressed up. I'm always rooting for a food fight, or someone to face-plant into a cake. I can't help it. The world always seems right on the edge of becoming a bad frat party."

"You're an anarchist, that's why. You'll probably be a perfect citizen until you're around forty, then you'll join some sort of fringe army and stride about in a uniform with a machete hanging around your neck. Are you drawn to machetes?"

"More than you know."

"South America, then."

"Oh, not a sweeping generalization there, I guess. Everyone in South America has a machete?"

"Of course they do. Didn't you know?"

"What weapon attracts you?"

"Hedge clippers."

"Hedge clippers, huh? Why's that?"

"I just think they're underappreciated."

"You linger right on the edge of annoying, you know? Sometimes you save yourself and you don't even know it."

"Some people call that dashing. Or swashbuckling. It depends."

Jack sipped his coffee and looked over the rim of the cup. Part of me wanted to kiss him, and part of me wanted to chuck my coffee in his self-satisfied face. But nothing about Jack struck me as neutral, and that was a first.

"How old are you, anyway?" I asked. "You should have a job. You should be working."

"How old do you think I am?"

"Ten."

He looked at me.

"I'm twenty-seven," he said. "How old are you?"

"A gentleman never asks a woman's age."

"You think I'm a gentleman?"

"I think you are very far from swashbuckling."

"You're not answering."

"Twenty-two," I said. "Soon to be twenty-three."

"Were you kept back a grade?"

"No!"

"You probably were and your parents didn't tell you. It happens, you know."

"I was a good student. You said so yourself."

"You were a good student because your parents kept you back a year and you had the benefit of a year's maturity on your classmates. I've met your type before. It's really terribly unfair. You had an advantage all through your school years."

"And you sat at the back of the class, didn't you? And pretended to sketch or be the misunderstood poet. It's such a cliché that it makes my molars hurt."

"What did I wear?"

"Oh, where to begin? Jeans, of course. T-shirt with place names on them . . . no, no, I'm getting a tool vibe. John Deere T-shirts, maybe, or like Ace Hardware. Something utilitarian or proletariat. And you wore your hair long, like you do now, only probably you deliberately pulled a front lock down across your forehead because, well, because you were just so darn caught up in your deep poet-y thoughts. Right? So you were the common-man guy, farmer boy, with a deep soul. Did you come in a kit? Or were you already assembled?"

"No assembly required."

"And grade-wise you rode the B train. Maybe B-. Good work, but not serious, missed a few assignments, could have done better, but you were reading and the teachers were okay with that. Girlfriend? Hmmm. That's a tough one. Probably a girl who raised sheep. Or goats—goats are better. She smelled of perfume and farm manure, but she, too, miraculously, loved to read and adored poetry. Kind of a Sharon Olds type."

"You nailed it. You're scalding my soul with your insight."

"She was probably named after a plant . . . or a season. Summer. Or maybe Hazel or Olive. Or maybe June Bug."

We didn't talk for a while. I wondered if I had gone too far. Then our eyes met again. The train rocked, and he lifted his cup and drained it to the bottom. It was possible we were heading toward a kiss. A serious kiss. I liked him way too much, I realized. Then a guy came out and lit a cigarette, which was entirely against the law, but he did it, anyway. He said something to us in English, but I couldn't hear him over the train noises. He looked like a bicyclist, all wire legs and a baseball hat with an abbreviated brim. I couldn't quite figure him out.

Then two more of his buddies came out wearing about the same thing, so it was some sort of team or tour group, I supposed, and Jack looked at me. Our eyes went down each other's tunnel a long way. He smiled, and it was a good smile, but also wan. It meant that this moment on the platform had finished, that we had caught it while it existed, then it disappeared. Something like that.

"Ready?" he asked, nodding his chin toward our car.

I nodded. And that was it.

6

....

Amy came back without Victor when we were a half hour outside of Amsterdam. Jack had gone down to the dining car.

"Where's Count Chocula?" I asked.

"OMG," she said and slid in beside me.

"Has Poland been conquered?"

"Let's just say the nations of Europe have once again given of their bounty."

"You're such a tart."

"Embrace the inner slut, Heather."

She did a little wiggle dance and sang something ridiculous. Her singing woke Constance. Constance sat up quickly and looked around, evidently unsure of her surroundings. A line from her U-shaped travel pillow ran down her cheek. When she saw she was on a train, and that Amy was wiggling next to her, she groaned and put her head down on her knees.

"Not another," she said, groggy.

"Count Chocula has some game," Amy said. "He's really quite adorable."

"You're hooking up with Dracula?" Constance asked, slowly rubbing her face clear of sleep. "Does anyone have any water?"

"Here," Amy said, reaching into her backpack at her feet and liberating a bottle of water. "Is anyone else starving?"

"Cheese and apples," I said, because I was more or less the quartermaster on this trip. I always had food. Sometimes, as I told Jack, I was a little too organized, a genetic hand-me-down from the Mom-a-saurus.

"Can you get to them easily?"

I dug around in my backpack. Amy pulled out a pear-shaped cutting board we had bought after a week. It fit in a backpack and made a decent impromptu table. We all took out Swiss Army knives while I laid out apples, a block of French cheddar, two stalks of celery, and peanut butter. I had to dig a little deeper to find a baguette I had broken in half to fit in my backpack. I put it beside the apples.

"How long did I sleep?" Constance asked. She smeared peanut butter on a slice of apple and chomped it down.

"Three, four hours, maybe," I said.

"What did I miss? Who is Count Chocula exactly?"

"The Polish guy who was sitting behind us," Amy said. "Victor was his name. His last named sounded like a sneeze. He invited us to a party in Amsterdam, by the way. I took down the address."

"Where is he, anyway?" I asked, arching up and looking over the back of the seat. "Did you sex him to death?"

"It was a fair fight," Amy said.

"I have to see this guy," Constance said. "I didn't notice him when we sat down."

I ate a bite or two of bread. Then I sliced cheese and ate that with more bread. Amy divided another apple into three sections. I ate that, too. For a minute or so, we ate without talking, and I felt happy. I looked at Constance, her face serious and concentrated, her blond hair beautiful in the dull light of the train compartment. She was the prettiest of us all and the least interested in guys. She was bookish, but not in the Hemmy sort of way. She liked research, imagined the saints as an extended family she could visit when everyday life became too dull, and she was the one we turned to when we needed the name of a figure in a picture or statue. She ate daintily, cutting things precisely and fitting them together in neat packages, while Amy, dark and slightly more abundant, slathered peanut butter wherever it landed and ate with a gusto that reflected her general approach to life. I had known them since first-year orientation at Amherst, had visited their homes, had seen them cry over boyfriends, get drunk, get As, get carded at bars, watched them dance until their legs dropped off, saw Amy play lacrosse like a demon woman, watched Constance cross campus on her sky-blue Schwinn, her books neatly organized in a front basket, her slightly myopic gaze finding the beauty in the campus oaks and the arches of the buildings. Seeing them in the soft, stuttering train light, watching them eat and smile and keep good company with each other, I felt enormous affection for them.

"I love you guys," I said because I felt it keenly in that moment. "And I want to thank you for doing this trip together, for everything. I don't want us to ever lose track of one another. Do you all promise?"

"What brought this on?" Amy asked, her mouth full.

Constance nodded at me and reached over and took my hand.

Amy made a little shrug, then put her hand on top of ours. The Musketeers. We had been doing the Musketeer hand stack since a drunken night in our first year outside the Lord Jeffery Inn when we realized we were pals, true pals.

"One for all and all for one," we said, which was our secret code. *"Un pour tous, et tous pour un."* As we finished, the train began slowing for Amsterdam.

7

·······································

D o you know where you're staying?" Jack asked.

We stood in the aisle, waiting for the train to empty. Amy and Constance were halfway down the car already, but a man two people in front of Jack had trouble getting a bag off the baggage rack. My neck already glowed just standing next to Jack.

"We have reservations in a hostel," I said. "It's called Cocomama. I liked the name."

"Do you make all the travel arrangements?"

"Not all. I just like things orderly."

"Said the girl with the Smythson appointment book."

I shrugged. He wasn't wrong.

"We might go to a party that Amy found out about from this guy Victor. It's supposed to be right in central Amsterdam someplace, overlooking a canal."

"My friend Raef, he's Australian, but he knows people here. He knows people everywhere. I count myself as pretty well traveled, but Raef, he's like Marco Polo or something. You'll like him. He's a sheepherder most of the year in the outback, and he saves up all his money, then travels. If you tell me where the party is, maybe we'll show up. I'd like to see you again."

"He sounds colorful. I don't know where the party is off the top of my head, the address, but Amy has it written down. I can ask her when we get off the train."

We didn't say anything for a moment. Finally, the man in front of Jack managed to swing the bag down off the baggage rack. People behind us clapped. Amy and Constance had already disappeared onto the train platform.

"Look," Jack said, his voice deep and pleasant and soft enough so only I could hear it. "Here's what I think we should do. If we get off the train and it has a lot of fog coming out from underneath, you know, like an old movie, then we should have our first kiss right there. We've both been wanting to kiss, so we shouldn't miss it."

I had to smile. I kept my eyes away from him and slowly crept forward as people began to move. My neck was beyond red.

"We should, should we?" I asked. "And you think I want to kiss you? Is that your best try?"

"Come on. It will be a story to tell our grandchildren. And if it doesn't work, if we don't meet at the party tonight, then what did we lose? Just a kiss."

"How big a kiss does it have to be?"

"Oh, we have to make it memorable."

"You're not without charm, as hard as that is for me to admit."

"I didn't mean to kid you about Hemingway. Earlier, I mean," he said, his voice dropping and becoming sincerer. "I think it's important to read Hemingway in Europe. I do. I like that you read him, and I like that you find his sadness interesting. I was just trying to connect with you."

"What if the kiss is a letdown? Not every first kiss is great."

"Ours will be. I think you know it will be, too. So you're agreeing to kiss me?"

"For our grandchildren's sake."

"I hope there's steam, and if we're lucky, it's raining."

"I just ate peanut butter, so I'm warning you."

"Duly noted."

It's amazing how long walking half a train car can take. I didn't dare turn around to look at him. My backpack dug into my shoulders. I bent down a little and saw Amy and Constance waiting, both of them looking back to the car for me. I waved. They waved back. Jack walked behind me, and I felt choked up and strange. I wasn't that kind of a girl, whatever that meant. Not impulsive. Not a girl to kiss a guy she had just met on a train to Amsterdam.

But it happened. When I stepped off the train, I turned to him, and he swung down lightly, big, muscular, and he took me in his arms. I wasn't prepared for his solidness, for the strength of his entire body as he pulled me close. It was ridiculous at first, both of us like turtles with our stupid backpacks bobbing behind us, but then it became something else. I had a vague sense of Amy and Constance watching, both of them slack jawed with amusement and wonder, and then his lips went deeper into mine, and I closed my eyes.

It should have been a joke. It should have lasted only a moment. But it was a great kiss, probably the best of my life, and I don't know why it was, or what he did, but when we broke apart, I didn't want to let him go.

When we finished, I turned to see the girls. They both had cell phones out to click pictures, and when they dropped them, I laughed at the amazement on their faces.

"What the hell?" Amy asked.

"When did this happen?" Constance asked.

Jack simply smiled. Amy recovered sufficiently to give him the address of the party. We exchanged phone numbers.

"Maybe we'll see you tonight," Constance said, polite as always, smoothing things.

"Isn't it pretty to think so?" he said, quoting the last line of *The Sun Also Rises* and letting his eyes rest on mine for an instant before he left.

8

Kitten, make sure you fill out ANY forms Bank of America sends you. Pronto!

On top of it, Daddy. Tell Mommy to pour you a big scotch and relax.

Don't require a scotch. Require my daughter to do what she has promised to do.

It will get done. I always get things done.

When?

When the moon is in the 7th house. And Jupiter aligns with Mars.

Stop fooling with me, Heather. I don't appreciate it.

Sorry, Dad. I will take care of it as soon as I can.

Not really good enough, is it?

Dad, I promise I will be on top of this. It's a little difficult from over here, but I have my eye on the ball. Swear.

Take pity on your father. Okay. Love you. No more lectures right now. Now I do need a drink.

There's always a moment when you enter a party when you think: *In or out?* Part of you wants to get the hell away from the noise and racket, the lights flashing, the people—strangers—yelling into each other's ears to be heard. You know immediately that the bathrooms will be crowded or impossible to use, that the dance floors will be sticky with beer and booze, that some wannabe playboy will come dancing toward you with his groin sticking out, his teeth tucked over his lower lip, his eyes giving you the you're-ten-minutes-away-from-having-my-baby look. For an instant, you see the party for what it is—a mating ritual, a celebration of coitus—and you start to turn away because you are smarter than this, cooler than this, quieter than this.

But the other part kicks in, too.

And you think, *One drink.* Or, *Why not?* And maybe, if the music is decent, you feel a little pumped up, you want to move, and you look at your girlfriends—they're looking, shrugging, trying to see some reason to fit in—and you raise your eyebrows. Usually they raise theirs back in reply. Then—because you've been doing it for years together—you slowly move into the crowd, turning sideways to squeeze past people, your hand sometimes reaching backward or forward to stay in touch with your buds, and you aim toward the bar. Fairly often some guy grabs your ass as you pass, and sometimes it's worse, sometimes you get the air grind—guy's hands up as if he's being held at gunpoint, his crotch inching toward you, his breath boozed up and awful—and you skitter forward and make it to the bar and try to shout for a drink. Up and down the bar, if there is a bar, guys glance sideways and send their eyes north and south over you, and you try to ignore them, try to pretend that getting a drink is the most important thing in the world because you don't want to risk meeting their glance, and eventually one of you, if you're lucky, makes eye contact with the bartender. Then you shout and he nods and you pull some bills out of somewhere and hand drinks back to your friends, each one immediately sticking the straw in her mouth to take a big sip because you're going to need it.

That's where we ended up five minutes after arriving at the party Victor had told us about.

At least the room was stylish. That probably made us want to stay. It was a big industrial loft, brick and metal and outsized lighting fixtures, with broad windows that overlooked a canal. The music sucked—it was European techno-pop, with a repetitive beat and a grinding, relentless forward drive—but it was also irresistible. I handed gin and tonics back to Constance and Amy. They nodded thanks and began sipping. I paid the bartender. He touched the bill to his forehead in a little salute and hustled off.

"Any sign of him? Of Jack?" Amy yelled into my ear when I joined them a few feet from the bar.

I shook my head. I hadn't heard from him, and I wasn't sure he would show. It would hurt if he didn't show, but I didn't want to think about it too much. I had been thinking about him too much, anyway, and had checked the photo of him asleep an unhealthy number of times. I remembered the kiss, and the look we had shared on the platform between the cars. My entire body remembered it. He had the look, the feel, even the size of the man I had envisioned for myself. It was weird to think that, but it was true. If I had gone shopping for a guy who fit me, and all the men from my history had been hanging on a dress rack in a well-lit shop, I would have picked Jack every single time. I could have held him up to me, taken one glance in a mirror, and known he'd fit me.

And I loved talking to him. I felt drunk when I talked to him.

"An amazing room!" Constance yelled at both of us. "Is this a bar or a private residence?"

Amy held her hand out to say she didn't know, couldn't tell, didn't care.

"It's still early," Amy said to me.

"It's almost eleven," I answered.

She shrugged.

So we did the chick thing, which is kind of lame and sort of great. We danced in a triangle, moving a little, sipping a little, drifting slowly into the middle of the floor. It had been a long time, I realized, since we had been out in a club scene dancing. It felt good. The gin began to work, and we did our signature moves: Amy wiggling her butt like a lightning bug and Constance sort of on her toes as if she wanted to reach something down from a high shelf but hadn't yet decided to lift her arms. It made me smile to watch them. You couldn't escape your personality when it came to dancing, I knew.

A few guys came up and circled us, dancing and moving, and we looked at one another and opened our eyes a little to ask, *Way, no way?* They weren't very cute. When Amy bit down on her straw and shook her head a millimeter, that was good enough to say no. We kept dancing and sipping. The drink tasted weak. The first group of guys drifted away, and we moved a little closer. Then Amy started doing ridiculous dance moves, ones we had seen a guy named Leonard back at Amherst make sometime in our first year. The guy was a mega-geek, but charming in a way, too, and he danced with crazy abandon that we had copied for four years. We did a dance called the *Guy Repellent*, which you could launch into if someone started dancing with you and you wanted him gone. Leonard had given us that, and that's the dance Amy started doing to get us laughing. She had mastered it and only pulled it out as a favor to us, but Constance and I both watched her spaz out, people around her trying not to notice. She did it perfectly.

Eventually, Constance grabbed her by the hand to get her to stop, and we made our way to the windows. It was a pretty sight. Light glistened on the canal below and turned the water into a crowd of stars.

"What do you think?" Constance said into my ear. "Do you think he's coming?"

"I don't know," I shouted back.

"Didn't you take his number? You could call him and ask him what the fuck he's doing," Amy said.

"That sounds desperate."

"It is desperate, but so what? You call for pizza or Chinese food when you want it, don't you?" Amy asked.

Constance shook her head. I wasn't sure she had heard the conversation.

"Well, if we're going to stay, we need more drinks," Amy said.

"Do you want to stay?" I asked. "We don't have to stay just for Jack. I didn't mean it to be like that."

But I was lying, and they both knew it.

"One more drink," Constance said. "Then we'll head out."

"Have you seen Victor anywhere?" I asked Amy.

Amy shook her head. It was making my throat hurt to talk. I drained the last of my drink and was about to turn when I suddenly knew Jack had arrived. I didn't know how I knew it, but I did.

Amy bit down on her straw and made a little bucking motion with her head to indicate, *There, right there, right behind you.*

9

....

I didn't turn. I didn't do anything except bubble my drink with my straw. Amy's gaze flicked back and forth from whoever was behind me to my eyes. She even tilted her head a little to say, *Come on, he's right there, come on, what are you doing?*

My neck started flaming. I took a final sip of gin and tonic. I kept my eyes on the other girls and pretended we had been having a great conversation. I didn't want him to think the night was suddenly much more interesting now that he had arrived.

But it was, and my neck knew it.

He came around into our circle and smiled. It was too loud to make any chitchat. I returned his smile and nodded. It wasn't clear what we were supposed to do next. In some clubs you could wait until a break in the music, but not in this one. Not in this apartment. The music kept pounding forward and people danced everywhere, and Jack appeared a little out of his element. He was not the dancer type, I didn't think.

"This is Raef!" Jack yelled to all of us, cupping his mouth with his hands.

He yelled at the top of his voice, and I barely heard him, but everyone nodded, anyway.

"He's the sheepherder from Australia," Jack went on with a second breath. "He's a great guy. We've been traveling together for a while."

"Hi, ladies," Raef said, his voice sharper and easier to hear through the music.

I looked at Raef. He was a handsome guy, though slightly husky and not as tall as Jack, with sandy-colored hair and a bright, happy smile. His accent—even in the two words he had spoken—sounded delightful. He wore some sort of Australian fleece-lined jacket, and it looked like it should be too hot to wear in a crowd like this, but it also looked like he *always* wore it. He had a big can of beer in his hand. He smiled and toasted us.

And it took me a second, and I'm not even sure I understood it at first, but his eyes were not on Amy, as we had come to expect in all our time together, but on Constance. And her eyes were glued onto his. Even Amy saw it, and she flashed a quick look at me, her eyebrows up again, as if to ask, *Really?* It was hard to imagine Constance with a less likely guy than an Australian sheepherder from the outback.

"Our grandkids are going to love this story," Jack said into my ear.

"Is that so?"

"Absolutely. Raef will have to be best man at our wedding. In fact, the entire wedding party is right here."

"Does this line ever work? This whole marriage thing?"

"It's working now, isn't it?"

I shook my head, but my stomach said something else.

"Time for a drink," I said, then yelled loud enough to the other three. "Hey, Jack Vermont is buying the next round!"

We headed back to the bar. We had crossed halfway across the dance floor when suddenly a bunch of people started yelling and scattering from something happening in their midst. It was all herd behavior; a girl slipped in her heels and went to one knee, and no one helped her up. Then someone else shot by, and I couldn't understand what he said, but he was laughing and shaking his head and saying something in Dutch. Jack grabbed me to make sure no one bowled me over, and I had a quick flash of Raef grabbing Constance. I had lost Amy, though I suspected she was just behind us, and I knew, whatever happened, she could take care of herself. I started to turn to look for her when I saw the cause of the disturbance.

Two guys, both horribly drunk, both skinheads, danced in the middle of the floor with their dicks out. They peed wherever they liked, their penises flapping, their hands up in exaltation. It felt good to pee, they seemed to say, and they danced with no self-consciousness at all. They wobbled on their feet, then occasionally seemed to get their balance. When they appeared steady, they wiggled their johnnies again and peed. Whenever they approached the surrounding circle, the crowd surged back, yelling and squealing, while the two guys high-fived and generally made jackasses of themselves. It was the worst kind of assholish frat party behavior, and I hadn't expected to see anything like it in Europe.

"Gross," Amy said from behind me. "Just fucking gross."

Then the guys danced toward us.

Everyone pushed back, but we didn't have anywhere to go. The bar blocked one end and the jam of people had made it impossible to move. I had a brief glimpse of the dancers' dumb, stupid faces as they gyrated forward. They appeared smug and happy, oblivious to almost everything around them except the beat of the music and their floppy joints. A glistening stream of urine looped out from their dicks every few steps, and the crowd pushed back and away, disgusted and mesmerized at the same time.

"Here they come!" Constance yelled, trying her best to melt into the people behind her. "Oh, God!"

"It's disgusting!" Amy shouted.

A few guys tried to dart forward and grab the dancers, but the dancers always managed to turn and threaten with their penises before the guys could seize them. The dancers had the sort of dumb, funny luck that sometimes happens to boozers. They laughed and kept drifting toward us, their hands on their wankers whenever they felt threatened.

They were the proverbial skunks at the garden party, and they were damn good at what they were doing.

Maybe he didn't step out of a moonbeam, or climb off the back of a white charger, but Jack stepped forward. Somehow he had gotten hold of a rubber trash can lid and managed to fit it to his forearm like a shield. As soon as people got an inkling of his strategy, they began to laugh and cheer. Raef called him over and handed him a shoe. It took me a second, but I realized eventually that it was Constance's heeled sandal. Jack needed it as a second weapon, one that he could use to whack their penises if they came too close. He held it by the toe and practiced twanging it down. The dancers didn't seem to care what Jack had planned. They drank from two enormous cans of beer, and you could all but see the liquid passing through them to their bladders.

I looked over at Constance and Amy. They both watched, their mouths open with surprise and delight. Raef had his arm hooked through Constance's arm.

Here's another thing: the situation was weird, inevitably thuggish, with the guys being skinheads and everything, but Jack, by playing to the crowd, defused it. He walked slowly around the perimeter of the circle, a Roman gladiator greeting the crowd, and the people began hooting and laughing. Twice he feinted toward the dancers, pretending to rush them, but they crabbed backward, their johnnies propped in their hands. Then, as if dumbly coming up with a strategy of their own, they began circling Jack in different directions, one trying to sneak behind him while he was occupied with the other.

I watched Jack, and I thought about our kiss and the way his arm felt around the small of my back.

Finally, he moved on the dancers. He held the shield in front of him, ready to deflect the urine back at them if they tried to squirt at him, and the skinheads proved to be no match. He took a big snap at one of the dancers' penises with Constance's shoe, and the guy wobbled away and began tucking his goods back in his pants. The other guy came sideways at Jack, but Jack moved too fast for him. Jack slammed the shield against the idiot, and the guy took three giant steps sideways, tried to right himself in his drunkenness, then fell like a plank onto his side. His beer skidded off into the crowd, and Jack, jumping on him, grabbed the guy's feet and began using him to mop up the floor. The crowd loved seeing that, and two other guys came forward and began running the dancer around the floor like a Hoover. The second dancer—the one who had escaped—made a halfhearted effort to intervene, but a bunch of people began booing him and chased him away. The skinhead wandered off, leaving his friend to be rolled around in his own mess.

Jack made a final triumphant circle, raising the shield in victory. I met his eyes and wondered if a prince could be a guy with a garbage can lid on his forearm, a shoe as a sword, his knighthood conferred by besting dragons squirting their noxious fluids.

10

Just your father being your father. You know how he is, darling. Have fun.

I am having fun. But Daddy's being a buzzkill.

He doesn't mean to be. Just Dad being Dad. He can't help it.

If anything, I'm TOO on top of everything. You know that.

He knows it, too. Just have fun. By the way, I cleaned out that back closet and gave away some old dresses.

Which old dresses? Do we have to do this now?

Just the blue one with the sleeves. You haven't worn it in years. I want my closets back!

Oh, Mom, good grief. How is Mr. Periwinkle?

He's outside a lot. Okay, have to run. Kiss the girls.
   . . . and make them cry?

Miss you.

Miss you, too.

R aef traveled for jazz. That's what he told us, and that's why
we followed him at three o'clock in the morning to a place
called Smarty's on a tiny little street off a tiny little street beside a canal somewhere in the downtown part of Amsterdam.
He promised us it would be worth it, and after shots and a half
dozen gin and tonics, after an Amsterdam joint the size of an ear
of corn, we were in no shape to refuse. He led us down a set of
cement stairs to a basement bar. I wondered how they could have
basement bars in Amsterdam because the whole place hovered at
sea level, but I was in no condition to discuss civil engineering. I
hung on to Jack and Constance hung on to Raef and Amy hung
on to Alfred, a Dutch guy whose fingers reminded me of typewriter keys.

Victor, Amy's Count Chocula, had never shown at the party.
Somehow or another, Count Chocula and Alfred knew each other,
but I couldn't draw a mental line to connect them.

A waitress with bulging biceps and a look that said she might
spit into your drink or take you home, either option open, pointed
us to a table by the WC. We had to turn sideways to make it through
the small tables, and the music wrapped around us and didn't let

go. A black guy played a deep sax, twisting the sound and making it yowl and bend and sip, and as soon as we plopped down, Raef leaned across the table and told us what we were hearing.

"That's Johnn P," he said, his voice bright and Aussie and fun to listen to, "and he's from Nigeria, but he lives here now. I don't think the other guys are well known, just session guys sitting in."

That was all I heard. Even that was difficult to hear. The waitress came by, and we ordered drinks—cognacs with waters on the side—and she nodded and headed off like a woman wading through a meadow of chairs. I felt hazy and a bit disoriented, but also happy. I wasn't Hemingway, and this wasn't Spain after World War I, but it was as close as I had come in my short life.

"I'd rate our kiss on the platform about a seven. How about you?" Jack asked, leaning close.

"That high? I was thinking more a six, maybe a five point five."

"You're a righty kisser. I knew you would be."

"How did you know it?"

"Most people are. If you meet a lefty kisser, chances are they have a small fin on the back of their neck. It's very hard to see, but it will be there."

"A fin?"

He nodded.

"A little-known fact," he said.

"Trouble is, I've never been ranked below a nine. My kisses can ruin a man for all other women. I'm just reporting what people say."

"That's why I held back, too," he said. "I could have brought it up to a ten, but I didn't want you to faint on the spot."

"What's the fin for?"

"What fin?"

"The fin you just talked about. The one on the back of the person's neck."

"People of Atlantis. They all kiss lefty."

"And that's how you can detect them?"

"Also, they will not eat tuna fish. Or any fish, for that matter. It's a question of cannibalism."

"I see. Can a normal person be a lefty kisser?"

"Not in my experience, no."

"Is it dangerous to kiss a citizen of Atlantis?"

"Desperately. You should always bring a tiny packet of tartar sauce on a first date just in case. Obviously, tartar sauce is Kryptonite to anyone from Atlantis."

"Do you always go on this way?"

"What way?"

"With your tall tales."

"You don't think I have a packet of tartar sauce in my pocket as we speak?"

"No, I don't think you do."

He leaned back. He made a tsking sound with his tongue and shook his head.

"Chauffeur, cook, or cleaner?" I asked him.

"What?" he asked, and he put his hand on my thigh and he looked me dead in the eye and it was nearly too much.

"Chauffeur, cook, or cleaner?" I repeated, trying to ignore his hand and his eyes.

"If I could have only one?"

I nodded. I should have removed his hand. My spine felt rubbery.

"Cleaner. I like to cook, and I'm a better driver than James Bond."

"But you look more like Wolverine."

"Should I move my hand?"

"In which direction?"

He smiled and took it away, and for a while we watched the guys playing music.

The waitress came back almost in time to the other musicians returning to the ribbon of sax, and Raef nodded and clapped, and so we clapped, too, because it was cool seeing the musicians match up, find each other in the melody, and it was cool thinking that Johnn P was a Nigerian playing sax in a European bar and that we had come from the United States and intersected with him here. Maybe that was the pot thinking, too—who knew?—but when I sipped the cognac I let it burn the roof of my mouth and tongue and looked over and smiled at Amy and Constance, both of them lizard-eyed and nodding slowly to the music.

My phone rang. It took me a moment to realize what it was, but when I dug it out of my pocket, I saw Brian's number on the screen. The ex-boyfriend. I hadn't heard from him the entire summer, and I suspected he hadn't been to bed and had a case of the phonies. Late-night boo-hoos. Nostalgia for something that wasn't much like the thing you remembered. Or maybe he genuinely missed me. Out of habit, out of curiosity, I almost hit the *green* button with my thumb, then thought better of it. Jack didn't even look over or seem to care.

I decided I didn't speak Brian anymore. I tucked the phone back in my pocket and put it on silence.

"Meet you at the hostel," Amy whispered in my ear when the band stopped for a break.

"You don't even know this guy," I said.

"*None* of us know these guys," Amy said. "Don't worry, I can call you. We're going to meet some other people for a drink. One guy is a magician, I guess. How often do you get to meet a magician in Amsterdam? Besides, the train isn't until the afternoon, right?"

"Two fifty."

I glanced at my phone to confirm my statement against the train schedule I had downloaded.

"Two fifty," I repeated.

"I'll be back at the hostel long before that, so don't worry. We'll see how things go with the Flying Dutchman. We can figure out everything tomorrow. Are you going to stay here and listen to more music?"

"I don't know yet. I'm getting tired."

"Carpe Jack-um. He's way into you. And he's off-the-charts gorgeous."

"What about Constance?"

We both looked over at Constance. She sat with Raef and John P, listening to a jazz conversation, apparently. She looked alert and happy and even had her hand on the small of Raef's back. We both looked at one another, then Amy shook her head.

"She's going sheepherder on us," she said. "I've never seen her so smitten."

"He's cute."

"He's really cute. I love his accent."

"Okay, then we're set," I said, trying to summarize, and because I always summarized. It was my singular talent. "I'll meet you back at the hostel. Call if anything changes. Don't get sawn in half."

I wanted to concentrate and make sure I understood everything correctly, but I was blurry and drunk and tired. I knew we
had a reason to leave Amsterdam pretty quickly, but I couldn't
remember why. It had something to do with a train connection,
and also something to do with meeting a cousin of Amy's in
Munich or Budapest, but I couldn't remember which. Besides,
the scenario reminded me of *Three Coins in the Fountain*, a corny old
black-and-white movie about three girls visiting Rome. They each
throw a coin in the fountain and the music swells, then a song
asks, "Which coin will the fountain bless?" The Mom-a-saurus
made me watch it on Netflix with her before I left. It was one of
her all-time favorite movies.

Too much had happened too quickly, and I didn't trust our
drunkenness. I also didn't trust Alfred, the Flying Dutchman with
the typewriter fingers; I had decided he was long and gangly, like
an overgrown asparagus plant, and I didn't like him. But Amy did
like him, or at least wanted to go with him, and I tried not to
judge when it came to her hookups, so I nodded and kissed her
cheek and told her to be careful. She said she would be, then she
grabbed Alfred and headed out.

That left me with Jack.

"Want to go?" he asked when Amy slipped up the stairs to the
street and into the night. "I know a place you should see."

"I'm tired, Jack."

"Of me, or just tired?"

"Not of you."

"Then the place I have to show you . . . Raef helped me locate
it on a map. We have to find it together."

Everything had softened. It was going to be morning soon,
and the street would come awake with coffee and baked goods,

and it was Amsterdam, the first time in my life, but I could hardly keep my eyes open. I didn't know what I wanted to do, although I knew I wanted to be with Jack.

"It's going to be light soon," I said, stalling.

"That makes it better."

"I'll tell Constance we're leaving," I said, and I stood.

I had made up my mind without knowing I was making up my mind. Jack called the waiter over and settled the bill with the money we had all contributed as I told Constance the plan.

11

....

After World War II, my grandfather made his way back home, but it took him a while. It took him about three months, maybe a little longer. Part of that was probably the devastation in Europe and the lack of dependable transportation, but he went on walkabout. That's what Raef called it when I told him about it. My grandfather never talked about it much. He seemed guilty about it somehow, or secretive. But he kept a journal, and now I'm following it. You asked what I'm doing, and that's it," Jack said, his body turned toward me. "That probably doesn't sound like much, but it is something I need to do. It's something I promised myself I would do, and now I'm doing it."

We had walked for a good half hour, and the streets *did* smell of coffee and baked goods. The sky hadn't become light yet, but the darkness had retreated and lost its grip. The windows and the canals had begun to glow with pink, but you could not see things distinctly. Once we saw a cat sitting in the window of an apartment, just under an illuminated lamp, and it stared at us for a moment before suddenly flinching and bending its head down to lick its shoulder.

"What were you doing before you started following his journal?"

"Journalism, mostly. Changing the world for good. Isn't that what they say? I graduated from the University of Vermont with a communications degree. I don't even know if journalism exists anymore in the age of the Internet, but that's what I was doing. When I got out of college, I took a reporting job in Wyoming at a small paper near the Wind River Range. I know, I know, little off the front line of journalism, but I thought I might be able to influence a community that size, whereas in a big city I would be a cub reporter with no clout. I've kind of come to think that small-town papers are the front line of journalism, but that's another story. It turned out to be an excellent paper, and I wrote everything, which was great training. I had a boss named Walter Goodnow, who was one of these old-time journalists you don't find much anymore. He gave me plenty to do, but he also let me write features, and he worked with me. Close editing. I wrote a lot of editorials, too, and I found out I had a tendency to be shrill when it came to topics that I believe in. Walter called me a pot-stirrer, but that wasn't all bad. I stayed there for about three years."

"Why did you leave?"

"Oh, I guess it was time to go. Walter said as much. After that, some things happened, not great things, and I decided to take a break. To interrupt my march to journalistic world dominance."

"And you also hatched the plan to follow the journal?"

"I was a little at loose ends. I needed a guide. I needed someone to help me start my life over again. My grandfather had to do it after the war."

"But you'll go back to journalism?"

"That's the plan. Walter called it the Clark Kent fantasy. You're a journalist, but you're also Superman. Once a news junkie, always a news junkie. You can't help it."

"I like that you're following your grandfather's journal."

"I'm actually hitting the most important spots in no special order, but I don't think that matters. And here I am going on and on and you want to eat, don't you?"

"You're not going on and on, but I do want coffee and bread. It has been a long night."

"Next bakery," he said, "we'll stop."

But nothing was quite open. We teetered on the edge of a fun night gradually becoming a march to hell. I still felt drunk and sloppy. My feet hurt, and I had started to worry about Amy and Constance. We had separated before on our travels, but usually after a couple of days in a city. This all seemed too fast, too reckless, and I was about to tell Jack I should grab a cab back to the hostel when finally he found an open bakery. It was merely a hole in the wall, a place to step in, order, then go, but an old woman opened the door for us when she saw us peering in, and she nodded when we ordered.

We ordered a lot. We took three baguettes in a paper bag, two croissants, one chocolate éclair, a chocolate bar, and two steaming coffees. Jack spoke to the woman in English, but she responded in Dutch. He tried German on her, and that worked fairly well, and he talked for a minute or two, asking directions, then he nodded and grabbed my elbow and led me out.

"Drink your coffee, but I have a place where we can eat," he said, his smile contagious, his excitement obvious. "She told me how to get there. We're close."

The coffee tasted fresh. I realized, holding it, that I had become chilled. Maybe it was hunger, or being drunk still, or the residue of the pot we had smoked, but I felt cold down in my spine. Jack held the paper bag open and made me put my nose in it. He said to breathe it in, that it was possible we would remember this single minute as long as we lived.

"I didn't take you for such a romantic," I said when he lifted the bag away. "You said I had it bad with Hemingway, but you have it worse."

"What's the opposite of a romantic? I've always wondered."

"An accountant, I guess. A person who knows the price of everything and the value of nothing."

"Whoa," Jack said. "Did you just Plato my ass at four o'clock in the morning?"

"Not that hard to do, Jack Vermont."

"You don't even know my last name, do you?"

"Do you know mine?"

"Merriweather."

"Wrong."

"Albuquerque. Postlewaite. Smith-Higginbothom. It's probably a hyphenate. Am I close?"

"Tell me yours first, and then I'll tell you mine."

"Now you're pulling some Rumpelstiltskin trip on me."

"Does your conversation ever go in a straight line?"

"Yes and no."

He smiled. He had a damn good smile.

"Let's keep our names to ourselves," I said. "That will make it harder for you to find me after you've fallen hopelessly in love with me. It will turn it into a quest."

"How do you know I'm not already hopelessly in love with you?"

"Too soon. It usually takes men a day and a half for them to pledge their lives to my service."

"Heather Postlewaite, for sure."

"Weren't you taking me somewhere?"

"You're making it difficult. Jack and Heather or Heather and Jack? Which way sounds more natural?"

"Heather and Jack."

"You're just making up anything now."

"Jack and Heather sounds like a candle store."

"What's wrong with a candle store? Jack and Heather is the euphonious order, and you know it."

"Euphonious? Is euphonious Latin for 'I'm trying to catch up to my smarter friend so I will throw in the biggest word I can think of'?"

We had been walking slowly. Before Jack could answer, a different smell took over. It didn't originate with the canals or the croissants, but something familiar and friendly, something I knew I recognized but couldn't quite place. Jack smiled as I struggled to make sense of it.

"Come on," he said, and I did.

12

....

The street sign hung from the side of the building read Nieuwe Kalfjeslaan 25, 1182 AA Amstelveen. The smell came from somewhere behind a dungeon door, a wide half circle of heavy black wood with equally heavy hardware. It didn't make much sense to me, but Jack began smiling, and he pulled at the hardware, causing it to make a loud bang. The door opened on creaky hinges, exactly out of a Frankenstein movie. Jack put his finger to his lips and smiled.

I wanted to tell him he had already been loud, that we probably had awakened anyone inside, but he slipped through the crack in the door before I could speak. I looked around, trying to understand what we were getting into, then did a mental shrug and followed him. Besides, he had the paper bag of food.

I smiled when I realized where we were.

It was a riding academy. De Amsterdamse Manege. And it was beautiful. It was old and meticulously cared for; the walls were white stucco, and pine shavings covered the cobblestones that lined the ground. A dozen coats of arms hung on the walls. The horses rested in ancient stalls around the perimeter of a large courtyard. Their heads hung over their stall doors, and they looked drowsy and peaceful, like coat hooks beside a fireplace. Jack grabbed my hand and led me to the first stall.

"The horse's name is Apple," he said, reading the Dutch.

"Hello, Apple," I said.

I petted his forelock and his cheek. He was a beautiful horse, not the knock-kneed nag you might find in a riding academy in some American towns, and slowly I slipped my arms around him. He smelled like everything good.

"My grandfather came here after the war," Jack whispered, his eyes a little wet, his hand petting Apple. "He wrote about this place, but I wasn't sure it still existed. He said the horses gave him hope after everything he had seen in the war. He always took special note of animals and children. He gave this place three stars. That's his highest rating."

"How did you know it was here?"

"I didn't, honestly. It was in his journal. I've read the entries a hundred times, but I'd always wondered if the horses still existed. The stable, I mean. I knew the general area of town, and Raef told me he remembered something about a riding academy being out this way. We looked it up when we got here, and that coffee lady gave me the last bit of directions."

"I rode a little when I was a girl."

"I'm glad you like horses," he said.

"I love animals," I said and let go of Apple and walked to the second stall. "I always have. What's this one's name?"

"Cygnet, I think. A baby swan."

I took out my cell phone to take a picture, but Jack stopped me.

"Would you mind," he asked, "if we didn't take a picture?"

I lowered the phone.

"Why not?"

He moved his hand slowly on Cygnet's nose. His voice was serious but sweet.

"I don't want to cheapen the experience," he said. "Or turn it into a little snapshot. I want to be here with the horses, that's all. And with you. I hate taking photos of everything. It means what's going on now is only this thing we perform so we can take pictures and look at them later. Stick them on Facebook. It dilutes whatever we're doing. That's kind of what I think, anyway."

"Do you take photos of anything?"

He shrugged. He shook his head.

"I want to remember being here with you," he said. "And I want to remember Cygnet and the smell of the coffee and manure, and the horse smell. I want to think of my grandfather being here, his pleasure and relief at seeing the horses. I don't know. I guess it's a little goofy."

"I don't think it's goofy, Jack."

I looked at him. This was a different side of him, and I liked it.

After petting the horses, we climbed up on a stack of hay in the center of the courtyard. A light rain began to fall, and the hay was piled under a pole barn. We climbed to the top of the bales and found a place to sit. The hay smelled magnificent, like open fields, and, mixed with the scent of the rain and the gentle movements of the horses, it couldn't have been more lovely. We ate the baguettes and the éclair and everything else. I couldn't believe how perfect the food tasted, how it felt to be with Jack in the horse academy. He seemed to read my mind.

"Pretty good first date," he said.

"Kind of up there on the list. Are you calling this a date?"

"What are you calling it?"

"Amy would say it's a hookup."

"I think it's a date, sort of."

"Okay."

"How long are you staying in Europe?" he asked, changing the subject.

"Another two or three weeks. I have to be back to work in the fall. I'm starting a new job."

"Where?"

"At Bank of America."

He looked at me.

"We can fix that," he said.

"It doesn't need to be fixed."

"Are you sure? I don't see you as a corporate suit."

"Judge much?"

"Things are what they are."

Our wires crossed a little. I wasn't sure why, or what it meant, but for an instant I felt a flicker of both of us reappraising things. I remembered what he had said about his editor calling him a pot-stirrer.

He gave me a look, then pushed one of the hay bales back and arranged two more on either side until we had a tiny couch. He lay back and then pulled me close. He put his arms around me. I rested my head on his shoulder and wondered what he would do next, if now came the big seduction moment, but he was smarter than that, better than that. He turned my face up to his and kissed me, kissed me with everything, then pulled me even closer if that was possible.

"Stay close," he whispered.

"You want to sleep here?"

"Well, we could sleep in bed, something we've both done a thousand times. Or we could sleep here next to the horses in Amsterdam in each other's arms and remember it the rest of our lives. Is it really a choice?"

"This is your code?"

"Something like that."

"Rough treasures?"

"Experience everything, I suppose. Drink it in. Is that a horrible cliché?"

I was still stung by his comments about Bank of America, but I understood him a little better.

"I'm still deciding," I managed.

A little while later, our breathing matched, and the scent of hay covered everything.

13

....

I woke to the smell of cigarette smoke. For a moment I had no idea where I was. Jack still slept beside me. The rain had grown heavier. Bit by bit, the pieces of the previous night came parading back. I sat up, slightly panicked. I had no notion of the hour, no notion of anything except that we had petted the horses last night. With the rain obscuring the sun, it might have been any time. The question of the cigarette smoke puzzled me until I realized someone smoked below us, under the cover of the pole barn, probably on break from doing something with the horses. Then I heard a voice speaking to someone. Jack slowly sat up beside me, his finger again to his lips, a smile spreading on his face.

"We're trapped," he whispered and almost started laughing.

"What time is it?"

He shrugged.

Ten or a million thoughts surged through my brain. For one thing, I had to pee. I mean, *really* pee. And I imagined the hay had made me look pretty much like a crazy woman. I put a hand to my hair and felt it going out in every direction. My lips and throat felt coated with chocolate, and my fingers felt greasy and dirty and horsey.

Then I thought about Amy and Constance. I glanced at my phone, but neither one of them had texted.

It was six forty-eight in the morning. That was the other thing the cell phone said. Brian had left a message, but I didn't have the stomach to listen to that at the moment.

"How are we going to get out of here?" I asked Jack.

"We'll just climb down. We haven't done anything wrong."

"How about breaking and entering?"

"We'll act like we just got done having sex," he said, grinning and balling up the paper bag and policing the area. "Everyone loves a lover. Besides, what can they do?"

"They can call the police."

"For two people having sex in a haystack?"

"We didn't have sex."

"But you wanted to."

I nudged his shoulder. He laughed. We heard a shoe scuff below us, and someone called up, his voice coated with nervousness.

"Who is there?" he called.

At least I think that's what he said. He called in Dutch.

"We fell asleep," Jack called down. Then he said the German word for *sleep*.

Then another voice joined the first voice, and I knew we had to climb down and face the music. Maybe they thought we were bums. Maybe they thought we were thieves. Jack went first. He turned back to me and helped me down. Two men—one young, one old—had backed away from the hay bales, their faces turned up to watch us.

"We came in to pet the horses and fell asleep," Jack said.

The old man shook his head. He obviously wasn't happy with us. But the young guy—who had the cigarette and probably had broken a rule by smoking next to the hay bales—spoke to us in passable English.

"This is not good what you have done," the young man said.

He had a thin face and a bunch of hair that went up a few inches from his scalp, then fell over into a hair hedge. He lips came together in a pucker.

"Sorry," Jack said. "We were out late. We didn't hurt anything."

The old man spoke rapidly to the younger one. The younger one answered. Then the older man hurried off.

"He's going to call the police. You'd better hurry. There's a station nearby here, so they won't be long."

Only he reversed the word order so that it came out, *long won't be*. He sounded like Yoda from *Star Wars*.

Jack grabbed my hand, and we ran for the door.

Halfway home—after stopping in a restaurant and going to the bathroom and getting more coffee—Jack made me stop to watch a swan paddle beneath a cobblestone bridge.

"My grandfather wrote about swans in his journal. I think it surprised him to find them here. He seemed to relish seeing any signs of nature, because that signified they had survived . . . that things would go on."

"Can you find a passage about swans?"

"I know one almost by heart, but let me see."

He dug in his pocket and brought out a small journal, Bible sized, that had a rubber band around the center. It *was* a Bible,

really, I realized, at least for Jack. He put the spine against the
railing next to the river and slowly opened the journal. I'm not
sure why, but I had imagined the journal as a big, wide book—
like a scrapbook, maybe—but when I saw its dimensions, it made
more sense. This was what a man might carry after the war. He
could keep it in his pocket, as Jack did, and pull it out when it was
time to make an entry. It wasn't much different from my calendar
book.

"I thought it would be bigger," I said, leaning close to him to
see the book.

"A woman should never say that to a man."

He kept his eyes on the book, carefully paging through it. I
bumped his shoulder. I loved seeing the tenderness with which he
handled the journal. He did not rush to find the passage, but lingered on each small portion of it. Twice he stopped to show me
pictures of his grandfather that were wedged among the pages: a
tall, handsome man in uniform, the pictures grayed and cracked
now with time. His grandfather's eyes, in each picture Jack showed
me, looked tired and hollow and sad. What made his expressions
sadder and more poignant was the attempt, at the borders of his
face, at the lines of his forehead, to smile for the camera. But he
could not hide his sorrow and his feelings at coming through the
horror of World War II.

I put my cheek against Jack's shoulder. I wanted to watch his
hands move slowly over the onionskin pages of the journal. Finally, he found the selection and tilted it for me to see. Then he
read. His voice became solemn and quiet and filled with love.

*"The swan swam on a small portion of water, its neck bent in a
perfect curve. The angle of the morning light threw the swan's*

reflection onto the surface so that it seemed to move with a companion, one matched to each slight movement."

Beneath the passage, his grandfather had drawn a small sketch of a swan swimming among lily pads.

"That's beautiful, Jack. It's poetry, really."

"I think he secretly wanted to write. We talked about it now and then. He read a great deal, mostly nineteenth-century novels. He shared books with me, and each year we read *Ivanhoe* together. We read it out on the porch at night before bedtime, and I loved that story and that memory. That's why I guess I gave you such a hard time about your iPad. Have you ever heard someone say that books are places we visit and that when we run into people who have read the books we have read, it's the same as if we had traveled to the same locations? We know something about them because they have lived in the same worlds we have lived. We know what they live for."

Jack blushed. It was the first time I had seen him blush, and I liked him for it.

"I like knowing you have that feeling for literature."

"Well, at least for my grandfather's journal."

"Is this the only copy? Would you mind if I held it?"

"I made a transcription. I typed it all in so that I would know each word. I guess that sounds funny. Honestly, I have most of it by heart."

"That's not funny at all," I said, slowly receiving the book from Jack.

The journal had a nice weight and balance. I opened it and saw the inscription. It simply said his grandfather's Christian name—Vernon, and his military ID number—and his address as Bradford,

Vermont, USA. Beside it was an inked sketch of a tank. Whether the tank was German or Allied, I couldn't tell.

"He was a farm boy, and he was dazzled by what he saw, and he really wrote beautifully. He was also hollowed out, I think. This trip filled him up again. I suppose I was hoping it would do that for me, too. This trip."

"I'd like to read his journal if it wouldn't be overstepping."

"You'd be the fifth person in the world to read it. My mom and dad and my grandmother."

I returned the journal to him. He put it carefully back together, reset the rubber band around it, and slid it in his pocket. Then he held my hand while we watched the swans paddle gracefully upstream. He told me to look for iridescence in the feathers. He said the legend was that the swans had once lived by eating light, but the gods had found their beauty threatening and made them hunger for grass instead. But the swans had eaten enough light that it could still sometimes be seen within them.

There was no need for a photograph.

There was no need for anything at all.

14

....

Back at the hostel, I had maybe the best shower of my life. I washed every inch of my body and shampooed and cream-rinsed my hair. Now and then, as I moved under the spray, I thought of Jack. Each time he came to mind, my body gave a small spasm. *Jack Vermont*. I didn't even know his last name, although I now knew his grandfather's first name and that his family came from Bradford, Vermont. For now, Jack was just Jack, my knight with a garbage can lid, my late-night horse whisperer. He had already taken too many of my thoughts.

When I stepped out, I found that Constance had texted me while I was in the shower. She had reached the same conclusion I had: it was weird to be passing through Amsterdam so quickly. We hadn't seen a thing, really, except the inside of a party, and she had half a dozen sites she wanted to visit. We were leaving because of Amy, I remembered. We had an appointment in Prague, and I couldn't recall all the details, but the plan permitted only a night and part of a day in Amsterdam. It was a bad plan, but because we hadn't heard from Amy, we couldn't change anything. I texted Constance and recommended we stick to the plan. She texted back, agreed reluctantly, and also said Raef called her *his Sheila*.

Back in the room, I sat on the bed and called my father. It took a long time for my dad to answer. When he did, I could tell he was in some sort of meeting or someplace he couldn't talk easily. My dad was usually in some sort of meeting. He spoke quickly, in short bursts, and behind him I heard glasses tinkling and other people conversing.

"Hi, sweetheart," he said. "How goes the grand European tour?"

"It's great, Daddy. We're in Amsterdam. It's a gorgeous city."

"How long will you be there?"

"We're leaving today, I think. We're bopping through because we have to get over to Prague to meet up with Amy's cousins."

"Well, that's good," he said, and then he evidently covered the phone and spoke to someone else. It was always hard to get his full attention, even long distance, when he was in a business environment. At home, he was a softie.

"Listen," he said when he came back on, "I talked to Ed Belmont, and he's really pleased you're joining his team. It's going to be long hours, but it will be worth it. You couldn't learn from anyone better. There's no limit on that position. But he said you didn't fill out the paperwork yet. You can't let these things go like that, Heather. You know better."

"I've got it covered, Daddy. I'll take care of everything, I promise."

"I missed that last part," he said.

"I said I'd take care of the paperwork," I said. "Scout's honor."

"Okay. It just puts me in an odd position with Ed. I thought you had already taken care of it. Business is all about first impressions and about follow-through."

"I'm on it, Dad."

"If you were on it, then we wouldn't be having this conversation, would we?"

There it was. The old two-step we did together. I wasn't sure what he wanted me to say. I wasn't positive *he* knew what he wanted out of the conversation. He had plenty of plates in the air, I knew, and at some level—business-wise—I was simply another plate. He had extended himself with Ed Belmont to get me hired, and now, to his mind, I had paid him back by not getting the paperwork in earlier than it needed to be in. I had not been sufficiently bushy-tailed and eager, and that was against the business ethos. If I entered his world, then I had to play by his rules.

At the same time, he had been happy to see me head off to Europe. His attitudes were contradictory and complicated. He probably wasn't aware of the mixed messages.

"Daddy, I am aware of my obligations and the expectations from Ed Belmont's team. I am. It's not your onion."

"What?"

"It's a French phrase. It means it's not your problem."

Something else made noise beyond his phone. He was in the middle of something and said as much when his voice came back to me.

"It *is* my problem, Heather! What do I always say? Either one meets his obligation or he doesn't. There's no in-between that's worth anything."

"I'm meeting it, Dad," I said, feeling my neck turning red and my blood beginning to percolate. "It's not your worry. I have an understanding with Ed's team. It's all going to be okay."

"Just call them, would you? Check in?"

"I can do that, Dad."

"Remember, Ed's an old bastard like I am. We feel better knowing where the thermostat is set."

"Dad, you're not an old bastard. You're a *really* old bastard."

He laughed. Whatever storm clouds had choked his sky seemed to lift a little.

"Sweetheart, I should jump off here. Glad to hear you're doing okay. How are the other girls?"

"They're doing fine. We're having a great time."

"Good, good. Well, you're only young once, right? Isn't that what they say? Okay, sweetie, I'll see—"

His voice disappeared, cut off by some unexplained transcontinental quirk. I didn't call him back. You didn't call my father back. Not when he was in a meeting.

15

....

I lost all my shit! Everything! Phone, license, passport, you name it! I am the worst, stupid-ass American tourist who ever lived!" Amy said when she finally got herself under control in the hostel cafeteria. After not showing up for most of the morning, she had finally borrowed a passerby's cell phone to call and tell us not to meet her at the train station, but to stay where we were. She hadn't explained much except to say she had been in a *situation*, a bad one, and that she only had her own idiotic self to blame. Now, sitting in the small hostel breakfast room, she looked like a wild woman—her wolf hair stood up like a British grenadier's hat—and she was angry enough to kill someone. "It must have dropped out when I put my coat on the couch at this party. I had it all together in that little, like, makeup bag thing, the one with frogs on it—you know the one. But who knows? I think it slid out when I lifted the jacket up, or maybe it was earlier. It's so fucking dumb it makes me cringe to think about it. Amy, the great and freaking powerful Amy, who can go anywhere, do anything, and here I am like the most dumb-ass tourist who ever left the U.S."

"Did you have it at the jazz club?" I asked. "The one Raef took us to?"

"Yes, yes, believe me, I've gone over it in my head a thousand times. I even went back to the apartment where I took off my coat, but it wasn't there. The apartment owner was very nice. He said he'd get in touch if anyone found it. He made me give him my information, and I took his."

"Do you think someone could have stolen it?"

"Possible, but not really. I think I just lost the fucker. What a reckless, stupid ass I am."

Constance sat beside her and held her hand. I had never seen Amy so shaken, and I couldn't blame her. The story didn't make much sense, at least not initially, because she had trouble telling it in sequence. We were all too drunk and too stoned the night before to be clear about any detail. But the basic elements came through.

Bottom line, she had no identification, no money, no phone, and no real way of resupplying herself.

"I am so, so, so, so, so bummed," she said. "I am such a complete rookie! What an idiot!"

"Okay, lighten up, Amy," I said. "Things happen. It's just a thing. We can get it ironed out. It's just a small setback."

I didn't dare glance at Constance, because I was certain she had come to the same conclusion. Amy had just fumbled away her trip. We didn't have time, I didn't think, to go through the headache of getting a new passport, new credit cards, and so forth. That's what made Amy so irate. She knew it, too.

"It's okay, honey," Constance said. "It's a setback. Heather's right about that."

"No, it's not. I almost couldn't even get back here! I can't travel without a passport. All my credit cards are gone, too. I have to cancel all those and call Mom and Dad. They are going to freak, I promise you. They *warned* me about this sort of thing."

"All our parents did," I said.

"Yes, but I always lose shit! I hate it about me. Even in second grade, I lost my mittens every day. I swear! My mom got so tired of it she made me wear my brother's socks on my hands!"

We couldn't help it; the comment made us laugh. It took her a moment, but Amy eventually saw the humor in the situation. She buried her head in her hands and laughed. It was a frustrated laugh, but at least it was a laugh.

Amy used my phone to make about a thousand calls. She rang her parents and told them what had happened, cried again, fought through it, explained everything, then took down a bunch of numbers and nodded as she did it. We called from a café not far from the train station. It was called Café Van Gogh. We sat outside and drank water and coffee and ate crackers and cheese. Little by little, Amy pieced the events of the night as well as she could, but the reassembled memories didn't shed any light on the makeup bag's disappearance. It was gone. Ultimately how it got lost didn't particularly matter.

In the late afternoon, we splurged on a room in the Hotel Hollander. Amy said she couldn't stand the thought of dealing with the hostel, so Constance and I chipped in and we got a charming room with a small balcony overlooking a canal. It was a major

splurge, and it cut into the meager budget we had so carefully con-
cocted during our spring semester, but it felt necessary. As soon as
we entered the room, Amy took a shower that went on so long
both Constance and I went in to check on her. Each time she said
she was okay. We didn't really believe her.

Her parents called a half dozen times, worried and trying to
manage things from stateside. They floated the idea that she should
come home. At first I thought that wasn't truly necessary. I asked
myself, *Can't something be done?* Although every time I asked it, I
failed to come up with a solution—but as the afternoon wore into
evening and Amy emerged in a towel, her face taut in a way I had
never seen it, I wasn't so sure. Although the credit cards had
already been canceled, the passport was not going to be easy to
replace. It took time, by all accounts, and we only had another two,
maybe three weeks left in any case. She had lost all her cash, close
to $700. I watched Amy calculating the pros and cons as she
talked to her folks. It was all a mess.

We joined Raef and Jack for late-night fondue, all of us squeezed
around a small table, a pot of cheese in the center, hunks of bread
and sausage scattered on a plate. It was a funny place called the
Bull Stone, as far as we could translate, well off the beaten tourist
track. Raef had known about it; Raef seemed to know everything.
But the silliness of the cheese pot, the communal nature of eating
around a crowded table, wound up being exactly what Amy needed.

You can never anticipate these nights. You can never expect
the kind of spontaneous fun we had. You can plan and plan for a
party, get every detail right, serve delicious food and excellent
drinks, and the party can still fall flat. We had no business being
happy and goofy, no business laughing at everything. Rounds of
beer punctuated each new burst of energy, and the cheese fondue

emptied slowly, the bread and cheese and sausage tasting more and more delicious as time passed, and I thought how I liked sitting here, how I loved my friends, how Jack fit me and Raef fit Constance, and how brave Amy was for rallying. A hundred times I looked over at Jack, or caught him looking at me, and I couldn't help thinking that I had never met anyone like him. I had never felt this *comfortable*, this *compatible* with a guy, and when he asked me if I wanted to go for a nightcap, I said I had to check with Amy, make sure she was going to be all right, then yes, yes, of course, if she felt comfortable.

16

Favorite movie?" Jack asked.

"*Babe.*"

"You're kidding. The movie about the sheepdog pig?"

"I love *Babe.* Favorite serious movie? Is that what you want?" I asked, my knees between his knees, the barstools pulled close. "*My Life as a Dog.*"

"I never heard of it."

"Scandinavian. Swedish, I think. What's your favorite?" I asked him.

"*Lawrence of Arabia* or *Gladiator.*"

"Good choices. If you have to pick one?"

"*Gladiator,*" he said. "Favorite season?"

"Fall. Cliché, I know, but it is. You?"

"Spring," he said. "It was a nice time to be on my grandfather's farm. It felt like everything had been asleep for a long time, and then morning came and everything began to wake up."

"The Vermont farm," I said, starting to see him, to understand something of his life. "With your grandma and grandpa when your parents had split up."

He nodded. I had no idea what time it was. Near midnight, I supposed, although I didn't care. The bar we sat in seemed to have no rules about closing, no plan to kick us out. The bartender was a tall, thin man with an enormous salt-and-pepper beard, who obviously got through the night by playing a game on his computer. He hardly looked up when people came through the door. A taxi driver had recommended the bar. It was called Abraham's.

"Are you tired, Heather Postlewaite?" Jack asked after a little bit. "Should I get you home?"

"Yes, of course. And no, not yet."

"Tell me about your job. You're going to work for Bank of America? New York, the whole thing?"

I nodded. That conversation didn't seem to fit the mood, but he waited, and finally I had to speak.

"Investment banking, really," I said carefully. "I'm going to be involved in the Pacific Rim side of the business—Japan, primarily. I speak a little Japanese. Well, that's not true. I'm fairly fluent. That's really what made me valuable to a couple of companies. I start September fifteenth. I'll travel a lot, back and forth, and I'll be expected to work long hours. It's a great opportunity."

"And a well-compensated position."

"Yes, better than I deserve. Better than anyone deserves, probably. It has potential that way."

"Is that important to you?"

"Is what important?"

"Money. Wealth. I guess the balance of work and life."

I regarded him closely. I wished I had been clearer in my mind, because I felt an agenda sneaking into his questions, a slight judgment, and I didn't like it. Didn't need it. I sipped my drink and looked out at the street. A single streetlight pushed the darkness away around the edges of the buildings.

"Sorry," he said. "A little reaction, that's all. You seem so . . . alive to the world in a way that I don't immediately connect with a corporate employee. With someone in investment banking."

"Investment bankers live in the world," I said, trying to keep my voice level, "and they even like it and admire it."

"Right," he said. "Point taken."

But I didn't think he believed it. He held my hand. Then he turned it over and kissed my palm. He put his eyes on mine.

"I'm sorry about what happened with Amy. Do you think she'll go home?"

"I guess so. She'll push through it, but from a practical standpoint, if she can't get a replacement passport and all the paperwork in reasonable time, she plans to head home in the next day or so."

"It's probably a better choice. It's a shame, but it is."

"It's sad, though. We planned this trip forever. It's all we talked about for the entire spring semester, and now it's gone, just like that. It's strange to think about how quickly things can change."

"You don't seem like a big fan of change."

"I guess I'm not. I don't know."

"A planner?"

"I suppose. You're not?"

"I'm a little lazy about planning. I like things to surprise me."

"I'm the Smythson planner type of girl."

"That's what I'm discovering. And I have an old journal held together by a rubber band. Tidy dresser drawers?"

"Organized closet. Shoes in rows. I alphabetize condiments and spices."

"I'm more of a dress-out-of-the-laundry-basket sort of guy."

"How do you fight wrinkles?"

"I let them live. I let them go free and find their way."

"See, I couldn't stand that. That's like going through life as a basset hound."

"I love basset hounds. What's wrong with a basset hound?"

"But I don't know if you want to be a basset hound. Kind of wrinkly and all jowly. You're not really a basset hound, Jack."

"What am I, then?"

"Oh, maybe a sled-dog type. I'm not sure. I don't know you well enough yet."

"Are you one of those clipped poodles?"

"I hope not. I've always seen myself as a Labrador retriever."

"You are definitely not a Lab. Labs are easygoing and happy with a dirty tennis ball in their mouths."

"I'm easygoing. I do draw the line at dirty tennis balls, though."

A little later, a man came in carrying a box containing a statue of the Virgin Mary. He had bad teeth and a hard face; his hands appeared heavier than any hands I had ever seen on a human, with dark, spatulate fingers connected to a palm as thick and purposeful as a hammerhead. He wore a red kerchief around his neck, but he was not a priest. He set the box on the end of the bar and asked us, and the bar in general, if we wanted to say a prayer to it. I had never seen anything quite like it: it had been made from a packing crate, covered in chicken wire, and he had fashioned a small spotlight behind the topmost frame, so that it appeared the Blessed Mother had been transfixed in a beam of celestial light. Constance, I knew, would have flipped over it. But if the bar owner or any of the other patrons found anything unusual about the box and the scene of the Virgin Mary, her palms turned out to welcome the world, her heel pinning a serpent to the earth, they showed no sign of it.

"Do we pay an offering?" Jack asked the man in English.

The man nodded.

"How much?" Jack asked.

"As you like," the man answered.

Jack dug in his pocket and gave him a few coins. Then he turned to me.

"Do you pray?" he asked.

"Not in a long time."

"I don't often pray, but tonight I feel I should. It's not every day the Virgin Mary walks into a bar."

"Sounds like the start of a bad joke."

"I worry that God might be lonely."

But then to my surprise, he closed his eyes and prayed. I examined his beautiful profile, his solemn expression, and I tried to join him, but I couldn't. When he finished, he crossed himself and nodded at the man with the boxed Virgin Mary. The man nodded. It was late at night, and the man seemed to understand the need for prayers.

17

I climbed into bed with Amy at dawn. It was good to be in a warm bed. She turned when I slid in, mumbled something in her sleep, then fell back into whatever dreams she pursued or ran from. Her feet moved for a moment, pedaling, then she stopped and began breathing steadily. I watched her face for a time and tried to imagine what she had been through. But I was too tired to do a good job of it.

Constance woke us near midday by appearing at the foot of the bed, coffees and bread and croissants spread on a tray in front of her. She had brought tiny plates and white, starched napkins, and she set them out for us on the bedspread. I pulled myself up against the pillows and tried to rub the sleep out of my eyes. The coffee smelled amazing; the croissants resting between tubs of raspberry jam and white bricks of butter reminded my stomach it was hungry.

"Your mother called me twice, Amy," Constance announced, pouring coffee out in the cups for us and adding cream. It was precisely Constance to turn the breakfast into a tea service. "I told her I would let you sleep until noon, then wake you. It's now past noon."

"I have to pee," Amy said. "Give me another half hour before I have to think about Mom and all that."

She shot out of the bed but returned in a few minutes. She had combed her hair and brushed her teeth. She climbed back in bed and fluffed her pillows behind her.

"I cannot think of a single thing I want more in this world right now than a cup of coffee and a delicious croissant," Amy said. "Thank you, Constance. You're a lifesaver."

"I got it from the dining room downstairs. It's surprisingly swanky, you know? The dining room, I mean. I guess this is a better hotel than we realized."

I waited for Constance to finish fixing me a cup of coffee. She handed it to me. I put both hands around it and cuddled it against my chest.

"Okay," Amy said, her voice rising in fun as it used to before losing her papers and cards, "let's go over the scoreboard. Who's in love?"

Constance flushed but did not look up. She continued stirring coffee and adding cream. I felt my neck go red as it always did in these moments.

"Wow," Amy said at our silence, "that means you both are. Jesus, it's really happening. No kidding? You two are not kidding me right now, are you?"

"*Falling* in love, maybe," Constance said, her voice soft. "Maybe. It's all too soon to say. But I like him a lot. I like him terribly."

She finished preparing her own coffee and raised the cup to her lips. Her eyes shone above the rim of the cup. She was happy and in love, or falling in love, exactly as she said, and it showed.

"You're going to end up on a sheep farm in Australia, and I can't freaking stand it!" Amy squealed, her eyes wide. "You're his little Sheila. How dreamy! How ridiculously dreamy! What do they call them? Not farms . . . stations. Sheep stations, don't they call them that?"

"I have no idea," Constance said.

"Oh, yes, you do, you little fibber. You've already dreamed it all out. The wind blows and the kangaroos hop by, and it's all red dust and sheep, but you'll have white tablecloths. Won't she, Heather?"

"If anyone will, Constance will," I agreed.

"And you—you're just as bad. Jack, Jack, the lumberjack! Okay, so I'll need two bridesmaids' dresses, unless you can figure out a way to get married at the same time—a joint wedding, a double wedding! That's what we'll do. It will save money all the way around. Now somebody tell me why I am destined to be the bridesmaid in all this? Always the bridesmaid, never the bride!"

"You might be rushing things just a bit. Jack can be superior and a bit judgy. That's a report from the front."

"Can he now?" Amy asked, glancing at Constance with a twinkle in her eye.

"He's very bohemian. At least he thinks he is. Aspires to be, I guess. He's dissing my plans to work for Bank of America. Says the corporate types are not alive to the world."

"Oh, that's just something he says. He's just posturing," Constance said. "He's crazy about you. Anyone can see that."

"One minute he's so sweet and sincere, and the next minute he's on his soapbox about how life should be. He's all carpe diem, let's go explore, let's not worry about tomorrow—"

"You *are* in love," Amy said and laughed. "You wouldn't care what he said if you didn't have a boner for him."

"Girl boner," I said.

"It's all way too soon to take seriously," Constance said, trying to shield me. "It's just fun right now."

"You girls are getting your frisk on," Amy said. "You're both so super slutty."

It was sweet and funny, but just underneath it, just along the seams, I knew Amy was trying too hard. She knew it, too, but she had to keep going. The rest of it—the phone calls with her mom and dad, the trips to the consulate for a passport, the ignominy of returning home before the trip was over—all lay in front of her. She knew it, and so did we, but we had to fake it and pretend and be brave.

We had the coffee and the croissants and the bright red jam. At one point, Constance slipped off the bed and opened the curtains and windows, and we gained a constant breeze flowing through the window. The breeze lifted the sheer white curtains, and I supposed we all thought the same thing: that this was Europe, that curtains lifting in a midday breeze against a French door was something worth seeing and remembering.

Then the phone rang again from far away, but we knew it was Amy's mom, or the consulate, or some day-to-day matter that demanded her attention. The magic left us, and we lifted the tray from the bed and swept off the crumbs, and Constance took a single spoonful of jam and put it in her mouth as if she wanted to remember, needed to remember, and the white curtain flapped softly and the day started.

"It's about the light, isn't it?" Jack asked.

We hadn't left Amsterdam. We couldn't leave until Amy's affairs were in order, or she had made the final decision to return home. Besides, we didn't want to leave Jack and Raef. Now we stood in front of Johannes Vermeer's *The Milkmaid*. It was odd, I thought, to see finally a painting that one had studied in art books for all one's school days. Here it was at last, the humble portrait of a kitchen maid emptying a pitcher into a bowl. Light—soft, morning light, I thought—streamed in through the window on the pail's right and coated everything with calmness. I knew from the small handout they gave at the Rijksmuseum's admissions desk that most art critics believed Vermeer employed a camera obscura to capture the image of the maid and reflect pinpoints of light onto the furniture of the painting. You could see the blots of light on the maid's apron and on the rim of the pitcher. But Vermeer had transcended the camera obscura and everything else to provide a moment of quiet domestic solitude. It was about the light, just as Jack said, and I stood transfixed by the painting. Out of every piece of art I had seen in Europe, it was my favorite painting by far.

"When I saw the *Mona Lisa* in Paris," I said, "I couldn't seem to care. But this?"

My throat caught.

"Yes," Jack said.

"She could be alive in the next room. And the light is still there, still waiting for any of us to discover it."

"I agree. That's how I see it, too."

"It's real, but it's more than real. It feels like it's the essence of everything. Sorry, I know that sounds inflated and pompous or just stupid, but it's not just about common light, it's about the whole world, isn't it?"

Jack took my hand. I was not sure why I felt so moved. It was a mixed-up day, with Amy calling and quarreling with her parents, with my own sense that soon, very soon, I would have to be on a plane back to New York for a career that felt—next to the beautiful simplicity of Vermeer's work—loud and difficult. Nothing felt settled; nothing seemed to combine in the way I had expected. The painting—in fact the entire afternoon in the Rijksmuseum, with Jack's hand finding mine, then releasing it, then finding it again—almost wounded with its beauty. It was not Hemingway's Paris, but it was the same thing, the same pursuit of the simple and sublime, and it hurt my heart a little to let it inside me.

"I know what we need to do," Jack said. "It's the perfect antidote for a day in a museum."

"I'm not sure I'm in a very adventurous mood."

"You will be. I promise. Come on. We need to get away from the past and move toward the future."

"If it were only that easy."

"What is it, Heather?"

"*Weltschmerz*," I said, feeling the heaviness of the word as it passed my lips. "German for world weariness and pain. It's the idea that physical reality can never meet the demands of the mind. I researched it for a paper my sophomore year. I remembered it because it kind of describes these moods I sometimes get."

"*Welt* . . . ?" he asked.

"*Weltschmerz*. Unnamed dread and fatigue of the world. That's the definition."

"Ugh," he said. "Do art museums always have this effect on you? If so, we'll have to avoid them."

"Sorry. I don't like to be this way."

"Don't be sorry. Come on. It's close by here. I found it the last time I came through Amsterdam."

I was in no shape to resist. Jack kept my hand in his and led me out. Five minutes later, we stood in a fencing studio at the edge of the Rijksmuseum Gardens. The idea of a fencing studio, the concept that you could simply trade everyday life in for a fencing foil, or an épée, or whatever the hell it was called, seemed so preposterous that I felt my heart lift a little. Jack spoke to the attendant and nodded at whatever he was being told. The attendant was a young man with a triangular goatee. He looked like Zorro only not as outrageously cute as Zorro was supposed to look.

"We're going to fence," Jack said, pushing his credit card toward Zorro and looking at me. "We're going to fight to the death. When you're feeling existential dread, you need to push the limits. You need to confront death."

"Jack," I began, then I realized I had no idea what I wanted to say. I didn't have a stance against fencing. No one in the world had a stance against fencing. I still felt jumbled up and jittery.

"You'll feel better, I promise. It's the best way to get out of . . . what did you call it?"

"*Weltschmerz.*"

"Okay, *Weltschmerz,* then," Jack said, pulling his credit card back from Zorro. "Trust me on this. It's impossible to feel world weary if you are fencing in defense of your life."

"I don't know the first thing about fencing, Jack. I've never even thought about it."

"Perfect," he said, accepting a roll of equipment from Zorro. Two white uniforms came ingeniously wrapped around a pair of fencing foils. Jack pushed one at me. Zorro shoved a beekeeper's hat toward me. It was a helmet with the front covered in mesh. Apparently, we could also plug ourselves into a sensing device to record hits. Zorro spent quite a few minutes explaining the hookup to Jack.

"You can figure this out, right?" Jack asked me when Zorro finished. "It's just a set of overalls, really."

"We're going to fence? Right now? That's what you're saying?"

"You won't think about a thing except combat. Trust me. It will get your blood cruising in the best way."

"This is crazy."

"Of course it's crazy. Everything is crazy. The whole world is crazy. Didn't you know that, Heather? Didn't you know everyone is an imposter and there are no real adults in the next room?"

"I'm very competitive, Jack. You need to know that about me. You need to know that if you want to sword fight with me, I will take no prisoners."

"Fence," he corrected me. "Now go into the ladies' locker room and suit up. There's a key, so you lock up your clothes in a cubby. Prepare to meet your untimely death at the end of my sword."

I looked him straight in the eye.

"Very Freudian, this whole fencing thing," I said. "Very penis-centered."

"Exactly."

"This could be your last moment on earth, Jack. Enjoy it."

"We'll see about that."

Zorro laughed. He had been watching our exchange.

"Americans," he said and shook his head.

"Fuck, yeah," I said, turning to him, then lifting the uniform off the counter.

You learn several things when you stand in front of a man you are drawn to while wearing a fencing costume and carrying an épée in your hand. You learn, pretty quickly, that it is impossible to look anything less than chubby in a fencing costume. You also learn, if you are lucky, that the man you are drawn to looks kind of amazing standing directly in your path, his body turned to provide the most difficult angle for potential punctures, his grin solid and amused. Annoyingly, you also notice that your discomfort somehow fuels his pleasure, so that when he tilts up his visor and smiles at you, suggests a small rearrangement of your elbow while lunging, you want to kiss him and kill him and, above all, land a solid stab to his chest so that you might exalt for an instant in the way he has exalted for the better part of an hour while turning you into a pincushion.

"You are really, really, a mad dog," Jack said after our twentieth, fiftieth, hundredth exchange. "Who knew? I had no idea. The real Heather is part sociopath."

"*En garde*," I said, mostly because I just liked saying it.

"Let me put my visor down."

I felt my arm shaking. I felt my *body* shaking. Whatever *Weltschmerz* I had felt before was gone. Jack was right about that. Now I felt my blood stirring, my competitive juices bubbling, while Jack slowly, slowly lowered his visor. He smiled, and the visor covered the smile.

Then I attacked.

Walking through the door of the fencing studio, if someone had told me that I would turn into a bloodthirsty savage with a foil in my hand, I would have called that person crazy. But I *was* a savage. Crazy savage. And I loved the feeling of a sword in my hand, the danger I embodied. This was one-on-one sport, the best kind. My body felt exhausted, but I couldn't resist attacking.

As soon as I lunged, Jack swatted my foil to one side, slid his blade down the length of my épée, and softly pecked my chest with the tip of his weapon.

"Touch," he said.

"Touch," I agreed.

But I kept coming at him. We stood in the *en garde* position. Whatever instruction Jack had given me was difficult to keep in mind. I wanted blood. I wanted to get him. I wanted to feel the pleasure of sneaking my blade inside his and landing *a hit, a very palpable hit*, as Hamlet's fencing supervisor once said in the final death scene. I even imagined being willing to be stabbed if only I could stab him in return. Insane.

But it didn't matter. I didn't make much progress. Jack slapped away my feeble thrusts and pivoted to one side. He quartered me for an instant, and before I could do a thing, he had tapped me again with the tip of his foil.

"Damn!" I shouted.

"It takes time."

"Knitting takes time. I want blood."

"Talk about a Freudian she-devil."

"You asked for it, Jack. You opened up this can of worms. I warned you."

"Okay, let's finish up, though. I only reserved the room for an hour."

"I can't believe how this feels."

"Feels good, huh?"

I nodded. Then I assumed a position to indicate I was ready. Jack nodded and said, *"En garde."* I charged forward.

But this time, before he could turn my charge aside, I pulled back voluntarily. I flicked my wrist over quickly and slapped his épée down. He was too strong for my parry to give me much of an opening, but I slid my blade quickly forward and caught the inside of his forearm. It was not a true hit, but it was as close as I had come in an hour of trying. Jack stepped back and pushed his visor up.

"I think that was a hit," he said.

I pushed my own visor up. We stood looking, breathing, panting, and I had never felt more alive and sexed up in my life. I shoved the helmet off my head altogether and ran at him and jumped into his arms and kissed him as hard as I had ever kissed anyone. He dropped his épée to one side, and his body swelled to take my weight, and then, in two steps, he had me against the padded wall of our tiny studio, his lips on my mine, the feeling of sweat and blood and anger and heat mixed together in a glorious, painful way.

We didn't speak. We had no need. He kept kissing me deeper and deeper, and I suddenly felt our bodies click, move to a second gear, a millionth gear, the ancient gear, and then the violence became gentleness, and he stopped and held me and looked in my eyes.

"This is a different Heather," he whispered.

"Same Heather," I said, finding it hard to catch my breath.

"You're spectacular."

"Shut up."

He kissed me again. This time he kissed me so hard that I felt my back and ribs flex against the wall. He was strong. Incredibly strong. I kept my legs wrapped around his waist and, yes, it was sex play, it was surely sex play, but it was something else, too, something beyond *Weltschmerz,* something that annihilated any false thoughts or cheap emotions. I wanted his body, all of it, but I also wanted something deeper, something that had to do with the light in the Vermeer painting, in the soft haze of a morning and the color of a bowl as if filled from the maid's hand, and I wanted his sweat and swagger and his sword thrusts. Of course it was insanely Freudian, that was obvious, but who cared? If he had pushed me through the wall, if we had created an ebony silhouette like a cartoon character blasting through the side of a mountain, I would have kept kissing him. It was only when someone began knocking, someone far away, and Jack turned slowly, peeling his lips from mine, that we saw Zorro standing in the doorway, looking sheepish, his right hand carrying a clipboard.

"Your time is up," he said, blushing. "Sorry."

Jack nodded, and I swung down from his body. Whatever blood remained in my body had turned to copper, and I had to put a hand out on the wall to keep from staggering. For a long time, we remained standing next to each other, both of us aware a touch from either of us could start everything again in a flash.

18

Raef asked me to go with him to Spain. It's near the end of our trip," Constance said. "There's a jazz festival in Málaga, and he wants me to go with him."

She didn't say anything else. We stood in the bathroom, both of us brushing our teeth, both of us looking at the other's reflection in the large mirror over the sink.

I smiled. But I had too much toothpaste in my mouth to do it properly, so I spit some out, then put my eyes back on Constance's eyes.

She stopped brushing and looked at me, her eyes getting teary.

"Could this be real?" she asked. "Can this be happening? Are we just making things up in our heads?"

She said it so softly that it broke my heart. It contained so much tenderness, so much longing, that it seemed to surprise her as she spoke the words.

"You and Raef? Yes," I said, "I think it is. I think you found your true."

True was an old word whose meaning we three had cobbled together to indicate things that felt indivisible. Amy and Constance
and I were true. Cold beer at a ball game, an open fireplace in a small
cozy bar, the scent of grass on a spring morning, lilacs, the sound
of a bee as it hit the screen door over and over—those were *true.*

"It *feels* like it is, but that's crazy, isn't it? I don't know what to
think about it. I really don't. I've known him for a day, maybe a
little more. And I promised my parents to stay with you."

"Don't think. Just go along. Follow it and see what happens.
We didn't come to Europe to be big chickens, did we?"

She looked for a while into my eyes. Then she spit out her
toothpaste and came back to reality.

"Well, I'm not going without you," she said, her face bent to
the faucet. "I would never do that, but I didn't know where things
stood with you and Jack—if we could all travel together, maybe. I
swear, I feel like I've been drugged. I've never felt this way."

"When is the jazz festival?"

"Probably the last week we're here."

"You should go with him. I don't know what Jack's plans are.
But even if I had to travel on my own for a while—"

Constance shook her head.

"No. Absolutely not. I won't even consider it. I'm not leaving
you alone in Europe."

"I think I want to go back to Paris, anyway," I said, feeling the
rightness of it even as I spoke. "Maybe I can talk Jack into that.
We're flying out of Charles de Gaulle, so I could just go a couple
of days early. We'll see. He has a friend who has an apartment in
Vienna, too. He has plans to go there. It will all work out. There
are plenty of people our age traveling around."

"He's your true," she said, straightening and meeting my eyes again. She dabbed a towel at her mouth. "I know that without question. You're like a picture that suddenly comes into focus when he's around. It's adorable. He's nuts about you, too. Raef said so."

"I don't know what to make of him. I'm like a guy who goes fishing and suddenly hooks an enormous fish. You never expected to be in contact with such a thing," I said. "It's all ridiculous, isn't it? First trip to Europe and we're gaga over a couple of boys."

"They don't feel like boys, though, do they?"

Constance wouldn't let my eyes go. She wouldn't let me dismiss Jack and Raef so easily. She wouldn't let me relegate them to college romances, silly flings that came and went quickly. She put her towel down at her side.

"No, they don't feel like boys," I said, my eyes still on hers. "But I think Jack has a secret. I don't know what it is, but there's something behind his travel in Europe. I can't tell if he's traveling to something, or away from something. But something's there. Something I can't put my finger on."

"Have you asked him?"

I shook my head.

"No, not straight out. It's a feeling I have. A sense that there's another piece to the puzzle and it's missing right now. He challenged me a little about going to work at Bank of America, kind of inferring that it would be soul killing. I told you about that."

"You could google him. I googled Raef and found out he's all over the jazz message boards. It reassured me to see that somehow."

"Oh, Lord, I don't even know his last name. He's just Jack Vermont. How absurd is that? Remind me to ask his freaking last name, will you?"

She nodded as she rinsed out her brush and then reached over and squeezed my hand.

19

....

We had our first fight, or squabble, or tiff, or who-exactly-is-this-person-and-why-out-of-all-the-people-in-the-world-am-I-spending-time-with-him-question-mark-question-mark-question-mark, at a table—one of those obnoxiously cute café tables I spotted everywhere in Europe but never in the States—beside a canal on the outskirts of the city. Constance and I had a train to catch to Berlin later in the evening, so Jack and I had decided to rent two black bicycles—the ubiquitous black bicycles that glide everywhere in Amsterdam (Jack had even made a lovely metaphor talking about the bicycle paths as ant trails, the Dutch so many black leaf-cutter ants bringing vegetation back to the nest)—and to spend the morning riding around the city. Naturally—because it was Jack—the weather cooperated. A perfect slice of sunshine, not too hot, not too cold, descended on the city, and the canals glistened and Jack laughed and held my hand whenever we stopped and we flirted nonstop, and we kissed twice in absurdly beautiful locations, the water glistening, the city clean and fresh, and the flowers, glorious flowers, every-where.

Then Wolf-Jack appeared.

He did not come to huff and puff and blow my house down.

He came with a smile, and he came with lunch and a tall pil-sner that sweated in the sun. He came looking handsomer than any man had a right to look, and he came with his bike leaned against mine, at a tiny restaurant on a tiny street near a tiny cobble-stone life-fucking snapshot.

"Are you sure you really want to hear this?" he asked innocently. "It's not that big a deal. It's just a theory, but you probably won't like it."

"Sure, I do. I'm always open to theories. Bring it on!"

"It's something I read, that's all. When you started talking about New York City, it came to mind. I read someplace that New York is a prison that the inmates have built for themselves. That's all. It was a concept that someone was kicking around."

"Go on."

"You sure you want to hear this? It's just a notion."

"Notions are good."

He took a deep breath and raised his eyebrows as if he had to outline the position even though it wasn't his. He repeated the proposition, he seemed to say, but he didn't want to own it.

"Well, if you follow the line of reasoning, it goes like this: The inhabitants of Manhattan live in this tiny area, jammed one next to the other, and to make it all worthwhile, they share the illusion that they are doing something important. If you can make it here, you can make it anywhere . . . all that horse crap. So they have art and first-run movies, and that's actually part of the prison pay. You have to provide that kind of thing; otherwise, people would revolt. But if you walk around the streets and really look, drop the scales from your eyes, so to speak, you see the dirt and the garbage and the homelessness. Part of that is true of any city, I grant you, but in New York there is a self-congratulatory element that says we are the best in the world. Meanwhile, most of the effort goes into keeping the everyday regimen in place. New York is all about status quo. It feels new sometimes, like when the circus comes to town, or some new movie premier arrives, but nothing really changes. The museums change exhibits and everyone talks about that, and then there are charity balls and everyone talks about the gowns and the new outfits and the fashions . . . I don't know, Heather. I'm probably not making any sense. As I said, it was just a thing I read."

But he had made sense. He had made more sense than he knew, but not in the way he intended. I didn't respond for a moment. I didn't know where it had come from, but a perverse part of me wanted to hear more, wanted to hear the full dimensions of his judgment. I wanted to hear why he had to blow up my world in order to make his better. Men did this sometimes. It wasn't the first time I had seen something like this.

"Can't you say that more or less of any city in the world?" I asked softly. "That it's simply an outcome of people living close to each other?"

He sipped his beer. He looked sensational sipping his beer. The muscles of his forearm twisted and popped in interesting ways.

"Maybe. Maybe you can. But that seems to be what people aspire to in New York. Everyone is climbing, and I'm not sure where people are climbing to be or to get to. Even the richest people in

New York have less land than my grandfather had in Vermont, and he was a poor man by financial standards. They live in apartments suspended above the ground, and they have doormen and nannies and life coaches and accountants. And you have to worry where Johnny and Jill go to school—it has to be the right school—and you go to the Hamptons in the summer, or up to Nantucket, and it all seems like a big conveyor belt. It doesn't feel real, at least not to me, so when you talk about going to New York, I don't know what that means. Not really."

"I see," I said, taking it in. "Not a very inspiring picture you paint. And I notice you've switched from the general to the specific. It's no longer a theory, is it? It seems to be more about me now."

"I knew I'd hurt your feelings, and I didn't mean to. It's the last thing I wanted to do. I should have kept my trap shut."

Yes, I thought, *you should have kept your trap shut.*

"I need a little while to absorb this," I said, sitting back slowly and trying to even out my breathing. "Kind of out of the blue."

"You're angry," he said. "I've hurt you. Come on, I'm sorry."

"What I don't get is why you wanted to hurt me."

"I didn't want to hurt you."

"Sure you did, Jack. I'm planning to go to New York in a few weeks to make a new start, and you let it drop that I am entering a prison of my own making. Why that random topic in the conversational spinning wheel? Is that supposed to make me feel good somehow?"

"I'm sorry, Heather. I am. Sometimes I think ideas are just things to play with. Little thought experiments. Sorry. I'm stupid about it."

"You're not stupid, Jack. If you were, I wouldn't take it so personally. But you picked this topic on what was otherwise a truly wonderful day. I don't get it. It's passive-aggressive to the hilt. Even when we slept on the haystack, you made a comment about how we can fix that. Fix me. That's condescending."

"I didn't mean it to be."

"That's the definition of passive-aggressive, isn't it? I'm trying to imagine another reason you might have had for bringing it up, and I can't think of anything. You've wanted to say something about my job choice for a while. Now you have. But you came at it sideways, didn't you? Not my opinion, oh, heaven forbid, this is simply a theory I read about."

"Why would I want to hurt you?"

"Because my life is different from yours. Because I have a job and a career that will provide me with a good living. Maybe you're jealous."

"Now who's trying to hurt who?"

"You picked the fight. I was happy to sit in the sun and drink my beer. Besides, your theory is so much nonsense I can hardly stand it. People have to live somewhere, Jack. Some live in Vermont, some in New York City. We all make trade-offs. I'm surprised someone your age wouldn't know that already. You're telling me everyone in Vermont in the middle of January is simply gleeful? Did you ever hear of cabin fever, maybe? People go nuts up there with all the snow and ice and darkness. Who's in a prison then?"

"You have a point, but if New York is such a great place, then a little social theorizing shouldn't rattle you. All this time we've been playing a guessing game about our backgrounds—who we were, what it meant—but I know who you are. That's why you're reacting. You're reacting because you're afraid you're going to live a cliché, an investment banker, for Pete's sake, and that I'm calling you on it, that your Smythson calendar knows your future and it's already written down in curlicue letters."

"I'm not rattled, you arrogant prick. Sorry, but you are an arrogant prick. You're just being a jerk. I should have seen this earlier, right? I'm not a little tootsie you're going to impress with your social justice theories. New York City is no more of a prison than anyplace else in the world. It's an island with a bunch of stuff on it. Some of it's good, some of it's not so good. But it's all life."

"It was just something I read, Heather. Something I thought was interesting to pass along. You're the one who is giving it greater meaning."

"I don't give a damn what you read, Jack. Honestly, I don't. What I care about is your need to tell me and your attempting to torpedo my world just to . . . what was it you said? Just to play with ideas? That's so charming, Jack. It's not even fair on a basic level of politeness."

"Oh, for goodness' sake, Heather, you're overreacting!"

"Again my fault, right? Not the great Jack Vermont's fault. All my fault."

"Jeez, this is a new side to the Heather coin."

"Is it? Well, then put it in your little ledger of marks against me. You are such a jerk you don't even know it. Seriously. You think you're all freewheeling and happening. Why do you get to judge? You're just over here drifting around."

"Now you're getting pretty personal."

"And you weren't personal when you told me I was about to incarcerate myself in a prison? That you can *fix* that? Fix me? What was I supposed to say? 'Gee, Jack, great and interesting point? I'll think about that as I slowly entomb myself in that horrible city.'"

"I can see where you would see it as insensitive."

"So it's my perception that's off-kilter? Is that it?"

That's when I realized I didn't have to do this.

I didn't have to win. I didn't have to argue. I didn't have to persuade anyone of anything. I didn't have to spend a minute longer with him. Jack was cute as the devil, was a beautiful man and he had his charms, but, really, why did I need to do this right now? I had a job to start. I had a career to get under way. It was pointless to argue. If we had been dating for months, okay, yes, I would try to get to the bottom of everything, but that wasn't the situation. It felt great to realize that I could simply stand up and smile and be graceful and say good-bye.

So that's what I did.

"You know what, Jack? I'm sorry. I truly am. I don't want to fight. I'm sure you're a great guy, but maybe, I don't know, maybe we're not matched up after all. Maybe we don't want the same things out of life. Who knows? I don't need your blessing to go to New York and start a career, and you don't need my permission to spend some time wandering around Europe. So I'm going to count this as a wonderful flirtation, a great what-might-have-been, and let it go at that. If you're ever back in New York City, visit me in prison."

"Are you serious? You're leaving? I thought we had a great morning."

"We had a magical morning, Jack. Thank you for that. But when someone tells you twice that they have a better plan for your life than you do yourself, well, those are warning bells. You need to pay attention to that. So no hard feelings, okay? I'm just going to go lock myself away on that miserable New York island and count the days until I can expire peacefully."

"Oh, come on, Heather."

"No, I swear, honestly, no biggie. Besides, that was a joke about expiring. I swear it's probably better this way. I have to be back in NYC in a few weeks, and I'm going to be flat-out busy. I go west and you go east, Jack. No harm, no foul either way."

"Heather, I apologize. You're right. I'm sorry."

Standing in front of him, a thought occurred to me.

I had read it a long time ago. It said something like: *It is imperative to complete a gesture once started.* You head out the door, don't stop. You start to drive away, keep going. Don't pull out the dresser drawers unless you intend to empty them.

So I had a divided mind. Part of me said, *Atta girl, get the hell away from this jerk.*

And another part of me thought, *He's right, I'm overreacting, why am I standing, why am I moving away from someone I care about, who might be important to me in my life, who seems to get me, who is as handsome as a damn movie lumberjack?*

But if you start a gesture, you must complete it.

I left the bill with Jack. He didn't chase me back to the bikes—*did I want him to?*—but I couldn't turn around to see what *he* was doing. As soon as I reached the bikes, I realized a couple of things to go along with my need to complete the gesture.

To hop on my bike, I had to move his. Fate played a part. When I lifted his bike away from my own, I realized that, without much effort, I could roll it toward the canal. The canal was slightly downhill from where we had left the bikes, and it happened that the fence bordering the canal gave way to a small landing spot. My mind again did a quick calculation, and I realized I could roll the bike toward the canal, although the chances of the bike staying upright, moving in a straight line toward the empty spot in the railing, was a long, long shot.

So I shoved it.

I wanted to shove Jack. He had burrowed under my skin that much.

His bike tottered forward, lazily moving toward the canal, and as I swung my leg over my bike and pushed down on the pedal, I saw his bike rap once against the railing and fall toward the canal. Part of me wanted to whoop, and part of me wanted to grab the bike and stop it and hand it back to Jack, but my blood burned too hot inside my neck and arms and legs.

I pedaled off just as his bike came to rest with the front wheel spinning languidly in the canal water. It would be nothing to retrieve it, which I supposed was a good thing, and by the time I was up to speed, weird boy-tears took hold of me and wouldn't let go.

Berlin

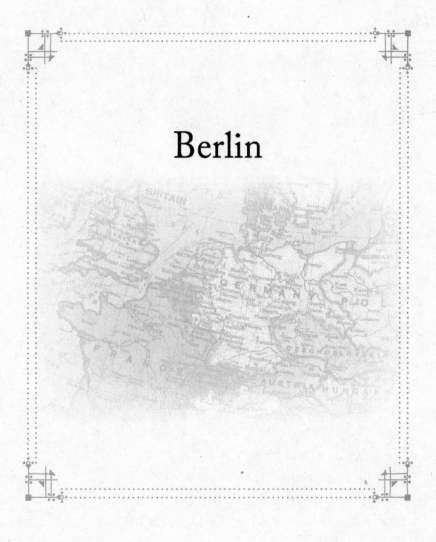

20

....

Have fun, bitches.

Love you, Amy.

Love you both. Don't worry. All good. Heading home tonight.

Travel safe.

I will.

Wish you were here!

Did you really just type that? Send lots of photos.

We will. Here's one of Constance.

Miss you already.

I need a man in my life like I need a hole in the head. Like a fish needs a bicycle," I said to Constance, even though she kept her eyes on the painting in front of us. "He was throwing me off schedule, gumming up the works. Seriously, now that we have a little distance, I can see it more clearly. I don't know what I was thinking. I wasn't thinking, that's the point, I guess. I was thinking with my Barbie brain."

"Your Barbie brain?"

"Oh, you know, Ken and Barbie in their Malibu house. Ken and Barbie going to the dance. Barbie brain. All that romantic foe-de-doe."

She nodded.

The sun had already dropped behind the line of buildings somewhere in the city and turned the shadows long. It was the Museum Island in Berlin at four o'clock in the afternoon. Rain expected, clouds already covering most of the sky. Constance and I stood in the Altes Museum. We had also stood in the Neues Museum, the Bode Museum, the Pergamon Museum, and the Alte Nationalgalerie. To say that the pictures and statues and pieces of textile and flaked arrowheads and spear points and pottery shards and razor wire had run together was an understatement. I loved museums and loved viewing art and cultural exhibits, but I was a complete slacker compared with Constance. She had turned my legs to rubber; she had beaten me down into a whimpering mass of jelly. We had spent three and a half days in Berlin being the best tourists two human beings could be. We had seen everything. We had done everything. You could not find an important site in Berlin where we did not pose for a shot, eat the appropriate food, shop for the kitschy doodad that signified and commemorated our visit. If Michelin or Lonely Planet gave out awards for "the thorough examination of a major European city," Constance and I would have won hands down.

Five stars.

And now it was threatening rain, and I was tired and grumpy.

"Then you don't need to see him again," Constance answered finally, her steps slowly moving her sideways to the next painting. "That settles it. Ignore the Barbie brain."

"Right. Simple as that."

"Raef may show up, anyway. Jack is off doing something with his grandfather's journal."

"I have to start a job in a month."

"Did you get your paperwork in?"

She didn't look at me; she kept her eyes on the paintings. Constance was never mean, but neither did she miss anything. She knew I had been stalling about the paperwork due to Bank of America.

"Most of it," I said. "Not every scrap."

"You, the girl with the Smythson calendar, not getting everything in? The girl who consults her Smythson more than people consult the Bible? Shocking."

"It will all get done. God, you're as bad as my father."

"Are you sure Jack hasn't made you rethink your choices? It's not like you to miss deadlines. He's made you question some things, maybe. That's healthy."

"Oh, he's ridiculous. *That's* ridiculous. Jack is a ship passing in the night. I see that now."

"Really?" she asked and raised her eyebrows. "Okay, if you say so."

"You think he isn't?"

"I suppose what I think doesn't matter."

"He is a ship. A big, ugly tourist ship that's about a mile high and unseaworthy and serves too much food and has bad steel-drum music playing all day long. He's charming, I'll admit that, but come on. I really don't have time for him right now."

"Of course you don't."

"If I were in a different place, you know, psychologically, I don't know, maybe. Maybe then it would be worth exploring. But he was awfully mean."

"So you check your messages a thousand times a day to make sure he hasn't texted you? Is that your tactic? That's a good plan to fend him off that way. That's not Barbie brain at all."

"Are you trying to kill me, Constance? First you make me look at every piece of art in Berlin, then you tease me about Jack."

"I thought you hated Jack."

"I don't hate Jack. We just don't fit in the same way I thought we did."

"Methinks thou dost protest too much."

"I need a drink. Maybe I'm a little confused."

"We'll get a drink shortly, I promise."

"Maybe a lot of drinks. You don't think New York is a prison we build for ourselves, do you?"

"No, I don't think so, sweetie."

"It's such an obnoxious thing to say to someone who is headed to New York in a few weeks. At the very least, it's impolite."

"Yes. Yes, it is."

"I don't care about the idea behind it, but why be so mean?"

"An imponderable of the universe."

"Men are idiots when you get down to it."

"They sure are. Always will be."

"Then why do we bother with them?"

Constance shrugged and slipped her arm through mine. It was

pretty in the museum, and the breeze hitting against the side of the building finally brought rain. I squared my shoulders and realized I had to stop perseverating—good SAT word—about Jack. It was childish, but I couldn't quite get rid of the sense that maybe I *had* overreacted. Maybe I had let something pretty good go. Maybe I should have ridden it out a little while longer. It was like looking at clothes in a thrift shop for a long time, then, when you finally found something cute or just right, you decide not to buy it. It's not that you can't live without it, but it does get under your skin that you walked away. You wonder if it's still there, if it was as flattering as you remember, and you realize if you had simply bought the darn thing you could have let your mind rest. Jack was the worst kind of question mark, a handsome, dashing guy who had made the mistake of saying exactly the wrong thing at exactly the wrong time.

What was the mental trick? If I tell you not to think of a pink elephant in a tutu, that's all you can think of. Jack looked good in a tutu.

After the museum, we went to Checkpoint Charlie. It was one of the rare instances with Constance when we didn't really know our destination but arrived at a must-see spot almost by magic. We walked and talked and wandered and window-shopped, and suddenly Constance told me we had arrived at the outdoor Allied Museum in Berlin-Zehlendorf. I made her swear that she hadn't deliberately led us to yet another sightseeing destination, and she crossed her heart and held up two fingers in some sort of Scout vow.

"I swear I didn't," she said. "I'm as tired as you are, I think. The last thing I wanted was another museum."

"You never get tired."

"I am tonight."

We stood for a while watching the foot traffic move around the open spaces. I knew the name Checkpoint Charlie, but I didn't know much more about it. Constance read from the Lonely Planet guide that it was the most famous "gate" in the Berlin Wall, known as Charlie for the letter *C*. I'm not sure why, but the sight of the Berlin Wall, the sense that people had been killed here trying to escape to freedom, got me choked up. Here was a real prison, I thought, not a make-believe one. I hooked my arm in Constance's, and we followed the cobblestone path that wove past various signs outlining the history of the checkpoint. We stopped for a long time to read about Peter Fechter, an East German teenager who was shot in the pelvis on August 17, 1962, while trying to escape from East Berlin. According to the brief history, his body lay tangled in a barbed wire fence, and he bled to death in full view of the world's media. American soldiers could not rescue him because he was a few meters inside the Soviet section. The East German soldiers could not help the boy for fear of provoking Western guards. Something about the idiocy of the situation, the pointlessness of borders and political divisions, made me feel restless inside.

"This may have been my favorite thing to see in all of Berlin," I told Constance when we finished following the cobblestone path and went to get a drink at last. "I find it fascinating. I don't know why exactly, but I do."

"It's a sad chapter in history."

"You can't fence things in or out. Not really. Not for long. That's what Checkpoint Charlie says to me."

"Let's get you a drink and bowl of soup."

I nodded. Something about seeing Checkpoint Charlie reaffirmed my desire to travel. To understand the world, you needed to see the world. For the first time in a while, I felt the rightness of my career, my job, the plan I had made for myself. As corny as it sounded, I wanted to be a citizen of the world. I was okay. Everything was okay. And when a little later in the café two German boys came up to us to ask if they could buy us a drink—boys the age of Peter Fechter—I told them no, no, they couldn't, because Constance and I were demon lovers, and we were here on our honeymoon, here without need of male company. It was the best way I knew to get a man to leave you alone.

I woke at 1:37 in the morning, thirsty and a tiny bit drunk still from the two martinis I had consumed the night before. My phone informed me it was 1:37, then 1:38, then 1:39. I checked for messages from Jack. Nothing. I checked for texts. Nothing. Nancy in HR at Bank of America had sent me an emergency contact form. I didn't read it carefully. I slid it into a folder marked Bank of America. I didn't examine the folder when the new file took its place among the other unanswered requests. I blamed Jack for losing my focus. I blamed Jack for making me ignore the requests and information coming from Bank of America. Jack the jackass.

Jack was not my *true*. He was just another boy.

I clicked the phone to sleep. I listened to the breathing around me. Constance's steady exhalations soothed me. Two other girls, both from Ireland, had come in late at night and fallen asleep with drunken murmurs.

I thought of the word *murmur*. I thought of it sounding like a word that sounds like itself. That did not exactly make sense, but it seemed clever at 1:41 in the morning. *Sludge* was another word that sounded like itself. *Sludge* and *murmur.* Sludge had to be sludge. Murmur expressed its essence perfectly.

I leaned out of my bunk and dug through my backpack until I found my water bottle. I unscrewed the top and drank a long time. I kept the water bottle next to me and considered going to the restroom to pee. But I didn't want to leave my bunk. I didn't want to wake up completely. My earlier buzz spun like a saw at the foot of my bed, and I slowly moved toward it on a conveyor belt.

I made a mental note to block all thoughts of Jack. Sealed tight. It was not difficult, and I felt proud of my new resolve. I had other fish to fry. Many other fish. I had Bank of America in my skillet and a new apartment and New York City and Japanese contacts and travel and Mr. Periwinkle, the world's oldest cat, and Amy and Constance and a dozen other friends who would be starting their careers. Looked at with realistic perspective, Jack was small potatoes. He just was. He was not going in the skillet. He was banned from the skillet.

Besides, I realized, we were not well matched. He was a freer spirit, impulsive and romantic, while I was steadier. He was correct about that. I was more career oriented, I told myself, more tortoise to his hare, more ant to his grasshopper. It didn't make either of us right or wrong, or superior or inferior, but merely different. That was a tidy way to look at it, and I felt pleased finally at getting a handle on it, a comfortable way to regard it.

"There," I whispered aloud, my voice surprisingly loud in the tiny bunkroom.

No room in the skillet. Too much in the skillet already.

21

·····························

The next morning, I spent some time in the bathroom holding my breath.

It's something I had always done. When I was a little girl, I went to the pool with my mother all summer long, and my favorite thing to do—the thing that brought me peace and serenity and a sense of calm—was to sink below the clear blue water and look up. By holding my breath, I could silence the world. I could hear the blood moving around in my body. My heartbeat became the sound of something big and important, and the world, the hustle and nuttiness of the everyday, faded backward like a concerned mother, coffee in hand, staring down in the water to check on her child. There I lingered, serene, breathing in check, the crystal ridges of water casting shadows down to the black lines of the deep end. It was punctuation. It stopped the world. So in the hostel bathroom, I closed my eyes and tucked in a deep breath, then opened my eyes to see the world drifting upward and away.

It worked. It always worked.

I stayed under. I looked up and saw the gnarly ceiling tiles above the sinks, heard the groan of a pipe somewhere below me, but those things did not concern me. I was a water creature, a manatee, even an oyster, and I watched the world slosh above me and recede, and it was okay, everything was okay. The sun pushed down into the water, and I felt the pull to go deeper, and I let my breath ease out in a long, tight whoosh as one of the Irish girls suddenly appeared, her hair wild, her pajamas turned almost sideways on her body.

"Meditating? That's ballsy," she said, clanging her way through the door. "All I can manage most mornings is a good, long pee, but I'll be out of here in a second, don't you mind me."

I nodded and held my breath again. *A turtle*, I thought. That's what I was.

For twenty-seven euros, I bought a day pass to a gym a woman at the hostel recommended. It was the last thing in the world I wanted to do, but I felt poisoned inside by the martinis, and I knew I needed to work out. To sweat. To put my mind elsewhere, preferably deep inside a tedious, repetitive hour of muscle expansion and contraction. Next to holding my breath and pretending to be underwater, exercise almost always helped.

Besides, Constance had calls to make. She had decided to take a miraculous morning off from perusing more art and history and saints.

As I navigated the exchange at the front desk and listened to the explanation of what machines I could use, I made a small cultural note: gyms looked the same, more or less, the world over. This gym, called the Worker, if I did my translation properly, had wide factory windows and two dozen exercise bikes lined up to look out on the passing street. Bikes were bikes, I realized, German or otherwise. I climbed on the second from the right, set my levels to an easy pedal (gradually gaining pretend altitude *up, up, and away*), and began the drudgery of motion.

I drank water. I pedaled. I pulled up some Checkpoint Charlie information on my phone and read that. I shot Amy a text and told her I missed her. I told her I missed her a lot. I wrote my mom and asked her to give Mr. Periwinkle a kiss and a brush out. I asked her to please play string mouse with him. I read more about Checkpoint Charlie, including a short essay on what it was like to go through all the paperwork and police interrogation to travel from East to West Berlin.

In a while, I had a good sweat going. My ponytail swept the back of my shoulders. A blond woman, German, smiled at me as she climbed on the bike beside me. I smiled back. She was about my age. I checked to see if she wanted to out-bike me, show off her stamina, but she didn't seem that type. She seemed relaxed and willing to let the time pass peacefully. She also had a ponytail. Hers rode higher on the back of her head than mine did.

At one kilometer, I smelled alcohol in my sweat. I rubbed a white towel across my neck and down my arms and kept going.

At two kilometers, I had to stand on the pedals to get up a pretend hill. My heart began pumping, and I wondered, for an instant, if my heart had decided to explode. But I kept going, and the virtual bike rider on the handlebar screen wobbled a little but kept up a steady pace.

At three kilometers, I saw Jack.

Sort of. I had to stand up straight on my pedals and look down, down to the street, and I had to squint. Jack did not simply show up, I told myself. Jack did not materialize out of nowhere. Maybe, no joke, I was having a stroke. Maybe I was hallucinating. I slowed my pedaling and looked at the woman on my right. She had a Kindle open on the reading rack in front of her. She did not pay any attention to me, but I needed her to be there to make sure I was not seeing things.

I counted to three, then four, then ten, before looking back down.

For some reason, I thought of *Mad Max*. Absurdly. I thought of people appearing out of the desert, the heat waves obscuring their images for a time before their growing proximity rendered them knowable. That's how Jack appeared. His image was not obscured by heat waves but by the everyday bustle of street traffic.

He had his eyes up on the building, watching. And he leaned against the most beautiful automobile I had ever seen: a tiny silver Mercedes convertible, its hood ornament so well polished that it glistened when the sun hit it right.

I got off the bike and stood next to the window and called him on my cell. I watched him click his phone and bring it close to his cheek. He smiled up at the building, but I didn't think he could see me.

"What are you doing here?" I asked. "What the hell, Jack?"

"Hello to you, too, Heather."

"Question unanswered."

"I'm here to see you. I'm here to apologize."

"How did you know where I was?"

"Constance told me."

"You're stalking me, Jack."

"I'm not stalking you, Heather."

I didn't say anything for a moment. I leaned closer to the window in order to see him more clearly. I put my forehead against the glass of the window.

I hated him a little for finding a cute sports car in Germany. And I hate-loved how he looked leaning against the car, because it was just a little unfair to see his killer handsomeness beside a topless car, his hair mussed, a navy sweater with holes in the elbows keeping him warm.

"What do you want, Jack?"

"To see you."

"What if I don't want to see you?"

"Then you tell me you don't want to see me, and I go away. It's not complicated, Heather."

"You were a complete jerk, you know?"

"Yes, I know. To make amends, I brought you this."

He reached into the car and grabbed something from the passenger seat. I couldn't make it out at first. Then gradually I realized what it was.

"Is that Ben and Jerry's?" I asked.

"Chocolate Fudge Brownie. Your favorite. That's what you said one time. See? I listened."

"So you show up with a Mercedes and Ben and Jerry's and you expect everything to be forgiven?"

"What I hoped is that you would know I'm trying."

"Trying what?"

"Trying to say I don't want us to be over."

Finally, he spotted where I stood in the window. My father used to ask: *Are you on the bus or not?* Sometimes life came down to choices as simple as that. *Are you on the Jack bus or not?* The answer wasn't in my iPhone, and it wasn't anything I could study and then regurgitate on a test. It wasn't anything I could manage by understanding trends or market analysis, arrange, set up, calculate, scribble on a pad of divided paper with pluses and minuses on either side.

Are you on the bus or not?

This was Jack. He would always be impetuous, always be a moving target, always be a surprise—delightful or otherwise. He would always make me wild and happy and thrilled, and he would always challenge me and hurt me in ways he probably wouldn't understand. He would show up without warning, and he would occupy far more than his share of my mental space. He would hand me a sword and tell me to fight him to the death. But even as my mind raced around all these thoughts, another part of me realized one simple thing: *our eyes hadn't left one another for a moment.*

I held up my finger to tell him I would be a minute. I hung up and turned around to wipe down my bike. The German woman surprised me with a single English word.

"Men," she said and shook her head.

"I was wrong, you were right," he said, coming around the car. "And I apologize."

"What was I right about?"

"Is this a quiz?"

"Maybe it is. Maybe it needs to be for the moment."

"I didn't study. This is a pop quiz."

"Hardly. See what you can do, anyway."

He was too damn good looking. I felt my gut flutter. It annoyed me that my gut fluttered, but I couldn't help it. He smiled. It was a smile similar to the one he had when he fenced with me.

"Okay, Heather. I'm admitting that I sometimes act insensitively.

I'm saying that I was wrong to bring up this whole New-York-is-a-prison thing to someone who is about to move to New York. I was a clod. It was a stupid thing to say, and it landed badly."

"Yes, you were a clod."

A few people on the street veered around us. We formed the proverbial rock in the streambed. We forced water to go around us. One old lady wearing a black kerchief over her head and carrying a bouquet of asters nodded as she passed and then moved down the street.

Jack stepped closer to me. I felt the back of my neck flush crimson.

"We can drive this one hundred miles an hour on the autobahn," he whispered, bending forward just enough so I could have his breath in my ear. "Have you ever gone a hundred miles an hour? You'll feel it everywhere. You'll feel it forever."

Then he pulled back. I stared at him for a ten count at least. He still didn't take his eyes off mine.

"First say you're an asshat," I said.

"You're an asshat."

"No, say *you* are an asshat."

"Okay, you are an asshat."

He smiled. I loved his smile.

He knew he had me. He held up the Chocolate Fudge Brownie ice cream again.

"It's going to melt if we don't eat it pretty soon," he said. "That would be a tragedy."

"Where do you want to go?"

"I have a place in mind."

"Where?"

"Give in to it, Heather. Trust me. You can trust me, you know."

"Can I?"

"I could take that in two ways. Should you? Or are you capable of trusting me?"

"I like you, Jack, but that really sucked."

"I know it did, and I'm sorry. I can't say it won't ever happen again, but I didn't mean to hurt you."

"I think maybe you did. That's the part that scares me. That's the part that hurt more than anything."

He nodded.

I was crazy about him.

And I did the girl calculation. I didn't like the way I looked. I didn't have a toothbrush. I didn't have a change of clothes, and I was sweaty.

My neck turned a hotter red. I felt it blistering the back of my shirt.

Taking a deep breath, I circled around the back of the car. At the passenger door, he turned me quickly and kissed me, and then an animal grew between us and I could not kiss him deeply enough, could not cling to him with enough force. It was the kiss we had experienced in the fencing studio all over again. He bent me back until I worried I would snap in half, and I nearly did. I put my hand out and braced myself against his chest, and suddenly nothing in the world mattered very much except Jack's kiss, his body, his smell of wood and mud and rivers.

Then we kissed some more. And it took me a few more minutes to realize my back wasn't snapping after all, but that the Ben and Jerry's pint had pushed against my skin along my beltline and turned it cold.

22

....

I looked down and watched the speedometer push above 137 kilometers per hour. Jack sat in the passenger seat, the spoon he had brought digging down into the Chocolate Fudge Brownie.

"Oh, this is a good bite," he said. "A really good bite. When I was a kid, we used to call a really good bite a Sing-Sing. This is a Sing-Sing for sure."

And he fed me a bite. A Sing-Sing, whatever the hell that was.

I pushed the accelerator and brought the car up to 145.

"I'm going faster," I said.

He nodded and went back to digging me another spoonful, digging for more Sing-Sings.

Somewhere around 161 kph in an open car, you feel the corners of your mouth push back. It's one hundred miles an hour, and the car is a bullet and you are simply riding it.

You also realize that anything, anything at all, could flip you and kill you and you don't care. You wait with your mouth open, the gorgeous taste of chocolate coming to you now and then like a divine explosion on your tongue, and you push more out of the car, give it gas, and you glance over and see that Jack, lovely Jack, does not cling to the hand rest or show any signs of nervousness. He is happy to go this fast, and he patiently doles out dabs of chocolate until you can't help it, you scream out in some weird caterwaul, and you wonder how you have never thought to go this fast, to rent a Mercedes for a day in Germany, or have a man feed you ice cream while the countryside passes by like a blur.

I topped out at 172 kph.

It was enough.

Jack nodded as I brought the speed back to a normal range.

It felt like falling to come back into the world.

"How did that feel?" Jack asked, giving me the last spoonful of Ben and Jerry's.

"Amazing."

"You looked beautiful driving that fast. You looked possessed."

"I felt possessed."

"I didn't like being apart from you, Heather. It didn't feel right."

I took a deep breath. I wanted to be clear. My body still tingled from the speed.

"New York is not a prison I am building for myself. It's the start of my professional life. I am going to work, and I am going to travel, and I am going to surround myself with good human be-

ings, and I am going to try to do charity work and be kind to puppies, and what the hell is so wrong with that, Jack? Why does that
constitute a prison?"

"It doesn't. And if I went with you, it couldn't be prison, could
it? We'd be in it together."

"You want to go with me?"

"You're not going to say we've only just met? That we need
time?"

"You didn't answer if you want to go with me."

"Would you have me?"

"You still haven't answered."

"I would go with you. Yes. Maybe, probably. Yes."

I nodded. I couldn't help it. I had no idea if we had come to
some sort of an understanding. I opened my mouth to ask for
clarification, but then I shut it. For once in my life I didn't have to
make everything tidy. It did not seem fair to go a hundred miles
per hour and then worry about precision in language. Not in the
same interval.

He took my hand and held it. He only let it go when I needed
to shift.

I checked in with nothing. No bag, no suitcase, no clothes carrier.
Nothing. I wore my hair in a ponytail, and I smelled of sweat. At a
hostel, it would not have been much of an issue. But this was not
a hostel. Not by a long shot.

It was the Hotel Adlon Kempinski, a five-star hotel on Unter
den Linden with a killer view of the Brandenburg Gate. A killer
view. It was a place my parents might have stayed. It was big and

stylish with royal-purple lobby chairs and potted plants as tall as Christmas trees. An enormous check-in desk took up one side of the hotel lobby, and a flurry of bellboys and luggage handlers zipped around wearing determined looks. The stone floor let out an occasional squeak, but otherwise the hotel had a decorous silence—a good silence, not an uncomfortable one, that promised the staff had not been distracted by the usual electronic nonsense that infiltrated most modern establishments. The hotel felt elegant without being old, serene without being library-like.

"A room for two," Jack said. "I phoned for a reservation."

"Yes, sir."

I *liked* this side of Jack. I liked his manner with the desk clerk; I liked that he felt comfortable in this environment. I suspected he could be comfortable on a Vermont farm, too, or in a lovely hotel, and I had to give him points for that. I also liked that he took for granted that we would stay together, that we would ride up in an elevator and take up residence in one of the rooms. It wasn't a particularly feminist stance, but I admired that he took some responsibility for our comfort. I had years of dating in high school and college when boys looked nervously around themselves and tried to figure out what was required of them. Jack provided a different experience. Clearly he had traveled enough to navigate exchanges like these.

"Before we go up, I think we should buy you a dress," he said when he finished with the desk clerk. "We can go up to our room in a while."

"A dress?"

"For dinner. We need to eat dinner, don't we? By reputation, they have a pretty great dining room."

"Jack, the expense—"

He leaned over and kissed me. He had it covered, I guessed. I knew I sure didn't.

"Are you sure?"

"It's a splurge."

He took my hand and led me back through the lobby toward a small row of boutiques just outside the hotel. I felt a little upside down. I had planned for a brief workout, then maybe a salad for lunch, but within the course of a few hours, I had taken a car over one hundred miles per hour, eaten a bunch of Ben and Jerry's Chocolate Fudge Brownie ice cream, and checked into the nicest hotel I had ever visited. Strangely, I also felt my stomach calm, as if being with Jack was something it knew I needed even if my mind did not. We had just the beginning, just the start, of the familiarity a man and woman can gain when they are left to their own devices. Nevertheless, it felt as if we had crossed an important line.

And we had gone over 100 mph together.

We ducked in a boutique that looked like a German version of the Gap. It looked like a nice boutique. I had trouble gauging anything for the time being. As soon as we entered, a German salesclerk asked if she could help me find anything. She spoke beautiful English. I didn't answer right away. Jack stepped up for me.

"We need something for her to wear to dinner. And maybe some basic things for day wear."

"Yes, of course. This way."

I looked at Jack. He looked at me and smiled. *Who is this man?* I thought. Then we followed the clerk, whose name, we learned a few minutes later, was Gilda. She had shiny black hair worn close to her head. I liked her boots.

We spent an hour shopping. I attempted to recall, as I tried things on and wore them out of the dressing rooms for Jack—*spin, yes, nice, okay, does it ride up, is it the right length*—if I had ever shopped with a man. The answer, I was fairly certain, was a definitive no. No way. But I liked shopping with Jack. I liked slipping into something, hearing his voice speaking to Gilda, then being astonished that he had a good eye when I came out and examined the dress in the three-way mirror. Moreover, he liked clothes, or at least liked seeing me in clothes, because before the hour had passed I had tried on at least a dozen dresses and day outfits. It was sexy, too, modeling for him. He watched me, but it was not all about the dresses.

"This is very strange," I said to him when we decided finally on a confetti fit-and-flare dress that swung flirtatiously whenever I moved. I liked the dress, and Jack liked the dress, and I liked that we liked the same thing. "I've never shopped with a man before. Do you really like to shop with women?"

"Not really. I like shopping with you. Shouldn't we get you some other things?"

"I'm going to wear this until you get sick of seeing me in it. We're going back tomorrow, right?"

"Yes."

"I can make it through the night with what I have."

We kissed while we waited for Gilda to price out everything and bag it. We kissed again out on the street. I made Jack wait while I called Constance. I didn't want her to think I had been abducted. But she answered calmly and revealed no surprise when I told her I was with Jack in another part of the city.

"Oh, sweetheart, I'm glad you're together with him," she said. "Even though you hate him, of course."

"You told him where I was."

"I thought you could always say no if you truly didn't want to see him."

"Thank you."

"You're welcome."

I found Jack in the hotel lobby. He didn't say anything. He took my hand and led me to the elevator bank. He held my hand as we waited. When the elevator doors opened, we stepped inside. It was a nice elevator, heavy and solid, with a brass rail that went around the interior at waist height. As soon as the door closed behind us, Jack pulled me into his arms and kissed me. It was more than a kiss, really. He devoured me. He pressed me back against the wall, and for a little while his hands traveled as they liked over my body. But we did not cease kissing, not for an instant, and when the elevator finally stopped, I had to put my hand out against the wall to steady myself.

"Best elevator ride ever," Jack said.

I nodded. I couldn't trust myself to speak.

He took my hand and led me down a carpeted hallway. I admitted to myself, as I walked beside him, that there was something about the anonymity of a hotel that aroused me. No one knew us. We were answerable to no one. I held his hand tightly. He managed the room door without letting go of my fingers.

We stepped inside, and he closed the door behind us. The room was lovely; the bedspread possessed a golden shimmer that might have been horrible in a lesser hotel, but the quality was good, and it worked. The carpet, dove colored, was thick and silent. Jack crossed the room and opened the curtains. We could see the Brandenburg Gate, though not fully on. It was a sideways view, merely a glimpse, but Jack asked me to come closer, and I did. He held me against him from behind. He kissed my neck.

And that was nearly unbearable.

"I'm going to shower," I whispered, my body churning, his lips on my shoulders now and back to my neck. "I have to shower."

"You don't have to."

"Yes, I do. But I am a fast shower-er. Trust me. I won't wash my hair or do anything else, but I need to rinse off."

"Okay, yes."

"Then I want to kiss you for a long time. Would that be all right?"

"Yes, of course."

"I think we made a mistake buying the dress."

"Why?"

His lips did not leave my neck. I felt my body turning slowly to syrup.

"Because I don't think we're going to dinner. I don't think we're going anywhere. I think this is our world, and we don't have to leave it."

He nodded against my neck.

"Okay," he said.

I pressed back into him. He was Jack. He was the perfect size for me. I slowly peeled his arms away and then turned and kissed him. It was an afternoon in Berlin, Germany.

The Hotel Adlon Kempinski should have won an award for the greatest terry cloth robes ever manufactured by human hands. I found two robes in the bathroom. I took the smaller one and put it on. That was all I put on. Then I went back into the main room and found Jack sitting in an enormous armchair turned to overlook the window. I made myself slow down to take in the sight of

him sitting there. He had turned down the lights; or he had decided not to turn on the lights at all. A quiet gray-blue light suf-
fused everything.

He pulled me firmly onto his lap, and I had to make a quick
catch at the hem of my robe to keep it closed. Then his lips kissed
mine. He kissed me gently and slowly, and for a long time that
was all that happened. I couldn't believe how easily I fit on his lap.
He kissed me again and again, and after a while our lips seemed
to gain knowledge of their own. I felt the moisture of my skin
from the hot shower, and I felt his body responding to mine.

After a time, he reached down and undid the belt to the robe.

He kept his eyes on mine. I had an impulse to be shy, to cover,
but he shook his head slightly, just a fraction of a movement, and
I let myself sink more deeply into his lap.

He pulled the robe apart slowly, slowly, inch by inch, and his
hands touched only the cloth. He bent down to kiss my lips again,
then he opened the robe a tiny bit more. I had difficulty remaining
still. Lightly, he put his fingers on the skin of my rib cage, against
my belly, on my hip. He moved as if unwrapping something valuable, something he could not rush to see. My body rose to his
fingers, retreated, rose again. He bent periodically to kiss me, but
he always pulled back, opening the robe farther, his hands growing
more solid on my skin. I felt myself opening to him. As absurd as
it sounded in my own head, I was the robe, I was being opened,
and he continued to move his hands over me, touching my skin
lightly and moving on. He touched my nipples carefully, gently,
and I had a difficult time staying still. But he kissed me and took
both my wrists in his hand, and he pulled my arms above my head.
I felt like an instrument spread on his lap, a thing to be played and
used and valued. And then he had difficulty containing himself,

because he pulled my arms higher and tighter over my head, and he slipped his other hand down between my legs, and I was ready for him, waiting for him, and he looked at me as if to say, *Yes, now, this part is mine now*, and I shivered and tried to raise up to kiss him, and that was when he gathered me up and carried me to the bed.

23

....

Flesh. His body on mine.

His lips on mine, slowly, softly, then more urgently. The white curtains at the hotel windows tucking into the room for an instant, breathing with us, then releasing, letting the curtains blossom and wave into the late-afternoon light. The smells of the hotel garden reaching us only in our silences, when our senses clear for a moment before he moves against me, stirring everything, everything important, and we kiss, and kiss again, and it is sex, gloriously sex, but not as I have known it, not exactly, not as sweet and rounded and filled with the earthy sting that I cannot know will take me until it does.

Jack. My Jack. His body beautiful, and mine white and soft beside his, around his, my legs over his waist, his force driving deeper and deeper into the bed, into me, then other ways, more lewd, more edge, more blood seeping into my skin, a wild, crazed feeling, balanced only by the return to his lips, his lips always safe and thrilling, and we look into each other's eyes—a stupid, absurd cliché—but what else can we do? It is the afternoon in Berlin, and all the world is quiet and the curtains continue to lift and fall, maybe rain coming, and we stay a long time, him inside me, deep, deep, not moving, not doing anything but kissing in this bed that floats in the island of Vermeer light. I kiss him and hold him, and for a long time we do not speak, do not try to, and then it builds again, becomes naughty and wonderful, becomes exploration and tongue and fingers and inexpressible surges. I want him to turn me inside out, to take me, every inch, but to give something back, something he has for me.

His body is perfect. Perfect. It is strong and long and fine, and he moves it gracefully; there are no gaps, no moments where skin leaves skin, and when his moment comes, when he is ready, he puts his eyes on mine and we do not glance away, do not surrender anything until he can no longer stand it, and I kiss him, pull him deeper, and then the white curtains flap harder and the breeze from the garden comes again to find us. I can barely keep from crying because if this is real, if one particle is real, then I am a dead pup, I am lost, I am so hopelessly gone that nothing can save me.

"I had sex with you, and I don't even know your last name."

"That's excellent. You should definitely slut-shame yourself."

"Do you have a bad name? Is that why you're keeping it from me?"

"How do you mean, bad?"

"Like, I don't know, Pancake or something."

"You think my name is Jack Pancake?"

I kissed his shoulder to hide my smile. It was a perfect moment. The wind had risen and now pushed against the hotel. We lay under a beautiful white down comforter, and the sheets glimmered white, contrasted as they were against the dark wood of the bed and bureaus. Jack's body felt warm, and everything felt lazy and quiet and smooth.

"Quiller-Couch," Jack whispered into my hair. "That's my name."

"That's not your real name."

"Yes, it is. I promise it is. I know how strange it sounds."

I pushed myself up and looked at him. He had his eyes closed. I couldn't read him.

"Your name is Jack Quiller-Couch? You're making that up, Jack. That's impossible."

"I am not making that up. It's really my name."

"Let me see your wallet. I want to check your license."

"You can call me Jack Vermont if you prefer. Or Jack Pancake."

"So some woman, someday, is going to have the option of keeping her own name or becoming Mrs. Quiller-Couch. I think we can guess how that will go."

"It's a perfectly fine name. My mother kept her name, Quiller, and hyphenated it with my dad's name, Couch. So I'm Quiller-Couch."

"That's just nutty. Jack Quiller-Couch. You sound like a pirate or something. Or like a British dessert."

"I could change it to Jack Pancake."

"Maybe Jack Vermont. I like that."

He kissed me and pulled me closer.

"Jack Quiller-Couch. That's going to require some getting used to. I'm not sure I even believe you. Are you joking right now?"

"I think it's too much last name for a simple first name. That's the problem. It's out of balance. I like your name better. Heather Mulgrew. What's your middle name?"

"Christine. Mulgrew always sounded to me like a mushroom you find in your basement. Oh, there's a Mulgrew."

"You're very strange. Heather Christine Mulgrew. I like it. So when we get married, you would be Heather Christine Mulgrew Quiller-Couch. You would be your own law firm."

"We're getting married now, are we? And I'm taking your name? It's all established?"

"It's inevitable."

"Do you simply say these things for effect? It's a bad habit. It's a habit you should denounce."

"I don't think you denounce a habit."

"What do you denounce?"

"Satan, I think."

He rolled me to one side and spooned me. His breath tickled my ear. I felt his body jump once as it relaxed into near sleep. For a long time, I watched the curtains move with the wind. This was Jack, I told myself. Jack Quiller-Couch. And we had met on a train and had our first kiss on the station platform, and now we had made love, and we were in Berlin, and it was all too fast, too easy to believe entirely, and I had driven a sports car over one hundred miles an hour, and now this lovely man held me and dozed, and I told myself I should remember this moment. I should trap it somehow, because someday I would be old and wrinkly and I might sit in the sun and remember Jack in this white, white bed, and the pleasure we had, and the taste of the Ben and Jerry's Chocolate Fudge Brownie, and his body covering mine like a tree growing around a stone.

Kraków, Prague, Switzerland, Italy

24

We took the night train from Berlin to Kraków, Poland. Poland had never been on my list of "must-sees," but Raef assured us it was spectacular, and I had learned to trust Raef's opinions about travel, restaurants, and jazz nightclubs. Kraków—the old city—was a World Heritage Site. It was, he said, the next Prague, meaning the next chic place to visit if you were young and mobile and in the mood for adventure. Jack had never visited Poland, either, and on the train we sat with Constance's Lonely Planet guide on our laps and turned the pages slowly, each of us reading and pointing to things we wanted to see. Raef and Constance slept in the seats across from us. Constance's head rested in the crook of Raef's neck as if she were his precious violin. I took a few pictures of them; I wanted Constance to know how sweet they looked together.

We were couples. That was the new understanding. It was so natural and unassuming that I had to shake myself sometimes to understand fully what had changed. Constance and Raef. Jack and Heather. Even in the darkness, with the lights from houses and stations and lonely farms flickering past our windows for a moment, I felt aware of Jack. I knew his body now, knew it better at any rate, and I knew the weight of his arm on my shoulders, the heaviness of his hand as it wrapped around mine. It's a cliché to say our edges blurred, that we became merged in some way, but it was true nonetheless. Everything felt accelerated as a result of our traveling together; we could not hide things or be slow to reveal our likes and dislikes. We traveled out of our backpacks, and the world was reduced to tiny instances of comfort and joy, of great, brilliant sights and sounds and smells. I saw with Jack's eyes, and he saw with mine.

Near midnight Jack and I slipped into the dining car and ordered vodka from an ancient porter standing behind the bar. He was a short man with enormous muttonchops outlining his jaw. The muttonchops appeared translucent, a blurry aurora, as if someone had tried to get his face into focus but then abandoned the project. Or as if a dandelion puff had decided to smile. He had a large mole on the center of his forehead, and his hands, when they moved over the bottles and cups, seemed to crawl rather than lift and drop. I put him at about seventy years old. His eyes had lines of yellow that reminded me of small strands of twine.

He poured two streams of vodka into our glasses. We smiled and drank them down. The porter shook his head.

"Americans?" he asked in solid English.

We said we were.

"My uncle died in Chicago," the porter said. "Long time ago."

"Sorry," Jack said. I nodded.

"I wanted to visit him, but never had. Is pretty, Chicago?"

"It can be," Jack said. "I haven't spent much time there. Have you, Heather?"

"No, sorry."

"Lake Michigan," the porter said and smiled. "My uncle, he always talked about Lake Michigan."

"It's a big lake," Jack agreed. "A great lake."

It was a pun. I liked Jack's tenderness with the man. I liked his willingness to listen and to talk.

The porter, meanwhile, held up his finger and bent under the bar. He brought up a bottle of vodka and showed us the label. It was Żubrówka vodka, a famous brand that we had just seen mentioned in the Lonely Planet guide. One of the travel tips was to consume Żubrówka vodka whenever possible. Now seemed as good a time as any.

The porter poured out second glasses for us. He turned our glasses around one full rotation to bring us luck and to say good-bye to misfortune.

"Will you join us?" Jack asked. "We'd be honored to treat you to a round."

The porter shook his finger at us.

"You cannot pay for this. Not young people like you. This is a gift. They say it is made of angel tears. You understand?"

"I do," I answered.

"Good drinks are always sad. They bring us life, but they also remind us of dead. You agree?"

I nodded. So did Jack. The porter made a motion to tell us to drink. We did. The first glass of vodka had burned on its way down. These few ounces of Żubrówka tasted like mountain water. I wasn't close to being a connoisseur of vodka, or of any spirits, really, but I discerned the difference. The porter put the bottle back down on the shelf.

"That was lovely," I said. "Thank you."

"Smooth," he said, standing straight again.

"Yes, very."

"Once America was very good," he said, his hands resting on the cups in front of him. "Now, too many bombs. Bombs everywhere, with drones, ships, just bombs. America never gets tired of bombs."

"I can see how it seems that way," Jack said. "We have funny ideas sometimes in our country."

"Not so funny for the people under the bombs."

"No," Jack agreed. "No so funny for them."

We paid. We left the porter a generous tip. When we returned, we found Raef and Constance awake. They had their feet on our seats and pulled them down when we squeezed back in place. Constance had the Lonely Planet guide on her lap, doubtless looking for saints to visit. She always excelled at planning activities.

"Did you guys drink without us?" Raef asked. "I smell vodka."

"The good stuff," I said. "The one that starts with a Z."

"Żubrówka," Raef said with pleasure. "That's like finding an old friend is still alive. I had some good nights on Żubrówka. It's considered medicinal, you know."

"It's made of angel tears," I said.

"Funny, I heard duck tears," Raef said. "Tears when the wind blows water out of a duck's eyes—only in winter."

"I need to taste this vodka," Constance said, not looking up. "These stories are too rich."

Then Jack said he saw the northern lights.

"Balls," Raef said, turning to look out the window where Jack pointed. "We're at about fifty-five degrees. We'd have to get up to sixty at least to see them."

"How do you know what latitude we're traveling?" Constance asked, looking up with amazement.

"It's a nervous tic of mine," Raef said. "Does it freak you out? I always know the coordinates of where I am. I know it's weird."

"Not really. It kind of turns me on."

It was a sweet interchange between Raef and Constance. Jack, meanwhile, lifted from his seat and tried to get a better angle on the northern lights. He kept squinting and putting his face closer to the window. Over his shoulder I could make out something, but it might have been just about any light source. Although I had never seen the northern lights, I assumed you couldn't easily mistake them.

"It's a gas station!" Raef said finally, his eyes on the same line as Jack's. "It's just neon lights!"

Jack turned around sheepishly.

"He's right," he said. "Isn't that a life lesson about something or other?"

"Think gas station lights before northern lights," I said. "Probably a good rule to follow."

"Oh, I don't know," Constance said, her voice quiet and solemn, her eyes still down at her book. "I admire a man who wants to see the northern lights so much that he sees them in a gas station sign. That's a man who understands dreaming."

"Thank you, Constance," Jack said with mock indignation as he sat beside me again. "Glad someone here understands."

"If you hear hoofbeats, assume horses, not zebras," Raef said. "Isn't that the phrase?"

"If you hear hoofbeats, assume unicorns," Constance said, bringing her eyes up to look at each of us. "That's the way to live."

The train passed a little closer to the offending gas station. It went by in a blur. The lights *were* green, and they *were* muted in the late-night mist, but they were not the northern lights.

I fell asleep a little later. Raef and Jack talked a long time about the nature of reality—how do we know a thing, how do we trust our senses, what can we take for truth? It had to do with Jack's vision of the northern lights, I supposed, and I tried to follow the line of their reasoning for a while. Little by little, sleep took me over, and when I woke, the train had begun to slow down for Kraków. It was early morning, not quite light, and the sound of the train wheels on the harsh metal rails sounded like all the waking in the world.

"I'm kidnapping you," Jack said the next afternoon. "I'm taking you to a place you would never want to go but that you need to visit. We both need to visit it."

"That's not a way to make someone want to do something, Jack."

"Trust me on this," Jack said. "Our lives are about to change."

I couldn't tell if he was serious or not. We stood at an outdoor lunch wagon eating cheese sausages and fried potatoes from a cupped bouquet of newspaper that had gone wet with oil. Jack loved to eat on the street, and he loved the feeling of Kraków. Raef had been correct again: Kraków possessed incredible old-world charm. We had already hiked to the Wawel, the lovely castle anchoring Kraków, and we had plans to travel north to the famous brick castle, Malbork, outside of Gdańsk. Kraków seemed less corrupted by tourists than Paris or Amsterdam, though it was still plenty busy.

"We need vodka with our meal," Jack said, clearly enjoying himself. He dipped his sausage into the sharp brown mustard served as a dot beside the sandwich. "We need to toast the ineffable."

"You can't toast the ineffable. The ineffable is impossible to know."

"Oh, yes, you can, Ms. Amherst. The ineffable is the only thing worth toasting. Every toast in the world is about the ineffable even if the people toasting don't know it."

"You're never lost for opinions, are you, Jack Quiller-Couch?"

"I am a font of ineffable opinions."

"And our lives are going to change today?"

"Without question."

"Ineffably?"

He nodded.

Then we had one of those love fogs.

Our eyes locked. It wasn't on a mountaintop, or beside a blue ocean, or in a flowered meadow. It was in the center of Kraków. I couldn't speak for him, but I wasn't feeling particularly in love, or gushy, or anything else. But then he turned to me and smiled, and I smiled back. We didn't say anything. The world kept going on around us, I was aware of that, but then the world no longer mattered. What mattered was Jack's gaze and his shy, soft smile that invited me in, invited me to share the pleasure of being here, in a foreign city, being in love, or the beginning of love, and knowing that we had the world by the goddamn tail if we wanted it, wanted each other, stayed with each other. The humor of the look slowly faded, and what remained deepened in the most profound way, and flitting around my head was a little mosquito of doubt that said, *No, no, things don't happen this way. It's not this easy, it doesn't happen so quickly, you don't love him, you just like him, and you're going to go back to New York and that's going to be that, and look, pull your eyes off him, because his eyes are a rabbit hole, and if you keep looking you are going to fall and fall and fall.*

But neither one of us looked away.

To his credit, he didn't try to kiss me, or try anything at all to heighten what couldn't be heightened. We stood and swam into each other's eyes, and I had maybe shared a baby cousin of this look with other men, but this was something different, something terrifying and wonderful, and if I didn't live a moment longer at least I would have known what it meant to hold someone's look with your own and to know, without question, that whatever we call a soul had answered your soul, and that going forward this look, this instant, would be carried between us like rare treasure, would be carried with the knowledge that neither of us ever had to be alone again, not entirely, not completely, not ever.

"Come on," he said when we broke off the look. "Finish and we'll go."

And we did.

25

....

Jack couldn't hide our destination for long. After a thirty-minute train ride from Kraków, we stood in front of the entrance to a salt mine. Of all the things I had thought to visit while in Europe, a salt mine might have been at the bottom of the list.

"A salt mine?" I asked. "You're taking me to a salt mine?"

"A salt mine," he confirmed.

"In Europe, in one of the most beautiful cities we've ever seen, we are abandoning that particular form of beauty for a—"

"Salt mine," Jack repeated. "But not just any salt mine. The Wieliczka Salt Mine. It's a must-see."

"Who must see it?"

"Should that be *whom*?"

"You tell me."

"I think it should be. Whom must see it? No, maybe not."

"I'm not persuaded," I said. "Why a salt mine?"

"You mean, why the Wieliczka Salt Mine, don't you?"

"Yes, of course."

"Because the mine no longer produces salt. It's now a national treasure of sorts."

"A salt mine treasure?"

"The chambers have been made over into chapels with chandeliers. It's supposed to be quite beautiful."

"As far as salt mines go."

"Yes, as far as salt mines go."

"You're a strange man, Jack."

"I've eaten a lot of salt in my life. It's time to see where it comes from."

"It's like salt's origin story, is that what you're saying?"

"Something like that."

We stood in front of the entrance booth. Jack held my hand. I looked at him several times, trying to gauge his interest. I knew him well enough to guess that he was, in fact, intrigued by the salt mine. He liked the unusual, the off the beaten trail. But a salt mine seemed like a new standard for him.

"What else is at the salt mine? And don't say—"

"More salt," he beat me to it.

"Besides salt. I'm assuming we'll see more than salt."

"You don't think it's enough to see a world constructed inside a salt mine? You're very hard to please, Heather."

"So this is the life-changing thing? We'll never look at salt the same way, will we? Is that what you're saying?"

He nodded. He was having a good time, I could tell. He liked everything about this: the train ride, the potential absurdity of a tourist destination formed inside a salt mine, the inevitable quirkiness of the people who had one day decided that of all things a salt mine might be, it served it best to make it into a national treasure. He bent down and kissed me. He closed me inside his arms.

"People who visit salt mines together are bonded for life. Did you know that?"

"I didn't know that," I whispered into his shirt. "Are you certain of that?"

"Salt is the foundation of life. Salt and vodka, of course. If we go in the salt mine together, it is a declaration of eternal devotion."

"The world isn't make-believe, Jack. I hope you know that. I hope you remember that it isn't for me."

"Who says it isn't?"

"No one says it. It's just the way it is."

"Right now, you're in my arms in Poland. On the way to a fantastic salt mine experience. If someone had told you that was your future three months ago, you would have thought it was make-believe."

I nodded. It was true.

We broke apart and paid our entrance fee and went inside.

I realized, quickly, that nothing in the buildup had prepared me for what was inside. Saying *salt mines* conjured up images of piles of white, snowy mineral compounds, a noble attempt by someone to turn a dead industry into something, anything, that might bring in a visitor's euro. But what awaited us, what we saw nearly at once, was something entirely different. It was designated a World Heritage Site, for starters, and I saw Jack's face turn to a slight smirk as it began to dawn on me what we had come to see. The brochure at the admissions desk informed us that salt mining had been going on at the site since the thirteenth century and that it had only closed for good in 2007. Meanwhile, the miners had begun carving four chapels from the rock salt, decorating them with statues of the saints, and boiling down salt to reconstitute it into crystals for the remarkable chandeliers that hung above. It was such an unusual combination of the everyday—what could be more common than salt?—and the sublime that I found myself moved beyond any expectation.

"Oh, Jack," I whispered. "It's beautiful."

"Copernicus and Goethe visited these mines, and Alexander von Humboldt and Chopin—and even Bill Clinton."

"I had no idea. Constance needs to see this."

"I wanted to see it with you."

"How did you know?"

But it didn't matter how he knew it. On the way down the wooden stairs to the 210-foot level, he told me the story of the Hungarian princess Kinga who came to Kraków and asked the miners to dig down until they hit rock. She had been forced to leave her native land and in her last moment had thrown her engagement ring into a salt mine in Máramaros. When the miners struck stone deep in the Polish earth, they also found salt. They carried a lump of salt to Princess Kinga and cracked it open. They shouted with delight when they found her ring inside the lump of salt, and ever afterward, Princess Kinga was the patron saint of salt miners.

"What?" I laughed when he finished. "That doesn't make any sense at all."

"Of course it does."

"She throws away her ring in Hungary and the miners find it in Poland?"

"You have no romance in your heart, Heather. That's becoming clear the longer I hang out with you."

"I need a little more story continuity, Jack."

He turned around when we reached the bottom of the wooden staircase. Then he reached up and grabbed me by the hips and slowly, slowly lowered me into him. He could hold my entire weight above him as long as he liked. It was erotic and beautiful and quietly lovely all at the same time. His lips waited for mine, and when we kissed we stayed that way for a long time.

What was the use? I gave myself up to him.

I couldn't resist him. I couldn't imagine our lips ever coming apart. I felt my body drip into his and his chest and arms, strong and steady and firm, slowly molded me against him, fit me to him as a man might fit a life jacket against his chest. Our kiss went deeper. It went on until I thought that I might pass out in his arms. I felt as if I had entered on a pair of train tracks that traveled into his body and mind and I could not escape, could not veer for an instant, that wherever Jack went so would I.

Gently—and after long minutes—he placed me on the ground. His lips slowly left mine.

"We have a habit of kissing on platforms," he said. "It's a good habit."

"It's a wonderful habit."

"Salt mines?"

"Anywhere, Jack."

He nodded. He kept my hand under his arm as we continued toward the underground lake, which the brochure assured was a marvel not to be missed.

26

Constance climbed on a mechanical bull in Prague, Czech Republic. She was drunk. She was happy. She was in love.

But she shouldn't have been on a bull, mechanical or otherwise.

"Ride 'em, cowgirl!" Raef shouted.

He was drunk, too.

We were all drunk, and it felt great. We had spent the afternoon in a tiny *heuriger*—a wine bar with cold cuts and accordion music—drinking the last of the spring vintage. Something about the constant travel, the difficult nights of sleep, had made us all slaphappy. We laughed a lot. We laughed in the way that old friends can laugh, with each of our personalities shining through the haze of alcohol and cheese wheels. We liked the Czech Republic even if none of us could spell *Czechoslovakia*. We liked the accordion music, too, and we talked a long time about why accordion music was not popular in the States or Australia, despite the fact—according to Raef—that it was the most versatile instrument ever devised by the hand of man. A debate about whether a squeeze-box and an accordion were the same thing occupied at least a pitcher or two of wine, and then we spilled out of the *heuriger* and poured ourselves into a westernized bar somewhere in the center of Prague near the Pražský orloj, or Astronomical Clock, and Constance climbed onto a bull.

"This could be a bad idea," I said to no one, to everyone. "Or the best idea ever."

Constance put her hand up above her head, cowgirl-style, and slowly began to spin with the bull undulating between her legs. It was sexual, of course, but beautiful, too, and I loved seeing Constance taking herself out of her usual prudence. She was the least overtly athletic person I had ever known, though she could be nimble and quick when she needed to be. She was always very balanced.

"She'll be okay," Jack said.

He had his arm around my waist.

Constance nodded every time she turned to see us. She had a gorgeous, funny expression. The expression said she had it, no problem, crank the bull, which was way more badass than anything Constance had ever done. The bull operator nodded at her, and she nodded back. They had an understanding of some sort.

Then she began to spin faster.

"I hope she doesn't get seasick," Raef said.

"She's a good sailor," I said. "Her family sails."

It struck me as a drunken comment, but I couldn't help it. A few people—it was early evening, or late afternoon, an in-between time at the bar, so the crowd was just arriving—whooped when

Constance took it up to the next level. She looked mythical on the bull. I would have bet a great deal of money that she had a myth in mind, maybe Europa and Zeus, because her eyes blazed, and she looked as happy as I had ever seen her. *Saint Constance riding the bull of Crete or some crazy thing.* I took a couple of pictures and sent them to Amy. This was something Amy needed to see. You did not get to see Constance on a mechanical bull in Prague, Czech Republic, every day. I didn't even glance at Jack, who always had a funny outlook about pictures.

Then the bull began to buck. Instead of simply moving around in a slow circle, it sometimes bucked its rear end up as if trying to throw her. Constance slapped her hand against the leather skin to balance herself for a moment, then she nodded as if she had once more figured out the rhythm.

"She's a natural," Jack said. "A freaking natural."

"She's the most beautiful woman who has ever lived," Raef said, his eyes not leaving her for an instant. "She's nearly too much."

"She's even more beautiful inside than out," I said.

Raef slipped his arm through mine. His eyes were a little damp.

Arms linked, we stood and watched Constance ride the bull. She didn't crank it all the way to the top, but she rode it hard and didn't show any signs of slipping off. When the bull operator slowed it down, people cheered for Constance. She waved at everyone, but she looked a little rocky. Raef walked over and lifted her free of the bull. Constance kissed him, and he kissed her back. I knew, watching them, that they would be married. It was as simple as that. Whatever it was that drew two people together had latched onto them both.

"He loves her," I said to Jack. "He loves her with everything he has."

"Yes, he does. Does she love him?"

"Totally."

"They're good with each other."

And there was a brief, passing instant, when one of us should have, might have, could have said something about love, about commitment, to the other. The knowledge descended on us inevitably. It wasn't that I didn't think we were falling in love, or already existed in love, whatever any of that meant. But we couldn't say it exactly, and I wondered why that was. I felt myself giving in to the ridiculous old notion that a man should say it first. According to common lore, a woman should never drop the L-bomb first. That was basic girl knowledge. We had hinted around about it, had come close in Berlin and then in Poland, to confessing everything. But the word eluded us. We watched Raef and Constance lean against each other as they cleared the matted area beneath the mechanical bull, and then we broke apart and said we needed more drinks, and I gave Constance a hug, and Raef volunteered to buy a round in honor of Constance the bull rider, and we were jolly once more, Jack and I no less than before, but a tiny pilot of formality took light in my heart, and I wondered how we could be so close and still be so careful with one another.

In the early hours of the morning, Jack talked us onto a milk barge. Raef and Constance had gone back to the hostel. Jack had picked up a card from a man he had talked to at the bar—the brother of the barge captain, if I understood it correctly—and we had an address to give to a cab, although the cab driver had to ask two other cabbies how to get to the pier. Then we drove around for what seemed a long time, the driver leaning forward to peer more closely through the windshield. I didn't have much sense of where we were going except that it seemed industrial. Now and then, a flash of water appeared in bright, surprising glimpses, the reflection of our headlights like small photographic flashes. We drove near the Vltava River, if I remembered my geography correctly. But it was hard to see anything with all the buildings and construction equipment barring the way.

When we arrived, Jack had to talk us onto the barge by giving the captain the card he had procured at the bar. He may have slipped the crew some money, too, because they went from reluctance to friendliness in a matter of seconds. The crew consisted of three men, all of them wearing dark clothing and black watch caps. They may have been wearing a company uniform, for all I knew, but they stayed busy and left us alone. The barge—a flat, messy boat with a small crane on the port side—pulled away from the dock sometime after midnight. The engine stunk of diesel, but eventually it pulled sufficient headway to make the exhaust stream behind us.

We sat leaning against the cuddy, as much out of the wind as we could manage. It was a dark, dark night, and I wondered how the crew could see where it was going. The canal, or waterway, was only a black rope through a black countryside. Now and then, the moon gave us a little light and the stars glittered and shook, and we heard an owl at one point, its call unmistakable, and then later, when the boat was steady and moving at a good pace, we heard a heron croak near us, and then we spotted him perched on a piling of a dilapidated dock.

We leaned close together. For a while, we didn't really talk; maybe Jack was a little nervous about taking me on a strange boat, with a crew he didn't know, but if he was, he hid it fairly well. When he sensed I was cold, he opened his barn jacket and tucked me inside it, sharing his heat, and we went along through the darkness listening to the engine sounds bounce back off the trees that lined the water. This was how Jack wanted to experience Europe, I knew. Anyone with the price of a ticket, he would say, can visit a museum. You had to be a traveler to scout out something unique in a place where so many feet had already trod. He wasn't content to visit museums and cathedrals and interesting cityscapes, then go home and feel he had bagged another destination. He refused to be a mere tourist. He desired a deeper connection with the land and people, and I had to admit that riding on the barge was something I knew I would remember all my life. The night after Constance rode the bull in Prague. The Vltava River. The scent of water and city mixed and the smell of diesel, making the air tinged with industry.

"I hope they're not taking us to Russia or something," Jack whispered. "Let's hope they'll bring us back to Prague when it's all over."

"Do you think we're being kidnapped?"

"Probably. I'm fairly certain at some point we'll have to dive overboard and swim for our lives."

I tucked closer to him. I looked at him a long time. He was still the handsomest man I had ever known. Sometimes I had to remind myself that I was beside him, that in some way or shape, he was becoming my own.

"I'm assuming your grandfather would have liked this kind of thing."

He shrugged. Then he tucked me closer still.

"He was a good guy," he said. "I don't know everything about this trip he took across Europe. I know he was traveling home after the war, but I don't really know why he went this place or that place. He seemed to be wandering. I'm sure he was shell-shocked from everything that had happened."

"I imagine everything was upside down. It had to be devastating."

"He was from a dairy farm in Vermont. That's the puzzle. I have a hard time imagining him here in Europe, just poking around. He had a big soul, Grandma always said. 'He breathed through both nostrils' was her phrase for it."

"I like that phrase. I hadn't heard it before."

He shrugged again. Then he nodded.

"I spent a lot of summers with him. My mom and dad didn't have a smooth marriage, to say the least. So during the summers, I went up and lived with Grandpa and Grandma, and I helped on the dairy farm. You were wrong about one thing on the train, by the way. I don't have a trust fund. I have a little bit of a nest egg from the sale of Grandpa's farm. I hate thinking about it. About selling it, I mean."

"And your parents are alive, right?"

"Yep. Mom's out in California reinventing herself. Dad moved down to Boston. They didn't have much interest in the farm, so they sold it. Dad grew up on it and was sick of it. I tried to talk them out of it. I actually wanted to be a dairyman at one point."

"And they gave you the money from the sale?"

"They split it in thirds. I guess partially out of guilt, they included me in the division. They knew I wanted the place. They sold it when land in Vermont was going for top dollar, and we did okay."

"I'm sorry," I said, and I was.

"The house wasn't much, honestly. It probably needed to go. But the land . . . and the barn. I always loved the barn. While I was in college, I tried to get Grandpa some money to fix it up from the National Registry. I researched the whole topic. As a nation, we're losing barns all the time, so there is some interest in trying to preserve them. Anyway, I was just this college kid with a grandpa he loved. I couldn't swing it, and the barn was wicked expensive to keep up. Once the roof starts to go on those old barns, it's over in no time if they're not replaced."

"I guess I didn't have you completely pegged on the train."

"I still had it a lot easier than a ton of people."

After a little longer, the boat began to shift to the left bank, and one of the workers, a thin, wiry young kid with buckteeth and now wearing blue overalls, asked us in German to move. They were going to start pulling in the milk, he said through Jack. Jack asked him his name, and the kid smiled a bunny smile and said, "Emile."

"Can we help?" Jack asked, standing and helping me up to my feet.

"Help?" Emile said and laughed.

He shouted something into the cuddy window, and the captain, a bearded man with an enormous belly and a deep, throaty voice, yelled back something that got drowned out in the engine sounds. The third crew member, likely the first mate, already stood up by the bow, ready to throw a rope to someone. The barge swung out of the current and rolled a little as it left the faster water and came into the slack. Emile ducked away toward the stern, probably preparing to throw a rope on that end. In the dimness, we could just make out the outline of a wooden dock beside a large field of emptiness.

The boat slowed, the engine reversed, and the ropes zipped out into the darkness with a whistling sound. The captain yelled something, and someone else replied, and then we shivered into the dock, rubbing it like a cat finding its way, a hundred, five hundred silver milk canisters arranged on the dock, waiting to be loaded.

We watched the first ten canisters come aboard. They swung in on small pallets; Emile worked as the ground man, guiding the loads while the first mate operated the crane. The captain did not bother coming out of his cabin, but we smelled his pipe smoke now and then when the wind brought it to us.

Five or six men moved on the dock. They didn't say much except to shout directions occasionally. A bright floodlight illuminated the scene, and moths fluttered under the light like miniature angels. After a while, Jack and I began helping Emile land the pallets in the proper order. It wasn't hard work, merely time consuming, and with three of us, it went faster. Emile laughed a lot as he watched us. The first mate said nothing, but the men on the dock commented about him having help for a change. The milk canisters came aboard sealed, but the bodies of the canisters perspired from the coolness of the night contrasted by the warmth of the milk. Light followed the loads and played off each one in short, soft glows.

When we had the milk secured, we off-loaded a pile of empty pallets. That was the hardest work, and Emile did not laugh as we helped him on that job. We handed the pallets down by crane, a dozen of them looped together for the men on the dock. The men let the entire load rest on the dock, then they unfastened the chain and swung it back to us.

"My grandfather would have liked this," Jack said when we finished and the boat moved off, pulling back into the current and running at a higher engine rev. "He would have compared it to what he did on the dairy farm back home. He was a good farmer."

"They must have trucks now, though, don't you think?"

"I'm sure they do. Maybe this is just an old way to do it that hasn't died out yet. Water is a cheap way to transport things."

We stood along the railing and watched the countryside. Most of it was dark and formless, but here and there we saw houses and lights, and dogs sometimes barked at us as we passed. The water hissed beneath us; the boat ran through a group of swans before pulling into the second landing, and the swans paddled off like origami fabrications, impossibly serene and white and comfortable in the water.

We helped Emile on the second stop, and the work went faster. This time, the captain came out and joked a little with all of us, his pipe an empty pointing tool in his hand. He said he wanted to hire us permanently, then he went off the boat and came back in a few minutes with rolled-up newspapers containing fresh bread. He gave us two long baguettes and a small plastic tub of honey. The rest he gave to Emile and the first mate.

We broke the bread apart and dipped the pieces in the honey. It tasted like the night, somehow, and like the grass that fed the cows. It tasted like the wooden piers. It was delicious and sweet, and Jack leaned over and kissed me, and his lips tasted of honey.

It was late, almost morning, by the time the boat returned us to the starting point. We had become friends of a sort with the crew. The first light of morning caught a portion of the river and turned it golden. It reminded me of days I could remember as a child. I could recall coming in from skating, or from sledding, and the world was quiet for a moment, was sincere in a way it could not always be sincere, and as eager as you were to be inside, to be warm and contained, it was difficult to leave the outside world, to say good-bye to all the air and wind and freedom. I always felt a traitor by going inside, as if I turned my back on a dear friend. I felt that now. When I stepped off the boat onto the solid framing of the pier, I felt my childhood beside me.

"Thank you," I said to Jack after we had said our good-byes to the crew. The captain had joked again about hiring us. He said something—the translation wasn't quite clear—about getting more work out of us than he got out of Emile. Emile smiled his bunny smile. Then it was over.

"That was an incredible night."

"I like how you live, Jack."

"Before," he said, "when we watched Raef and Constance . . ."

I turned and looked at him.

"I know what we wanted to say to one another. I do. But I don't want to rush it. I don't want to say a single word to you that isn't true."

"Okay, Jack."

"I'm filled with you, Heather."

"I know. I feel that way, too."

"I don't want to name it yet. That's too easy and too predictable. I want it all to rise on its own."

"So you were paying attention?" I said and pushed my shoulder into his.

"I try to."

"Now you have to buy me breakfast."

"We always end up at breakfast."

But he took my hand. And we walked down the dock, and when we turned back to wave at a shout from the crew, we discovered the crew had not called at all, but that a gull had made the sound of a human and forced us to turn.

27

....

July 12, 1946

    I arrived in a small encampment near Vallorbe, Switzer-
land. I'm exhausted now and hardly feel I can stand on my feet.
A friend suggested I go to see the Col de Jougne Fortress. The
fortress was carved from stone and is kept active to guard
against invasion. The friend—a thin man from Brooklyn
named Danny—said it was a marvel of engineering. I like such
things, but right now my thoughts are filled with longing, and I
wish I could be home. It's the evening light that always reminds
me of the farm. My heart is heavy, and I wish I could free it
somehow.

I t happened here, I think," Jack said, pointing at the ruins in
front of us. I had never seen a building that had been bombed
before—at least one that had been bombed and then abandoned.
You could say it was the skeleton of a building, but it failed to retain
even that much identity. It was the corpse of a building, the empty

skin of something that had once been vital but now had been opened and its entrails scattered in haphazard directions. If Jack hadn't followed his grandfather's journal, if we hadn't asked a thousand directions on both sides of the French-Swiss border, we would never have found the site. The surrounding forest had reclaimed much of the stonework and the pig iron struts that had apparently served to span the roof. Birch trees, mostly still young, shed a dappled light on the mounded relics of the factory. A cold breeze fell southward along the Alps. Raef and Constance had gone off to Spain to a jazz festival. Jack and I were alone.

"So he stood here?"

"It was here. He described the bombed-out building. He was exhausted, he said. His heart was heavy."

"You can feel it a little, can't you? You can feel something horrible went on here."

Jack nodded. His eyes scanned everything, looked to understand what had occurred. He squatted next to a pile of bricks and turned a few over, looking for names, any clue to the building's history.

"What was the building?" I asked, stepping carefully off the old rutted cart path. Nothing, it seemed, had been down this way in ages.

"A rope factory. My grandfather said three families lived here in the burned-out building. He gave them some of his rations, and they gave him coffee, which was a true luxury then. They had stolen the coffee, he thought, but he didn't say anything. He said in his journal that the coffee was black and horrible, but they served it with such pride that he pretended to enjoy it."

"You really loved your grandfather. It comes through everything you do."

"He was good to me. We understood each other in ways I haven't found with many people."

"How did he come to this place?"

"I don't know, honestly. I think he grabbed rides when he could. He hiked and was on different trains and transports. I can't reconstruct all of it because he didn't always write about how he arrived in different locations. He went to see what the war had done to the world, I guess. He was traveling home."

Jack stood and used the toe of his shoe to nudge more bricks around.

"So I think my grandfather stayed at least a week in Berlin. I think he found it horrible and fascinating. Everything, every particle of life, had to be picked up and reexamined. You couldn't go back to believing the same things about human beings as you did before. You just couldn't. He says that any number of times in his journal."

"Then he came here? After Berlin?"

"With some stops in between. Not a straight line at all."

We circled the building as well as we could, bushwhacking through clumps of brush and alder. We had to be careful, because you could not tell what was underfoot. Jack stopped several times to inspect the few piles of rocks or bricks that retained a semblance of a structure. But the forest had consumed the building; the birches and aspens fluttered in the early fall light. Whatever had occurred here, whatever had transpired in the wake of a world war, had now been reclaimed by the land. It seemed to me a fitting memorial.

Jack was different when he looked for sites from his grandfather's journal. He became more serious. We had uncovered two on our travels. This was the third. It was as if he tried to establish himself with his grandfather, to journey back in time to understand what his grandfather understood. The effort made him melancholy. I was never certain if he wanted me with him or not in those moments. He continued to be affectionate, often reaching for my hand as a support, but he might just as easily pull it away to concentrate on his memory. He was like a man inspecting a sailboat, worrying about dry rot and unseaworthy features, while at the same time loving the sense of the design and imagining how it might flow through the water. I made it a practice to speak as little as possible at these moments.

"Well, we should get going," he said eventually, stopping on our rutted path with his hands on his hips. "Nothing to see here, really."

"When you're ready, Jack. No rush."

"It's strange for me to think of him here. I don't know why. I feel as though he was in pain."

I nodded.

"Maybe he was afraid to go home," Jack said. "Maybe that was part of it."

"Why would he be afraid?"

He shrugged. I saw he had grown emotional. I resisted the impulse to comfort him. It broke my heart to see him in such anguish. As much as he loved his grandfather, and spoke of him often, he was also haunted by this trip, by the journey his grandfather made after the war. Something didn't add up, or added up in a way that he found disturbing, and I couldn't ask without intruding. I decided early on that if he wanted to tell me, he would. I wouldn't dig or ask to know.

"I guess I'm all set. We should find a place to stay."

"Okay, Jack."

"Thank you for coming with me."

I put my hand on his back and brushed it lightly.

"It's a puzzle. I don't understand what he was looking for."

"You said you didn't think it was any one thing, right? He might not have known himself what he was searching for."

Jack nodded.

"Would you take a few pictures?" he asked me.

I slipped my phone out and took a dozen shots. He didn't direct me. I tried to be as comprehensive as possible. I didn't ask him why these pictures were all right, but pictures of us having a good time were problematic. I guess he would have told me we were documenting something he needed for research.

We left late in the day and arrived at dinnertime in Vallorbe, Switzerland. Jack wanted to visit the Fortress Vallorbe, the fort his grandfather had described in the journal. It was located in the Col de Jougne mountains, an easy trip the next day. It was too late to investigate it that night, so we found a restaurant and ordered the prix fixe.

And that was where we fought again. Our own World War II.

28

....

A million years ago, my family drove west on a vacation to Yellowstone. I was twelve. When we reached Nebraska, my father got it into his head that we should watch the sand cranes in their annual migration. It was the proper season, and he claimed that none other than Jane Goodall, the famous primatologist, had recommended it as one of the great world animal migrations. My mother simply shrugged, and off we went. It was more or less on the way in any case.

I remember the cranes, but I remember even more the approach of a rainstorm across the wide Nebraska plains that we experienced on I-80 one late afternoon. It came from the west, and it blocked out everything. We had been driving along, playing the inevitable game of spotting various state license plates, when suddenly my father leaned close to the windshield, looked up with a strange expression on his face, and said, "We're in for a little weather."

I had tasted the storm in my teeth, in the soft palate of my mouth, sensed it in the nerve endings of my fingers. We did not enter the storm so much as puncture it; our car became a pliant needle that probed deeply into the rain cloud's epidermis until, at last, we understood its nature.

"Is it a tornado?" my mother asked, her hand out to brace herself on the windshield, her other hand holding a camera.

My father shook his head, leaned closer to the windshield in order to look up, and said again, "We're in for a little weather."

That was the phrase that came to mind when Jack suddenly clouded.

We had been going along, sipping a salty consommé, waiting for the waiter to refill our wineglasses when suddenly I recognized the signs of a storm approaching, and nothing I could do or say could prevent its devastation. Jack smiled. And then the weather took us.

"I want to know what the next day will bring. Not everything—I don't want to know everything—but I want a degree of certainty," I said, my neck flashing red. "At least I want that option. Is that such a horrible thing?"

"It's just . . ." He smiled and looked away.

What was happening? I wondered. How had we gone from these lovely, lovely, lovely weeks, traveling together smoothly and without argument, to arrive suddenly—in the mildest of environments, a perfectly acceptable tourist restaurant with checked tablecloths and soup bowls hung from hooks along the walls for decorations—at the edge of another argument? *We're in for a little weather*, I thought, even as Jack became vivider and leaned forward in his seat.

"This is not about New York this time," he said. "It's not about New York being a prison we build for ourselves. This is about an approach to life and to living."

"You sound very young when you talk like that."

"Like what?"

"When you make these grand proclamations. Didn't you just finish saying New York might actually be a good thing for you career-wise? That it might be a place where you could start your climb to world domination in journalism? You just finished saying that, Jack. Or am I crazy?"

"It's not all one thing or another. It's not."

"I don't even know what you're saying anymore. Do you want to go to New York and try it with me? You don't have to. There's no gun to your head. We've been talking about it, but we haven't committed yet, have we? We haven't."

"I'm worried what it means."

"What *what* means?"

He smiled again. I realized I hated his smile at these junctures. It wasn't so much a smile as the camouflage for a snarl.

The waiter returned with more wine. We smiled at him. We had plenty of smiles to go around. Jack said something in French. The waiter smiled. I wondered if I should get up, pretend I needed the WC, do anything to break the trajectory of where this seemed to be headed.

At the same time, I felt my heart breaking.

When the waiter moved away, Jack took a drink and sighed.

"You were my biggest fear," he said. "You really were. You, Heather Christine Mulgrew."

"Me? Why me?"

"A person like you. A person who I would want to join. I didn't want to meet anyone like you. I had a pretty good plan, I thought. I had six months I could use for traveling. I think that's why I'm reacting."

"You still can."

"Maybe I don't want to. Maybe that's the confusion I'm feeling."

"Jack, we're making a problem where there isn't one. You can continue on your trip. I wouldn't blame you if you did. Not in the least. It might even make things easier for me. I can settle into New York—"

"There is a problem, though. You know it, too, at some level. You're trading in freedom for security. You're trading in this wide world," he said, and he gestured to the restaurant with his right hand, "for a nine-to-five job. It doesn't matter how well paid you'll be; you're deliberately trading something for your life. We both know that life. We know what it can offer and what it kills. It's predictable. That's why people are drawn to it."

I tried to be calm. He seemed to be all over the place with his ideas. If I hadn't been beside him all day, I might have wondered if he had been drinking. I tried to remember how the sand cranes had looked when we finally reached them. They had been more impressive, in many ways, than Yellowstone. They had fallen out of the sky like origami kites, their wings outstretched, their feet shifting slightly to balance their pitch and yaw. Their large wing feathers shifted like piano strings in the air, and they called plaintively, searching for their mates even before they landed, the vast Nebraska plain sending motes of grass and dust into the sunlight to color it.

Somewhere outside of what Jack said to me, the cranes waited.

But for the time being, for this horrible, horrible quarter hour, the storm had us, and we could not leave it.

I forced myself to slowly sip my consommé. It was too salty, but I didn't care. I ate with a straight back, the soup traveling in a dignified square to my mouth. Up, right angle, to the mouth, sip, out, right angle, down, bowl. The waiter passed by and checked on us. We smiled at him. He was a young kid, maybe eighteen, with shaggy hair and a Texas bolo tie. Why he wore a Texas bolo was anyone's guess.

"Should we just drop this discussion for now?" I asked after a little time had passed. "It seems to be a point of conflict for us."

"I'm sorry. I guess this is my personal demon, right?"

"Just so I understand, Jack, are you worried that you will lose something by joining your life, in whatever way that means, to mine? Is that it?"

"I don't know."

"You have to know, Jack. I don't mean this minute, but you have to know eventually, right?"

He drank more wine, then pushed his soup away.

"Salty," he said.

I nodded.

"The last time we fought, we more or less exploded. I don't want to do that this time, Jack. I want us to be honest with each other. The last thing in the world I want to do is invite you to be with me in New York if that's not what you want."

"The thing is, I *do* want that. That's why I said I didn't want to meet someone like you. Not now, maybe not ever. Part of me is drawn to everything about it. About you. And another part, the one that I can't quite understand, that part wants me to keep moving and keep experiencing things. New things."

"We could do that together. We already have. We've been traveling together and seeing new things every day."

"I know. It's true."

"And you've made me look at my life and how I lead it. It isn't all you bending to me, Jack. I haven't even filled out all the stupid forms from Bank of America. That is so not like me, you can't even begin to imagine. My focus is wider now. You've made me examine my choices, and that isn't easy. You've put a crink in my plans, too."

The waiter came and took our soups and replaced them with a pork chop of some sort. It was the specialty of the house. I had no appetite for it, but I smiled anyway and told Jack it looked good. He reached across the table and took my hand.

"I had a friend named Tom, Heather. He was an older guy, but not that old. Maybe midforties. Great guy. He was a bit of a mentor for me. I worked with him on that newspaper. He wanted the same things I did, more or less. Wanted to be a journalist, all of that. Then one day when he was shaving, he found a lump right above his collarbone. He went to the doctor, the doctor diagnosed it as cancer, and nine months later, he was dead. I don't know if I've ever fully acknowledged what it did to me. Mentally, I mean. He went from being a fortysomething-year-old in perfect health to a cancer patient in a matter of weeks. You don't just get over that. Seeing that happen to someone. So I made promises to myself, and one was to see as much of the world as I could, to experience as much as I could as fully as I could. I know that's impossible, I do, but I also know we are going to die one day, and it won't be as

long off as we imagine. It can happen anytime. Trust me, I heard
the mortal knock when Tom got sick. It's one thing to know that
in the abstract, sure, sure, I'm going to die someday, but when it
suddenly becomes a possibility that you might die now, this week,
tomorrow, then something changes. It changes, Heather, believe
me. I *know* that I am dying. Tom taught me that. This is my problem, Heather, not yours. It's my worry. You're perfect. You are. If
there's anyone in the world I want to be with, it's you. But I'm not
sure what I can give you."

He kept my hand in his. His color had gone up and red.

"Okay," I said after a long pause. "I get it. I do."

But I didn't really get it. I couldn't think. I couldn't put two
words together. I sipped my wine. My brain felt like a crab scut-
tling for someplace to hide. Was he breaking up with me? Was he
saying this had been fun, we were great, while warning me not to
get hooked on him? If so, he was too late.

"Are you all right?" he asked.

"Sure. Just sad."

"I didn't mean—"

I stood very, very carefully. *Poise*, I reminded myself. I needed
to be away from him. I needed time to think. The back of my neck
felt like it might burst into flame.

"I'm sorry about Tom's cancer, Jack. I really am. I'm sorry he
died. I'm sure that was a shock, and I'm sure he was terrific. It's
not something you get over. But even so, it's not a free pass to hurt
other people. You don't get to do that. You don't get to think of
people as simply another experience. Not like this, you don't. You
don't get to play around about being in love and then pull back
because you never wanted to be involved in the first place. That's
using people. So you can talk about New York and building prisons

and making choices that limit you, but you're the guy who flirts about getting married and what my name would be, and the whole time you're wondering how you can get out of this and keep going on your walkabout. Well, don't give it a thought. Go on your quest, Jack. Don't let me stand in your way."

"Heather—"

"I'm not angry. Honestly, I'm not. But I'm also not a trap, Jack. I'm not a dead end you need to avoid. You know where the real prison is? It's in your mind. It's in your head. We live in our heads, Jack, and you can travel your legs off, but you're still going to be right inside your brain when the day is done. You made me think it might be nice to have someone along for the movie, someone who might be next to you eating popcorn and watching the same show so you could discuss it and compare it later. But if that's not what you want, if being free means watching the movie alone, okay, I get it. Good luck with that, Jack."

Carefully, carefully, carefully, I walked out of the restaurant. I made sure not to storm out, not to show any impatience in my walk. Besides, I didn't feel angry. I felt I had a hole in my heart, that's all. I held my breath and pretended I was at the bottom of a pool. I kept my chin up and tried not to look right or left. A small part of my brain started sending messages and asking questions— *Where is my backpack, where am I going, where is Constance, how can I reach her?*—and at the same time, my head began to pound. I wanted to cry, but I wouldn't let myself.

When I stepped outside, I realized it had become cold. Truly cold. And the mountains said it was almost time to go home.

29

I did not charge off and leave. Dramatic departures cost money, and I was down to the last pennies of my budget. Besides, I wasn't sure where I wanted to go, how I wanted to get there, what the next step should be. We had a room in a cheap hotel, and I needed a place to stay. Simple as that. You have to have a roof over your head. That was the first law. It was time to be practical. I decided I didn't hate Jack. I decided he had a right to be frightened by his friend's illness. He had behaved badly by involving me, but he wasn't the first person in the world to make a mistake. I had made plenty of mistakes. I told myself that I should be relieved. I had enough to do in New York. I had too much to do, honestly. Back in the room, I pulled out my iPad and answered every form, every request, every e-mail that waited for me while I traveled around Europe with Jack. I had simply lost focus, I reflected. Jack had lost focus, too, in his own way. We didn't have to be enemies. It was all a simple question of emphasis.

I changed into my pajama bottoms and an Amherst hoodie.

Then I held my breath for a while again. It helped. Afterward, I propped up the pillows behind me and read Hemingway.
Hemingway, I reflected, left his first wife for greater experiences. The
greater experience was a woman named Paulette, or Pauline something or other. It was a question of emphasis. Emphases. Everyone had to decide where to put his or her money on the roulette
table.

I turned off the lights a little later. I wasn't sure I could sleep.

Jack came in quietly about an hour later. He used the flashlight
on his phone to see where he was going. I kept my eyes shut.

"Can we talk?" he asked softly. "Heather, are you awake? Can
we talk?"

I considered pretending to sleep, but what was the point of
that? I reached to the lamp beside the bed and turned it on. Jack
sat on the bed and put his hand on my leg. I shoved up into the
pillows and tried to push my hair out of my face.

"That didn't go so well," he said. "The dinner, I mean."

I shrugged.

"Do you think we can repair it?" he asked.

"I don't see how. Not the way it was before."

"I'm sorry I was ambivalent about going to New York with
you. I don't want to lose what we have. I'm drawn to you, Heather,
but I'm scared of what that means. Here's what I want to say: I
was like you a couple of years ago. I cared about promotions and
climbing the ladder, but one day Tom came to me and explained
what had happened. I realized through his death that I hadn't
done the things I wanted to do. I know that sounds melodramatic,
but I promised myself that I would never spend another day in an
office. I asked myself if I wanted to change my life, if I *could* change
my life. I took this trip, this mission to follow my grandfather's

journal in the hope that it would restore me somehow as it re-stored him. Then I met you."

"Jack, I'm sure I can't understand what it means to watch a friend die that way. Not really. But you have to understand that you're free. You can do what you need to do. You don't owe me anything."

"It's not about owing, Heather. I'm sorry I'm so bad at framing this conversation. I keep saying things I don't mean exactly."

"I'm listening, Jack."

He took a breath. I could see he wanted to say things clearly.

"It's not just about you exactly. It's about work and getting back into journalism. It's a whole range of things. It was Tom's death, too. He had a shunt put in his chest and had a bunch of interferon pumped through his system. That went on a long time, and he was sick every day. It made me pretty gun-shy to watch that, Heather. It made me not trust the world. I'm afraid you got swept up in all those thoughts, but it's that, not us."

"I understand, Jack. You don't need to explain yourself to me or to anyone. I think I'm going to head to Paris. We're flying out soon, anyway, and my money is low. I already let Constance know. She's coming up from Spain soon."

"I'm coming with you. I want to be in Paris with you."

"Not sure that's a great idea."

"We talked about being in Paris together."

"We talked about a lot of things. I won't kid you, Jack. I'm falling for you. I know it's a cliché, but you take my breath away. You do. I don't know if we would have been perfect, but I was willing to try. I didn't see getting together with you as the end to anything. I saw it as a beginning. An exciting one. I want to keep traveling, Jack. I'll be going to Japan and Indonesia . . . all over the world, really. Yes, I'll be working, and yes, I will have to pay my dues at the office, but I'm happy to do that. It's part of my life. I thought you might be part of that life, too. I hoped, anyway. But if it's not meant to be, okay. It hurts, but I can accept it. I still love what we've had here."

"I just need a little more time."

"Time for what? That doesn't sound very likely. Or practical. It's just going to dig the hole deeper, isn't it? I don't want to give you an ultimatum, but I suppose we're coming to the fish-or-cut-bait stage of things. It means too much to mean just a little. I can't make it casual at this point. If we had met in a town in the States, we could have kept dating and let time help us decide what to do. But that wasn't our fate, was it? We met on a train going to Amsterdam. Maybe spending so much time together, traveling, you know, maybe that raised the ante. Maybe it rushed things without our knowing it. I'm not sure. I'm tired of thinking about it, Jack. I have to go home soon. I want to see Paris one more time before I go because I've always loved the idea of Paris even before I saw it. But I don't want to see Paris with you. Not anymore. Not if you're coming to see me onto a plane. I don't want to remember Paris as the place I went and broke up with a sweetheart. Remember a long time ago you asked me what I liked in Hemingway, and I said I liked his sadness? Well, I do like his sadness, but I don't want to bring that sadness with me to Paris."

He looked at me a long time without speaking. Then slowly he removed his shoes. He leaned over and put his head next to mine on the pillows. I turned to him. Our faces rested inches apart.

"I choose you," he whispered and stroked my cheek. "I do. I choose you. You've given me back some hope I lost along the way. Will you still have me?"

I nodded. I didn't have a doubt from my end of things.

"Are you sure?" I asked. "Don't say this kind of thing anymore if you don't mean it. We can't have this conversation again."

"We'll go to Italy first, then Paris. We have time, and I want to see one last thing from the journal. Then I'm going to Paris with you, then to New York. I don't know everything yet, but I know I want to be with you. I'm sorry if I've been difficult. I don't mean to be. I was scared, Heather. Maybe I told myself not to have too many hopes, and then you came into the picture."

"You've changed me, too, Jack. You made me question some of my assumptions, and you made me slow down. I've learned from you. I'm thinking of getting rid of my Smythson."

"I'm not sure the world is ready for a Heather Mulgrew without her Smythson."

"I'm the new, freer Heather. Wait and see."

"We'll meet in the middle."

"Yes, that's the plan."

His eyes crinkled. He kissed me lightly, his lips barely resting on mine.

"You must be starving," he said. "You didn't eat anything at all in the restaurant."

"I am starving."

"What if I told you I had Ben and Jerry's in my backpack?"

"You'd be lying."

He nodded, and he kissed me again, and a little later we fell asleep. The sand cranes did not trouble my sleep, and the storm passed away to the east. But what had happened, what it all meant, still wasn't clear to me.

30

His name is Jack Quiller-Couch, and I met him on a train going into Amsterdam . . . yes, no, you will like him, Mom. So will Daddy."

I spoke to her on the train on our way to Italy. Jack had gone off to the bar car. The train, for once, was fairly empty. We had the luxury of a pair of facing benches entirely to ourselves.

"So what does it mean? That he's coming back with you?"

If I didn't miss my guess, she had a cup of tea. I knew she sat in the solarium, her favorite place in the summer, the room filled with houseplants and geraniums. She loved geraniums.

I heard her being deliberately even. I heard the mistrust of Jack in her voice—of everything Jack represented—but I knew she was trying to be motherly and calm, and that only made it worse.

This was the conversation I had dreaded. If Jack was coming with me, then it meant Jack was going to stay at our house, at least briefly, and I wanted to clear that with my mother.

"In what sense?" I asked, mostly to give myself time to think.

"Well, I don't know, Heather. I really don't. I mean, are you two engaged somehow?"

"No, Mom. It's not like that."

"But he's coming with you?"

"That's the plan."

She didn't say anything. She was the absolute master of not saying anything. She never made it easy. She paused long enough to make it awkward, and then I usually vomited something out to kill the silence.

I tried to wait her out, but I couldn't.

"We've been traveling together," I explained. "In Germany and Poland and Switzerland, Mom. We're going to Italy now—I told you that. Obviously, we care for each other. We're deciding what that means."

"I see."

"I'm not sure you do *see*," I said, flashing a little. "He's a terrific guy. He's very handsome. He's a Vermonter. He grew up on a farm, at least mostly."

Again, the Mom-a-saurus, master of silence.

"And I think I'm in love with him, Mom. Do you understand? I think I love him. I think we might be right for each other in a big way, in the way you and Daddy are right for each other."

I felt close to tears.

The train continued to knock along. The mountains and pines outside the window sometimes held pale ghosts of snow and ice.

"So when you come home, he will be with you?" Mom asked.

"Yes. Jack. Jack will be with me."

"Are you planning to live together?"

"I don't know. We haven't discussed things fully."

"But if he's coming home with you—"

"I get it, Mom. I get what you're asking. There are some practical matters we need to iron out. I understand. We'll do all that. We'll come up with a little more of a plan. I'm sorry to drop this on you this way. It's new to me, too, so I don't have all the answers. But I wanted you to know what was going on."

"I'm glad you did. You know, you could just bring back a souvenir. You don't have to go to Europe and bring a man home with you."

I took a deep breath. It was a joke. I think she meant it as a joke.

"I want you to be happy for me, Mom."

"I am, honey."

"Really happy. Not reservedly happy. Not standing-in-judgment happy. I don't know if what we are doing is the right thing, but it feels that way. I'm not being rash, believe me. I'm not losing my head. Jack is real and solid—as solid as anything. And he sees the world in such a beautiful way. It's different from the way I see the world, but we complement each other in that regard. I don't know. I'm tired of trying to fit everything into convenient boxes, Mom. I feel I've been doing that all my life. Jack doesn't fit neatly into any sort of box, and I love that about him. The world feels more open with him beside me. It does. I've thought about all the sensible objections. We're too young, we're not established . . . there are a thousand valid cautions, but there are always a thousand cautions, right, Mom? You taught me that. Sometimes you have to accept what is given to you and hold it close. Please tell me you understand, Mom."

"Of course I do, honey," she said, and it was the good mom, the warm mom, the perfect mom who caught a picture of my friends and me at commencement oozing all that hope and the one who maybe, maybe, maybe, understood me better than anyone else on earth.

And I could imagine her conversation with my dad later that night.

Heather has met someone.

Someone?

A boy. Well, I guess he's not a boy technically. A young man.

And . . . ?

My father sitting in his chair, maybe watching a Yankees game, maybe sipping a dark, single-malt scotch out in the solarium with her.

And she's going to bring him home.

The Dad look. The slow study. The quizzical lift of his eyebrows.

She's starting the job, he would say.

Mom might nod.

Hmmmm.

Then he would look back at the TV, or peer out at the setting sun, lift his glass, sip.

He would think the pieces don't quite fit. He would think I was being hasty and lacked seriousness. He would wonder what I was possibly thinking.

"How did that go?" Jack asked, sliding back into the seat across from me. He handed me a hot chocolate. He looked handsome and rested. It occurred to me I now knew how he slept, what he felt like each day.

"As well as it could, I suppose. It's a lot to spring on them."

"Good. Give me your feet, and I'll rub them. That's the least I can do."

"My feet are filthy."

"I accept that condition."

"You do have a foot fetish. It's becoming clearer and clearer."

I sipped my hot chocolate. It was pretty good. He patted his knees to get me to put my feet up. I did. I told him to leave my socks on.

"When will you call your folks?" I asked.

"Oh, we're not that kind of family."

"What kind of family is that?"

"I don't know. The kind that actually likes one another."

"More pathology?"

"It's what gives me my edge. Did you talk to your mom or dad?"

"Mom. But that's the same as talking to both of them. They share relentlessly."

He hit a nerve in my toe, and my foot jumped a little. We were back on our even keel. We were back on even a better keel, because now things were out on the table. For the first time, we had begun talking about New York not as a hypothetical destination but as a place we intended to live. It changed the music for both of us.

"Sleepy?" he asked. "Sometimes a foot massage makes me sleepy."

"What are we going to do in Italy?"

"Eat spaghetti. Look around."

"We're going all the way to Italy to eat spaghetti?"

"It sounds pretty badass when you say it like that."

"Your grandfather went there?"

He nodded.

"Then Paris?" I asked.

"Then Paris. And Raef and Constance will be there. And then the trip is over. Just like that."

"It will be good to see them."

"I wish they could meet up with us in Italy."

"I guess there's not enough time, really. Did I ever tell you I used to think Venice was on Venus? That it was a place on a different planet?"

"And you with a degree from Amherst."

"I think it was just the Vs. I don't know. I remember being disappointed when my friend told me Venice was a city in Italy. I didn't believe her at first. I thought she was misinformed. I thought the gondoliers wearing striped shirts . . . I thought that was a space uniform."

"You have your moments of strangeness, Heather."

"It was an easy thing to mistake."

"Like thinking an aardvark is a car ark. That's what I thought when I was a kid."

"An aardvark is a car ark? I can't even pronounce that. It's a tongue twister. What is a car ark?"

"I thought Noah built an ark for the animals, so why wasn't there a car ark? Or, as I thought of it, as an aardvark."

He held my toes. Things felt light and happy and solid. We still looked into each other's eyes when my phone sounded. I glanced down and saw it was my father. I showed it to Jack, and he nodded and climbed out of the seat.

"All yours," he said.

He kissed me lightly and headed back to the bar car.

31

....

So tell me about Jack," my father said. "Your mother says he's accompanying you home."

Accompanying, my father said. He made Jack sound like a valet.

I knew he had been put up to the call by my mother, by her insistence that he find out what this all meant. It was an old pattern with us. And, man, they worked fast.

"Jack is a man I met on a train to Amsterdam."

"He's an American?"

"Born and bred."

"And your mother said from someplace in New England?"

"Vermont," I said.

I hated giving him short answers, but I didn't trust myself to go on at length. It was better to speak in short, declarative sentences without volunteering too much.

"And what are his plans? Do you know?"

"Regarding what?"

"Well, just his general plan. For life, I guess. Have you had that kind of discussion?"

"Dad, you're prying."

"I don't mean to, sweetie. Sorry. I'm curious, I guess. So is your mother. This is a big step. You just graduated this spring."

"I'm aware of that, Dad."

I sipped my hot chocolate. I determined not to step into any traps with my dad. If he wanted answers, he would have to lead the conversation. After a pause, he continued.

"And with the new job—Ed Belmont's team just went through the roof, by the way. Their sales, I mean. They had a big write-up in *The Wall Street Journal*. Anyway, Jack is going to be living with you?"

"We don't know exactly, Dad. Probably. We only know we want to be together. That's the crux of our plan."

An intense, narrow headache lodged like a bullet in my front cortex. I put the cup of hot chocolate against my forehead, but that failed to help.

"And what is his line?" Dad asked.

"His line?"

"His trade, his ambition. What does he want to do?"

"He's been following his grandfather's journal through Europe. That's what he's been doing, mostly."

"His grandfather's journal?"

"His grandfather traveled through Europe after the war. Jack is retracing his steps with the idea of maybe doing a book. He loved his grandfather. Jack was a journalist before that at a paper in Wyoming."

My father didn't say anything. The tide of electric whatever-buzz that connected our phones made the sound of the sea swelling and subsiding.

"Okay, then, I guess you know best, Heather. We're a little concerned—your mom and I—we're a little concerned about the timing. You're young, kiddo, and this is your first big love."

"Dad, come on. Stop, please. I'm not doing this lightly. I'm not. Neither is Jack. We didn't plan to meet or fall for each other. It just happened. We want to be together. He's a great guy. You'll love him. He makes me feel solid when I'm around him. I know it may take a little juggling at first, but I'm good at that. And don't worry. I'm still fully committed to the job and my career. You don't have to worry about that. I won't embarrass you, I promise."

"Nothing you've done has embarrassed me, sweetie. Don't even think that."

We didn't have much more to say, at least not without getting into a major fritz with each other. I wasn't going to defend Jack as an abstraction to my father. They would have to meet, to size each other up, have to do that maddening boy-boy thing that I never quite understood.

"How's Mr. Periwinkle?" I asked to break the awkwardness.

"Doing fine, I guess. I haven't heard anything to the contrary."

I took a deep breath and then tried to frame my thoughts carefully for my father. I started once, stopped, then started again.

"Dad, I don't know for sure what it all means with Jack. I love him. I know that. And I think he loves me. I know some of the timing may be a little awkward, but there's always a glitch, right? Isn't that what you say? Life is one long fight against glitches? Well, I'm starting this new job, and I will give it everything. I promise you that. But Jack counts for something, too. We could postpone everything, tell ourselves what we experienced here doesn't count, but you didn't raise me to think like that. You didn't. Life doesn't happen someplace in the future. You said that. You said life happens here and now, and it's a fool's bargain to let something good go now in the hope of something better at a later date. That's almost a direct quote. So trust me, Dad. This is a good man. He sees the world in a way that interests me. We make a good team. Maybe it's not the most convenient set of circumstances, but life is always full of glitches, right?"

"Always full of glitches," Dad agreed.

It was his adage. He had to agree.

"Okay, sweetie, I guess that's it. We're looking forward to seeing you home here. Will Jack be with you here?"

"We haven't discussed it, but yes, if that's all right with you."

"It's your home, too, sweetheart. You're always welcome no matter what."

"And Jack?"

"If Jack's okay with you, then he's okay with us."

"Thank you. I appreciate your saying that."

"You're not supposed to be growing up so fast, you know?"

"Not that fast, Daddy. I still feel like a ten-year-old."

"Well, we all do in one way or another. All right, I'll report back to headquarters. Mom will want to know the scoop. See you in what? A little over a week?"

"A little over a week."

I thought for a second he hung up. But then he said what he always says.

"You're still my pumpkin, you know."

"I know, Daddy. I always will be."

32

....

July 30, 1947

*I arrived in a beautiful Italian city called Finale Ligure.
It's not really a city, I suppose. More of a village. It's on the
seacoast, the Gulf of Genoa. The war didn't consume it as it
consumed other places. Being near the sea air has improved my
appetite. I ate two large bowls of tomato and noodles at lunch.
Afterward, I slept a long time beside the ocean. I had one of
those strange sleeps in which the sound of gulls plays in your
dreams and you hardly know what is the dream and what is
waking life.*

These must be the stone pillars he wrote about," Jack said, the
journal in his hand, his head turning back and forth from
the café nearby to the line of pillars that now towered above us. They
were heavy spears of stone jabbed into the earth as if someone had
thrown them. No one seemed to pay them any mind except other
tourists. One short, round man with enormous forearms stopped

near us and explained in Italian that the pillars had once belonged to a Roman brothel, but I had a feeling he was having us on. I tried to google *Roman brothel and Finale Ligure* on my phone, but the phone claimed it was out of range. The Italian man laughed and walked off. We were the American dupes.

"Is the café name . . . ?" I asked and borrowed the journal from Jack. The journal read Café Excalibur. The café now was called Café Caprazoppa, named after the great limestone rock that formed the mountains, but that did not necessarily mean it was not the same café.

"Put the journal in your backpack, will you? But wait. It says seven pillars, doesn't it?"

I searched the entry. His grandfather had drawn pillars, fat tubes of rock, but he did not give a number in the text that I could find. I read it up and down while Jack wove in and out among the pillars, his eyes up. It was late afternoon, and the cafés had begun to fill with crowds taking late coffees or having their first cocktails.

"The drawing has seven pillars," I said, my eyes going back and forth from the stones to the journal, then back again. "But I don't see it in the text."

"Imagine if he was here. I like thinking that he was here."

"I suppose it could be plenty of places, but this seems like it has all the right ingredients. You don't see pillars like these every day."

"I'm still picturing this Vermont farm boy wandering around Europe all by himself. It's strange in some ways."

"How do you mean?"

"Well, I guess most people's impulse would have been to get home as soon as possible, but not Grandpa. I don't think he left the farm more than a couple of times the rest of his life. It's almost as if he knew he wanted to gather up some images for later reference. I don't know. It's kind of funny. I wonder if he resisted going home for some reason."

"We passed the Benedictine abbey, didn't we? That's in Finale Pia, I think."

"Why do you ask?"

"Just triangulating. Trying to get the layout."

It occurred to me how different it was to travel with Jack. Here we were investigating random pillars in a small Italian town, when most people would have been on the beach or traipsing through the ruins. If I had been with Constance, there would not have been a question: we would have seen the sights suggested by the Lonely Planet guide, and that would have been that.

"Are you bored?" Jack asked, his hands on the pillars, his eyes up at the smooth rise of stone. "You're probably bored, right?"

"I'm always bored around you, so it's hard to distinguish one time from another."

"Must be."

"I wanted to learn more about pillars while I was in Europe. It was on my to-do list."

"I figured."

"I am going to take a couple of pictures of you," I said.

"You're so pushy."

"If you do a book, you'll want them. And even if you don't, you'll still want a picture of you standing where your grandpa stood."

He started to say something, then he shrugged. I snapped a half dozen pictures of him. He smiled. He had a dazzling smile.

"Am I going to like your mom and dad?" he asked as I slipped my phone away, changing subjects, his hands still on the stone.

"Sure. Why not?"

"They probably think I'm digging for your gold. They probably think I'm your man-candy."

"And that would be wrong how?"

"So you admit I am your man-candy. I thought so."

"It's okay. Men are the ultimate accessories. I thought you understood that."

"Let's go to the beach and find a nice café and have a good dinner," he said. "You can show me off."

"I'm pretty broke, Jack."

"We need a good dinner in Italy. At least one. My treat."

"And wine?" I asked, tucking the journal in my backpack.

"Plenty of wine."

The next thing slipped out of my mouth before I could catch it. It had ghosted our conversation since the night of the mechanical bull. I couldn't stand it any longer.

"Are we going to start saying we love each other out loud?" I asked.

I watched his expression carefully.

"You first," he said.

"No, boys always have to go first in that situation."

"Why?" he asked, dropping his hands from the pillars and coming to put his arms around my waist.

"It's one of the rules of the universe. I think it's on the periodic table, actually."

"I love you, Heather. There you go. Right out loud. The whole thing."

"I love you, too, Jack."

"So now that's part of us. We can't go back. We can break up, but we can't go back."

"True."

"I feel as though I've loved you from another life almost."

"Me, too. Feels that way, I know."

"We don't have to stop falling in love, do we? We can fall deeper."

"We will."

"We can make our own world. We can live how we like," he said, his lips close to my ear.

"Yes," I agreed.

We stayed for a while longer and looked at the pillars. I liked that we didn't know their exact purpose. I liked that we committed ourselves to one another in a spot where Jack's grandfather once stood. It was a gorgeous little village, a perfect Italian *comune* on the Italian Riviera. In a way, life seemed to be beginning right in that instant, immediately after our words had passed from one to the other. Everything before it had been mere prelude; everything afterward would be Jack. We stood until a flock of pigeons circled near us and landed. They came forward hoping for handouts, their glittering necks holding the light of the sun and turning it green and blue and yellow.

Paris

33

Whatever you bring to Paris, it takes away and uses for a time, then it returns it to you. But what it gives back is altered, sometimes subtly, sometimes more noticeably, but the city guards a small part of whatever you brought and keeps it for itself. Paris is a thief. It is a smiling thief, one that lets you in on the joke but steals just the same. And you can't resist, because it is Paris, and the city falls into darkness at ten o'clock on summer evenings and the cafés turn on their lights and the streets fill, and the scent of coffee, of perfume, of cooking eggs and onions, is everywhere. In recompense for the theft, Paris returns small, glorious pictures, beautiful moments when it gives you back the thing you brought and hints that you can have more, go deeper, if only you accept the bargain. Sometimes it is only the swell of the Seine as it throbs against its ancient bank, or the absurd open mouth of a sword swallower at Montparnasse, or the feral glint of a traveler looking to lift a wallet on a crowded train platform.

Paris is the cupped hand of a woman accepting a match light from a man at a small round table under a chestnut tree thirty minutes before a rainstorm.

I spotted Constance from half a block away, and my heart leaped up.

I ran toward Constance, and she ran toward me—her look as ethereal as ever—and we embraced in a do-si-do that threatened to knock us over from the weight of our backpacks. After a deep, satisfying hug, we pushed away from each other to fill our eyes with the other person, then hugged again, this time more fiercely, and some small thing that had been missing returned to me in a great, gushing relief.

"You look amazing!" I said, because she did. She looked radiant and happy, and one glance told me everything I needed to know about how her time with Raef had been.

"You do, too!" she said, nodding, and our eyes worked on one another's, trying to send messages, to interpret everything in a mad rush to understand what the other had experienced.

"Did you love Spain?"

"I loved Spain," she said. "And Italy?"

"It was wonderful. We only saw a little, but it was wonderful."

"And what about Switzerland?"

It was too much to tell all at once. We realized, gradually, that Raef and Jack stood back from us, giving us a chance to catch up. We both laughed as it became clear that we had ignored the men. I hugged Raef, and Constance hugged Jack. Then for a moment we didn't know what to do next.

"I have a line on a place," Raef said when we settled in a small circle together, blocking too much foot traffic, it was true. "Maybe we could leave our bags with you two while Jack and I go sort things out. You said you're okay with a cheap hotel?"

"Sure," I said and looked at Jack. He nodded.

That became the plan. Jack and Raef walked with us to a café near the train station and left us with all the baggage. We ordered two coffees from a stringy old waiter, his white hair like a Roman's laurel wreath around his temples. The waiter nodded and wandered off. I put my hands across the table, and Constance placed her hands in mine.

"So?" I asked.

Her eyes filled.

"He is the kindest, gentlest man I have ever met," she said, understanding instantly what I had asked to know. "I'm so mad about him I don't know what to do with myself. Honestly, I don't. I keep telling myself this is nutty, this can't be happening, but then he does something else, something so sweet and thoughtful that it knocks me over again."

"I'm so glad, Constance. I'm so happy for you."

"And Jack?"

I nodded.

She squeezed my hand. The waiter returned with our coffees. She spoke again.

"We went to Spain, and at first I had difficulty with the language and the pace of things. It was slow, and I felt this nervous need to keep going, to see more, but Raef worked his magic on me. I started asking myself, is this some kind of race? Is it a game where someone wins a prize by seeing more museums, visiting more cathedrals? Why hadn't I ever thought of that before? It's so basic and so obvious, but it wasn't until Raef helped me see it, gave it a context, that I understood a little of what I was doing here in the first place."

"I felt the same way," I said. "With Jack. I had this absurd checklist in my mind, and if I didn't notch all the squares, then I had somehow failed. I wasn't the good tourist. I wasn't getting full value. I don't know if it's an American attitude, or just one of my own. Maybe it has something to do with being a good student, but suddenly with Jack I no longer felt in a rush to get somewhere that I had never wanted to get to in the first place. Not really."

"Raef wants me to go to Australia with him. To not go home, but to go with him instead. He wants me to meet his family."

"Are you considering it?"

She looked steadily at me. My lovely, intellectual friend, the young woman who studied saints, merely shrugged.

"I don't know," she said. "It's not at all what I came to Europe to do. My parents would think I've gone insane."

"Have you told them about Raef?"

"I told my mom. She's supportive but wants me to be cautious. I've hashed it all out in my head. I don't have to start work until later in the fall. I could do it, go to Australia, I mean. It's tempting. Raef has to go back for the summer sheepshearing. I think that's what he said. The seasons are reversed, so I get confused when he talks about it."

"You're that serious?"

She nodded. She sipped her coffee.

"Apparently we are," she said.

"I'm happy for you. I know I said that, but I really am."

"I'm not ready to say good-bye to him. Not yet. Can you say good-bye to Jack?"

I shook my head. I didn't feel I could ever say good-bye to Jack, but I didn't want to say that aloud. Seeing Constance, listening to her plans with Raef, made me realize Jack and I could go on. We didn't have to end in Paris or New York—or anywhere else, for that matter. It made my stomach feel buttery to think it.

The waiter brought us more coffee. For a little while we watched the café, the crowd moving around, people coming and going. The crowd looked different from the crowds in Berlin or Amsterdam. Younger, perhaps. Lighter. I felt the ache that I had felt the last time in Paris: that life was here as it was present in few places. And although that didn't make logical sense, I still felt it, still needed to know it somehow.

"Let's call Amy," Constance said after the waiter left. "It doesn't feel right to be here without her."

"Okay," I said, because it was the perfect idea. "Let's call her."

We Facetimed Amy.

Constance hadn't heard from her except for a few random texts; I hadn't, either, even after I sent the pictures of Constance riding a mechanical bull in Kraków. Somehow being united again persuaded us to believe that she had to pick up and answer our request. Constance texted her first to tell her we were calling. Amy didn't answer the text. But a few second later, when we clicked on Facetime, Amy immediately picked up and answered with a signature line.

"What's up, bitches!" She laughed.

It was Amy, our Amy, and she looked happy but strange confined to the small computer screen. She looked thinner, too, bonier. Her eyes sparkled. She looked like someone who had run many miles but wasn't quite put back together.

"Oh, it's so good to see you!" I said. "I missed you so much. We both have!"

"No, you haven't! You've been slicing off some sweet boy flesh for yourselves! I watch your Facebook posts! All those Instagram shots."

Maybe, maybe she was overcompensating a little with her enthusiasm. Constance leaned close to the screen, her glasses glinting a little.

"What did you do to your hair?" she asked Amy. "I can't quite see on the camera."

"Cut it. This gay guy grabbed me in my mom's salon and insisted on a new hairstyle. I'm officially middle-age bobbed! I look like I just had a baby or something!"

"It's just wonderful to see you, Amy," I said. "You look fantastic."

"I feel great. I've been going to the VFW hall in town and flirting my ass off with a bunch of old soldiers. They're like training wheels for me. Getting back in the game little by little."

"Good," Constance said. "I'm glad you picked up our call. It's been too long. We miss you so much."

"And you two! Is love in the air over there? What the hell? I leave you alone for a couple of weeks and you go over the moon on me."

Constance blushed. So did I. Neither one of us answered.

"Oh, jeez, you both have it bad!" Amy said, her voice slightly lagged in time. "Really bad. So now where are you? Are you back in Paris?"

"We just got here," I said. "We're staying for four days, then we're flying home."

"Are you coming alone?"

I glanced at Constance. She didn't take her eyes off the screen.

"Jack is coming with me," I said.

"I might be going to Australia," Constance said. "It's not for sure yet."

"You love these guys, don't you?"

"Yes," I said softly. "I guess we do."

"Well, then, don't be a pair of prudes. Ask for what you want. I'll tell you this, the dating outlook around here is pretty grim. All boys or old men. I've got this one married jerk who won't leave me alone. He has a belt buckle with an entire buckboard wagon on it. You wouldn't believe someone like him exists, but he does. Every Saturday night, he shows up at the VFW hall, only he doesn't say *Saturday* night, he says *Date-ur-day* night. He's a weird little man."

"Are you dating him?" I asked.

"Nooooooo," she squealed. "No way. Oh, good God, no."

"But everything is okay?" Constance asked. The question was deliberately vague. Despite discussing it a thousand times, Constance and I were unsure what Amy thought about leaving, about the whole wrap up of her time in Europe.

"I'm okay," she said. "I know I haven't been a good friend lately. I'm sorry I wasn't in touch more. I couldn't do it right away. It was hard coming back. Embarrassing. My parents were pissed. They couldn't leave it alone. My mom likes to drop my fiasco—that's what she calls it, Amy's fiasco—into conversation every now and then just to keep me humbly under her thumb."

"Mothers and daughters," I said.

Constance nodded.

"It was just a big bust," Amy said. "Just Amy's fucked-up summer trip."

"Things happen," I said. "Crazy things. It wasn't all that bad."

"Yes, but not to you two."

"You never know what's going to happen," Constance said. "The saints teach us that much, at least."

"Trouble is, I'm far from a saint," Amy said.

"You're pretty saintly," I said.

"Honestly, though, I'm pulling back a little. I'm being a little less wild, a little less robust, you might say. I've been cutting down on my drinking, and I've been running again. It's been a long time since I had steady exercise. I need it. I ran a 10K last weekend. I'm in surprisingly decent shape."

"You look good," Constance said. "Healthy."

"Well, I'm trying."

We talked a little more, mostly focused on gossip about recent Amherst graduates. Amy had a good supply of tall tales about our old group. Finally, Raef and Jack returned. They sat and had a coffee and smiled at Amy and said hello, and then Amy was the fifth wheel and felt it.

"Okay, I'm going to scoot," she said. "Later, bitches."

"Take care of yourself," I said.

"Always," she answered.

She hung up or whatever it is you do when you sign off from Facetime. The screen shrank down and swallowed her, and she was gone in an electric burp that sounded odd in the café, sounded as if she had returned to the mother ship and wouldn't beam down again anytime soon.

34

....

We checked into the Hotel Trenton, a modest pension on the Left Bank, not far from the Jardin du Luxembourg, a block or two from the Sorbonne. It was an extravagance on our limited budgets, but Jack argued it was worth it. We would only be in Paris together for the first time once—and only once—and to huddle together in a hostel wouldn't do to commemorate such a moment.

As always, Raef knew somebody, worked a deal somehow. There was no end to Raef's handiness.

The rooms were not much; they had not been updated in ages, but each room possessed a tiny balcony, large enough for a chair if you sat sideways. Raef and Constance had a room on the second floor, slightly below and to the right of our room. From our balcony we could see the rooftops, the red-tiled gutters and aluminum vents, and Jack promised me that Quasimodo, the Hunchback of Notre Dame, might swing into our bedchamber at any time, day or night.

He sat on the bed and watched me unpack. I put some things in the small bathroom, trying to be orderly. The double bed made the room difficult to navigate. I banged my shins twice on the bedframe, the second time so hard that I had to stand for a second and close my eyes. Jack seemed to have the better idea. He looked ready for the nap we had promised each other—Raef and Constance had the same idea—before meeting to go exploring.

"You okay?" Jack asked when he saw me standing and grimacing against the pain.

"This damn bed."

"Why don't you get on the bed with me? Then it wouldn't trip you up."

I nodded and crawled over to him, my shin still stinging like a crazy torch. With our heads on the pillow, we could look out on midday Paris. I smiled, thinking how good it felt to be in Paris. The sun did not appear to be strong; a few lazy clouds worked against the gray sky and seemed to gather the day's color into their billowy centers.

"I have a bit of a headache," Jack said.

"You okay?"

"I'm fine."

He shrugged.

"Can I get you anything? Do anything?"

"Sex," he said. "Kinky sex."

I pushed up and looked at him. He smiled. It was a weak smile. He didn't feel great, I could see, and his color was lousy.

"I mean it, Jack. Are you okay?"

He shrugged again. He tried to put a brave face on it, but he clearly didn't feel well.

"Let me close my eyes," he said. "I'll be okay in an hour."

"Okay. If I'm not here when you wake up, it means the Hunch-back has taken me."

"Good to know."

I kissed him gently on the cheek. I felt his lips curl in a smile, but he didn't move.

We slept a long time. I woke in midafternoon, and Jack still slept soundly beside me. He had turned away so I couldn't see his face. I didn't want to shake the bed or risk waking him, so I slipped carefully into the bathroom, rinsed my face, brushed my teeth, brushed my hair quickly, then wrote a note and stuck it to the mirror.

"Sleepyhead, call me as soon as you wake up," I wrote. "I hope you feel better."

I slipped out the door and went to explore Paris on my own.

I bought a *crêpe du fromage* and a café au lait from a food truck outside the Jardin du Luxembourg and carried it to a table beside a statue of Pan not far beyond the entranceway. I was hungry, but I also wanted the sensation of having a small meal by myself in the park that Hemingway made famous. I sat beneath a large chestnut tree, already in its final fruiting, the heavy nuts scattered around its base, some of them exploded from footfalls. I ate slowly, picking at the crêpe, which was delicious. It tasted of grass and meadows, and the cheese was warm and sweet. The coffee had a dark, heavy viscosity that I had never tasted in coffee before. The two flavors and textures—the soft, yielding flesh of the crêpe balanced against the oily richness of the coffee—made me happy in a peculiar, pleased way. Here I was again on the Left Bank of Paris, late summer, and I sat in the Jardin du Luxembourg, the massive trees and green lawns surrounding me, the exact spot where Hemingway and Hadley and Bumpy sat decades before between the wars.

It was slightly silly and overly romantic, but I didn't care. I pulled out my iPad and read Hemingway. I read from *A Moveable Feast*, which I had read during my first trip to Paris. I scanned through the pages, stopping to reread sections I had noted or underlined. Hemingway still got to me. He wrote: *We ate well and cheaply and drank well and cheaply and slept well and warm together and loved each other.*

I read that several times. I thought of Jack and of what I wanted.

I took the last, tiny sip of my coffee and turned the plate over so that the crumbs from the crêpe could be taken by the multitudes of pigeons that roamed near the table, never far away, always burbling, like water or birds made of glass.

I was still sitting, empty but pleased, when the phone beeped.

Where is Quasimodo holding you? the text read.

The Jardin du Luxembourg, I wrote back. *Come sit with me.*

"We need to go on a secret mission," Jack said as he kissed me quickly and slid in beside me. "We're not meeting Raef and Constance until late. We have the evening to ourselves."

"First tell me how you're feeling."

"I'm fine."

"Are you really? Or are you just being brave?"

"No, I feel fine, honestly. I swear."

"You slept really hard. You didn't wake at all when I left."

He smiled and reached over and tucked my hair behind my ear.

"Did you eat?" he asked.

"A crêpe and a cup of coffee."

He nodded. He looked serious for a second and turned to me. "This is Hemingway's park, isn't it?"

"Yes."

"When he was young, he walked his baby here, didn't he?"

I nodded.

"He used to kill pigeons and stuff them under the baby blanket," I said. "They were so broke they needed the pigeons for food."

Jack smiled softly.

He reached across the table for my hand.

I loved the weight of his hand. I loved its size wrapping around my own.

My phone buzzed before we had a chance to move. The Mom-a-saurus was on the line, but I didn't pick up the call.

We sat for a while and watched the park grow darker. It was a beautiful evening. Later, a tall man walking a Jack Russell came by, and we watched them continue down the path. They looked funny together; the dog's short little legs seemed to go a thousand times faster than the man's. The dog was well behaved. It moved like a balloon tied to the end of a stick.

We headed back to the room at twilight. I felt full with happiness. Jack stretched out on the bed again and fell asleep. I guessed he wasn't feeling 100 percent. I sat on the chair on the balcony and looked out at Paris. I opened my iPad, but I didn't read. I wanted to breathe Paris into my core. I wanted to trap some part of it so that I could carry it with me. I saw the pigeons alight on the slate roofs for the night and watched a tiny plane pass overhead. One by one, lamps came on down in the street, and soon the build-ing shimmered with yellow light, cocktail light, where people came inside and sat and began their evenings. I watched it all and said not a prayer, not a memo to God or a mysterious creator in the sky, but instead to life, to whatever it was that propelled Hadley and Ernest and all the people who had come to Paris to discover what they didn't even know they needed. I had come, too, and now I was going to say good-bye, but I vowed never to leave Paris entirely, to carry it with me, to keep it as my own secret to visit whenever life permitted it.

A little while later, Constance tapped on the door.

"Is he still asleep?" she whispered when I opened the door and stepped into the hallway.

"He's asleep. I'm not sure he feels great."

"Raef said the club we're going to isn't far. I texted you the address. We'll see you later?"

"I hope so."

Constance gave me a quick hug. She smelled of the outdoors and of her favorite soap.

"We're going to eat something with some of Raef's friends, then we'll go from there. But the plan is to go to the club. I'll text you if anything changes."

"What time will you get there?"

"Late, probably. Everything is late in the jazz world."

"Okay, shoot me a text to let me know what you're doing."

She nodded. Then she left.

Sitting on the small balcony after Constance had gone, I read parts of Jack's grandfather's journal. I held it on my lap and maneuvered my chair until I had sufficient light to read it.

It was a remarkable document. The writing was fiercely literate, and the paragraphs and observations were delivered in a sharp, sure hand. He was an excellent draftsman, too. He sketched his impressions of buildings and flowers, boulevards and bridges. He seemed drawn to architecture, especially, although he possessed varied tastes. He had a good eye for images and small details.

It was easy to see what about the journal attracted Jack. His grandfather had been a kind, compassionate soul. He wrote about children and animals suffering the effects of the war. He wrote about the bombings and the smell of thermite still lingering in the air. He also found beauty in all the devastation, and his pictures—plain, simple figures, for the most part—possessed an elegant primitivism that needed no words.

I was still reading, fully involved, when Jack whispered to me.

"Hey," he said.

"You awake? How do you feel?"

I put the journal down and climbed into bed with him.

"Better."

"Really better, or just trying to be brave better?"

"No, I think I'm on the mend. It might have been some food poisoning. I have a chronically weak belly. You might as well know that."

I put my hand on his forehead. He felt warm but not feverish.

"I was worried about you. I'm still worried about you. Do you think we should find a doctor?"

"You're sweet. But I'm all right."

"You must be starved."

"What do we have around?"

"Odds and ends, Jack. I'll run down and get you something else."

"No, let me try whatever's here. It will be okay."

I kissed him lightly and climbed out and took a few minutes to put together a haphazard snack. It wasn't much. I gave him the remainder of the bread we had from my backpack, an apple, and a bottle of iced tea.

He went to the bathroom while I got things together, and I heard him washing. When he returned, he looked a little better.

"I haven't even asked if you can cook," he said as he climbed back into bed. "Do you have any kitchen skills?"

"Not many. You?"

"I'm not bad. I have about ten dishes I can make. That's about it, though. Plus the basics."

"Well, don't judge me on my little snack here. I don't have much to work with."

"I appreciate you doing it and staying with me."

I gave him the makeshift tray, the food arranged on the cutting board Amy had donated to the cause. I sat next to him. He ate slowly, picking at things and chewing carefully to judge how the item sat with him. He drank the iced tea in two gulps. I gave him the rest of the water bottle.

"I was reading your grandfather's journal," I said. "It's wonderful, Jack. Have you ever thought about trying to publish it?"

"I've thought about it. I talked to my dad about it once, and he wondered why anyone would be interested in a man's journey through Europe after the war."

"Why wouldn't they be? I would think anyone would see the value of that."

"That was my position. My biggest concern about writing a book of alternating chapters is whether I can match his style. He's better than I am."

"I doubt that. But how did he learn to write so well?"

"You mean as a farm boy in rural Vermont? I don't know. I've thought about that. His father was a veterinarian. They had books at home, that sort of thing. His mother was a midwife. He read mostly classic literature. Ovid and Sophocles. He hid his learning, but it was always there. The nights can be long in Vermont, and when you're a farmer you don't have as much to do in winter. He read by the fire or woodstove. I once saw him speak to a classics professor from the University of Vermont, and I watched the professor's face change as he realized how much my grandfather knew. He was a remarkable man."

"You're lucky to have the journal. Did your dad or mom ever read it?"

"Not as I did. Or do, I should say. I don't think my dad knew quite what to make of it. It made him uneasy somehow. I suspect he thought the journal proved my grandfather was discontent with his farm life—that he had bigger ambitions but settled for life in Vermont. I think my father read it almost as a warning. I'm guessing, but that's my take on it."

We didn't talk for a little. Jack continued to eat at the same pace. Now and then, he stopped to see what reaction his body had to the food.

"So did you know Constance is thinking of going to Australia with Raef?" I asked when his eating had slowed. "She thinks maybe she'll go instead of returning home. At least for a while."

"I know he's nuts about her."

I looked at him. Our eyes locked.

"And you're crazy about me. That's the next thing to say, Jack."

"And I'm crazy about you."

"Too late. Doesn't work when I have to show you the cue card."

"I am crazy about you. But I've always wondered what that meant. Is that really a compliment? Do we want people to be crazy around us?"

"It's an idiomatic expression, I think."

"But what if they really were crazy? Would that be good? Isn't a stalker crazy about the person he loves? I don't think anyone should say he is crazy about someone unless he is a bona fide stalker. Then, sure. And also, I don't think it's politically correct to say *crazy*. It makes fun of those who really are off their rockers."

"You have a strange mind, Jack."

"I'm feeling better. I think we should try to go out," he said. "If you're up for it."

"Do you feel well enough?"

"Sure."

"Are you positive? You still look a little pasty."

"I'm really okay," he said, loading his voice with sex, but it was a fake.

He grabbed me and pulled me close.

35

....

Jack and Raef disappeared the next day. They said they would be back by dinner, not to worry.

Constance and I went to Notre Dame.

We had been there before on our earlier visit, but to Constance, who studied the saints, Notre Dame was a living, breathing building that revealed secrets at every glance. She was systematic in her approach: we sat outside the building for a long time and let our eyes travel where they liked. She knew the history of the cathedral, of course: how it had been built commencing in 1163 and took more than a century to complete; how it had hosted hundreds of important political and religious events; how it perched on the Île de la Cité; how the "Te Deum" was sung there at the end of both World Wars I and II. But that was all background to Constance.

She came to see Mary.

It was an obsession with her. Of all the saints, she loved Mary the most, and Notre Dame—Our Lady—contained thirty-seven statues of Mary. But Constance's obsession within her obsession was the statue of Mary holding the Christ child in the trumeau of the Portal of the Virgin. The statue came originally from the Chapel of Saint Aignan in the ancient Cloister of the Canons, and it replaced the thirteenth-century Virgin knocked down in 1793.

"Here it is," Constance told me when we finally entered the building and stood in front of it. She put her arm through mine, and her eyes began to tear as she described it. "This is the Altar of the Virgin. It's been here since the twelfth century—the altar, but not always with the same statue. *Regardez!* It doesn't look particularly momentous until you stop and consider it. See her? She is a young mother, Heather. That's what I like about it. She is a young woman who has been asked to hold in her womb and arms the divine. What I admire about this statue is the ambivalence. You can see she is charmed by the child. See him? He is playing with a brooch on her cloak and not looking at her exactly, and her hip is out. I love women's hips, especially when they're poked out. See? Poked out to hold her child, who is the salvation of the world, and it all rests on a woman's hip. But inside all that majesty is this small, timid woman and her beloved child. That's why this statue kills me. I've read about it over and over, and now to see it . . . you know, there have been many transformations here in front of Our Lady. People have been converted in a single instant by one glance at her. I know, I know, I don't believe much of it myself, but, Heather, I believe in the human need to believe, and this is the embodiment of that."

I loved Constance. I loved her as much as anything in the world.

Jack took me to bed in the late afternoon and devoured me.

The balcony doors stood wide open, and the warm Paris sun

heated the first foot or two of the room floor, and he put grapes between my lips and kissed me with them, and it was funny, and silly, and incredibly passionate. Our bodies moved perfectly. He was rough at times, as if he'd fallen through something to be with me, as if his body contained an element that was fish and DNA and seawater, and that had to be released, must be cast forward, and I thought of Mary—absurdly—and of the surprise of pregnancy, and the weight of the Christ child on her hip. It all mixed together, Jack's splendid body, his mysterious absence earlier, the sun, the warmth of the day, the scent of Paris, dirty and choked as any city with exhaust and human activity, and I gave myself to him, pulled him deeper in me, opened myself to him and lost the line between us.

Afterward, I rested with my head on his shoulder. He tickled my back slowly, calmly with the stem of a violet he had purchased from a woman selling forget-me-nots for a soldiers' fund. He drew little pictures on my back, and my breathing matched his.

I did nothing but stay against him, our bodies cooling together.

"How's our sex?" he asked a little later. "Is it kind of spectacular or only okay?"

"Oh, you first on that one, buddy boy."

"It's a horrible question, isn't it? If you say it's great and the other person thinks it's only so-so, then you've created a huge communication gulley. If you say it's good but not great and the other person thinks it was *terrific*, then you've insulted your partner. It's one of the great conundrums of modern living."

"It's like going to Phoenix."

He pushed up a little and looked at me.

"It's an old story in my family," I explained. "A long time ago, my mother and father had a chance to go to Phoenix. They went and had a horrible time. The entire trip, my father thought my mother wanted to go, and my mother thought my father wanted to go. That's called a trip to Phoenix in my family."

"And the moral of that story is . . . ?"

"You have to tell the truth to your partner."

"I think you're delicious in bed," he said. "I love making love with you."

"I'm glad you feel that way. For me, it's only so-so."

His hand slowed on my back. I turned my head so he couldn't see me smiling.

"You're a rat," he said. "A horrible rat."

"You turn me inside out, Jack. You ring all sorts of bells."

"Good, I'm glad."

"In a so-so sort of way."

He tried to push me out of bed. I grabbed around his belly and held on. Then he pulled me on top of him—and I loved his strength, I loved how he could move me as he liked—and kissed me with everything. We kissed a long time with the balcony door open and the Paris light beginning to turn away for the night. Each told the other how sweetly we loved. The kisses became a chain, and we followed each link for fear of leaving anything to chance, anything to part us.

At sunset, Jack took me to plant a tree.

He could not have surprised me more. After leaving me for about an hour, he came to our room at the Hotel Trenton with a small ash tree wrapped in a burlap holder. The tree looked vigorous, but it was a sapling, a slender plant no taller than my knee.

He carried it out to the balcony and made me do a *Lion King*

salutation. I held it up and introduced it to the plains of Africa—
or Paris. It was lighthearted and fun. He sang the *Lion King* song
and made me join in on "The Circle of Life."

"So what is this about?" I asked, delighted. Already delighted.

He had two bottles of red wine, both of them without labels. It
was like Jack to find wine from a private vendor. He made me
hold the tree—he treated it like a baby—while he opened the first
bottle. He pulled our two seats onto the balcony. It was a tight fit,
but we both managed to have our legs out, at least.

"We drink to its health," he said. "To the long life of a tree."

"To its health," I said, raising my glass.

He sipped the wine and appraised it. "Not bad," he said, smiling. He looked incredibly handsome and happy, alive to everything
around him. He knocked me out the way he looked in that moment.

"A tree is an arrow into the future," he said in mock seriousness.
"We're going to plant a tree tonight. We're going to cut locks of
our hair and bury them with the tree. We're going into the Jardin
du Luxembourg and plant a tree to shade any future Heming-
ways. You can visit it whenever you come to Paris. Everything else
in the world will go along, sometimes failing, sometimes prospering, but your tree—*our* tree—it will keep growing. Our grandchildren will be able to visit it."

"Are we having children soon? That would be good to know."

He looked at me and made a funny face. His eyes looked lively
and happy above the rim of his glass. He wiggled his eyebrows a
little.

"The world is unpredictable," he said. "You can't plan everything. Not even with a Smythson superdeluxe calendar thingy."

"Do you think the authorities are going to let us plant a tree in
the park without any objection?"

"Oh, Heather, my careful, dot-the-i's Heather. We are going to plant it without them knowing. Ninja gardeners. Who can hate a planted tree? Who would pull it up? Once it's in the ground, it will be safe. Do you see how clever this is? Maybe we won't even go into the park, although that would be the best habitat for a tree. We could plant it in one of those little plots of earth on one of the boulevards. The tree would live a riskier life, but that might suit it. Maybe the tree is a rebel tree. Maybe the bucolic life is not for our tree. It might be an alternative, punk kind of tree."

"Why an ash?"

"European ash," he said, drinking off half his wine. He topped us both off again. "It's long-lived, for one thing. And it's common. No one will think it out of place. The man gave me a little card— the gardening shop guy. Ash has its own runic sign—an AE merged. They think it comes from the Old English or German meaning *Esche*."

"You've done your homework. I'm impressed."

"You should be," he said, and he leaned over to kiss me. "If it goes our way, the tree will live a century or more. Think of that! *Look upon my mighty works*, or *Look upon my works, you mighty*, or something like that. Was it Keats? Or 'Ozymandias,' by Shelley? Anyway, one of the Romantics, right?"

"I remember reading it in high school."

"So while the world falls and collapses, our tree, the great ash, will be rising into the sky, triumphant! What do you think about that?"

"I think yes. I think yes to everything, Jack."

"Good, now finish this glass of wine, and then we can be on our way. Do you have nail polish?"

"A little, I think. Hold on."

Where did this man come from? How had he tumbled into my life? And why did his pleasure in life infect me so readily?

I went into the bathroom and returned with a small bottle of red nail polish. It was nearly empty. I handed it to Jack. He had a flat rock that he had found somewhere, and he carefully brushed it off.

"Our immortality," he said.

He shook the nail polish, then carefully, precisely, wrote our names out on the rock. He enclosed them with a silly heart. He took out his Swiss Army knife and handed it to me.

"Here, cut a lock of my hair, please. Then I'll cut yours."

I cut off a curl above his right ear. He took a small shank from the line of hair near my left shoulder. He tied both locks of hair together with piece of twine he cut free from the burlap holding the tree.

"Ideally," he said, his hands busy, his eyes still fresh and happy, "we would plant it like this, without anything to guard it, but then the hair would decay and the nail polish would become indecipherable. Here." He snatched a plastic container that we had from an earlier purchase of watermelon. "Not as romantic, maybe, but maybe it will make it last longer. What do you say? Anything else you want to add?"

I nodded. I took the stone from him and wrote under our names my favorite line:

Hate what's false; demand what's true.

Jack read it, nodded, then kissed my lips.

"Didn't Raef and Constance want to come?" I whispered.

"I didn't invite them. This is about us, not them."

I squeezed his hand.

It was dark. The Boulevard Saint-Michel sent enough light for us to use, but we kept to the shadows. Our gardening tools were pathetic. We had a single dinner knife, a plastic bottle of water, our plastic container, and nothing else. But it made me tingle to be doing something illicit. The park was closed, but Jack promised that other people got in during the night. It only stood to reason, he theorized. Even if we were apprehended, he said, we would not be arrested. The French, he promised, could not resist a love story.

It felt like being ten years old in the middle of a hide-and-seek game.

This, I realized, was something I would remember all my life. More than a photo. More than a museum visit. For a century, a tree would grow in a park in Paris, and my name, and Jack's name, would be at its root. That was Jack's way in the world.

"We're looking for an innocent sort of plot, a place that is inconspicuous. Nothing grand or showy, okay? We want the tree to be a nonentity for the first twenty years of its life. Then, oh, baby, it's going to begin to dominate its surroundings. Then it will become the most badass tree around. Are you with me?"

"Yes. Hell yes."

"Okay, here we go. What do you think of that spot? It's not fancy, but it's safe, I think. It's near the café tables. We can come back and visit it tomorrow. Wouldn't that be something?"

We snuck carefully across a wide lawn, attentive to our position relative to the lights on the Boulevard Saint-Michel. When we reached the dirt plot, Jack canvassed things quickly and then suggested a spot on the right-hand corner.

"No big trees here," he said, falling to his knees and beginning to dig in the dirt. "No competition. It will look like a volunteer plant, or a tree that some department planted and then forgot about. There won't be any reason for someone to dig it up. Not back here away from things. Is this good? Are you liking this spot?"

"It's perfect. It works."

"Okay, the soil is soft. This is easy. Are you ready? We'll both slip it in together. Here we go."

My hands shook. I couldn't control them. They shook until Jack put his hands around mine and steadied us both.

"It's our tree," he whispered. "No one else's. It will always be ours."

"In Paris."

"Our tree in Paris," he said. "The mighty Esche."

I put the plastic box containing our hair and the rock down in the hole beside the tiny roots. Then we backfilled the hole and smoothed dirt around the tree stem. We did our best to make it appear that the tree had always been there. Jack handed me the bottled water.

"Water gets the air out of the soil," he said. "Gives it its first drink in its new home."

I poured the water carefully around the base of the tree. Pan, not far away, watched us in the still light at the entrance to the park. It seemed likely he would approve.

36

....

August 2, 1947

Spent the night in Paris and went to the races at Long-champs on Saturday. The racing wasn't much; the horses looked neglected. It was a wonder they hadn't been eaten or killed outright by a bomb. I liked seeing the riding colors: the bright green and yellow and scarlet. During one race, a dog got loose and chased after the pack of horses. A man behind me said he should have bet on the dog, for at least the dog ran as hard as it could, unlike the horrible nags he had wagered on. It drew a general laugh from the people around him. He laughed, too, but his eyes didn't.

Constance standing with Raef in the early morning light. A waiter sweeping the sidewalk outside his restaurant. Five pigeons clucking around her feet, a few sometimes dashing forward to see what the waiter had swept into a pile. Constance checking her purse, her backpack, patting her pockets to make sure she had remembered everything. Raef, her man, fiddling with the bags, making a final check, looking to see if this or that buckle had been properly snapped closed. Constance's hair softly blond and beautiful in the light, her outfit carefully selected from the few clothes that we had, her attention, just for an instant, drawn to the pigeons gathered behind her.

This was Constance in Paris, I told myself. *This is a memory to hold. This is Constance going off to Australia with her true.*

I smiled. My lovely Constance, the girl on the Schwinn, the lover of saints, the gazer at statues of the Virgin Mary.

She turned and saw me watching. She was on her way. She was going with Raef to the train station, then to the airport, then onto a plane that would take her to Australia. She had days of travel ahead of her, hours on buses and in cars, out to Ayers Rock, out to the red sand and clay of Western Australia. It was an adventure, a what-the-hell flyer, and she stood for a moment on the edge of everything. She smiled at me, and then she took her scarf and threw it into the air. The pigeons, sensing a hawk that was only a scarf, exploded around her feet. They shot up into the air, and their wings clapped and clawed to get higher, and Constance smiled broadly. She knew what she had done: she had sent the pigeons into the air on purpose. She stood in the morning light, leaving me, but putting herself into my memory one last time.

Jack and I went to Longchamps, the horseracing course in the Bois de Boulogne, on the last day. We picked a marvelous day. The temperature had dropped off, and true autumn had snuck in at night. I wore a sweater, and so did Jack. We took a jitney recommended by the hotel, and it was nearly empty. The driver, a fat man with a walrus mustache, listened to a soccer match as he drove us. Jack said he thought the soccer match must be a replay, because it was too early in the day for a live match. The bus traveled out of the city and into the wooden environs of the Bois de Boulogne. Jack said several times it looked like Vermont.

"Do you miss Vermont?" I asked him.

He nodded. He squeezed my hand. The other riders studied racing forms. Jack kept his eyes on the wooded border to the road.

"I love Vermont," he said after a little while. "It may not even be love. It's just inside me—the seasons, the open meadows, and the damn cold winters. You don't take anything for granted in the winter in Vermont. Everything rests on the edge of freezing and busting, and as brutal as it is, it's also fragile. Very fragile. If you look carefully, you can see that fragility everywhere. I remember seeing the edge of a stream one time, and the ice had trapped a frog. I don't know if the frog was living or dead when the ice surrounded it, but you could see the body clearly beneath the ice. It was entombed, but it was beautiful, too. I don't even know how to say what it made me feel. I still wonder if something had stunned it, or if it had failed to get out of the weather, or if it thought it had one more good day and then the weather turned. Isn't that a metaphor for life? We all think we have one more good day, but maybe we don't. Anyway, the ice looked blue except where it covered the frog, and then it was green blue. That's what you see in Vermont if you pay attention. It exists everywhere, of course, but I am attuned to it in Vermont. So when I say these woods remind me of Vermont, I mean it."

"Could you buy a farm like your grandfather's? Are those kinds of things still available?"

He stuck out his lower lip.

"Hard to say. Some, I guess. Usually the house would be in horrible repair, the chimney falling down. All that. The land would be overgrown. Everything tries to break down a farm. That's just the way it is."

The bus took a turn onto what looked to be the final run-up to the racecourse. Hundreds of cars parked in an open meadow. I had only been to a track once, at Monmouth Park in New Jersey, but this looked nothing like that. Longchamps looked as if a fair had decided to pitch a tent for the night and that it might travel tomorrow. It made Jack smile to see it. His grandfather had gone to a day of racing in Longchamps.

The bus dropped us at the front entrance, and it took a few minutes to make our way inside. We bought a racing form and found some seats back under the grandstand. I had no point of comparison, but the crowd seemed sparse. It gave us room—easy to get a drink, easy to get to the ladies' room—and that made the proceedings more festive. The melancholy that could sometimes accompany people losing more money than they should did not seem as prevalent as it might have been at some racecourses. It seemed like a holiday instead, a day out on a fabulous fall noon.

We bet the 5 horse on the first race, and it won going away.

"What do you think of that?" Jack shouted, pounding the racing form against his leg as the horse won easily. "We're a pair of handicappers! How do you like that?"

Oh, Jack. So young and handsome. So happy. So much mine.

We did not have a winner the rest of the day. We drank sidecars and got drunk and rode the bus back through the Bois de Boulogne, back into the city, back to the eternal Seine and the hiss of coffeemakers and the brush brooms on cobblestone. I clung to Jack's arm and put my head on his shoulder. Silence covered us, and he was in his world and I was in mine, and Paris accepted us once more.

"Want to go see the tree?" he asked when the bus dropped us off in the Centre de Ville.

"Sure."

"We may have to climb the fence."

"I don't care."

"We can bring it some water."

"Or we can go back to the room and make love and fall asleep, and in the morning we can have coffee in the park and say good-bye to the tree and to Pan and to everything else. How does that sound?"

He kissed me. He lifted me off my feet and kissed me.

After we had made love, we stood naked in the Paris night and watched the light move over the rooftops. We held hands and looked out, unembarrassed, body beside body, the cool air passing over our privates, over our hair and faces and everything else, summer *ending ending ending.*

37

We danced at the Club Marvelous on our last night in Paris. It was an old-style nightclub that Raef had recommended. It could have come directly out of a vintage 1930s Busby Berkeley movie, with cigarette girls roaming—selling chocolates instead of cigarettes—and some men sporting tails. It felt like a masquerade party, with everyone dressed to play at her or his favorite movie period, except that it truly existed in modern-day Paris. A ten-piece orchestra played dance music, and the arrangements were heavy on muted horns and whispery snare drums. We were colossally underdressed, but it didn't matter. Jack was so powerfully handsome that it sometimes surprised me to turn to him and discover him at my side. He was a Vermont boy, sweet and gentle, his shoulders square, his demeanor open and welcoming. When he danced with me, he held me securely, his right hand flat on my lower back, his left hand holding my hand. He smelled like Old Spice.

I wore a wrinkled travel dress that I had tried to steam out in the shower. It hadn't worked. But we made a good-looking couple. We did. I could catch it in the glances we received, in the smiles we captured as we walked back and forth to our tiny table by the left-hand side of the orchestra riser.

"We're only drinking martinis," Jack said after we had danced to a tune I faintly recognized. He held my chair for me and tucked me into the table. "And two exactly. More than two, and we will regret it. Less than two, and we will also regret it."

"When did you become such an expert on martinis?"

"It's a family curse. We are good at martinis and pepper jack cheese."

"Vodka martinis?"

"No, no, not proper, I'm afraid. You need gin. It's a dangerous business to drink a gin martini, because gin turns people into savages. Everyone knows that. A vodka martini has no danger. Gin is the way to go."

"Olives or onions?"

"I'll pretend you didn't ask that," he said as the waiter appeared.

Jack ordered two martins with olives. Then he reached across and held my hand.

"Last night in Paris," he said.

"For now."

"Yes, for now. We'll always have Paris. Shouldn't one of us say that?"

"You just did. You should pay a penalty of some sort."

"Tomorrow we leave for New York."

"Yes."

"Do you think your parents will try to poison me?"

"They might."

"Do you think they will let us sleep in the same bed?"

I looked at him.

"Hard to say," I said. "But it should be interesting."

"Do you still have stuffed animals on your bed?"

"Two. Hopsy and Potato-Joe."

"I'd like to meet them."

"I'm sure you will."

The music picked up and played something with more speed. Sitting at an angle, I could sometimes watch the horn players' spit spray when they hit a hard note. I had never noticed that before.

The waiter came back with our martinis.

"They're beautiful, aren't they?" I asked as he served them. "Stunning and lethal."

"Sip them. Don't drink them too quickly. Now what should we toast to?"

"I hate toasting."

"You do?" he asked. "I would have thought you were a fan."

"Why's that?"

"You're a sentimental mush."

"You should talk."

"What do you do, then, if you don't toast?"

"We tell each other's fortunes. You first."

He looked at me. He picked up his martini and waited until I had mine in my hand.

"You will meet a tall, dark stranger," he said.

"No, a real prediction. That's the rule."

He smiled.

"You will be a great, smashing success in New York. You will visit Paris often over the years. And you will own goats at least twice in your life."

We sipped. It tasted like glass if glass melted and surged onto your tongue.

"Now your turn," he said.

"You will also be a great, smashing success in New York, and you will travel to Vermont whenever you have free weekends. And a puppy you dream about will turn into a footstool that will comfort you in your old age."

We sipped again.

"Lean forward," he said. "I've always wanted to look down a woman's dress as I sipped a martini."

"You never have?"

"Not once."

"Why do boys look down girls' dresses?"

"Why wouldn't they? Because it's fun."

"Do you actually want to see nipples, or is that not the object?" I felt the martini in just a few sips.

"Not really the object."

"What is the object, then?"

"To see lingerie, I think. And to peek when you're not sure she knows it, but she kind of knows it, but she would never admit that she knows it. She has to kind of want to be seen, but not really, but definitely wants to."

"Makes perfect sense. The *she* in that construction meaning just any woman?"

"The décolletage-er. She has to be in on it for it to be alluring."

"I'm learning a great deal tonight," I said.

"Lean forward a little more."

"Should I look away? How does that work?"

"You're letting me look, but not letting me look. That's the trick."

"I think I kind of knew that."

I sat straighter and raised my glass. He mirrored me.

"You will have pinkeye twice in your life," I said, "and a hamster you own will escape and die underneath your refrigerator."

"That's horrible," he said and sipped. "And you will develop a love of root beer in later life and take to wearing kilts and matching berets."

"I like that look."

"Sip," he said, and I did.

"Should we dance again?" he asked.

"Yes, we should."

"Do you recognize this song?"

"No, do you?"

"No. That's good. I don't want us to have some sappy song we always associate with our last night in Paris."

"Good point."

He came around and held my chair while I stood.

"I saw down your dress," he said. "It was very satisfactory."

"I'm happy for you."

Then we moved onto the dance floor.

It was late, very late, and we were still on the dance floor. I had my head on his shoulder. I felt tired and melted into him. We did not want to go to bed. It was the trick for trans-Atlantic flights. Stay up all night and then drip onto the plane.

"We've been to Paris now," Jack said. "Some couples, they wait their entire lives and they never get to Paris."

"We've been to Paris."

"We've had martinis in Paris."

"Two precisely. You were right about that."

"Martinis are a science-based drink."

"Is it always bad form to have a vodka martini?"

He nodded.

"You could have one in Sheboygan, maybe."

"Where is Sheboygan? I like saying Sheboygan."

"Is it in New York State? No, I think it's in Wisconsin."

"Sheboygan. She-boy-gan. It's an Indian word, I bet."

The music stopped. We didn't break apart right away.

"We can't be the absurd couple that keeps dancing even when the music stops," Jack said. "It would make me rethink our entire relationship."

"Okay, let's go."

He kissed my neck. Then he kissed the top of my head. Then he stopped moving, and we slowly split apart.

"There," he said.

It felt cold without his arms around me. I leaned back into him.

"If we stay up all night, we'll sleep on the plane, right?" I said.

"That's the plan."

"I want to walk and see the city. I want to say good-bye to it."

"It's late," Jack said. "Maybe a little dangerous."

"Find a bar, then. Find a place that's warm."

"Let me ask," he said.

He walked over and asked one of the band members where we should go. That band member didn't seem to know, but another band member, a guitarist, said something, and Jack nodded. When he came back, he put his arm around me and walked me to the table.

"Not far from here," he said.

"Remember when we slept in the stable in Amsterdam?"

"Yes, I remember."

"I thought you were going to try to seduce me. A roll in the hay, I guess."

"I knew just how to play you."

"You did, did you?"

I grabbed my purse and checked the table to make sure I didn't leave anything. Jack pushed in the chairs. He came and put his arm around me again and started walking me toward the door.

"That was the first night we slept together. In a haystack in Amsterdam. That's a good story to tell. We can dine out on that story for quite a while."

"That's an old expression," Jack said. "Dining out on a story."

"What do you think the puppy I included in your toast really means?"

"I think the puppy symbolizes innocence."

"So do I," I conceded. "And the hope of something pure."

"Puppies symbolize sexual perversion," Jack said. "Freud said as much."

"He did not."

"Sure he did. You can say that about anything, and no one will know. Freud said as much. Try it."

"Men who play clarinets have a phallic obsession. Freud said as much."

"See? It works."

"Better than it should."

We reached the door and pushed through. It was not sunrise, but the sun was in the neighborhood. You could feel it as much as see it. The city felt like a flying carpet, a carpet that possessed magic but lacked the will to get up and move. A few pigeons stepped sideways on their perches on the building window ledges. Jack pulled me closer.

"You frozen?" he asked.

"A little."

"Why are women always cold?"

"Because we wear things that boys can look down."

"True. And we are grateful."

"I always thought you were after nipples. Now it's not as disturbing."

"Freud said as much."

"Of course he did. Do you know where you're going?"

"Just up here, I think."

"My father is going to be a bit standoffish at first. I have to warn you. Then he will lighten up. I promise."

"At some point, you have to meet my parents, too, you know?"

"I know. I want to meet them."

"So you say. Wait until you do."

"Are they horrible?"

"Not horrible. Just self-involved, I suppose. I paint them to be worse than they are. It's part of my self-mythos."

"Freud said as much."

"It didn't work just then. I can't give you that tool if you misuse it."

Then he stopped and kissed me. We kissed a long time. It was not chaste, and it was not fully passionate. It was a companionable kiss, as if we had entered a different level, a more comfortable level, in what we meant to each other.

"Sun's going to be up soon," Jack said when we broke apart.

"I liked dancing with you. I liked the martinis. I liked everything."

"We could fall in love this way, you know?" Jack asked.

"Freud said as much."

Jack smiled. Then it was morning.

38

....

"You don't believe in Bigfoot?" Jack asked on the bus to the airport, his eyes inspecting me as if I had said something preposterous. "How can you deny science? Bigfoot is pure scientific fact. Haven't you followed the expeditions that have proven, beyond doubt, that Bigfoot exists and is hanging around the rain forest of Washington State?"

"Freud said as much."

"See? You are using that way too much. That's an improper use of the Freud card."

"I thought you said it always worked."

"Not always, Heather. Nothing is always. Nothing in the universe is always. 'Freud said as much' is a line that fits in some places but not others. The trick is to know when."

"Freud said as much."

"See? Again, penalty flag. You're like a parrot that has learned to say, 'Polly want a cracker.' You keep repeating it without any understanding."

"Why would a parrot want a cracker, anyway?"

"You really don't get this stuff, do you? Sorry, but you're a little joke deaf. I didn't know the extent of your disability until now. I apologize if I have been insensitive."

He looked at me and put his finger to his lips.

"Don't say it," he warned.

"Freud said as much."

He sighed.

"Maybe we could get you into a program. Maybe we can get you some kind of joke help. You're a deserving minority. You are humor impaired."

I put my head on his shoulder. I felt sleepy. I felt calm and happy. I didn't like flying especially, but I liked where flights brought me. It was time to go home. I wanted to see my parents and Mr. Periwinkle, and I wanted to be in one place for more than a night or two. Travel sheds skin, and it takes time at home to grow it back.

"I have to ask you something else," he said, sounding more serious. "Are you in the mood to take on something kind of important? It could change our relationship."

"What?"

"Are you?"

"I guess. Is this a joke?"

"It's not a joke, Heather. I need to know your attitude toward air guitar. I need to know if you think playing air guitar is acceptable."

"Why? Do you play a lot of air guitar?"

"Au contraire, Ms. Heather. I believe anyone who plays air guitar should be forced to look at a never-ending loop of themselves playing air guitar."

"You hate it that much?"

"Oh, more than hate, Heather. Much more. Hate does not begin to describe it. I mean, what is air guitar? What does it mean? A person holds out his hands as if he—or it could be a she, but more typically it's something guys do—as if he were playing a guitar. Of course the guy just happens to be able to play the best guitar licks in the world, usually without practicing anything at all. And then he looks around as if he's actually doing something, and he makes these rock-and-roll faces like he's getting the last squeal out of a note he just played. It's an insult to everything that is holy on this earth."

"So I can never air guitar?"

"You can air guitar, Heather. Be my guest. I will never stop you from air guitaring. I will simply have to leave the room, that's all. I could never look at you in the same way afterward. I just couldn't. It's kind of the white man's overbite of musicianship."

"So yes to Bigfoot, but no to air guitar. Got it. Anything else I should know about? Is there a manual that accompanies you?"

"Oh, there are caverns within caverns here, Heather. It's one big car ark."

I closed my eyes. The bus came to a wider road and accelerated, and when I looked out the window, I saw planes coming down out of the sky. Jack held my hand. I thought of Mr. Periwinkle. I thought of my mom and dad and what they would say, and what they wouldn't say, how Jack would fill up our house. I held my breath and went under the pool water and all above, all the bars of light and liquid, became soft and quiet and tender. Then the bus pulled onto a ramp and the tempo changed and we were here, we were leaving, and Jack stood up to get our bags, then did a quick air guitar lick, his tongue out, his grin the Jack-est ever.

. . .

Airports suck. But Charles de Gaulle sucked a little less with Jack beside me. With a second pair of hands and eyes to manage the baggage, things went easier. We had arrived early enough to go through security without feeling like a convertible going through a car wash. We showed passports, bumped our phones on the desk clerk's computer to record the boarding pass, slipped our shoes back on, restrung our belts through our jeans, bought gum, bought magazines, drank a quick beer in a quasi-French sports bar named Alas, then sat for a time in a pair of rockers the management had placed near the windows overlooking the tarmac. It was nice sitting in the rockers. I felt quiet and dizzy and exhausted. But I felt satisfied. I had done Europe. I had seen it. I had strayed off the path and seen different aspects of a place so many people visit, and it felt good. I held hands with Jack. Sweetly, he stood and moved his rocker closer so that we could have greater contact.

"I really didn't expect to meet anyone like you," Jack said in his softest voice when he had settled back into his chair. "I really didn't."

"Ditto. You're a surprise."

"Do you want me to tell you why I love you? Would that be a good thing to do right now?"

"Sure, of course."

I kissed the back of his hand. I always wanted to kiss him.

"First, I want you to know that I love you despite your disability. Your joke deafness. It started out as a problem, but I've learned to overlook it."

"Thank you."

"And because you read Hemingway. I love you because of that."

I nodded.

"And because you complete me."

"Oh, good grief. Quit quoting movie lines."

He leaned over and kissed my neck. I moved my lips to his. We kissed for a while. The world went away whenever I kissed Jack.

"The real reason I love you is because we share an eye," he said when we parted. "Have you ever heard that?"

"I don't think so."

"You've heard of the Gorgons? They were three dreadful sisters with snakes for hair. They were all blind, but they had a single eye, and they had to pass it back and forth to see the world. We share an eye like that, Heather. We look through the same lens."

I started to make a joke about him calling me a Gorgon, but then I realized he was being serious. Although I couldn't quite believe it, I heard his voice crack. I sat forward and looked at him.

"Jack?"

"Sorry."

"Don't be sorry. Are you okay?"

"I love you, Heather. I want you to know that."

"I love you, Jack. You okay? What's going on?"

"I'm fine. A little tired."

"You shouldn't stay up all night dancing."

He smiled and kissed the back of my hand now. He let his lips stay on my skin.

"What do you think the Esche is seeing right now?"

"Two lovers. They have a small dog that sits by their feet. The dog is very old and comes to the park every day with them. The dog can barely see, so it has mistaken a squirrel for a lady dog, and it dreams of running through the park with the squirrel, except the dog is too old and has bad hips."

"Does the squirrel have a name?"

"No, I don't think so. The dog's name is Robin Hood."

"That's not a dog's name."

"Yes, it is. It's a beagle. It has brown dots right above its eyebrows."

"That's a good thing for the Esche to watch. I'm happy the Esche has something like that to see on a good morning."

"The Esche will always be watching."

A few minutes later, he said he had to use the restroom. He got to his feet and grabbed his backpack. I asked him to snag a piece of fruit if he saw one. He nodded.

"It was pretty to think so, wasn't it?" he said more than asked me.

He had said it to me once before. Maybe twice before.

"Are you quoting Hemingway at me?"

"It's a nice line. I always wanted to use it."

"I don't get the fruit connection. I mention fruit and you quote Hemingway."

"I guess there wasn't one," he said. "I guess it seemed like a cool thing to say. You looked beautiful sitting here, Heather. If I had six lives, I would want to spend them with you. Every last one."

He smiled and hoisted his backpack higher on his shoulders.

What was going on? He seemed too emotional for the everyday atmosphere of the airport. A glancing thought passed through my mind to ask why he needed his backpack to go to the men's room, but I let it go. Maybe he wanted to change. Maybe he needed something out of it. Our eyes met. I watched him walk away, and in an instant, the foot traffic had swallowed him.

I dug out my phone and checked messages. I shot a text to

Amy. Told her I was heading her way. I texted Constance and asked if she had seen a kangaroo. I texted my mom—knowing that was the same as texting my dad, too—and said I was at the airport, all good, tired, ready to come home, couldn't wait to see them. I checked a dozen e-mails, mostly from work, and then looked at a picture a friend named Sally had posted on Facebook of a cat wearing a pirate hat. It was a good picture, and it made me laugh. I *liked* it and wrote *Aaarrrgggghhhh, matey* under it. I stopped short of adding an emoticon. The cat looked adorable.

I felt, for a while, that I had entered the phone-world. It was just me and a virtual world that didn't actually exist, but did exist, and when I looked up, I was surprised to see time had passed. The light had changed slightly out by the airplane. The flashlights the ground personnel used to guide the planes, to flag them forward or left and right, suddenly seemed brighter when contrasted against the dull sunlight. My neck began to prickle, and I put my phone away slowly into the breast pocket of my shirt.

I looked down the passenger way where Jack had gone. Then I pulled my phone out again and checked the time. He had been gone . . . I didn't really know how long. What was the sense, I asked myself, of checking the time if I didn't know when he had left? If I didn't know that basic piece of information, whatever time it was now was pointless.

Then before I could do anything, or come up with a plan, a man in a nice-looking business suit, his ear to a phone, pointed at the spare rocker beside me. I held out my hand to block him, but then realized that was a pretty ballsy reaction. I dropped my hand and nodded to him. He smiled a thank-you and dragged the chair away. It had been close to me from when Jack had sat in it. It bothered me to see him drag it off.

"Would you mind?" I said to the man, pointing to my backpack.

I wanted him to watch it. He covered the mouth of his phone and shook his head. He told me in French he was going to be only a minute.

"Please watch it as long as you can," I said. "I'll be right back."

The man gave me a French lip purse. As if to say, *Americans*. As if to say, *Maybe, maybe not*. I didn't have time to negotiate a deal with him. I walked in the direction Jack had taken. People walked toward me, and for an instant I had an image of *The Catcher in the Rye*. It was a novel we had read in high school, and I never liked it much, but I did recall the image of the main character, Holden, as a catcher in the rye. He wanted to be a boy who went through the tall meadow and kept children from falling, his arms outstretched, his eyes trained on their safety. That was how I felt walking against the grain on the passenger way. Jack had to be in there somewhere, in among the people, and I walked with my arms nearly outstretched, trying to see him.

A little farther on, I pulled out my phone and texted him.

Where are you? I texted.

I held the phone in front of me, expecting his reply to come instantly. But it didn't. I realized I had stopped in the middle of the moving traffic, a boulder in a streambed, and people moved past me, clearly annoyed, their faces bright little bubbles of mini-rage. I was violating rules. I was an imbecile. It was all they could do not to strike me.

I tucked my phone back in my pocket and went down the passenger way until I found the men's room. I looked at various men as they went in and out, and I wondered if I could ask one or the other to check on Jack for me. He could be sick, I realized. Something could have happened. But then I thought, *The hell with it*, and I ducked inside, keeping my eyes innocent and glanced away, and called out in what I knew must sound like a shrewish wifely voice.

"Jack? Is Jack Quiller-Couch in here?"

The bathroom attendant, a thin, tall African man in a blue coat, came toward me and held his arm out to prevent me from penetrating farther into the bathroom.

"*Mademoiselle, non,*" he said. "*Non, non, non.*"

"Jack!" I shouted louder. "Jack, where are you?"

The bathroom attendant backed me out of the bathroom. My voice had echoed in the tile chamber.

"I am missing my traveling companion," I said, trying to speak in French but failing horribly. "My boyfriend, he went in here, I think."

"*Non, mademoiselle. Les garçons—seulement les garçons.*"

"I understand, I do, but he is missing."

A text came in on my phone. I pulled my phone out so quickly that I dropped it. It skidded on the floor, and I had to scramble after it. I thought it might be broken, but it seemed all right when I examined it. The text was from my mother saying she couldn't wait to see me. I didn't even want to think about my phone skidding across a bathroom floor.

I texted Jack again.

Jack?

Almost in the same moment, the PA system called our flight.

New York City. JFK. Group four now boarding.

"*Mademoiselle,*" the bathroom attendant said again, and it wasn't until I heard him speak that I realized I remained in the outside portion of the restroom. I backed up. The main streamed of passengers felt as busy as ever with people rushing down toward their flights, their roll-on luggage trailing behind them like obedient dogs.

My brain began speeding up, and I thought, *My backpack.* What kind of idiot leaves a backpack unattended in an airport? I started back toward our gate, and I realized, as I went, that Occam's razor applied here. I knew the rule from a first-year philosophy seminar. I even knew it in Latin as *lex parsimoniae.* Simply stated, it recommended when confronted by conflicting hypotheses, the one with the fewest assumptions should be selected. In short, keep it simple. Assume the easiest line of reason. I was letting my mind get carried away. I needed to follow Occam's razor instead.

Another voice—a voice outside my head—came over the PA system and announced a flight for Algiers. That stopped me. A small flood of panic kicked into my bloodstream. I turned and began jogging in the direction Jack had taken. It was nearly impossible to jog with the people coming toward me, but I did my best. My breath felt like a sword plunging in and out of my lungs. The fact that Jack might have left, had gone, was such a raw thought that I could not allow it space to emerge, to uncurl like a ghastly baby bird pecking its way horribly through a gray egg wall.

But then a saner, more measured voice began whispering calming things. *He did not leave,* it told me. *No one does that. He would not simply walk away.* It told me to take it easy, to go slow, and I slowed to a walk and continued another five minutes down the long footbridge, trying to be a normal tourist, trying to look unconcerned, trying to believe that when I went back, when I returned to the backpack that I had recklessly left in the middle of an airport loading gate, he would be there, air guitar in hand. I even forced

myself to stop in a magazine and candy shop, pretending to browse,
my stomach as raw and horrible as if I had swallowed a cat covered
in Crisco. I snatched up a copy of *Match* and flicked through the
pages. I wanted Jack to have time to return. I wanted him to be
unrushed.

I took my time returning. I looked at the faces passing by
me, coming at me, or whisking by, and I wondered what secrets
they had held that they could not reveal. Everyone appeared to be
searching. Everyone seemed to be looking for someone else,
something else, and twice I nearly collided with people wheeling
bags. Then, without meaning to, I saw my backpack, and I smiled
to see it, glad it was still there, happy that I had taken a small risk
and won, but I did not see Jack. I walked closer, and still he did
not appear, and I turned to inspect the waiting area, the small
check-in desk, and he was not there, either.

I went and sat next to my backpack. I stared straight ahead.

I was aware of time passing, but only in a marginal way. When
the people around me began to stand and move, I realized, almost
in a haze, that it was past time to board. New York City. JFK. I
stood and bent and lifted my backpack. I chucked it up onto my
shoulder, and it bounced against my back, and a tiny gurgled grunt
worked out of my lungs. I bent and made it hit me again. It felt
good to be hit, to feel the solid weight strike like a pendulum
against my back and beltline.

I snatched my phone and looked to see if Jack had texted,
called, done anything. Then my finger snapped on my contacts,
and I hit Jack's name, and I poked it. My phone connected with
Jack's phone, and I thought madly about things to say—*Hey, Jack,
where are you? You disappeared. Hey, Jack, I'm standing at the gate,*

and they're calling our flight, and I thought you might want to hustle along now . . . but he did not pick up. The call went to his answering message, and I took a deep breath, opened my mouth to speak, then softly hung up.

The airport people announced they were now boarding section one on the plane, please have your boarding passes ready and your passport opened.

I moved slowly into the boarding line. I looked down the walkway in the direction where Jack had disappeared, and I thought, *Now he will show up, here he comes, he must be moving toward me now, what a funny joke, what a nut, how kooky is this guy?* It occurred to me he might even be on the plane already. Maybe it was all an insane mix-up. Then one of the airline people asked for my passport, and I handed it to her. She scanned it and handed it back to me. I said okay, thanks, but mostly I watched her mouth move, and then we went down a long passage toward the plane door, and I stepped on, removed from France's earth at last, and I handed my documents to a flight attendant, a woman with plenty of makeup and a smile that came too easily to her lips, and she nodded and pointed me toward the back of the plane. I passed the bulkhead that separated first class, and I kept going, and then I arrived at my aisle and row, and I slipped in, sat down, and kept my eyes forward. Jack was not sitting next to me.

I threw up in the plane's restroom before we had taxied an inch.

It came like a wave, and I couldn't resist. I voided everything. After a while, after throwing up three times, someone knocked on the door and asked in French if I was all right.

"*Ça va*," I said. "*Merci*."

The person said something rapidly in French.

I repeated, "*Ça va*."

After great pain, a formal feeling comes. That's what the poet Emily Dickinson said. As I sat waiting for my flight to start its taxi, the minutes passing, the reality slowly, painfully becoming incontrovertible, I felt a rigidity enter my posture. I sat more upright. Yes, I would be formal. I would accept what I could not change. I would not, could not, cry anymore. It sounded like Dr. Seuss. *Would not, could not*.

I put my phone into my pocket and turned it off.

I did not try to read. I did not check my e-mail. I did not drink or eat. I sat and felt strangely solid. This had happened. That's what I told myself. I had been played for a fool, and I wasn't the first woman to believe a man's lies, nor would I be the last, but this counted for a lesson learned.

I did not permit myself the luxury of searching the faces of my fellow passengers for Jack. I didn't pass any longing looks toward the front of the plane. He was not coming; he did not come; he did not want me after all.

A little later a bright, red-lipsticked flight attendant told me to buckle up, and I did. She smiled. I smiled back.

We took off a little later. The plane lifted, and Jack was not with me. We passed through a cloud, and Jack was still not with me. I asked the attendant for a gin and tonic, drank it, asked for another, drank it, asked for a third, drank it. She refused to give me a fourth. I put my head back against the headrest and closed my eyes.

It's over, I told myself. Maybe it had never been, had never ac-

tually existed in any sense that mattered. I reached down to my
purse and slid my Smythson out of my bag. What I could do, what
I had always done, was to stay organized. I had ignored the Smythson too long. I opened it carefully, as if calling a friend I hadn't seen
in a while, and my hands moved slowly through the pages. Appointments. Assignments. Forms. Birthdays sketched in pink ink
through the year. I leafed through the pages slowly, resolutely, and
I did not cry. Why cry? We had had Paris and Amsterdam and
Prague and Kraków and salt mines and milk barges. That was a
good summer. That was a good trip. I slipped the pen out of the
tiny holster on the Smythson and darkened a square around my
work start date. I darkened it until the pen tip nearly pierced the
paper. The clouds floated below us, and nothing seemed solid any
longer.

When I tried to slide the Smythson back in my bag, it refused
to enter. I jiggled it, angling it so it had to go in, but something
continued to block it. I reached down inside the bag and pried
things around. My hand fell on Jack's grandfather's journal. I knew
its feel before I even put my eyes on it. It turned me cold. I felt my
chest compress, and it made it hard to breathe.

"Would you take this and throw it out?" I asked the flight attendant the next time she passed by. I held the journal out to her. It
still possessed a perfect weight and size for my hand. I believed that
if she took it, if she freed me from its touch, I would be restored.

"Sure, honey," she said.

She gave me a fake smile and tossed the journal in a tiny refuse
bag she had carried down the aisle. She did not examine the journal
at all. She smiled brightly and continued on, the journal no more
or less than a saggy weight in a bag reserved for peanut wrappers
and swizzle sticks.

She covered half the distance back to the galley before I screamed for her to stop.

I made, in the vernacular, a *scene*. I was aware of making a scene even as I performed for it. Deep inside, I blamed it on the drinks. I blamed in on my emotionally overwrought condition. But self-knowledge didn't prevent me from surging down the aisle, my balance off, tears starting to cloud my perceptions.

Watching me advancing toward her, the flight attendant made a face that said clearly: *Calm down, you little bitch.* The last thing she needed was a madwoman passenger.

"Sorry," I said, leaning in to whisper to her. "Love letters and things from an old boyfriend."

"Oh," she said.

Only she said it this way: *Oooooooooooo.*

Then she held out the bag, and we enacted a reverse trick or treat, with me digging through the trash to secure the journal. When I finally fished it out, I clutched it to my chest.

"I've been there," the flight attendant said. "Exactly there."

"Thank you."

"I'll bring that last gin and tonic, okay? But you just get some sleep after that."

I nodded and bobbed my way back to my seat. The rest of the world felt far, far away.

Part Two

New York

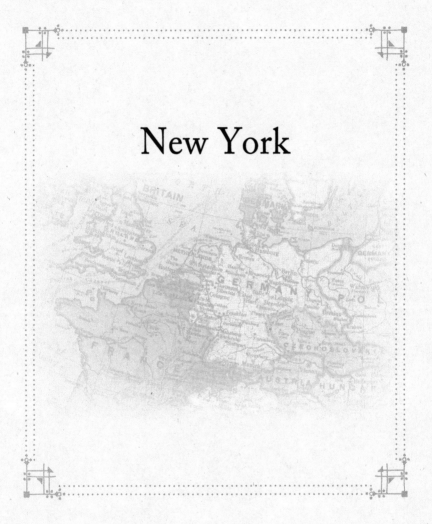

39

If you're going on a date, a fix up, would you rather be in the bar waiting for the guy to show up, or would you prefer to make an entrance, scan the diners and drinkers, trying to pick out the friend of a friend who is supposed to be cute?

Worst-case scenario, you don't know if you are early or late, because your heart isn't into it, but you have come out of some sort of prescriptive push from two friends at work, and this is what people do, this is one way they meet, so you have said yes, okay, all right, I'll meet him, thanks.

His name is Gary.

That's what you were told.

It's after work, 7:30, which is an early night for leaving work when all is said and done. In the month and a half since you started at Bank of America, you have earned a reputation as a grind, a work grind, so you have changed your shoes, combed your hair, put on a touch of eyeliner, a bit of blush, and unbuttoned one button to reveal the top of your laciest bra. It all feels phony, like putting peanut butter on the lever of a mousetrap as bait, but Eleanor, the girl closest to your age and experience at Bank of America, has coached you, even made you sign up for a dating site—*Come on, Heather, don't be ridiculous, you need to get out and about, it's not a big deal, everyone is online, it doesn't mean you are some sort of dating failure*—and now you are putting into practice what you are expected to do.

You pause after stepping through the door, carefully moving a little aside to let other people pass by. It's Friday night, the start of the weekend, and the bar, Ernie's, is awash with young energy. It's a scene, a meet and mingle, and you suppose you fit in here, you are the correct demographic, but it doesn't feel as festive in the bottom of your gut. A loud roar goes up at the east end of the bar; someone has done something at the center of a group of guys, and people clap and shout, and a hat of some sort goes into the air.

A text comes in on your phone.

Running late, Gary says. *B riht there.*

So now what?

And can he spell? Or is that text code? A typing mistake?

The bar is jammed, but you forge ahead and look for seats, but nothing is open. This is supposed to be fun, you remember. This is why you work, so you will have money to go out and meet guys in crowded rooms. Something like that. But that is cynical thinking, and Amy and Constance have hectored you about negativity, telling you it is not right to turn into a lemony pill after being jilted by He-Who-Shall-Not-Be-Named. You agree, sort of, but can't always help it. So when a pair of seats opens up off to the west end of the bar, a couple heading out, you force yourself to see it as a good omen, a propitious sign.

Before you can save the second seat, however, another woman, your age, your look more or less, slides in, and it is everything you can do to hold on to your own seat. You swing your butt up onto the seat and hang your purse over the back, and you twist around so you can watch the door. Casually, though. You don't want to appear too eager, a golden retriever jumping on the house door as his provider gets out of the car in the driveway, so you decide to turn back and try to catch the bartender's eye, but he is down at the other end watching whatever it was that made everyone shout a moment before.

You turn back to check the door, and you see Gary.

It has to be Gary. You know it's Gary by the look, the glance around the bar, the way he stands. You've been told he is into working out, and it seems true; his body is solid and tight, and he has an athlete's bounce when he catches your eye and makes his way over to you, his finger poked to his chest, then to you, then back to his chest.

"You must be Gary," you say. "Eleanor's friend, right?"

"Heather," he says, but before he speaks another word, his phone goes off, and he holds up a finger and smiles.

"Okay, okay, yes," he says into the phone, smiles at you again, then nods at something the other person has said.

Which is okay, because it gives you a chance to examine him. He's not bad, not precisely your type, but not bad. He's a little suit-y, a little corporate New York, a little man on the go, man about town, man pretty in love with himself. He is blond, though his hair is thinning, has already pulled back from his forehead—*He's a fivehead*, Amy would say—and he is clean shaven, with a thick chin that reminds you of an ice cream paddle. His suit is good, blue with pinstripes, and his tie is a bit too attention seeking, *a boner tie*, Amy would call it, bright blue and slightly iridescent.

He smiles again at you, raises his eyebrows to say he is sorry, then makes a drinking motion with his hand to indicate the bartender has appeared behind you.

"Club soda for me," Gary says to the bartender, then returns his attention back to the phone.

"I'll have a white wine," you say, then realize how pathetic and clichéd that sounds, so you switch it to a Stella Artois.

"Sorry," Gary says when the bartender walks away.

He slides his phone into his jacket pocket and leans over to kiss your cheek.

"So you're at Bank of America?" he asks.

"Yes, I am. Just started this fall. And you're an attorney?"

"Guilty, Your Honor."

"Contracts?"

"Well, for now. I'm trying to work my way into sports contracts. I'd like to be an agent."

"Oh, cool."

Your drinks arrive.

And you are already not into this guy. And you are pretty sure he is not into you.

Call it chemistry. Or lack of chemistry.

"Cheers!" you say, toasting.

"Cheers. Sorry to let you drink alone, but I'm training. Trying to avoid carbs."

"No worries."

"I'm doing an endurance thing. Do you know about them? These mega-endurance things? You run, you go through mud, go over obstacles . . . it's awesome."

"Do you compete in teams?"

"On this one, yeah, but not always."

It's loud. Everything he says is just on the edge of too garbled to hear. You have to cock your head and keep an ear, like a small microphone, pointed in his direction.

"So what did Eleanor say about me?" he asks.

"She said you were a nice guy."

"Nice isn't very exciting."

You take a second sip of beer. You don't mind letting him stew on the possibility that he is not exciting. In tiny pulses, you realize you don't particularly like him. At all. Then his phone goes off, and he plucks it out of his jacket again, holding up his finger to promise he will be only a moment.

As he talks on the phone, obviously setting things up for later with someone cooler, more attractive, more interesting, you compare him to He-Who-Shall-Not-Be-Named, and it doesn't work. It's no comparison. Jack was bigger, for one thing, and more at ease, worldlier, more natural, much cuter. No, not cuter, you think, just much handsomer. This guy, this Gary, is like an ersatz Jack, a faux Jack, and you take a pull on your beer and wonder how you can get out of here politely. You need to be on a train out to New Jersey for the long weekend, the Columbus Day weekend, but if things had gone well, really well, you suppose you could have postponed that a day.

But Gary solves the situation for you.

"So I don't beat around the bush," he says when he finishes on the phone. "You're not digging me, are you?"

"I wouldn't say that."

"It's not working on this end, anyway," he says, smiling. "I don't get that we're into the same things."

"Should we be into the same things?" You can't help yourself from asking.

Suddenly, absurdly, Gary has become a *project*. You love projects. You cannot resist a project, and though you don't want Gary, you don't want him to not want you, so you try to flirt a little. His phone rings a third time, and as he picks it out of his pocket, you understand you don't need to do this, so you make a little bye-bye sign with your right hand, then spin around and take a good, long drink of your beer. Gary reaches beside you, puts his half-empty drink on the bar, smiles wanly—oh, you love a wan smile—and then pats your back in farewell as he walks away, his phone still attached to his head.

You think of the Esche, the mighty Esche, growing in the Jardin du Luxembourg.

You think of the riding academy and the moment in front of the Vermeer painting, and you can't help it, won't help it, you think of afternoons in Berlin when your bodies collided and stopped against each other like sticks searching for sparks inside themselves, and He-Who-Shall-Not-Be-Named slowly takes over all your thoughts, your vision, your memory, and you drink the rest of the beer with your eyes on the mirror behind the bar. Single girl, Manhattan, Friday night.

40

On the train to New Jersey, to home, you text Eleanor at work:

Nice guy. Glad we met. No magic. But thanks.

Downy face emoticon.
You text to Constance and Amy:

Nice guy. Glad we met. No magic.

Dad met me at the station.

"Hey there, sweetie pie," he said when I climbed in beside him. "You're riding the rails late."

He smelled like butter and popcorn. I threw my overnight bag in the backseat, then leaned over and kissed his cheek. He wore a white shirt from work, but it was one of his older ones, relegated to his casual wear. Over the white shirt, he wore a Carhartt vest, his favorite weekend Dad-fix-it-manly-man wear. He looked tired, but calm, as if perhaps he had been dozing before picking me up at the train station. His hands, heavy and useful, hung from the two and ten positions on the steering wheel. He was a good-looking man, I decided, but not flashy. His hair, grayer now, had thinned a little on top, and I knew, from my mom's reports, that it was a source of injured vanity for him. He possessed strong cheekbones, well defined, that lent strength to all his other features. He was fifty-two years old, a man in his prime, a calm, steady force in all our lives. I found him very dear in that instant, my dad, and it felt good—no, more than good—to be sitting with him in our car, the lazy weekend ahead of us, the refrigerator, I knew, stocked with my favorite treats, the TV couch in the den comfortable, my mom doubtless being the Mom-a-saurus.

Then, out of left field, I put my head on his shoulder and started to sob.

"Hey, hey, hey, what's this all about?" he asked, his voice consoling, his voice the one that picked me up off my fallen bicycle when I was seven, after a failed tryout for the lead in *South Pacific* in high school. "Hey, hey, sweetheart, take it easy. Are you okay? Did something happen?"

I shook my head.

He kissed the top of my head and slowly pushed back my hair from my face.

"What's going on, cupcake?" he asked and reached forward with his other hand to turn down a college football game on the radio.

I felt absurd, but I couldn't stop crying. The car idled. It was cool outside, and he had the window down, and the air smelled of leaves and October and fire. He reached over quickly to his glove box and pulled down the door, rummaged inside for a second, then produced a handful of Dunkin' Donuts napkins. He handed me a few. I put one against my eyes and blew my nose in another one.

"You okay? What is it, sweetheart? What's going on?"

I lifted my head from his shoulder. I shook my head. What was worth saying that hadn't already been said? I missed Jack. I missed what we had and what we might have been. That was established family legend. For all intents and purposes, I had been left at the altar.

"Just the blues, Daddy," I said, covering. "Just a long day."

"Work okay?"

I nodded.

"But on the social front?"

I shrugged. I couldn't risk speaking.

"But you're liking your apartment."

Which was a safe conversation point. He knew I liked it. I nodded.

"It's small, but I like it. It's miniscule, really. You've seen it."

"Well, New York living. That's what it is. I heard the other day about some condos over in Jersey City just coming online. Newark is coming back, too."

"Hmmmm," I said.

I dabbed at my eyes.

"Mom's got all your favorites in the fridge."

"Oh, good."

"And I am going to make my Magic Chicken Dinner on the grill. The one and only."

"Then all is right in the world."

I expected him to move the car. Cry over. But he didn't push it into drive. I squared my shoulders and blew my nose again.

"Listen, Heather, I'm afraid I have some bad news. I hate to add it to your unhappiness right now, but Mr. Periwinkle died yesterday."

I felt, incredibly, the same stillness I had felt in the Paris airport. In Charles de Gaulle. Something so horrible, so irrevocably painful, had happened, and it took the air from my lungs and the blood from my heart.

"What?" I asked, tears returning. "How?"

My voice went up on the last word, and I could barely contain a sob. My father took a breath and patted my knee.

"He didn't come inside. Your mom hadn't seen him. He was out in the garage in that place he liked to go. In the morning sun. He was just dead, honey. Old age."

"Not Mr. Periwinkle."

Dad put his arm around me. Mr. Periwinkle, cat of cats, my childhood friend, my tear pillow, my comfort, my kitty, was gone. And nothing I could do, or say, or hope, would change that one iota.

Appropriately, it rained as we buried Mr. Periwinkle the next morning.

I dug the tiny hole for him. Down in the basement, I had scrounged up an old hatbox—at least it looked as though it had once been a hatbox, with a six-sided top and a pale blue cover—and had found a discarded pile of raffia my mother had used for some sort of crafty project years before. I made a raffia-lined coffin for my kitten, for my old friend, and I put him carefully into the box and taped it shut, content that I had done what I could. I left the box in the garage while I dug the hole.

It was early, just past eight, and the leaves stuck to the earth in wet patches of muted colors. When I had the hole three feet deep, the turned soil on a piece of cardboard box stationed next to the hole, I stopped and regarded the work. It felt good to have my hands on something solid, a shovel handle, not more numbers on a computer.

"Deep enough?" Dad asked, coming out with two coffees. He handed me one.

"I think so, don't you?"

He nodded and said, "He was a good cat."

Dad wore an Irish tweed hat he had bought on a trip to Limerick years ago. I liked seeing him that way.

"Tell me something you remember about Mr. Periwinkle," he said. "What was your best memory of him?"

I thought a moment and sipped my coffee.

"I used to think he was wishing."

"When?"

"When he stayed on my chest or sat on a couch, he put his paws together and closed his eyes, and I used to think he was wishing for things."

"Good things?"

"Yes, mostly."

Cat wishes, I thought. My dad put his arm over my shoulders, and I almost burst out crying.

Before we could talk more about it, Mom appeared carrying something in her hands, and it took me a moment to realize she had collected most of Mr. Periwinkle's toys. A cat fishing pole, a knitted robin, a wind-up mouse that contained catnip, a jingle bell swat ball. Whether she meant it as an act of kindness or simply wanted to be rid of the clutter of owning a cat, I couldn't determine.

She loved Mr. Periwinkle, I knew, but she loved him from a distance, as you might love a sunset or a snowstorm.

Then I realized if she meant it simply as a means to rid herself of the cat junk, she could have thrown it out and I would have been none the wiser. Over the last years, while I was at school, she had been the cat custodian. Somewhat grumpy, and grudging with her outward affection, she had been as fond of Mr. Periwinkle as I had been. She was simply more private about it. I realized that was something I had to keep in mind about my mother.

"That looks nice," Mom said about the grave. "You did a good job, honey."

"Thanks, Mom."

"Are we ready?" Dad asked.

I went and carried the box from the garage. It weighed next to nothing. This was the second thing I had buried, I realized, in less than a half year. That probably had some meaning, but I couldn't divine what it might be.

I held the box and asked everyone to put a hand on it.

"Good-bye, Mr. Periwinkle," I said. "You were a good cat and a good friend, and no one can ask for more than that."

Mom, my sweet mom, put her face down and began to cry. My dad knelt on the other side of the hole and helped me put the box inside. Then Mom handed us the cat toys, and we buried those on top, turning our Mr. Periwinkle into a tiny Viking warrior, in his hatbox ship, who would need his weapons and inspirations of joy if he intended to feast in Valhalla with Odin on this gray October morning.

41

....

"Y ou still haven't heard anything about him? No word from him, of course," Mom asked.

It was late. Dad had gone to bed. We sat in the solarium with two cups of tea. Mom wanted to try a licorice-flavored tea that was supposed to be good for muscle and tendon ache. She always tried various teas, few of them effective, but I liked the scent of the licorice in the chill interior of the solarium. I held the cup close to my chest.

I shook my head. I hadn't heard anything about him.

She didn't have to spell out whom she meant by *him*.

"Well," she said and let it hang.

"Constance says Raef refuses to talk about it. He'll talk about anything else, but not about Jack."

"And they're engaged? Constance and Raef?"

"Yes."

"That's wonderful. I wouldn't have pictured Constance being the first to go in your little group."

"You mean to be married?"

"I would have put my money on Amy."

"Amy, not so much, Mom."

"Do you still have his grandfather's journal?" she asked, switching subjects.

I nodded. I didn't have an address for Jack. I had to keep it.

She sipped her tea. I did, too. I didn't much care for it. I had a *Vogue* magazine open on my lap, and I occasionally flipped a page. Mom had the *Times'* Sunday crossword cut out and clipped to the clipboard she always kept for that purpose. It was Sunday, and I should have been on a train back to Manhattan, except that it was Columbus Day weekend, and Monday was a holiday. I planned to take an early train back, then work in the afternoon.

"Do you like these blazers?" I asked my mom, and I held up a page of the magazine for her to peruse. She pinched her folded glasses against her eyes and looked at the pictures. This was an old game with us. We had always talked clothes, even during the stormier days of high school. One of the few highlights of being home after Paris was shopping for my business wardrobe with Mom. She liked coming into New York and having a daughter to meet for lunch. I liked those days with my mom.

"I've never been much for blazers," Mom said, dropping her glasses down and returning to her struggle with the crossword. "They always remind me of Catholic schoolgirl uniforms. I see their utility, but I just never went for them."

"I have that camel one, but I hardly ever wear it."

"It's hard to find an occasion to wear one."

I flipped some more pages. Mom sipped her tea.

"Do you like the tea?" she asked.

"Not a lot. Do you?"

"It tastes too licorice-y."

"But good for your joints and tendons."

She reached to the table beside her chair and used the remote control to turn on the gas fireplace in the corner of the solarium. It popped into action immediately. She loved running the gas stove. She said it made her feel like a pioneer woman. Mostly, I thought, she liked the contrast of the cold glass pressing against the warmth inside the room.

She smiled at the fire and pushed the crossword off her lap.

"Did I ever tell you about the pumpkin war I fought?" she asked. "I don't know why I've been thinking about it lately. I guess it's just the season. Did I tell you the story?"

"No, Mom. Pumpkin war?"

"Oh, that makes it sound more dramatic than it was. But I fought it alongside a few of my friends. We must have been in, oh, seventh grade or so. And we got to talking about the unfairness of boys coming by and smashing the pumpkins we'd spent so much time carving. Are you sure I didn't tell you this?"

I shook my head, fascinated.

"It was my idea, I suppose, but I talked all my friends into pushing pins from the inside through the pumpkin skin so that each jack-o'-lantern became as prickly as a porcupine. I don't even recall where I got the idea; maybe I read it somewhere. Anyway, it was us against these imagined boys—the boys who smashed our pumpkins. We pictured them sneaking up to our doorsteps, reaching for the pumpkins, then jumping back when they were pricked by the pins. It was actually a pretty devilish idea. Each night that the pumpkins survived seemed to be proof of our cleverness. It was really very fun. We'd meet in school each day to report that this or that pumpkin had made it through the night. It was the first thing I ever led—counterterrorism, right?"

"Mom, you rebel! So did the pumpkins make it through until Halloween?"

"We ended up smashing them ourselves. I've always wondered about that. One night we got on the phone and decided to smash them. We all found gardening gloves so we could pick them up or whatever, and we smashed them. I think we missed having the boys' naughtiness or something. I've never been able to understand our motive."

"Did you clean them up?"

"No, of course not. Lazy little twits that we were! My dad poked his finger on a piece before I told him what happened. I remember he gave me the strangest look when I explained it to him."

"I think you were guarding your virginity, Mom! It all sounds very Freudian."

"You know, I thought the same thing!" she said and laughed. "I've always thought exactly that. The masculine surge and the feminine repulse! I don't think I've ever told this story to anyone. How odd that it came to mind."

"Why tonight?"

She shrugged, obviously amused with the recollection.

"Why not tonight, I guess? I imagine I've been thinking about Jack, too. I didn't know him, of course, but he might have been a little like the girls and me smashing the pumpkins before anyone even approached them. Sometimes it's easier to ruin a thing than to guard it. Does that make any sense?"

"It does, Mom, but we don't have to figure out Jack's motives.

I'm trying to let all of that go under the bridge, so to speak. Bygones be bygones. That's what I want now."

She nodded. She poked the remote control and nudged the stove a tiny bit higher. Then she picked up the crossword puzzle clipboard and propped it on her lap.

"Not loving this tea," she said.

"Me, neither."

"My joints don't feel any better, either."

"Isn't that always the way?" I asked.

42

....

What you do is work. That becomes the answer for everything. You dress in the early dawn, showered, powdered, hair cut to a smart set, the clothes in your closet mirroring back an image of *a gal on the go*. That's absurd, you know, but that's what you think of when you address your wardrobe. What you want, mostly, is a good-looking outfit, not dowdy, that can transform, when necessary, into something chic and hip and provocative. *Why not?* you ask yourself when you bend to the mirror in your apartment—an apartment that is either tropically warm or refrigerator cold—and apply makeup, why not have your times in New York City? Why not enjoy what it is to be young, free, single, in one of the great cities of the world? Jack was wrong about that. New York City is not a prison the prisoners built for themselves. No, no, it is something rich and fun and festive, something occasionally desperate and frightening, an edge of some sort of world, and you like knowing you belong, had conquered a small corner of it, had it licked.

Sort of.

Not too much makeup, by the way. Never too much. Just enough to give yourself a glow, an outline, a definition. The bathroom is still foggy, but when you step back, you can see your cloudy form. *A gal on the go*. You turn this way, back, the other way, back, check the line of your skirt, the tuck of your blouse, the height of your heel. It works, it usually works, and you are aware of being young, very young, and of being in demand for your youth, because what did your division boss quote? He said the most powerful people on earth are rich old men and pretty young women. Maybe he was right—who knows?—but right now you simply assess that you are competently dressed, correctly dressed, and on the way down in the apartment elevator, you go through your purse and say the modern rosary of Cs: *cell, comb, credit card, condom*.

Then it's New York City. You step out, and it's cold, cold as hell, the wind pushing through the buildings, everyone moving quickly, trying to get indoors, to get to work, no lollygagging. You'd like to take a cab just for the luxury of it, and you have the funds for it—not a bad salary, not at all a bad salary, it turns out—but at this hour of the morning, the traffic, especially the crosstown traffic, would be torture. So you hustle to the nearest subway entrance, go down into the cave, a mythological creature Constance would be able to identify, then you slide your monthly pass through the turnstile, knock the three-armed fanny patter with your thigh and hip, check your phone as you find a place to stand on the platform. The subway station smells like panting, you've always thought, like the lair of some awful creature whose breath, year after year, painted the walls until no other smell could find a purchase. As you think it—you think it every day—you look at your phone and check a dozen things. Stock market. Basic headlines. Messages, texts, e-mails.

You do not look for anything from Jack. You gave that up long ago.

You didn't give it up, but you pretend that you did. You tell yourself that you did. And that amounts to almost, kind of, the same thing.

Then the train comes in, and you step on, turn sideways, find a pole to hold on to as the train begins to move forward. It's okay. It's early enough that it's okay. And the reception on your cell disappears, and you sling into the darkness of the between-stations world, and you think of Vulcan, for Constance, and of all the creatures below the earth, the dirt animals, and that strikes you as strange, not a healthy thought, and when you finally reach your stop you are glad to get out, glad to move quickly toward the light, a square of daylight, and the cold brilliance of winter in New York City.

Then you are career girl, a girl on the go, because you like what you are wearing, like how it feels, and you can tell some men you pass are appreciative, and you stop at a coffee truck and order a medium, skim, two artificial sweeteners, then decide to splurge on a fruit salad kind of thing that comes in a plastic container. You carry everything toward your building, the coffee's warmth entirely welcome, and you push through the revolving door to find Bill, the security officer, standing behind the check-in desk, his eyes passing to the cameras that show him every corner of the workplace.

"Hey, Bill. How's it going?"

"Fine, Ms. Mulgrew."

"Glad to hear it. Am I the first one in?"

"Just about, I think."

You ride the elevator up—again something mythological about this up-and-down life, this above the ground and below the ground—and for a blinding second you think of the mighty Esche, the European ash, covered now, probably, in snow. You think of Pan's statue watching the Jardin du Luxembourg, and then the elevator arrives at your floor, twenty-third floor, and you feel yourself tighten and come more alive, work, work, work, sacred work. It's okay, you like work, and you move to your desk, hang up your coat, put your coffee down, toss your bag into your bottom drawer, look around. One of the supervisors' office lights is on—Burky's, you figure—but you are not game for him, not so early, not yet, so you sit down, boot up your computer, plug in your phone to the spare power cord you keep on your desk, and that's that. Open for business.

You take a minute to wiggle the top free on your fruit, put on last night's economic report from *The Wall Street Journal,* eat the taste of sunlight and sweetness, and behind you, and around you, lights begin coming on, a little foot traffic noise arrives, and the day has begun, and Jack is still missing, and your heart, your treacherous heart, refuses to let him go.

43

....

There is a feminine protocol to these things.

Before we slid into the banquette of the restaurant on Fourteenth Street, before we settled in at all, Constance held out her hand, and Amy and I gave out the obligatory girl squeal.

Amy grabbed Constance's hand and held it close.

"Get out of town! It's beautiful," she said, examining it. "Classic setting. Platinum, right? Not white gold. Oh, it's beautiful, Constance, just beautiful. An Empire cut?"

All of this happened on our way to the table. I couldn't believe the stars had aligned to bring us all together. Constance had returned from Australia ten days before—engaged!—and Amy had arrived from Ohio on a job-search swing through New York. Our get-together had happened almost by itself, which only went to make it seem even more miraculous. It also made me feel surprisingly adult. Here I was, a denizen of New York City, having lunch with girlfriends in the middle of my working day. It gave me a kick. I knew the other girls felt the same way.

The maître d' tolerated us and held the menus while we slipped into the green banquette. It was a Vietnamese restaurant named something Crab. The Beautiful Crab or the Enchanted Crab. Constance had read about it in *The New Yorker* and suggested it. We had arrived at the door almost at the exact instant, Constance and Amy sharing a cab over from Penn Station.

We put Constance in the middle. Amy and I took turns passing Constance's finger and hand back and forth.

"Okay, I want the whole story," Amy said. "Did he propose cute? What happened? And we're going to need a scorpion bowl for this. Three straws, please."

The waitress—a petite Vietnamese woman in black trousers beneath an olive tunic—hadn't even fully arrived at the table, but Amy had already given her a mission.

"Three straws," the waitress said, confirming.

"Three straws," Amy agreed.

Then for a second, before Constance started, we went silent. It felt so good to be back together, to be one group again, that we all felt—I guessed—a little shy. We looked around the restaurant, pretending greater interest in the furnishing than we probably felt. But Amy saved us by snagging a busboy and asking for water.

"You have to ask for water in every damn restaurant now," Amy said. "Are they trying to save dishwashing fluid or water or what?"

"I guess in case of a water shortage," I said lamely.

"This is New York! There's no water shortage here, is there? Not that I've heard of, anyway. Okay, Constance, give us the story. You know we want to hear it. Don't leave anything out."

Constance blushed. She hated being the center of attention.

"We were out checking the fences on the station," Constance began. "And Raef—"

"Wait, how big is this station?"

"Big. Very big. Hundreds of acres, but the land is dry and not very useful. I guess you can still get big parcels of land up in the desert for next to nothing in Australia. Raef's family owns a lot of the land around those parts. He has an extended family, so everywhere you go, there's an uncle who has this plot, an aunt who has this one, a cousin . . . you get it."

"So you're out checking the fence?" Amy said. "I can't believe our prissy Constance is out checking fences in Australia."

The busboy came with our water. He poured out three glasses. Constance paused while the busboy finished. Then she continued.

"He leaned against the fence, and he looked out at the desert, and he asked me if I could imagine spending my life here. It wasn't dramatic. He said he would make sure we traveled and that we could spend time in the United States, but that he wanted me to consider being his wife and living in Australia with him. That was all."

"Did he get down on a knee?" Amy asked.

"No. We're not like that."

"You mean sort of . . ."

"Just those outdated roles. I don't know. Raef doesn't go in for much in the way of formality or tradition. I've never met anyone who lived more for the day. He doesn't stand on ceremony. Most of the Australians I met despise ceremony. They have a bit of a hangover from the British rule, but most of it is pure Aussie."

"What did the desert look like?" I asked.

"Oh, beautiful colors. Red, mostly, but that doesn't do it justice. All the doors to the house are kept open, screened, but opened. And you spend a lot of time on the porch. You visit different porches depending on what time of day it is. It's a farming society, really, although I guess herding is more accurate. They run thousands of sheep. Everywhere you look, you see sheep."

"And his family?" Amy asked.

"Sweethearts. Very welcoming. They made sure to tell me Raef had never brought any other girl home. It was comical how each one pulled me aside and told me that. Pretty funny."

"Have you set a date?" I asked.

"Spring," she said. "In Paris."

She reached quickly and took my hand. It was typical of Constance that she would not want her happiness to bring me sadness of any kind. She smiled and made sure she caught my eye. I nodded. It was okay. Everything would be okay. Paris was fine.

"No word from He-Who-Shall-Not-Be-Named?" Amy asked me after a second scorpion bowl arrived. "Is that's what we're still calling him?"

"We call him *asshat,* mostly," Constance said.

"Constance!" Amy laughed. "You calling someone an asshat? All that Aussie stuff is rubbing off on you. Well, my stars and garters!"

"I don't care," Constance said, sipping the straw that angled into the scorpion bowl. "My friends' enemies are my enemies."

I leaned over and kissed Constance's cheek.

"Nothing," I said. "Gone into the wind."

"He's removed everything, Raef said," Constance said. "Facebook, Instagram, even his cell. He's disappeared from everything."

"What the fuck?" Amy said. "Who does that?"

"Next topic," I said.

"Wait, who are you dating these days?" Amy asked me. "Anything cooking?"

I shook my head.

"I am a celibate priestess," I said. "I could be sacrificed to a volcano."

"Girl, you got to get back in the game."

"That's what I tell her," Constance agreed, nodding and sipping.

"I mean," Amy said. "I mean, just even a little ride 'em cowboy. Your ginny is going to dry up like an old pumpkin."

"Ginny?" Constance asked and laughed.

"I work," I said. "That's what I do."

"So that's going well?" Constance asked. "You like that?"

"It's . . . interesting. I keep hearing He-Who-Shall-Not-Be-Named's voice in the back of my head. *New York is a prison we build for ourselves*," I said in a monster voice. "It's not a prison, but it's not a picnic, either. He was right about that."

"You need to get out more," Amy said, sipping and talking, talking and sipping. "You need to join something."

"All these hipsters playing dodgeball and joining bowling leagues," I said. "It tires me out just to think of it."

"Have you been on any dates?" Constance asked. "You've gone on a couple, haven't you?"

"Three," I said. "Not disasters, but not great, either. Mostly people kind of get together. There's always a function at the office. Someone's getting married, or a promotion, or—"

"Or an ass lift," Amy jumped in.

"Or an ass lift," I agreed.

"My mom always says boys spend their twenties chasing girls, and girls spend their fifties chasing boys," Constance said. "How about you, Amy? Give us the lowdown."

"Nothing to report on the man front."

"I thought you were dating Mr. Belt Buckle," Constance said. "The guy you told us about."

"Bobby," she said and smiled. "He's an idiot, but I like him. Nothing serious. We're just play pals."

"And work?"

"I don't care about work, really, but I'm hammering nails for Habitat for Humanity on the weekends. I'm kind of digging that. I get to wear a tool belt. I want to buy a pickup truck. I swear, I'm going redneck."

The waitress came with our bill. I put my credit card down on it and told them it was my treat.

"Are you sure?"

"I'm sure."

"I would have ordered another drink if I had known you were picking up the tab," Amy said. "Thanks, Heather."

"I have one more thing," Constance said, and she grasped both of our hands. "I want you both to be my bridesmaids. No maid of honor. Just you two. Co-bridesmaids or whatever that's called. It's going to be small. Very small. In Paris. I'm sorry to drag you all the way to Paris, but if we book early enough, it won't be too bad."

"We wouldn't miss it for the world," I said. "And it's Paris, not Cincinnati."

Amy nodded. Then she burped. It was a long, hissing burp that sounded like air seeping from a punctured tire. She smiled when she finished and then exclaimed, "Constance, how could you?"

The waitress picked up the check. Lunch was over.

44

....

A my left first.

"See ya, dolls," she said, and she plunked herself in a cab. She had an appointment uptown.

We waved her off, then I walked Constance to the Port Authority. On the corner before we left and went our individual ways, Constance told me Raef had still not heard from Jack. It was our usual conversational touchstone. We always reviewed the Jack situation when we got together.

"Nothing?" I asked, my stomach rising, the pedestrians around us moving fast.

"Nothing. He said Jack hasn't been in touch. The few contacts they had in common . . . no one knows where he went. It's really very odd."

"So he's gone? Truly gone?"

She nodded softly.

"What does that even mean?" I asked. "Do we know if he's alive? Should we try to track down his parents? I might go see his parents or at least call them. I could say I want to give back the journal."

"I wouldn't do that, sweetie. He's dropped out. With all the ways to be in contact now, it has to be by choice, right? Pick up a phone, Facetime, text, e-mail, tweet—you name it. He has removed his electronic footprint. He's not on Facebook, and you know how freaking hard it is to get your account deleted from Facebook. Nothing. Raef is worried about him. Really worried about him."

"Does Raef think he's dead?" I asked, naming my deepest fear.

"No, I don't think so. Do you remember that day in Paris when they went off together and we went to Notre Dame and looked at the statue of Mary?"

"Sure," I said.

"Raef refuses to talk about it, but I've thought about that day a lot. It was a curious thing to do at that moment. Why leave us when we only had a little time left in Paris? And what did they have to do that was so secretive?"

"Right," I said, pulling Constance a little to one side to avoid a teenager pushing a clothes cart on the sidewalk. "Jack never said where he went. I guess I never actually asked. I assumed they were up to some sort of boy mischief. Or maybe they were planning a surprise for us. I was a dope, now that I think about it."

"Well, I've always wondered what that might have been. I wonder about that a lot."

"You think something changed his mind? Something that he went to see that day?"

She shook her head to indicate she didn't know. It was a mystery. I kept my eyes on hers. She smiled softly.

"Sorry, sweetie," she said. "I would tell you if I knew. I promise. I don't have a clue."

"I can't even put my mind around this."

"Does it still hurt as much?"

"Yes. As much as ever. More in some ways. You know what adds to it? Because he was so adamant about not taking pictures in important moments, I have next to nothing to look at. It's like a dream. I mean it. Was he real? I can't even go back and look at him, really. It's almost as if he planned to disappear right from the start."

"Well, stay strong. I promise to get in touch the minute I hear anything about him, but I honestly don't have an inkling. He's just gone. He evaporated."

"I have his grandfather's journal. But I can't predict where he will be or when."

"Does he have a copy?"

I shrugged.

"He does. But he memorized a lot of it. He probably cares more about that journal than anything else in his life."

"And he let you keep it? And he hasn't called or written to ask for it back? That seems significant to me, cowgirl."

"I don't speak Jack any longer. I'm trying to forget that language. I had a Jack-a-cism."

Constance leaned forward and hugged me.

"I have to go. I miss you already."

"And I you."

"It was good to see Amy. She's still the tiger woman."

"She's strong. We're all strong, right?"

She nodded, then hugged me one last time and hurried off.

Saturday mornings, a jog around the reservoir. A Bloody Mary afterward at the deli on Fifty-Sixth that you like, or maybe an early drink with a friend, a show down in Soho, a new gallery to visit, an opening. *The New York Times* on Sunday morning in your apartment, the paper, The Gray Lady, spread out on your couch while you text and answer e-mails, try the crossword puzzle, read the editorials, force yourself to look at the stock reports. Then something cultural, something solid and good, the MoMa or the Frick, your special favorite, a walk through the park to look at the ducks, to rub Balto's nose, to see Alice in Wonderland remaining perpetually childish and overlarge. Winter is here, no longer threatening, and you spend some time with your mom talking about wardrobes, a few shopping trips, some good basic gear. You make a reservation for skiing in Vermont. You talk to your boss, three bosses, actually, about Japanese accounts, and they suggest you brush up on your language, so Thursday mornings you drink tea with a Japanese instructor, Mr. Hayes, who is only part Japanese, you discover, but speaks a high-quality language. You practice calligraphy, painting with brushes and ink, and once Mr. Hayes brings in vases and sprigs of forsythia and involves the class—five of you, all young- ish corporate types—in ikebana, the traditional art of flower ar- ranging. You are given three wands of forsythia, and you are told to find their proper balance, which is not easy, in Japanese or in English, but you go forward and converse with the other students, with Mr. Hayes, and when you report back to your office you nod at the questions and say the language training is going well.

New York, New York, a helluva town.

Yoga Monday nights, a spin class on Wednesday, mostly women, all pedaling like crazy, sometimes in the dark, and you cannot help recalling Jack's words, his idea that New York is a prison the inmates build for themselves, because, given a different perspec- tive, spin class could be the activity of madwomen. But you go on, and there are moments of beauty, true rewards, the sun setting behind the Chrysler Building, an amazing drummer in Union Square, a monologue by a woman named KoKo who pretends to be King Kong's wife, who is mad at him for leaving their island home. Funny stuff, New York stuff. Hip, in the know, tastemakers.

A few faux dates here and there. A drink session with one attorney and a quick flirtation with a hockey player who said he played for the Rangers but his name wasn't on the roster when you googled it. Your girlfriends calling, trading experiences of ruinous dates, gallows humor in every sad tale of men's inadequacy or capricious hearts, your dad dropping in to take you to an elegant dinner right on the park. Not bad, nothing bad, you have it all, you have everything, and your mom comes in on Saturday afternoons sometimes to take in a show, sometimes with her friend Barbara, and you join, a third lady in a cloud of suburban perfume, the actors onstage often hilariously hammy, but this is Broadway, and if you can make it here, you can make it anywhere.

New York, New York, a helluva town.

You try not to think of He-Who-Will-Not-Be-Named. Jackie-O, Jackass, Jack and Jill, Jack-o'-lantern, and so on. You do not think of that night in Berlin when your bodies clung together, or the time you stood beside the canal in Amsterdam and watched the swans swim under the cobblestone bridge. You do not think life would be better, truer, more genuine with Jack. You cannot let your mind go there, and you flitter online in the faint blue cursor lights looking for signs of him, electronic tracks, his whereabouts.

Touch football in Central Park, the Sheep Meadow, then a group retreat to a sports bar on the East Side, wings and beers, full-grown men in sports jerseys, blue jeans, and grass-stained sneakers. Hooray for the Giants or the Colts or Notre Dame or USC, and you keep it light, go along, remind yourself that this is what you wanted. You are making it, you are, good job reviews, good feedback from your team leader, up early on Mondays to start it all over again. It is not a prison, no way, and you can think of a thousand girls, a thousand dudes, who would be happy to trade places with you. Even your dad smiles when he hears how you are doing, because you are a cheetah, fast and lethal, and you refuse to be outworked. Twice you go out dancing and drink too much and take a few tokes of a rancid joint, and you let a few guys grind up on you, their johnnies obvious and lurid, and you dance away, remember Amy and Constance, remember Amsterdam, and sometimes it all seems like a dream, like a tossed salad of experiences and hopes and sensation, but part of you admits you are lonely for even that creepy touch, and you go to find your girlfriends and order another round.

New York, New York, a helluva town.

On rare and stormy nights, you read Jack's grandfather's journal. Only when the heart needs rain. You sit by the window and look out, air coming in, your pain sharp and brutal and nearly welcome. You read and dream and remember, and you feel old, feel like a person looking back instead of ahead, and you wonder where Jack is this night, this minute, if he thinks of you at all. For a millionth time, you go back over it, recall the deadened feeling in your heart when you knew, you knew, that he was not coming with you. That everything that had gone before it was a myth, a story we tell ourselves in the little hours before sunrise. You say you would send the journal to Jack if you had an address, but you don't, you surely don't, and the words and pages go together and become blurry with a third glass of wine, and the wind comes in and makes it colder, and the rain falls out of the sky and makes flecks of moisture on your windowsill.

45

I pulled up in front of Jack's Vermont land on a cold March morning, my rental car pushing as much heat as it could out of the tiny vents along the dashboard. I parked in front of his house— the former address, anyway—and plucked my coffee out of the slot on the console. I looked at the GPS on my phone, then at the line of stores that had obviously taken over the land around Jack's grandfather's farm. No mistake. I reached over and plucked Jack's grandfather's journal from my backpack. Jack's grand-father's farm, the source of the journal Jack had followed into oblivion, lay buried under a couple of acres of parking lot, a craft store, a kitchen store, the Maple Syrup Restaurant, and a Curves outlet.

I didn't do anything for a while except drink my coffee and stare out the frosty window. A little later, my phone buzzed, and I picked it up.

"Did you find it?" Amy asked.

"I guess. It's just a mini-mall of stores now."

"Well, that's what he said, right?"

"Right. I guess I had a different image in my head."

"And what image was that?"

"Oh, beautiful old farmhouse, white picket fence."

"But, Heather, he told you what had become of the place. He said it was all sold off."

"I know, I know, I know."

"How far was it, anyway?"

"An hour and half, but the roads were bad. It's wicked cold out."

"I know. Constance isn't even skiing this morning because of the cold. She's going out in a little while if it warms up."

We were staying together in a condo at Sugarbush. Girls' getaway week. This side expedition was my little research trip to Jack's ancestral home. I was supposed to get groceries, too, and wine, plenty of wine.

"It was silly to come up here," I said, understanding it fully for the first time. "I don't know what I expected to see."

"Come back and hang out with us," Amy said. "If you're around, I won't feel so much pressure to go ski with Constance."

"I'll be back in a while. I just want to poke around."

She didn't say anything. My friends, I realized, had become good about not saying too much to their nutty friend who remained obsessed with a man she had met on a train traveling from Paris to Amsterdam. They held their judgment, and their tongues, and I understood that was no easy trick.

"If you're up there, anyway, you should go to the library and look up his family. Local libraries have a lot of information."

"Maybe I'll do that."

"Don't kill the whole day there, Heather. It's not worth it. Come back and be with us."

"Just a little while," I said.

"Is this healthy, sweetie?"

"It doesn't really matter if it's healthy or not. I have to do it. I'm thinking about calling his parents to see if he's all right. There's some other element here, Amy. I swear it."

Amy didn't say anything.

"It's just that . . . ," I said, trying to think, trying to frame what I wanted to say. "It's just that if Jack wasn't true, then I don't know what else to believe in. I really don't. Everything feels false."

"I know, sweetie."

"If I could be that wrong about something—"

"You weren't wrong. It was just one of those things. One of those things that didn't quite work out."

"I wish I could hate him. That would make it much simpler."

"Maybe you can hate him in time. There's always hope."

She meant it as a joke. She meant it to lighten things up.

We hung up after adding a few things to my theoretical shopping list, then I sat a little longer.

What *was* I doing here? I wondered as I drank the rest of my coffee. It had been half a year since I had last seen Jack. Now, on a ski vacation with my two best friends, I had decided to leave them for a day so I could explore . . . what? What was I hoping to find? Even if I did discover something about Jack's background, that still didn't tell me where he was today, what he was doing, why he had dropped out of my life, everyone's life, entirely. Besides, it felt pitiful to be checking up on Jack's past; I felt like a celebrity stalker, although Jack wasn't a celebrity, and I wasn't truly a stalker, I hoped.

I turned off the car and climbed out. The cold hit me like a solid force. The weather report had called for an Arctic depression, and during the night the temperature had fallen through the floor. It was twenty degrees below zero out and overcast. I hustled across the parking lot and pushed into the kitchen store. A little doorbell tinkled above me.

"Cold, isn't it?" asked a woman wearing a red apron.

She had been arranging tea towels.

"I can't believe how cold it is," I said. "It's bitter."

"March is supposed to be warmer, but for me it's always the worst winter month. It promises so much and always fails to deliver."

"Yes," I said. "It can do that."

"Can I help you look for anything?"

"No, just browsing, but thanks."

What I wanted to ask is: *By the way, I met this guy and fell for him, and he used to own the land under these stores, his grandfather did, and now he's gone and you're here and can you tell me anything about him?* That sounded crazy even to me.

46

The bad drunks, the ones that get you in trouble, are the ones that sneak up on you. If you set out to get drunk, then you go at things with a plan in mind, a pacing that a sneaky drunk slyly slips around. During a sneaky drunk, you start with a drink, maybe in the afternoon, and one thing leads to another, and maybe you haven't eaten enough, at least not enough for the kind of drinking you are about to engage in, and before long you are drunker than you should be, sloshy, and because you haven't planned for the drunkenness, it seems like a pleasing surprise, an unexpected guest, and you keep offering more drinks to this visitor, delighted to find yourself in a state of glow when you hadn't even meant to have more than one.

I found myself drunk in an après-ski bar with five young men from the University of Vermont's ski team at four o'clock in the afternoon on the last day of our girls' getaway week. Constance and Amy sat beside me, equally drunk, the merriment of feeling happy and loaded beside a fire with five attentive young men locked deep in the experience.

We talked about eyebrows.

We talked about eyebrows because one of the Vermont boys, Peter, posited the theory that the denseness and thickness of a woman's eyebrows served as a reliable indicator about the denseness and thickness of a woman's privates. What denseness and thickness meant in relation to a woman's vagina was hard to pin down, but it was an afternoon discussion, a drunken debate about the impossibility of eyebrows having anything to do with our anatomy south of the equator. But Peter—who was tall and cute and hopelessly full of himself—insisted it was true.

They all wore Carhartts. They all wore fleeces and silly wool hats. They were like a pack of puppies, and Amy, at her wicked best, liked to play with puppies.

"So you're saying," Amy said, getting everyone to define terms for a moment, "is that what hands and feet are to men, indicating size and scope of the male organ, eyebrows are to women? That's a fascinating theory."

She pulled out the waistband on her jeans an inch and looked down. Then she looked up at the boys, her eyes wide. The boys laughed hard.

"By god, it's true!" she declared.

The boys laughed again.

"I just read that there is no correlation between hand size and penis size," Constance said, ever the scholar. "I read that is a myth."

"Thank goodness," one of the puppies said, holding up his hand.

I took his hand and examined it. It was a small hand.

"One more round," Peter, the ringleader, said to the bartender, Tomas.

We drank beer. Vermont Long Trails. And twice we did shots of Jack Daniel's. It felt like a couple of rivers joining in my belly.

"What might make sense," Amy said, "is to think the thickness of a woman's eyebrows has something to do with her passion. That might make a little sense. Women with thick eyebrows are passionate, more than a woman with thin, delicate eyebrows. That only stands to reason."

"I have thin eyebrows!" Constance said.

And that made the boys laugh once again.

"The mound of Venus, the thick meaty part under your thumb," I said, finding it surprisingly hard to speak clearly, "is supposed to indicate a lover's passion. A thicker pad at the base of the thumb is a sign of a good lover."

All the boys felt their thumbs. Of course.

It was afternoon drunk talk. That's all it was until Peter asked us if we wanted to smoke a joint. And when he said *smoke a joint*, what he meant was: *Let's get out of here, let's go somewhere, let's see what else this afternoon can become.*

And maybe, probably, he meant his invitation chiefly for me.

"He's way into you," Amy said in the bathroom, inspecting herself in the mirror. "Peter, the cute one."

"They're all cute," Constance said from the bathroom stall.

"They're puppies," I said, because they were.

"Puppies or not," Amy said, digging in her purse for lip gloss, "they're adorable. And they have nice bodies. And they don't judge. They're just out for fun."

"So do we want to go smoke a joint?" I asked. "They said something about a hot tub."

"I am not going in a hot tub!" Constance said, and she flushed her toilet and came out. "No way. They're a bunch of boner boys, believe me."

"Of course they're boner boys," Amy said. "That's the whole point, isn't it?"

Without meaning to, we found ourselves standing in front of three different sinks and mirrors. We all became aware of it at the same instant, and our eyes went from one to the other, back and forth, our smiles broadening as we realized what fun we were having, how much we cared for each other, how the boys, one way or the other, were just diversions along the way—friendly, cute diversions, but mere diversions.

"I just want to hold one on my lap and pet him," Amy said.

"Which one?" Constance asked.

"The little one. What do they call him?"

"Munchie, I think," I said. "It was hard to tell."

"I don't remember boys being so innocent," Constance said. "They have a lot to learn."

"They're young," I said. "As young as we were not long ago."

"We're not much older now," Amy said. "Don't go freaking granny pants on me."

"But we've been through a lot," Constance said. "I get Heather's point."

Amy held out her hand, and we slid our hands on top of hers. We didn't say our little ritual saying, but simply held our hands together. It was somewhere around five o'clock on a snowy day in Vermont.

47

I kissed Peter, and it was pretty good.

It was pretty strange, actually, because it had been six months since my last Jack kiss. Six months since my body felt tangled up in another person's tangle, and I felt a little on guard, a lot drunk, and happy to have broken the spell.

"You're like the prince who wakes Sleeping Beauty," I said. "I've been asleep for a long, long time."

"You're not asleep now, are you?"

"No. I'm awake."

"I'm into your eyebrows," he said.

He kissed me again. It was a light, easy kiss, but underneath it a bunch of other impulses asked for consideration. Begged for it. And we sat in a hot tub, and I had smoked a joint, and Amy was due to arrive any second with another wave of ski puppies, but they hadn't come into the pool area yet. Children played in the shallow end of the regular swimming pool. Their moms sat at a table and watched them, but the hot tub was far enough away, down at the other end entirely, to let Peter reach across, take the back of my neck gently, and pull me toward him for a kiss.

For a kiss in a bathing suit, which had to count for something extra.

He had a great body. He looked like a young British actor, one of those gallant lads who appear on the PBS dramas, a thin, tall scion of the ruling class, nice hair, nice teeth, and a gaze that suggested long walks with Labrador retrievers circling his legs and later, in the evening, a gallop and a cup of tea. He was handsome, in other words, but knew it, and that was a bit of a fatal flaw for him.

"This is a family pool," I said after he had kissed me a second time.

His hand had roamed a little under the water. Not inappropriately, just exploring.

"We could go someplace where it isn't so public."

"Is that so?"

"It is so."

"And what would we do in this not-so-public place?"

He kissed me again.

I didn't stop it. But I didn't encourage it exactly, either.

Several thoughts: *How much had I had to drink? How drunk was I? How much did I trust this Peter character? Where was Amy?*

And what about Jack?

Well, what about Jack? I asked myself. Jack wasn't precisely in my calculations at the moment. He wasn't in my calculations when Peter leaned forward and kissed me again, and this time his hands grew bolder, and I felt myself caving in a little, drunk, warm, and he *was* cute. Definitely cute, but full of himself, full of that young guy conceit that says he can get pretty much what he likes, and plenty of it, and I told myself I would not reward such a jerk, but then his hands brushed over me and the water was warm and I asked myself, *Why not, why not, why not? What am I waiting for?*

Amy arrived just in time.

"And what's going on here, you little lovebirds?"

She had two boys in tow. She dropped her towel without ceremony and climbed into the hot tub. The two other boys, Jeff and Munchie, climbed in after her. Munchie smiled a druggie smile. He was the chief pot smoker, apparently, because most of the jokes surrounding him had been about weed. His smile was wifty.

Jeff, who was sharp featured and muscular, wiggled his eyebrows at us.

"Orgy," he said. "Who's in?"

"Definitely," Munchie said. "Orgy for sure."

"Dream, you little twits," Amy said.

Munchie smiled at her. Jeff sank into the water up to his nostrils.

Peter's hand brushed my thigh underwater.

"Heather and I were thinking about heading out," Peter said. "Weren't we, Heather?"

I tried to clear my head. Had we said anything like that? I understood how he could come to that conclusion, but I wasn't sure that we had confirmed anything between us, not in the least, and I shook my head softly.

"Not sure we said that," I said. "No promises made."

Peter's hand brushed my back and the side of my ass.

"You guys are going to go have sex," Munchie said. "You lucky bastards."

"Shut up, Munchie," Jeff said.

"But they are. Look at them! They got that low eyelid thing going. Like they're all smoky and ready and hot and bothered."

Peter smiled. It was a guy-to-guy smile, and I didn't particularly like it.

"Don't count your eggs before your chickens," I said.

Which was not the correct phrase. I tried to edit the comment, but I couldn't remember how it went.

Peter smiled some more. Jeff popped higher in the water.

"We need more to drink," he said.

"And more to smoke," Munchie said.

Peter stood and reached for my hand.

He had an erection. He had folded it up under his waistband, but it was still obvious.

"Ready?" he asked.

I didn't feel ready.

"Let's just hang for a while," I said.

Peter smiled. He reached down for my hand again.

"Come on," he said.

"I'm going to hang for a while," I said. "Just sit down. We're having a nice time."

He reached for my hand again.

And that's when Amy punched him.

She punched him so quickly, so unhesitatingly, that it stunned everyone.

One second she had been half-submerged, watching, joking with the puppies, and the next she had crossed the diameter of the hot tub, had surged up in the water like a great white shark

beheading a seal, and she punched Peter on the chest with a force
that knocked him to a sitting position on the side of the hot tub.

"Not now means not fucking now, douche bag!"

She screamed it. Even after she stopped, her voice reverberated
around the natatorium. Everything, every little thing, went silent.

"You saw us leave the bar," Amy said. "Alfred and me. Or is it *I*?
No, it's *me*, right? But do you remember him? I picked him up,
and he had those horrible, long fingers."

"Of course I remember him," Constance said. "So does Heather."

I nodded. We sat at a butcher-block table in the small kitchen
area of our condo. Constance had made us a salad with a side of
mac 'n' cheese. We were done drinking. Amy sipped tea. We all
wore pajamas. I felt exhausted and hungover and foolish. I had a
bottle of water in front of me. The mention of Peter, the afternoon
hot tub punch, had started Amy talking about Alfred of Amsterdam. She knew more about what had happened with Alfred now.
Therapy had brought things to light.

"Anyhow," she continued, "we went back toward his apartment, or something, and we stopped along the way and ate a
brownie that he had with him. I mean, this brownie kicked my
ass. I have never felt so high in my life. Added to that was all the
pot and booze we had had that night, and I was stretched out."

"Do you think he extra doped the brownie?" I asked.

She shrugged.

"Hard to say. He might have. Or maybe it's just really strong
stuff. I ate too much of it, because, well, that's what I do. That's
what I've done all my life. Amy can do it because she's Amy! You
know the deal. It's my badass, self-imposed identity. That's some-

thing, by the way, that Tabitha, my therapist, is helping me deal with. She says I don't always have to lead the charge. That came as a news flash to me."

She sipped her tea. She looked radiant sitting in the stupid little kitchenette, her hair wild as always, her gray-green eyes slicing through everything around her.

"So I don't want to give all the gory details, but we started making out, and then he said, 'Here's a friend's boat,' or something, and we climbed down onto it, and I had more or less made up my mind not to be Alfred's ho, when suddenly I couldn't stand up straight. That's about all I remember with any accuracy. You know the rest of the story almost as well as I do. My stuff was gone. He wanted to rip me off. That's why he hung out with us. With me, anyway."

Her eyes did not tear. She sipped her tea thoughtfully, almost, it seemed, astonished that this thing had happened to her and that, at last, we all knew the final details.

"It had to be the brownie, right?" Constance asked after a moment had passed.

Constance, of course, would want real, demonstrable reasons. I wasn't sure Amy believed in those kinds of answers. Not about this.

"I think so. It tasted chemical, but who knows? Something knocked me out. I'll say this for Alfred. He didn't do anything to me. I'm pretty sure about that. My clothes were in place, no sign of rape. He was a gentleman about all that."

Constance reached across the table and held Amy's hand. Amy nodded.

"Well, come on, you both wondered. I'm solid that he didn't molest me that way. It's a thing. It happened. No real repercussions except the mental part. And maybe even that was good, because it made me start asking some serious questions. Like, what the fuck was I doing with a guy I had just met at some ridiculous hour walking around a city I didn't begin to know?"

"It was our fault," Constance said. "We shouldn't have let you go. I hate that we let you go."

"Do you really think you could have stopped me? Haven't you both wanted to say I should cool down a little with the whole men thing? I know you have. I wasn't able to listen at that point. Now, it's different."

"And that's why you punched Peter," I said, stating the obvious.

"And that's why I punched Peter, stupid-ass little puppy. It's all about ladies' choice for me. If the woman isn't into it, then nothing is going on. Not while I'm around. Sorry if I overreacted. He seemed like he was pushing it. You didn't seem ready, Heather."

"I don't know what I was, honestly. I can't pretend I wasn't thinking about it."

"Well, maybe I overreacted. I don't know. But I'd rather err on the side of caution, right? You can always pick up with Peter. With any Peter."

She finished her tea and went to the sink and rinsed out the cup. Then she came back and sat down again.

"That's it. That's the story," she said.

"There had to be something in the brownie," Constance insisted. "I've seen you party, Amy, and nothing can bring you down."

"Well, something did. Something definitely did. The truth is, there had to be something in me to put myself in that position. You can't imagine Ellie Pearson walking the streets of Amsterdam with a vampire like Alfred, can you?"

Ellie Pearson was the most goody-goody girl at Amherst College. We always used her as a counterpoint to whatever mischief we had engaged in.

"No, Ellie Pearson wouldn't have been walking around the streets of Amsterdam late at night with Alfred," I conceded.

"So the fault was in me," Amy concluded. "Nice to think otherwise, and I hate Alfred's guts and would stab him in an instant if I could, but I take my share of the blame. You know what I think about a lot, though? I think about the fact that he didn't cover me. That he didn't have enough kindness toward me that he would at least put something over me. I hate thinking another human being could treat me like that. I don't know what he would have had on the boat to cover me with, but it would have made it a little more bearable to think back to. It's probably just an absurd quirk of mine. I wanted to have a blanket over me and stay home from school, I guess."

She reached across the table and squeezed our hands.

"I'm okay," she said. "I am. Just don't make a big deal of it, okay? Don't ignore it and pretend it didn't happen, and don't get a worried look on your face every time the story comes up. It's a fact of my life now, and it does no good to try to pretend anything about it. You with me?"

We nodded.

"I probably should apologize to Peter, though," she said.

"Fuck no," Constance said.

Coming from her, the word was such a shock that Amy and I both laughed.

"He had a boner when he stood up," I said. "He had it tucked into his waistband."

"Poor little idiot," Amy said. "He thought he was getting some."

"Well, the thought had crossed my mind, I admit. Okay, I

have to sleep," I said. "I'm beat. I'm not used to drinking beer in the middle of the day."

I hugged them both. Later, I heard Constance talking to Amy about her wedding plans. I liked hearing their voices in the darkness.

Paris

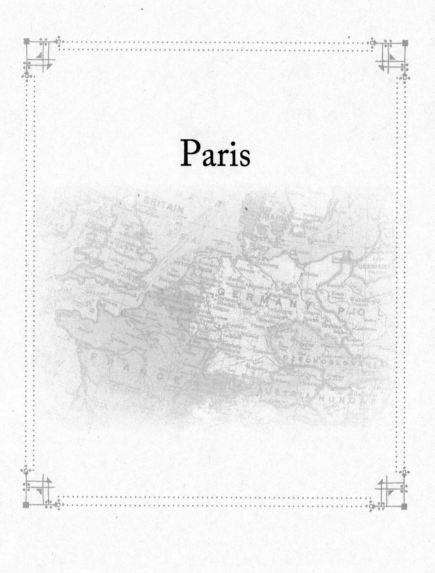

48

Paris again. Paris in spring. Paris when the chestnuts are in bloom. Paris when the Seine runs at its fullest, and when the cafés, sleepy from winter, begin to shed their weight and heaviness and waiters in white aprons crank up their awnings to let the new sunshine find their customers. Countless brooms whisk the cobblestones awake, and the oxidized roofs shimmer green as pond moss, and the tulips, thousands of tulips, surprise you with a wink of color and a promise of warmth. Women find clothes deep in their closets and pull them out, unsure, because the weather can still change, still turn chilly, but it is worth the risk to wear something you love, and hats suddenly appear, fantastic hats, and your eye is pulled this way and that because it is Paris and it is spring and you are young.

In the days before the wedding, Constance is in love, about to be a bride, and she brings to everything such loveliness, such grace, that you think, *This is how weddings should be, all weddings,* and Raef, handsome Raef, dotes on Constance and does not leave her side, not for a second, not for a breath, and you wonder how this has happened, how Constance, the pale beauty on a Schwinn bicycle pedaling around a college campus less than a year before, has the maturity and wisdom to preside over these charming festivities, her sheepherder in her thrall. She strikes the perfect tone at each event, at the tea with the mothers as they meet for the first time, at the shops when ordering the last of the food for the ceremony, at the florist's when she speaks in her eloquent French, bending beside the stout proprietress over flats of violets to smell the shy fragrance—who knew studying French would truly be useful in the end?—so that she herself at times seems a new growth, not a flower, but a sedge, a six-sided grass that arrives slowly and calmly in time at the edge of a meadow and whose beauty one must stop to appreciate. You stand beside her, a bridesmaid, and watch her prepare herself to love and to honor and to hold, and tears fill your eyes a thousand times, and Constance, sweet Constance, brings you and Amy to Notre Dame, where she kneels before her favorite statue of Mary and prays, not to God, maybe, not to any entity, but to the commitment she is making, to the desire to be good and kind in her marriage, to her promise to forsake all others and to become one flesh with the man she adores.

A hundred instances of perfection, small, delicate tones that only Paris can offer. And Hemingway, your Hemingway, lived here in deep love with his Hadley, and you hate the bastard for leaving her, as Jack left you, and you love him for feeling life so deeply, as Jack also felt life deeply, and you feel fluttery and wild and happy being in this wedding, being beside your friends, waiting for the day. In Paris. Always in Paris.

. . .

In the three days before the wedding, I tried my best not to be haunted by Jack. I hated that I thought of him, that I placed him beside me, mentally, a thousand thousand times; I hated that Constance had to give a single thought to my position, my situation, because she had a billion details to occupy her, and she didn't need to concern herself with my mental state. When we put up at the Hotel Sampson, a beautiful Edwardian building on the outskirts of the seventh arrondissement—the same arrondissement that contained the Eiffel Tower—I found myself entertaining the possibility that Jack might attend the wedding. I mentioned the thought to no one, because I understood, in a deep part of me, that it was my own invention. No one had spoken of Jack to me at all. My daydream was so pitiful, so embarrassing, that, if anything, I went overboard attempting to be the life of the party to compensate for my moody dream-state. Without meaning to, I came perilously close to being "that" wedding girl—the girl ready to do shots with the boy side of the wedding, to stay up and find a new bar in the center of Paris—how I loved being able to guide people in Paris!—the girl who sometimes looked a little rumpled, a little too partied up, a tad too tarty. I *knew* what I was doing, but I almost couldn't stop myself from doing it. I felt as if I stood outside myself—a ridiculous image, I know—to watch this crazy girl behaving as if she belonged in Sheboygan, not Paris.

Besides, who needed Jack? That's what I wanted to prove to anyone who cared to notice.

Long before the wedding date, Constance had mentioned a friend of Raef's who would be my partner in the wedding party, and that, nearly as soon as we landed, became a standing joke. His name was Xavier Box, an absurd name that made Amy and me laugh whenever we spoke it aloud. He was a tall, severe-looking

Australian, with blond hair and eyes so blue they seemed made of ice, whose angular appearance belied the sweetness underneath his exterior. One of the ridiculous side notes of the wedding— everything was graceful, everything was beautiful because of Constance, but still it was a wedding and there was plenty of wine—was Xavier's ability to speak something he called "sheep talk." Apparently, it was a thing in Australia—although I had never heard it from Raef—and it involved saying everything in a bleating voice that was, supposedly, the stuttering speech of a sheep. It made no sense whatsoever and was not in the least funny, except that Xavier, maybe six foot three and as thin as a greyhound, used it so often that it became funny despite its chunkiness. Pretty soon everyone had a sheep talk voice, so that, if you wanted a drink, you might say, "May I have a drinnnnnkkkkk?" with the tail of the sentence going up like the voice of a baby lamb calling for its mom. Who knows why things like that become funny, but it did, and it became the wavering lament that wove through the wedding despite Constance's ethereal beauty.

Xavier Box was the master of sheep talk—partially because he came from Australia but also because he looked a little goatish— and as partners in the wedding, we became adept at playing off each other. I spoke sheep well, and when we stood to say our toasts at the groom's dinner held in a nearby pension (think checked tablecloths and grumpy waiters and wine bottles with straw bottoms) the night before the wedding, both of us managed to slip in a sheepish phrase. I said something like, *Raef is the beeeessstttttttttttt man in the world*, and Xavier topped me by saying, *You beeeeeeetttttttttt.*

It was funny. It made everyone laugh. We almost came across as a couple.

As I sat and watched Xavier finish his speech, Amy leaned over and told me I should sleep with him.

"I am not sleeping with a man who speaks sheep talk," I whispered to her. "Are you nuts?"

"You need to get back in the game, sister. You're going a little loopy. Constance says all you do is work and read."

"He's way cute in a sort of sheep way, but he's not my type. I do more than that, by the way."

"What exactly is your type? I'm looking around, and I'm not seeing him. You no longer have a type, Heather. You have an ice cream flavor that you like to eat late at night by yourself, but no boy type anymore."

"You don't have a type around here, either, Amy."

"When has that ever mattered to me? Sleep with Xavier Box. You're snakebit. You need to shake things up."

We both had had too much to drink. It wasn't a great line of conversation. Absurdly, I kept flashing my eyes at the door, half expecting Jack to show up. I had no idea what I would say to him if he did show up, or what I would do, but the idea of his potential arrival drove me slightly insane. It felt a little like anticipating a surprise party on your birthday, half hoping it doesn't materialize, the other half wondering if this or that person wasn't slipping off to buy a cake. After all, Jack could be impetuous. He liked to be dramatic.

I still hovered in the *no-Jack-land* of speculation when a woman holding a baby sat down beside me. I had seen the woman over the last few days, had even been introduced, but I couldn't recall her name. She had auburn hair with a wide, broom-like bang cut straight across her forehead. She looked to be in her midthirties, a Mom-a-saurus in training, and she smelled of lemon and baby powder. She was from Raef's side of the wedding, and when she spoke she had a thick, adorable Australian accent.

"Will you hold him?" she asked, extending the baby to me. "I need to run and pee. I won't be a minute. It's much easier without bringing him along."

"Of course," I said, taking the baby and lifting him into my lap. "What's his name?"

"Johnny."

"Hello, Johnny."

Before I could ask any more, the woman slipped away. I had never been super comfortable with babies, but this one, I had to admit, was cuter than a box of puppies. He had a stout little body and beautiful eyelashes, and when I danced him on my legs, he smiled and gurgled and reached out for my hair. He couldn't have been more than a few months old. He wore a sailor-type outfit, with a blue blouse and white shorts and cotton socks on his tiny feet.

"You notice she didn't give him to me," Amy said, leaning over to look at Johnny, putting her finger in his tiny fist. "What a cutie pie."

"What a little man. What a perfect gentleman."

"He looks serious. He looks quite self-possessed."

Then Amy was called away, and I found myself, strangely, sitting alone with Johnny. Xavier had gone off to the bar, and most of the party had gotten up to stretch its legs, and I realized Johnny and I had the space to ourselves. I danced him on my lap, and he stared at me, apparently not for or against our association, and for an absurd ten count, I thought, *Now is when I want Jack to walk in.* I wanted him to see me with this gorgeous child, my maternal impulses on full display, though why I thought that would be attractive to Jack I couldn't say. We had never even talked about children. I realized, thinking about it, that Jack was a virus that I couldn't shake. I had officially gone crazy.

Then all of that passed away, and I was left with Johnny, with his beautiful eyes staring into mine, with the simple fact of his personhood arresting me. He was not a "baby," not a "rug rat," but was, instead, a perfect little human, a sweet, adorable child who gazed at me to discover what he could trust. I had never experienced a moment like that with a baby before. Our eyes rested on each other for a long time.

I lifted him carefully into my arms and held him against my chest. I felt close to crying.

"Hi, Johnny," I whispered. "You're a beautiful, beautiful boy. You're a sweet little boy, aren't you? How precious are you?"

I put my nose against his skin, the back of his neck. He smelled like the powder that his mother wore and also of that ineffable baby smell that was like no other smell on earth.

"Oh, he's taking to you," his mom said on her return. She popped into the chair beside us. "He doesn't normally let himself be held by strangers. You must have a good, solid character for a child to trust you so easily."

"I feel like I've known Johnny for a thousand years."

"Careful on," the woman said. "That's the way it starts. Next thing you'll be married to a bloke and have six kittens to care for."

"Do you have six children?" I asked, shocked at the possibility. Maybe, I thought, I had misunderstood this woman.

"No, no, no, just Johnny here. But he's enough. He keeps me busy, but he's a lamb, as you can see."

"He's a beautiful boy."

"You know, I had one like yours," she said. "A love, I mean. One that went away."

I looked at her over Johnny's soft shoulder. Was my story that well known among the wedding party? It embarrassed me to think it might be. Did people say, "Gee, there goes Heather, who once had a man she loved leave her at the Paris airport?" Was that my legend at this wedding? I supposed it had to be for the woman to know my story. I imagined it was the capsule explanation: *Oh, that woman next to Xavier Box, that's Heather, her boyfriend was a friend of Raef's, and he left her at the airport in Paris*. It was a shorthand means of identification. *There's Raef's uncle, and Constance's cousin, and, oh, her, she's the one who lost the boyfriend.*

"Excuse me?" I asked.

"Oh, I know. It's painful. Mine was a sailor. He took parties out to the Whitsunday Islands. Ran them over to the Great Barrier if they liked. Oh, he loved being at sea. I should have learned from that, of course, but I ignored it. Ever notice how women who see almost everything can ignore the biggest clues imaginable? It's always baffled me."

I held Johnny closer. I heard his breathing next to my ear.

"People say you get over it, but you don't. Not those kinds of men. They leave scars. I only mention it because I can't talk about it to anyone else. It's a taboo subject, you see? And I'm married. Happily so, honestly. But not a day goes by that I don't think of my lost sailor."

"I'm not sure—"

"I know, I know. It's still raw. It will be for a long time, believe me. I actually felt sometimes as if I had been burned. It felt like my skin had to regrow around these horrible burns. I don't mean that as a metaphor, either. It's more painful than any metaphor could be. *Great love inevitably carries with it great loss.* That's something I read. I've held it close to me ever since. I remind myself of it now and then. In our beginning is our end."

Then she reached over and held my hand.

I almost pulled my hand away. I didn't know her name. I didn't know the first thing about her, honestly. She leaned closer to me and put her lips somewhere near my ear. It was as if she wanted to confide the most perfect secret to Johnny and to me. We formed a conspiratorial triangle.

"It will heal in time," she whispered. "Not entirely. It never goes away entirely, but you will go on, I promise. And Johnny's a great love, too, so you see? More comes along, and it will; it will for you, too. It's probably not fair to my husband to remember the sailor in such a way, but I do remember him, and it would be a lie to say I didn't. Don't ever think you're alone in this. I've met many women who have had the great love walk away. You'll see him all your life—at a bar, in an airport. Something will remind you, and it's spark and flint again."

She smiled at me. Her eyes looked soft and kind and tired. Then she reached for Johnny and lifted him to her. I held on to his tiny fist until she smiled again and stood.

"Thank you for watching him," she said. "You have a good heart, I bet."

"Good-bye, Johnny."

She nodded and lifted him against her shoulder. Then she made her way through the scattered chairs, Johnny's tiny face like a pale moon riding against her neck.

49

Constance's parents knew the Jeffersons, part of the diplomatic mission in France, and it was at their temporary estate that Constance got married. It was a glorious location, with sumptuous grounds and a large, yellowish Georgian mansion made of pale stone anchoring the land at the head of a white gravel circular drive. Paul Jefferson had been a college roommate with Constance's dad, Billy, and the idea that a roommate would be so kind to a roommate's daughter—to host a wedding, albeit a small wedding—seemed somehow to confirm something about our own friendships, we three. We would do the same for our college chums, we knew, and when Mrs. Jefferson, Gloria, led us upstairs to help Constance dress in the late morning on a perfect April Saturday, she opened the French doors communicating to the spacious grounds below, and for a moment we all stood on the balcony and watched as men in blue coveralls set up chairs and the florist misted the violets that Constance had chosen to commemorate the day.

"It's so beautiful," Constance said. "I can't thank you enough, Gloria. It's what I've always dreamed."

"Oh, I've always wanted a wedding here," Gloria said. "I've just had sons, I'm sorry to say, and they refuse to oblige me. Sons may be a little easier in some ways, but they're not nearly as much fun."

She was a tall brunette, with a tight head of hair and wide, capable shoulders. She had been a swimmer, a breaststroker, and she had met her husband, Paul, at the Olympic trials one late winter. She still possessed an athletic body, and it did not surprise me when Constance's mother, Gail, told us that Gloria swam every day to keep her form.

Constance turned and hugged her. Constance, beautiful Constance.

True to her nature, Constance did not want a makeup person or a hairstylist. She had selected her dress for its simplicity. It was a white shift, tea length, with a sheer lace bodice, and she wore white ballet slippers. When she stood in front of the floor-length mirror, her hands trembling slightly as they held her bouquet of baby's breath and irises, she looked as perfect as a bride could be. Her mother had gone out of the room to find her seat, and we stood behind Constance, and she said nothing but moved her eyes from each of us to the next. Through the window we heard people assembling, and we heard the music—a jazz quartet, naturally, for Raef—begin to play lightly in the background, and Constance turned to us and spoke.

"Remind me in the years to come how happy I was in this moment," she said to us. "Remember it for me in case I ever forget. Never let me color it with any other emotion. Whatever happens between Raef and me, this moment is a *true*, I know it in my heart, and I'm asking you to know it, too."

"I promise," I said, and so did Amy.

Then it was time. Gloria came in and smiled at us.

"We're ready," she said simply.

Amy and I walked down the aisle together. Constance did not want the bridal march to be a long, drawn-out affair. She came down the aisle shortly after we did. She clung to her father's arm, and she kept her eyes on Raef. Raef stood near Mr. Jefferson, Paul, who had been asked to preside over the ceremony.

The jazz quartet did not play when Constance came down the aisle. Instead she walked to a recording of Yo-Yo Ma playing the music of Ennio Morricone. The delicate sounds came from all around us. Constance, I knew, loved the cello and loved Yo-Yo Ma more than nearly anything else in the world. She owned all his recordings and played them often in her apartment at school and sometimes, when she was a little tipsy, she made everyone stop and listen and marvel to the beauty of his haunting music before letting us resume our drunkenness.

Constance walked down the aisle gently, sweetly, her smile passing over each person there and warming whichever person it fell on. At the altar, she kissed her father, and they had a tender moment where he whispered something to her, then he kissed her again. She went to her mother and kissed her. Then she gave her hand to Raef, and for a moment nothing else mattered in the world.

Xavier Box asked me to dance. We were well into the reception, and we had both had plenty to drink. His tie had come loose; his hair stood up like a shoeshine brush turned upside down. His eyes glittered with moisture, not from emotion but from the straight line of booze he had been drinking. I had kicked off my shoes and liked walking on the smooth, slippery wood of the dance floor. I felt . . . good. Pretty darn good. I had searched all over for Johnny and his mom, but I hadn't caught sight of them.

I hadn't caught sight of Jack, either, but that was another thing altogether.

Remarkably, Xavier was one of those guys who could actually swing dance.

And he wasn't show-offy about it, either. He grabbed my right wrist and shot it to the side, and I spun and he caught me around the waist, bent me back a little, then shot me out the other way. I felt like a yo-yo. Like a Yo-Yo Ma. Like a paper party horn, rolling out with a wheezy blast, then rolling up again. His icy blue eyes followed me everywhere, and I was aware of him being kind of cute, kind of honestly cute, and I wondered, in a distant part of my brain—as I went shooting off again with the whiplash of his arm—why I was so resistant to his charms. Why was I so resistant to every man's charms for the past nine or ten months? It was useless and pointless, and so when Xavier pulled me back in and held me close, I thought, *Hmmmm*. I thought double *hmmmm*.

When I happened to look over at the head table, I saw Amy nodding happily at me. She had obviously given her blessing to whatever was going to happen between Xavier and me.

"Where did you learn to dance like that?" I asked Xavier when we finished. "You're really very good."

He put his arm around my waist and led me off the dance floor. Was this it, then? Did I lean into him, swing my hair a little, look up into his polar-blue eyes with a smile and a come-hither glance? I felt out of practice. It felt wooden and absurd. It felt artificial and false. I told myself not to have another drink. I told myself another drink would cloud things horribly.

"Oh, round about," he said, escorting me to the bar. "My mother taught me some of it in our kitchen. She loved to dance, my mother did. We had dance parties to liven things up when my father was away on business, and he was away a good deal. My sisters had lessons, and they could be quite severe teachers. They bullied me into it, but I'm glad they did."

"The lessons took."

"I'll be sure to tell them."

Then we exchanged a little look. It wasn't *that* look, but it was a look. I broke it off with difficulty.

"I'm going to run to the loo," I said, using a sheep riff . . . *looooo*. "Be right back."

"Okay, don't be too long. You'll be missed."

I went to find Amy.

"Bridesmaids are *supposed* to get laid at weddings!" Amy said when I found her and told her about my confusion over Xavier. She held a drink in her hand, her hair slightly mussed from dancing with one of Raef's many cousins. They had found her early in the reception and kept her moving. "I mean, isn't that the point of dolling everyone up? Everyone's here to get a little something. Heather, you're not a nun!"

"Oh, good grief, Amy. I never said I was a nun."

"It's a decision you don't have to make right now. You're not a Roman emperor giving a thumbs-up or -down. You could just go with it and see where it takes you."

"I know where it will take me, Amy. That's the point."

"I wish I had someone around here! I wish I had someone to decide about."

"Those cousins would oblige you," I said. "The ones you've been dancing with."

"Wouldn't they ever? Horny little toads. Australian boys have a lot of energy. I'll give them that. But I don't see any men here. Not eligible men. Men at weddings are either too young or too old. Otherwise, they're married themselves."

"You're not helping me a damn bit with the Xavier question," I said. "He's honestly not my type."

"What is your type? Never mind, I know, I know. Jack. Yes, okay, Jack is your type. I get it. But Jack took off for the hills, honey. Jack is doing his boy walkabout or whatever the hell he thinks he's doing. He's a great guy, I like him a lot, but he's no longer around. Poof. He disappeared. That woman who did massage on me always said to get over a man, get under a man."

"You're horrible, Amy. That's obscene."

She smiled. She wiggled her eyebrows. She had had a lot to drink, I realized. But then she waxed philosophical.

"Here's the thing. If you sleep with Xavier, you'll wake up with a headache and probably the same heartache. Plus, you run the risk of him thinking you hit it off, so he will call and want to talk, and every time you hear the phone ring, you will be hurt that it's not Jack."

"I thought you wanted me to sleep with him!"

"Just *someone*, Heather. I want you to return to life. You can sleep with anyone you like, of course, but I don't want you to hold that hurt, that Jack stuff, so close to you anymore. It's time to let some of it go. I know it's hard, honey, but you need to let it slip away."

I nodded. My eyes filled. She put her arm through mine. We stood for a while and didn't talk. It was a gorgeous early evening. I wondered if I should go find Xavier. I wondered if I should go to the loo. I felt all sixes and sevens, as my mother used to say when she was out of sorts.

We were still standing there when Raef came by.

"I want to have a dance with you, Heather," he said. "Would you dance with the groom?"

"I'd be flattered."

"What am I? Swiss cheese?" Amy asked, releasing my arm.

"You're down the road. Just hold your horses."

Amy grumbled and went off. I stood with Raef.

"I'd love to dance with you, Raef," I said.

"I'm not much of a dancer. Not like my friend Xavier."

"Xavier has many talents, it seems."

"Oh, you don't know half of them. Do you like him?"

"I do. I like him a lot. He's a character."

"He's actually quite a good man. We've been friends a long time. Since boyhood, really. You two would make a nice couple."

"Are you in the matchmaking game now, Raef?"

"I've become an expert now that I'm married. Didn't you know? Married people always know exactly what single people should do, who they should see, how they should live."

He smiled and held out his arms, and I stepped into them. I realized, moving close to him and beginning to step after his lead, that I was enormously fond of Raef.

"You know that you have the best girl in the whole world," I said, finding it the tiniest bit strange to dance with my friend's husband. Her *husband*! "She's like a light that the world needs."

"Yes, I do know that. That's a good way to put it. I'm a lucky man."

"She's even more beautiful than you might know, Raef. Her beauty touches everything. Her love and feeling for beauty. I don't know anyone else like her, honestly."

He nodded. We danced clockwise around the floor, but his

body felt tight and nervous. I almost spoke to ask him if he was all right, when he leaned close and whispered into my ear. He gave me the real reason he had asked me to dance.

"I wanted to talk to you about Jack," he said. "Our Jack. Your Jack Vermont. I thought on this day of all days I might be given permission to speak."

He pushed me away a little so he could look me eye to eye. I felt my heart drop to the ground. He had kind, warm eyes. The band played a nice, gentle beat that seemed out of keeping with the expression on Raef's face.

"Is it okay if I talk a little about Jack?" he asked. "I need to say something, and I've been holding on to it too long."

I nodded. My body felt as if it had lost its bones.

"Go ahead."

"First, I have to ask for your understanding, and maybe your forgiveness. I made a promise to Jack that I would not speak of this matter to you. I've never mentioned it to Constance, either. No one in the world knows except Jack and me and his parents. He confided it in me."

"What is it, Raef? Tell me. You sound terribly formal."

"Sorry. I don't mean to be. I feel funny about saying anything at all."

"Go ahead and tell me."

The music shifted time and slowed to a soft, brushy beat. We danced on the parquet floor. I was conscious of every detail: the music, the firmness of the floor, Raef's handsomeness, the color and texture of his suit, my own gown, tea length, touching the skin beneath my knee. Raef seemed to be caught on what he needed to say. He started to speak, then stopped.

"What is it, Raef?" I asked again. "Please tell me."

He took a deep breath, seemed to think one last time if he had made the correct choice to tell me, then spoke softly.

"That day in Paris, here—I should say, *here* in Paris—do you remember that day?"

"Which day, Raef?"

"The one when Jack and I disappeared for a day. We played it off. We tried to make it mysterious. I think you and Constance went to Notre Dame to see the Mary statues. That's where she always likes to go."

"Yes, of course, yes, I remember it. Jack never explained where he went. We didn't press it, because we thought maybe you were planning a surprise of some sort. We didn't want to spoil things."

He nodded. My recollection apparently conformed to his.

"That's just the thing. That day when Jack and I went off on a mysterious mission and we joked about it and refused to tell you two about what we were up to . . . that day we went to a hospital."

"What hospital?" I managed. "What are you saying, Raef?"

"I don't even remember the name, Heather. Saint Boniface, I think. It was on the outskirts of Paris. Jack didn't tell me everything, but he has a condition of some sort. Something he needed to check on, I guess. He didn't explain the details. He wanted me along because my French was better than his."

"He's ill? Are you telling me he's ill?"

Raef looked carefully at me. I saw how much it pained him to break Jack's confidence, how much it pained him to injure me. Part of me held sympathy for Raef's position, but another part of me, a wild, feral side, wanted to jump at his mouth and pull it apart and swim down to wherever the words were kept and then dig through them until I found what I required. He could not speak quickly enough; he could not break the news rapidly enough to satisfy me. But I held on and let him speak. I did not want to frighten him off or cut short his explanation by rushing at him.

"I think Jack's symptoms had reappeared. He was sick before he came to Europe. I think that's it. He never came right out and explained everything. I can't say whether or not that was the reason he decided not to go home with you, but I've always thought it was. It's the only explanation that makes sense. I reckon he wanted you to think poorly of him, to let him go, because whatever he found out at the hospital maybe confirmed something he suspected. I don't know the timing on all this, but he had to wait for some test results to come in. That's what he told me."

"But Jack wasn't sick," I said, though now doubt had begun to spill into my brain. "He told me about his friend Tom, but he never—"

"It wasn't Tom. There was no one named Tom, Heather."

"His friend. A man he worked with. What are saying, Raef?"

"There was no friend named Tom. Sometimes he referred to his condition as 'old Tom.' He turned it into a joke. He'd say things like, 'Old Tom's not letting me sleep.' I don't know where he dreamed that up, but that was the name he used."

"I can't understand what you're saying to me, Raef. I hear the words, but they don't add up."

"Tom was something he made up so that he could talk about the need to experience everything without going into the exact reason. He gave the illness to an imaginary friend. Maybe it wasn't fair. I don't know. He didn't want people to pity him. He didn't want to be treated differently, to answer all the questions his condition would raise. I'm sorry, Heather. I've wanted to tell you many times, but I can't stand by and see you suffer any longer."

I couldn't think. A thousand questions flooded into my brain.

It was the one explanation that fit all the various questions and objections. Hearing Raef's confession, tiny pieces began clicking together.

"He's sick, then?" I asked, remembering, remembering every word, every glance and gesture that shed any light on Jack's condition. "Is that what you're telling me, Raef? Please, I need to know."

Raef nodded, then he made a face to indicate he didn't know what Jack had intended. He couldn't say because he truly didn't know. The music stopped. We stood for a moment facing each other.

"I don't know if it's true or not. I don't know if he's sick," Raef said. "I don't know what it means, even, but it was important to Jack. That day, I mean, and the visit to the hospital. It would explain why he disappeared. He didn't want to be a burden to you, and the only way he could get a distance, so to speak, was to disappear entirely. And probably to make you hate him in the bargain."

"Are you serious, Raef? Are you kidding me? This is just too much."

"Please forgive me, Heather. I don't even know if I should be saying anything now. I have divided loyalty on this. Jack made me give him my word, and I did, and now I'm violating that. I couldn't hold it as a secret anymore and watch you go through it over and over."

We stood looking at each other. He reached and took my hands in his.

"You have suffered, haven't you?"

"Yes. Yes, I have."

"I'm sorry, Heather. I wish I had more to tell you."

"Was it cancer? Did his symptoms return? Is that why he went to the hospital? Was he Tom all this time?"

"I don't know. I think it was leukemia. Probably whatever symptoms he attributed to Tom actually belonged to him. Yes, probably that."

Then he was called away by one of Constance's cousins. Cake to cut, something. Raef dropped my hands slowly, still holding my eyes with his. He didn't leave, though.

"Let me find Amy," he said. "Let her sit with you awhile until you've had a chance to digest all this."

I shook my head. I couldn't stand to think of talking with anyone. Not now.

"You should take a minute to absorb this. A lot of minutes, actually. I'm sorry, Heather. I hope you don't think I was cruel to withhold this information. It was Jack's story to tell, not mine. That's what I told myself. Then I saw you dancing with Xavier, and I saw that you were unhappy, and I knew I had to say something."

"I'm glad you did. Thank you."

"I know Jack pretty well, Heather. He loved you. He told me that more than once. He refused to be the sick invalid with you. He wouldn't want to put that on you. That's how I put it together, anyway."

"No," I agreed, "Jack wouldn't want that."

Raef reached over and hugged me. He hugged me hard. Then he held me by the shoulders and looked directly at me.

"Are you going to be okay?"

"Sure."

"I don't believe you. Take a minute, though, please. Take some time to get your mind around it. I feel terrible springing it on you like this."

"It's okay, Raef. Go ahead. You need to cut some cake. I'm all right. In some ways, I'm better now. You were right to tell me."

"I don't know, Heather. I hope I didn't make a mistake in telling you," he said, and then one of his cousins came over and insisted he come along. She grabbed him by the hand and dragged him away. I stood and watched and felt that I might lift and float away like the smoke of a candle drifting upward a moment after it dies as a flame.

50

....

At two in the morning, I went to find the Esche, the tree we
had planted together in the Jardin du Luxembourg.

I brought along a fork from the hotel. To dig. To defend myself. Because I had nothing else.

I could not think or speak or plan in a linear way. I took a cab
from the reception. Amy had gone to bed. Constance and Raef
had left on their *lune de miel*. Their month of honey. Their married
life. I had told no one what Raef had told me.

The cab driver was from Burkina Faso, Africa. He wore a black,
red, and green hat swollen with his dreadlocks beneath. I counted
six pine tree car fresheners dangling from the rearview mirror.
According to his license, his name was Bormo. Zungo, Bormo. He
looked at me in the mirror whenever we stopped.

"You okay, miss?" he asked in French.

I nodded.

He studied me.

"You sure?" he asked.

I nodded again.

"It's late to be around the park," he said. "The *jardin* is better during the day."

I nodded.

He pulled forward when the light changed. We drove a long time in silence. His eyes checked on me frequently in the rearview mirror.

"This is not the best place," Bormo said when he pulled to the curb outside the *jardin* and flicked off the register. "Forty-seven euros. It can be dangerous at this time of night."

He turned around in his seat so he could speak to me directly.

"It would be my honor to take you for coffee . . . to bring you someplace with lights."

"I'm fine," I said, paying him. "*Ça va.*"

He took the money. I gave him an extra twenty euros. One of the good things about working tirelessly and having no social life was that I always found money in my pockets. He took the twenty euros and slid them into the brim of his lumpy hat.

"It's very late," he said. "You were in a nice hotel, and now . . . it's not good out here."

I smiled and climbed out of the cab. Then I stood for a time facing the iron gate of the Jardin du Luxembourg. Bormo pulled away from the curb.

He was correct about everything.

The *jardin* was better during the day.

I had no light except the flashlight on my cell phone. Park lights did not quite illuminate the bed where the Esche was located. It grew in a shadow. It took me surprisingly little time to recall precisely where the tree lived.

I used the fork to dig in the soil. The soil was damp and cold.

You can visit it whenever you come to Paris. Everything else in the world will go along, sometimes failing, sometimes prospering, but your tree—our tree—it will keep growing.

When I struck the clear plastic container holding our braided locks of hair, I pulled it slowly from the earth. I saw the new note—the note from Jack—immediately. It had been placed inside the plastic container after we had buried it. It was clear that he had dug it up and placed a note for me inside. He had used our own secret mailbox to leave me a message I would find if not today, then tomorrow, then a thousand tomorrows later. No one else in the world would know to look for it. And the Esche, the honorable Esche, had stood guard over it until I could come for it—had stood next to it in the winter, through the long, gray days of autumn and bursting fruits of spring. Hadley and Hemingway had been here, as we had been, and it did not surprise me to see his careful handwriting.

Heather, the writing said.

A plain business envelope enclosed whatever note he had written. A little dirt had soiled the bottom-right corner. For a moment I couldn't touch it, couldn't breathe, couldn't do anything.

In that instant I knew he had not forgotten me, not forsaken me. He would not have written a note, not bothered to return to the mighty, mighty Esche if he had not cared. I knew he had thought of me kneeling in the same place that I now knelt. I knew that he understood I would search for him, that I would come looking until I found him at last. I felt an enormous torrent of love and hate and every emotion under the sky. I lifted the absurd plastic container and kissed it. I removed the letter carefully and then closed the plastic box again and buried it once more. I thought of Mr. Periwinkle and of all those creatures that try to go on bravely. I knew about Jack now. I knew he had left me for all the reasons Raef had explained.

And I also knew he was dying.

"Drove past here twice and wasn't going to come back," Bormo said, "but I had a feeling something was going on."

I opened the door and climbed in.

"Thank you. Thank you very much."

"You got dirty."

I nodded.

He regarded me in the rearview mirror.

Then he shook his head, apparently unable to figure it out.

"Back to the hotel?" he asked.

I nodded.

"You're not going to tell me, are you?" he asked.

I shook my head.

"Love," he said. "That's the only thing makes people act that crazy."

I smiled. He smiled back. Then he drove off, and my heart felt empty and frightened. I held the letter against my chest. I could not open it. Not yet. Not until I could breathe again.

51

Amy called me before we made it back.

"Where the hell are you, Heather? I woke up and you weren't here."

"I'm okay, Amy."

"That is just not fucking cool! To leave without saying anything—"

"I'm sorry. I really am. I apologize."

"I thought . . . I don't know what I thought. That is so, so, so not cool, Heather. It rings some bells for me when people disappear like that. You're not with Xavier, are you?"

"I apologize. No, I'm not with Xavier. I wouldn't have left if it hadn't been important."

"What was so goddamn important that you had to leave the hotel in the middle of the night? We have to be on a plane at noon, Heather. Have you left the hotel? Are you in someone's room?"

"I had to go look at something. Something Jack related," I said.

Amy didn't say anything for a moment.

"Where are you?" she said eventually.

"On my way back."

"I'll wait up."

"Thank you, Amy. And I'm sorry."

"So am I. Hurry."

Dawn light pushed from behind low-hanging clouds by the time I arrived back at the hotel. Bormo swung the cab into the porte cochere, and a doorman stepped forward to handle my door.

"Thank you, Bormo," I said, paying him.

He would not accept a tip.

"The fee, that's business. But the tip, that's between us."

"Thank you."

"Hope it was worth it."

"I hope so, too."

He flipped down the meter and drove off.

I went in and found Amy sitting in the lobby.

She stood when she saw me and crossed the lobby floor and hugged me hard. Then she pushed me away, examined me, and hugged me again. I couldn't raise my arms. I couldn't dare lose sight of Jack's note. I put my forehead against Amy's shoulder and wept. She pushed me away, looked again at my face, then hugged me as hard as I had ever been hugged in my life. For the life of me, I could not stop weeping.

"That's the letter?" Amy asked. "He left that in your secret place? The tree that you two planted?"

"He knew I would come to look for it someday. Only I would ever know where to find it."

I sat hunched forward from the waist. I still had trouble breathing; I had almost begun to wonder if I would ever catch my breath again. Amy kept her arm around me. The long, slow shudders that come after a cry trembled up and down my body.

"Raef should have told you before. I'm super angry at him right now."

"He had given his word to Jack. You should like that Constance married a man who keeps his word. I don't blame Raef. He was in an impossible situation."

"Then why tell you now?"

"I think he thought I was in too much pain."

We sat in a small love seat in the corner of the hotel lobby. A forest of potted ferns hid us from direct observation. Across the lobby, two sleepy kids worked at getting a tray of pastries displayed for the coffee shop. Now and then an older woman, apparently in charge, swung by to speak to them and to push them to hurry up. The smell of coffee filled the lobby.

"So you think he's sick?" Amy asked. "Is that it?"

"I think he's dying. I know he is. Jack is dying."

"Oh, come on," she said, and she reached across to grab my hand. "You don't know that."

"He was sick. Raef told me. He has leukemia. He went to a hospital with Raef to check on a condition. Don't you see? He came with me to the airport because he wanted me to know that he had made a choice to go with me. But he couldn't. He couldn't cross that line. It wasn't about New York or jobs or anything like that. He just let me think that."

"And that's why he didn't come with you?"

I nodded.

"Yes," I said. "That would be the way Jack would handle things."

"That's a bunch of bullshit, though. Why wouldn't he tell you what was going on?"

"Because that's not how Jack lives. He wouldn't want my life to be diminished by his."

"It wouldn't be diminished."

"He wouldn't see it that way, Amy. What would he do? How would it go? Was I going to be his nurse? Is that the life he wanted me to have? Think about it. Would you want that for someone you loved? If we had been married for twenty years, okay, then that's part of it. But we had just met. We were just finding out about each other. He didn't want to be a patient."

She weighed that. Despite Amy's sometimes wildness, she saw the world as an orderly place, and this did not fit into that mold.

"And that's why you loved him," Amy said. "That's part of who he is. That's who Jack is."

"Yes."

"The world is just too damn complicated for me," she said. "Do you want some privacy while you read the letter?"

I nodded.

She squeezed my hand and then leaned over the table to kiss me.

"I'll grab us some coffees if it's ready," she said, leaving. "Remember to breathe."

I nodded again.

I put the letter on my lap and stared at it. It took me a long minute or two to force my hands to touch it.

52

....

I slid the letter out of the envelope carefully. I separated the two pieces of paper—the envelope like a pursing bird mouth—and placed them side by side. I wanted to absorb every detail. The two young people arranging the pastry display paid no attention to me. I smelled coffee still brewing and the faint odor of cleanser. Far away, a clock chimed. I didn't count the chimes.

I looked inside the envelope to make sure nothing remained inside it. It was empty. I bowed it open farther so that I could be sure, then turned the envelope upside down over the table. I shook it several times. Satisfied, I placed it carefully back in its position.

Then I unfolded the letter and read:

Dear Heather,

I am writing this after leaving the airport. I'm sorry. I know I caused you pain, and I grieve about that. If your pain matches mine at this moment, then I am doubly sorry.

I couldn't follow you to New York, because I am not completely

*my own to give. I'm sick, Heather, and I'm not going to get
well. I can't—I won't—shift that onto you, onto us. Believe me
when I say I am not being melodramatic. I am being as hard-
headed as I know how to be. Call it what you will—fate, a roll
of the dice, a bad card. It came up against us this time. Our luck
didn't hold.*

*But it was pretty to think so for a time, wasn't it? It was
for me.*

*You made my days rich, Heather. I loved you from the bottom
of everything. Love finds us, passes through us, continues.*

J.

I read the letter three times, ten times, read it until my hand
shook so hard I could no longer hold the paper steady. I placed it
back on the table and held my breath. I looked up through the
deep blue of the pool water and tried to empty myself. I held my
breath for a long time.

Then I went to Amy.

"Will you do me a favor? Will you run up to our room and
bring me down my book bag? You know the one."

"Sure, honey. Can you tell me what the letter said?"

"Bring me the bag, please, and then I'll know. I'd go myself
but I don't trust my legs right now. The bag. It's on the table."

She nodded, touched my hand, then left. She returned in no
time to our tiny island behind the ferns. She put the bag in front
of me. I slid out Jack's grandfather's journal.

"You have it here with you?" Amy asked.

"I carry it everywhere. I carry it to work sometimes. When I
have it I can almost believe I will run into Jack."

"Oh, you poor lamb. You've got it bad. So bad."

I pulled out the journal. It had a familiar, kindly feeling in my hand. I knew the passage. I opened to the beginning of the journal and found it almost immediately.

In the square they danced with cowbells draped around their necks. The sound was riotous and unendurable. I saw a woman and man dancing together, and they danced with something akin to fury. The man stood tall and angular, and something had happened to his face to remove a divot from his forehead. He wore the half mask of a wolf. The woman danced with her skirt trailing out like the blade of a mower, and she spun and spun, her beauty heightened by the way she appeared as a wick in the center of her own candle. I watched them a long time. Evening came on, and they continued to dance, their movement absorbed and sent back by their compatriots and fellow townsmen, and for the first time since the war ended, I felt my heart lift. Yes, they danced to send winter back into the mountains, but they also danced because winter always ends, wars end, and life is victorious each and every time. Watching them, I learned that love is not static; love does not divide. What love we find in this world is coming toward us and traveling away from us simultaneously. To say we find love is a misuse of the word find. Love finds us, passes through us, continues. We cannot find it any more than we can find air or water; we cannot live without either thing any more than we can live without love. Love is essential and as common as bread. If you look for it, you will see it everywhere, and you will never be without it.

"I know where he has to be. It's spring, and he'll be there. It's here in the journal. I know where he has to end up. The journal begins at a place in spring. That's how his trip will end. It just makes sense."

"You're starting to spook me now, Heather."

"Look at the date on the entry. It's now. It's two days away. And the phrase he quotes in the letter—it's from the journal. *Love finds us, passes through us, continues.* Do you see? It's right here."

"But that doesn't mean he is following the journal exactly, does it? Sorry, Heather. I'm trying to go with you here, but it's just a line from a journal."

"It's the last entry. It's where the journal begins. It's a festival. He'll be there. I know he will. He told me about this place. He said the night before the Nazis invaded, the entire town went out and danced. They danced in the face of death. That's why he'll be there. He wouldn't miss it. He wants to dance in the face of death. *That's* Jack."

I stood.

"I'm going to pack now," I said. "I'm going to go to him."

"Heather, hold on. This is crazy. You can't know that he's there. And you can't know even if he was going that he's going to be there this week, or in a few days, can you? Come on, think. Are you sure? Are you sure you know where he is?"

"You're right, of course. I know that. I know I'm being irrational, but I can't let it go, Amy. Don't you see? I've tried to let it go, but I have to see him. He has to be there eventually. He will be there. It's spring, and he has to follow the journal to the end."

"What about your job?"

"Fuck my job."

"You're not saying that. You're not thinking clearly."

"Maybe not. And maybe I am thinking clearly for the first time. I should never have let him go."

"You didn't have a choice."

"I am going to stay until I find him. I don't care anymore. I can't live this way. I have to see him again. One way or the other, I have to know I wasn't crazy to believe in what we had."

Amy took a breath. I saw her weigh things again in her mind. I saw the old Amy, the wild Amy, return and take possession of her soul. Her eyes became bright, and she grabbed my forearm and squeezed it.

"You go to him," she said, her voice irresistible. "You go and find him, and you don't stop until you have what you need. Do you hear me? You'll regret it all your life if you don't find him and know, once and for all, what happened to him. He's your great love."

"He's sick. And he went away to let me be free."

Amy squeezed my forearm harder.

"I believe you," she said. "Either that, or you're having a nervous breakdown."

I hugged her. I hugged her hard. I laughed, but it was a short, abrupt laugh more like a cough than anything else.

"I can't live halfway. I can't go forward until I understand what happened. I can't."

"And if you have it wrong?"

"Then I'm love's fool. That's not such a bad thing to be, is it? To be a fool for love?"

She let me go. She nodded. I nodded back at her. Then I ran upstairs to pack.

Batak

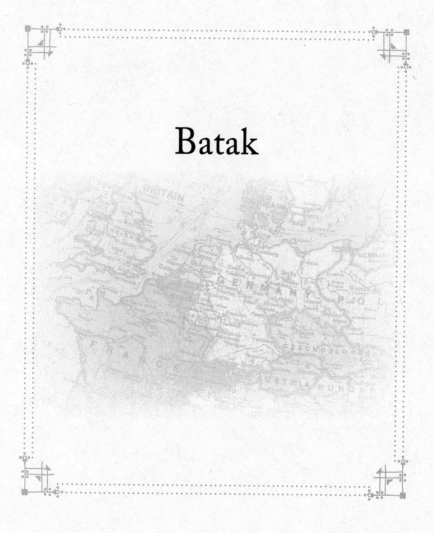

53

....

Batak, Bulgaria, April 1946

The man tilted the bottle back into his mouth and squinted. He staggered from his drunkenness; now he had collected a crowd around him with the promise to empty the bottle of "savage gin." The gin, I knew, was anything but gin. It was a combination of rubbing alcohol and barley. Clearly the man no longer cared. Several onlookers rushed forward to pull his arm down, but he fought them off, pushing them away and dodging until he could get his lips around the bottle's neck again. I would not have noticed his tears if the last light hadn't caught him in profile. He was an ugly man, made uglier by the bestial face trapped to the bottle that fed him, his jacket torn, his pants bare at the knees. He appeared desperate to have the liquor inside him, desperate to forget, and each nod of his Adam's apple declared a victory of suicide. At last he tossed the bottle to one side and held out his arms, ta-da, and no sooner had he made a small bow to the crowd, he collapsed in a pile on the ground. Even in war I had never seen a man go down so heavily. He collapsed in a pile, as if a force above him had driven him into the ground, and I turned away so I would not watch him vomit. But he did not vomit; he rolled on the ground, seizing his stomach, and one of his friends got him onto his knees and pounded on his back until the man finally disgorged a clear arc of liquid. The crowd cheered, and the drunken man sank onto the earth once more and looked up into the evening light. His tears had left a trail down his dirty face, and his mouth, glimmering with vomit and drink, glowed in the last light. The two marks of moisture connecting at his lips looked like an hourglass.

The taxi driver—a large man with an enormous mustache and a barely disguised delight in the opportunity to practice his English on a young American woman—drove me to the Hotel Orford in Batak, Bulgaria, the beginning point of Jack's grandfather's journal. During the drive, he told me he doubted the Hotel Orford would have accommodations.

"Too many dancers. It is the Surva Festival. Everyone, from all the region, they come to the dancing. They wear masks. You know this reputation? This town? The people hear Nazis coming, they look up at the mountain, and they dance. Crazy peoples, they dance in the face of death. It is very photo worthy."

"What do you recommend?" I asked. "Where could I stay?"

"Hard to say—depends. What are you looking for?"

"I'm not sure. Just a room of any sort."

"Sometimes families . . . you understand, families? Sometimes they rent rooms for rent. They post them on a board—paper on a board."

"Bulletin boards?"

He nodded emphatically.

"Yes, messages."

"When does the dancing begin?"

"It's already begun. Everyone dance. They dance for three days. Some people, they rent out their cars to sleep. It is still cold at night. We have snow up in the mountains."

I surveyed everything as we entered the town. The village wasn't big, I knew. The population was only about four thousand people, maybe fewer, but the town had obviously swollen to accommodate the festivalgoers. The streetlamps and buildings and stairways wore festoons of pine and spring flowers, and now and then I spotted what had to be a dancer carrying an outsized papier-mâché head, usually painted in bright, outlandish colors. The masks invariably wore terrifying faces; they reminded me of Mardi Gras masks, only more primitive and more connected, somehow, to the deep forests surrounding the town.

"Is it going to snow?" I asked, wondering, halfheartedly, if I could sleep out. "Do you know the weather report?"

He buzzed his lips in reply. Who knows? He didn't know, certainly.

As we drove a little deeper into the town, I began to feel triumphant. I was a madwoman; it was that simple. I had no idea if Jack was in fact here. Even if he was, I reflected, I couldn't be certain of finding him. He might come for a day, then leave before I ever saw him. But I had done the first truly impulsive thing in my entire life. I hadn't weighed it out, determined the proper course of action, made careful calculations. For once in my life, I had acted on my gut, taken a flyer, followed my heart. Jack had taught me that; Jack had made such freedom possible. Whatever else he had meant or been to me, he had unlocked something inside me that had been rusted and clotted with disuse. He had given me hope and taught me to trust that life held surprises if you allowed it to reveal itself. You did not clutter it with camera shots and Facebook postings. You gave yourself to the situation. That was Jack's great lesson.

The driver, meanwhile, cruised slowly past the village square. Police had lined off a large area with yellow tape. Dancers had already begun to collect. Many wore large strings of cowbells around their necks, and the noise increased the deeper we penetrated the square.

"I can get out here," I told the driver. "This is probably as good as anyplace, isn't it?"

"Yes, good, yes," he said, navigating the foot traffic that swirled everywhere.

"Those are the dancers?"

"Everyone is a dancer in Batak. It is everyone's job to end the winter and promise a good spring."

"Yes," I said, watching everything. "Yes, of course it is."

The noise of the bells increased the moment I stepped out of the car. Dancers arriving in the square jumped up and down, or moved in spins to get their bells to ring. Most of the dancers were young, but not all. A light snow had begun to fall. I glanced up at the sky. It didn't appear to threaten a true storm; the snow seemed to fall with reluctance, drifting down in the gray atmosphere. The surrounding buildings had already turned on their lights against the early evening.

I stood for a long time as the cab pulled away. I didn't move.

I watched the dancers congregate—large masks of fanged lions, dragons, terrifying canine faces and wild, engorged children—and

I wondered if I had not entered a nightmare. But the expressions on the festivalgoers' faces saved me: they were lighthearted and happy, and it was clear that this was a cultural event that carried with it a great deal of merrymaking. Jack's grandfather had come here after the war, and I could imagine the pleasure he had taken in the celebration, in the village's determination to drive back the darker human forces. And the *crazy peoples,* as the driver said, had in fact danced in the face of death. I had read about that. The night before the Germans invaded and took over the town, the villagers could think to do nothing more forceful but to dance. I knew that from Jack's grandfather's journal.

For what felt a long time, I didn't move. I waited—I hoped— for the music to infect me. I wanted its primitive pull to take me over, but I could not give in to it yet. I envied the dancers. They seemed to let everything go, to join with the music, to swirl their cowbells at the dark mountains. I had never learned to let go in that way. Jack had been teaching me to do it, but I hadn't been able to take the final step.

That's what I thought standing in the town common in Batak, Bulgaria.

Then, as quickly, I realized that I was cold.

54

It is not much," Mr. Roo said.

I didn't know if I had heard his name correctly. Mr. Roo? Mr. Kangaroo? Surely, I thought, the name meant something more. I had heard it indistinctly when he had introduced himself. Now I followed him down a long hallway that smelled of cabbage and snow and cat. It seemed to be an apartment house of some sort, but even that was hard to determine. Outside, the noise of the cowbells filled everything with cacophonous sound. Mr. Roo—a man with an enormous stomach plow and deep, sympathetic eyebrows—turned back to me and tried unsuccessfully to talk over the noise. He held up his finger to tell me to wait.

Mr. Roo wore a blue work shirt and a black boiled wool vest tucked into his pants. He struck me as the Eastern European character actor who holds a lantern at the inn and warns against going in the mountains toward Dracula's castle. But he seemed pleased to have me as a guest, and as he led me down a second hallway, this one more removed from the clamor of the bells, he explained the building's history.

"In another day, a military barracks. A dormitory. You understand? Small rooms. Just cot beds. You understand?"

"I understand."

"We charge a lot for such rooms, more than is should, but we cannot help it."

"It's festival," I said, agreeing.

I thought of Hemingway attending the bullfights in Pamplona, drinking from sunrise to sunset, drifting from bar to bar, but this festival had a different feeling. It took place in the mountains, in what the guidebooks called the great karst areas with deep river gorges, large caves, and carved sculptured rock formations where the spirits of winter hid until the spring dancers frightened them back to their frozen lands. Hemingway celebrated death in life; the Surva Festival asked for life in death. It made a difference, somehow, but I could not yet determine what that might be.

Mr. Roo opened the door to my room.

"Simple," he said, holding open the door.

Primitive might have been a more accurate word, but the room suited me. He had not misled me: it was an eight-by-ten box with a gray painted floor, a cot with a wool blanket tucked over it, a single pillow, and a yellow table and chair pushed against the far wall. It had no heat that I could detect. A fair-sized window looked out onto a courtyard. I liked the look of the window: it let in the gray afternoon light, and I watched the snow drift like moths into the air below me.

"Good?" Mr. Roo asked me.

"Fine," I said.

A look of relief spread over his face. It occurred to me that perhaps he had been slightly embarrassed to show a foreigner the humble accommodations he offered. Now with that settled, he turned on the overhead light and showed me how to put a coin into a small heater on the wall. The heater resembled a Cupid face, with an innocent pouting mouth that spewed heat once the coin had been digested. Mr. Roo stood with his hands out to the heater as if he had just ignited a magnificent campfire. I decided that I liked Mr. Roo, and if he told me not to take the carriage to Dracula's castle, I would heed his warning.

"Better?" he asked as I swung my backpack down onto the yellow table.

"Better," I said.

"Do you know the mountain history?"

I shook my head.

"Rhodopa and Hemus—very famous. They were brother and sister. Then they began to desire one another. Very wrong. Because they were beautiful, they called each other by god names. Zeus and Hera. You understand?"

"I do," I said.

"Day come, and the real Zeus and Hera, they become disenchanted with Rhodopa and Hemus, say it was wrong to use the god names. So, poof, the real Zeus and Hera, they turn the young brother and sister into mountains. That is Bulgaria."

"Jealous gods," I said.

The room had become warm in just the time it took Mr. Roo to tell the story. It made me sleepy. Mr. Roo smiled.

"I leave you now. We serve soup at seven o'clock. Good soup. You sleep now. I can see you need to."

"Yes," I said. "I guess I'm tired from traveling."

"Of course you are. When you travel, your soul . . . how is it? It is up in the air."

"And when you are home?"

"We believe here that your soul is divided and that half it lives in your native soil!" Mr. Roo said, laughing. "When you are in your own country, your feet can find the soul beneath, and it is whole. But when you travel, you are a half soul. You believe such things?"

"I believe everything," I said, feeling that I needed to lie down or faint.

Mr. Roo bowed, nodded, and went out. I closed the door behind him after agreeing, again, that I might come down for soup. The room felt warm and smelled faintly of a gaseous discharge that came from the Cupid face heater. I wondered, absently, if the heater could kill me with carbon monoxide if it didn't function properly. I imagined it could.

I went to the cot and stretched out on it. I wanted to cry, but I was too stunned, too out of my element, to permit even that slight weakness. If I gave in to that, I realized, I might run up into the hills to conspire with the winter spirits. I might live in the karsts and grow moss in my hair and live among savage stone and quivering pines. I reflected, as I fell toward sleep, that the dancers did not dance to chase the spirits away but danced instead to mock them for what they could not have.

I woke in the last light of day, and I did not know where I was. I was cold; I knew that much. I shivered and pulled the wool blanket around me, then remembered that Mr. Roo showed me how to use the heater. I stood with the blanket still draped over me and dug in my backpack until I found a few coins. The currency was strange to me, so for a moment or two I bent over to inspect them. I imagined, as I did so, how I would appear to anyone watching: a strange, hair-tousled woman wrapped in an olive military blanket, standing in the last light of day going through her coins. It was not an inspiring image.

It took me three coins to get the Cupid heater blowing air at me. I held my hands out to the tiny mouth, just as Mr. Roo had done. Then I crawled back into bed.

For a long time, I commanded myself to do nothing, think nothing, until I was at least marginally warm. That seemed like a good way to approach things: take one small thing at a time and accomplish it. First, make myself warm. Second, maybe, go eat soup. Third, figure out what insane impulses had led me to flying to Batak on such an absurd whim. To do the last thing required serious introspection, so I put that aside and concentrated on soup.

What kind of soup? I wondered. Beet soup, probably. Something made of root vegetables and onions and dark, smothering water. No, not smothering water, but mountain water, water that drained from the winter spirits' baths, water that flowed like roots down from the karsts to the village square. That was the kind of soup Mr. Roo would serve.

Thinking of soup satisfied me for a time. The heat gradually took over the room. I tried to guess what time it could be. My phone lay on the desk across the room, and that seemed an insurmountable distance. But I forced myself to climb out of bed and grab it. I fell back in bed, this time letting out a small *oomph* as I gave in to gravity.

It was 6:37. Approximately twenty minutes to soup.

I dialed Amy's number on my phone but canceled the call before it went through. I sent her a text instead and said I had arrived safely, I was okay, all was well. I told her the place was astonishing, *smiley face, smiley face, smiley face.*

55

Potato-leek soup.

Mr. Roo and a nameless woman—she wore a blue *putzfrau* dress like the ones the washing women wore in Berlin and Vienna and Kraków—ladled out bowls of potato-leek soup for the clientele in his sparsely populated dining room. To call it a dining room, however, was being generous. It was a large gray room with refectory tables. Its only saving grace was a ponderous woodstove that burned in the corner of the room. It was the kind of woodstove with open doors, so that it doubled as a fireplace, and the light from the burn filled the room with golden flickers.

I took my bowl of soup from the nameless woman—Mr. Roo's wife, his sister, his *mother?*—and carried it to an open chair beside the woodstove. Mr. Roo passed around the room with a plate of black bread. I took a piece, and I could not help being reminded of communion. The soup was too hot to eat. I held it in my lap and let it soak me with heat.

"Warm?" Mr. Roo asked on his second round in an attempt, I imagined, to make me comfortable.

"Warm," I said, although whether he meant the heater upstairs or my spot in front of the woodstove I couldn't tell.

Eventually, the soup cooled, and I ate it. I was hungry, and the soup was quite good. It tasted of onions and summer lawns. Mr. Roo gave me a second piece of bread. I ate that, too. In some ways, it was easier to eat than to think. Thinking meant I had to decide on a course of action. My inclination was to climb back up to my Spartan room and sleep the night away. I felt exhausted and confused. My plan to come to find Jack in Bulgaria now seemed so impulsive, so demonstrably ridiculous, that I wondered how Amy hadn't thrown me down on the ground and tied me up to prevent me from leaving Paris. But she had accepted my assurances—*Honest, Amy, he has to be there, that's where the journal begins, I swear it makes sense if you know Jack, if you've read his grandfather's work*—and I had been so intent on persuading her that I had persuaded myself.

"Are you going to watch them burn the old man?" Mr. Roo asked when he began clearing plates. The other diners had wandered off. I sat alone in front of the fire.

"Burn the old man?" I asked, not understanding.

"Old Man Winter. They carry him to the square and burn him. Then spring can come down out of the mountains."

That will be warm, I thought. My world had suddenly become binary: warm or not warm.

"Is there a way to find someone in the festival? To leave a message for someone?" I asked.

Mr. Roo leaned his rear end on one of the tables and looked at me.

"You okay?" he asked.

I shrugged. I needed to shrug or cry.

"I need to find someone here," I said when I had my emotions under control.

"A lost boy?"

Yes, I thought, smiling at the mention of lost boys, the wild boy-men of Peter Pan. "A lost boy."

Mr. Roo gave it some thought, but when he pushed himself off the table he merely smiled and reached for my bowl.

"It's chaos," he said, "the festival, so you can never know what you will find. Or what will find you. But sometimes the gods remember us. Go out and look. What do you have to lose?"

Old Man Winter had a tough ride.

I watched him coming—held up by a winding procession that spanned two city blocks or so—on a decrepit dining chair carried aloft by a team of large men. Old Man Winter was a scarecrow, but a well-crafted one, with a wry smile somehow inked across his face. He looked to be at least as tall as a normal man, and he wore a suit coat with a boutonniere sticking out from his lapel. The men transporting him wore formal top hats and had their faces painted white. I had no idea what symbolic importance the top hats or white faces played, but I was willing to go along.

I *wanted* to go along.

I wanted to feel myself swept up and carried along, much as Old Man Winter was carried, to some burning conclusion that would cauterize the memory of Jack from my brain once and for all. The cowbells rang with wild energy, and their sounds reverberated against the old walls of the city, and for a while they chased even the simplest thought from my head. I stood on an avenue, squeezed back into a shop door, watching the procession dance by, the hilarity and drunkenness—I smelled a vaporous tinge of alcohol, like a great wave of corn and wheat as the crowd surged and danced—exploding in small clusters as the revelers passed. When the last of the procession had tailed out into the common, I fell in behind, determined to watch the Old Man meet his fate.

That's where things stood when I saw Jack.

Where I *thought* I saw Jack. Where Jack floated out of the crowd for an eyeblink, then disappeared again.

It felt like a punch to the gut. It felt like someone had taken a sharp, delicate file and tapped it with the palm of his hand into the meaty furrow between my brows. I couldn't move. Someone jostled me and said excuse me. I assumed he said excuse me, because I couldn't understand him. I turned and nodded. Then I returned my eyes to the patch of people where Jack had been an instant before.

Where Jack Vermont, my Jack, had been dancing in celebration, his arms raised, a beautiful woman beside him.

A gorgeous woman beside him.

But was it Jack? Had it been? I couldn't say with certainty. On one pulse I felt absolutely positive that Jack had appeared like a specter dancing with his arms upraised, in his barn jacket, the same barn jacket he always wore. In the next instant the rational part of my brain dismissed the vision as wish fulfillment. As delusion. As the product of exhaustion and a heightened emotional state.

And was he with another woman? Is that what I had seen?

Had I seen anything at all?

Stop, I thought. Make everyone stop for a moment. I needed everyone to stop as if I had dropped a contact lens on the ground. Keep your position. Then I would pass among them, the world's largest duck, duck, goose game, and tap one after another and ask them to leave. One by one, I would whittle them away until whatever remained, whoever remained, would be Jack, or Jack's doppelgänger, or a man who resembled Jack so closely that it defied rational explanation.

I hurried forward. Something in the village common roused the people into a cheer, and by the time I reached the assembly, Old Man Winter had already been ignited. He burned at the top of a large bonfire, his scarecrow body turning into a wick inside a piercing yellow flame. The crowd yelled and danced, and the cowbells, the perpetual, insistent cowbells, rang like a hellish chorus jibing at the Old Man's suffering. Everywhere I looked, the masks changed form by catching the light from a new angle. I could no longer determine what I felt: a wild appeal to a primitive self, fear, joy, anger. Maybe that was the point, I realized, as I circled the crowd, turning this way and that to make my way between the crazed dancers. Maybe the winter that counted, the one that needed to be burned most of all, lived inside us.

I searched for an hour. Two hours. I searched until the Old Man and his throne of fire had burned down to a smoldering heap of ash and charred tree trunks. I searched until the local constabulary came and backed us away while the fire department hosed down the last of the fire. Then I watched as a backhoe scooped up the remaining ash and waste and dumped it into the bed of a blue truck.

The Old Man was gone. Jack was gone. I walked back to my room, to Mr. Roo, to the Cupid heater with the pursed lips and the breath of hot air. My lost boy was still lost.

.   .   .

I couldn't sleep.

I couldn't come close to sleeping. I fed the Cupid heater coins and stayed on my cot, trying my best to come up with a plan. To come up with anything. Mostly I argued for or against the proposition that I had seen Jack. One second I thought, *It had to be Jack.* I knew Jack's shape, his build, his walk, down in my bones. As soon as I grew comfortable with that assertion, doubt crept in on thorny little mouse feet, nose twitching, ears flexing, whiskers rising up and down.

It was not Jack, the mouse told me in those moments. *Girl, you really need to get over this guy.*

And if it *was* Jack, and Jack had been dancing in that crowd, was it possible his new girlfriend was beside him? Was he hooking up with someone new just as he had hooked up with me? Was this his pattern? A romantic sociopath? A serial sexual predator?

No, no sleep for me.

No clear thinking, either.

Then the room suddenly began to shrink. I knew it was all in my head, but I couldn't quite deny the evidence of my senses. I stood and did some stretching. I did at least a quarter hour of yoga. Afterward, I got out my iPad and checked for Wi-Fi. Nothing. The room continued to shrink. Finally, I grabbed my jacket and went outside. It was cold and bitter and dark. If the villagers were sending Old Man Winter back up to the mountains, or at least murdering him, they weren't doing a good job of it. The entire town smelled of charred bonfire remnants.

I had no idea if I was safe wandering around town by myself. Now and then, a couple or a group of revelers passed me. I always nodded. I told myself to turn around, to go back to the Cupid heater and try to sleep. I also told myself that I needed to call the airport as early as I could the next day and book a flight out of Bulgaria. I even considered calling my parents, maybe my mom, just to reassure them that I had not gone completely mad. But then I realized needing to reassure my parents I wasn't crackers sounded like a bad piece of reasoning. If you have to tell someone you're not crackers, you probably are.

I walked for another half hour before coming on *the couple*.

That's what I would call them ever afterward. They wore wolf masks, only their mouths and lips exposed, and beautiful clothing. The man wore an ancient cutaway, the kind of jacket George Washington wore, with knee-length pants—plus fours—and a blond wig of some sort over his scalp. The woman dressed in the style of Marie Antoinette, with a full gown of brocaded material, and she wore a gray wig on top of her head and a narrower, more vulpine mask extending upward from the bridge of her nose. Their appearance made no sense whatsoever. Initially, I could hardly credit my eyesight. What did costumes out of the 1700s have to do with the festival? But before I could advance toward them— they stood near a working fountain, the water splashing up in a white arc of light—I heard their music. The male wolf—that's how I came to think of him—put on a vinyl record on a tiny turntable and stood back to make sure it ran properly. When the music came on fully—it was a waltz of some sort—he turned and bowed toward the female wolf. She curtseyed and moved into his arms.

Then they danced.

They danced quietly, expertly, and as they moved, the spray from the fountain sometimes seemed to leap and ask to be ice. They danced on cobblestones, and I was the only witness. I couldn't say for certain, but I believed they danced only for one another. They did nothing theatrical besides their outlandish costumes. They did not turn to look at me or engage me in any way. They merely continued to move and spin, the vinyl record spotty with pops and clicks, the fountain water providing a glimmer to their movements. I watched and felt my eyes filling. I yearned to see it as a sign, as a token that I would find Jack, but a part of me didn't even care for that hope. No, it was enough to see them dance, to believe they were sufficiently in love to bring a portable turntable onto a plaza in the small hours of the morning in order to waltz with one another.

I watched them another minute or two, then backed away as silently as I could. In the muted light of the fountain, I saw them spin and revolve together, a wolves' dance on a cold spring night.

56

The next morning, I ate breakfast in Mr. Roo's dining room. He made good oatmeal. He served it with cinnamon and a thick piece of black bread from the night before.

I told him the story of seeing Jack for an instant. Of thinking I had seen Jack, anyway. In no time, it became an idée fixe with him that I must find my lost boy, as he called him. But he had no solid plan to offer. He kept saying destiny would have a hand. He liked the word *destiny* and said it often. He said when we stop looking for something, it usually shows up. Then he asked how I liked the oatmeal. I said it hit the spot.

My phone rang before I finished my oatmeal. It was Amy. I excused myself and walked away to an empty table to talk with her in privacy.

"Are you okay?" she asked as soon as we connected. "Tell me you're okay."

"I think I saw Jack last night."

"What do you mean, you think you saw him?"

"It was crowded, and he was only there for a second. I couldn't get to him fast enough. And he was with another woman, I think."

Amy drew in her breath. She didn't say anything for a moment. Then she spoke.

"You'll find him, Heather," she said.

"I will."

"I know you will."

"I will."

"But if it becomes torturous, don't feel you have to stay. You are captain of your own ship, remember? You are the wild, new, freer Heather. The one who takes off and tells her employer to fuck himself."

"I'm not torturing myself. And I did not tell Bank of America to fuck itself. I give the company good value. I'm a good employee."

She didn't say anything for a second.

"Is the festival fun?" she asked.

"Yes, it is. In a strange way, it's very fun. I'm having a wonderful time. I've never been to anything like it."

"I'm worried about you. I'm also more inspired than you might know. You're doing one of the bravest things I've ever heard about."

"I'm all right, Amy. I'm strong enough for this. I am. Maybe it wasn't even him that I saw. It's hard to say. People were dancing, and the light wasn't good. Maybe I imagined him. Maybe I conjured him into existence just because."

"Was there really a woman near him?"

"Maybe. If I saw him at all, then yes, yes, there was. I'm okay, Amy. Honestly. I feel stronger, in fact. I feel like he is here," I said, understanding it to be an honest statement even as I spoke it. "And it's not just about him, Amy. You know that. It's about what we had. If what Jack and I had wasn't real, didn't mean as much to him as it did to me, then I need to know. I need to know life can fool you that profoundly. If it does, then okay, I'll keep going, but I'll have a different feeling about it all. It will hurt, but it will be a lesson learned."

"It will make you cynical. I'm worried it will make you give up on things."

"Maybe it will. Maybe it's part of growing up. Sometimes growing up seems like a simple process of casting things off. What do I know?"

"Stay as long as you need to. Don't do it halfway."

"I won't, I promise. Honestly, the old Heather might have done it halfway. Not now. I've changed. But the festival isn't enormous. If he's around here, I would probably run into him eventually."

Amy blew out air in a hopeful release. I tried to imagine what time it was there, but my brain couldn't handle the calculations.

"When do you go to Japan?" she asked.

"Next week."

"Okay," she said. "That's good. Go to Japan and get a new haircut or something. Buy a samurai sword. Shake it up. Good luck today."

"Mr. Roo says it's all about destiny."

"Mr. Roo? Who is Mr. Roo? That can't be his name."

"It is today," I said, and I disconnected.

I walked. And I looked.

Gradually, I learned the form of the festival. Dancing went on at all times. In fact, it was the job of the festivalgoers to keep the dancing continuous so that winter would not have a chance to take root again. Several people told me this. The sound of cowbells permeated everything. It dug so deeply into my consciousness that it disappeared eventually like the noise of a clock ticking or a railway car going by. *Bells, dancing, Batak. Surva Festival.*

As I walked, I wondered what in the name of God's last word I was doing in Batak, Bulgaria. I tried to imagine what I must look like to the passersby. Here was a young woman, reasonably attractive, dressed well, who seemed to wander aimlessly throughout the day. She was obviously American, obviously a tourist, obviously out of her element. She lived now in a single room, sleeping on a nunnish cot, while a white Cupid-faced heater blew hot breath over her to keep her from freezing.

It was absurd.

I was absurd.

Olly, olly, oxen free, I whispered five times, a hundred times, a thousand times. It was the come-to-base call from childhood, the signal we used to say the game was over, come out now, stop hiding. Jack didn't hear me. Jack did not come in or stop hiding.

I ate a late lunch at a café off the common. I ordered more soup. Vegetable. The waiter brought it to me and asked if I wanted wine. I said no. I ordered a beer. I told him to bring me the darkest, heaviest, local-est beer he had in the restaurant. He smiled and nodded and hurried off. He was a short, runty man with enormous forearms. He put the beer on my table and nodded to indicate that he wanted to watch me drink it. I did. It tasted black and heavy, tasted of tree roots and dwarf toes, for all I knew, and I had never tasted anything better.

"Yes," I said. "Beautiful."

And that's when Jack walked by the window of the restaurant.

. . .

I jumped up and leaned over a window table—a couple eating lunch leaned back, terrified, or annoyed—at this body that suddenly hovered over them. "Excuse me, sorry, excuse me," I said in a rush. I tapped on the window. I tapped until I thought the window might break. But Jack didn't hear me. He didn't stop. His barn jacket disappeared in the crowds.

"Here," I said to the waiter, spidering back to my table. "Here, I'm paying. Here."

I threw money down on the table. The waiter began to dig through his pockets for change, but I didn't wait. I ran to the door and pushed outside.

I sprinted after Jack. I ran as hard as I had ever run. I knew he could disappear in an instant. He could duck in a store or decide to go into his hotel. Anything could happen. But at least he headed for the town common, where the dancers kept up their constant movement. Going in that direction, he likely would watch the celebrations. It was nearly evening, and the light and noise drew us all toward them.

I caught him half a block away from the town common. I recognized his back, his walk, the shape of his neck and shoulders. I wondered how I could not recognize him, his body was so familiar to me. I circled out and away, flanking him so that I could see his face if possible. I didn't want to run up to him and jerk his shoulder around, screaming into his face, *Hello, Jack. Remember me? Remember the girl in Paris?*

Maybe he was going to meet the other woman.

For a half a block, I walked on the other side of the road from him. It was easy to do. The crowds clogged the streets. He had no reason to look for me or to believe anyone observed him with special attention. The only reason he would turn to me was if I happened to be in the center of an explosion of noise. Otherwise, I blended in to the festivalgoers. I kept his pace. We arrived at the town common at the same time.

I stopped. So did he. We stood for a few minutes not moving. He kept his eyes on the dancers. I followed his eyeline to see if he sought anyone special.

How many times, I wondered, had I rehearsed this in my head? How many times had I been able to say this or that, just the correct phrase, that instantly cemented us together, made him understand the absolute error of his ways, of his entire thought process, so that he would crumple before me and beg me to take him back? My insides felt stirred and rattled, and I wondered if I could speak at all. I had never imagined this. I had never imagined how hard it would be to approach him. At the same time, I realized I still loved him. I loved every molecule of him, every glance, every fact of him.

I also saw that he was sick. He had thinned. His skin looked sallow.

Turn to me, I thought. *Turn now.*

And he did. As simple as that.

But his eyes passed over me. They did not see me. His eyes went back to the common and the dancers, and I held my breath, wondering how it had come to this. Was I going to let him go now? For the first time, it occurred to me—it truly, truly sank in—that I had an obligation, too. Maybe it was my duty to let him go. By approaching him, maybe I would infringe on his privacy, his right to leave the world on his own terms. He had a right to be left alone, and I felt foolish and selfish that I had never taken that into account at a level that I should have.

Destiny did play a part after all.

His height saved us. He looked again in my direction and, without fully meaning to, our eyes met. I watched the recognition bloom in his eyes. I made a vow, silently, that I would not advance toward him. I would not move a muscle. It was still within his power to walk away, and I understood, at last, that I would let him go if he did.

We looked at one another a long time. People danced around us, but they didn't make any difference.

He moved toward me. I didn't move. That was my promise to myself. I watched him coming closer, his face drawn now with illness, his body not nearly as solid as it had been. He had to stop several times to dodge around people, and then, miraculously, he stood in from of me. Jack Vermont. The man I loved beyond all hope or reason.

He lifted me and kissed me and held me. He spun me slowly, and I knew, I knew, that he had lost strength. I knew everything now, every word or thought, and I clung to him, kissed him over and over again. He kissed me, and he set me down slowly, and he kept kissing me, breaking away and kissing me again, as if kissing was thought, was breath, and what was the point of talking any longer? He was dying, and he had decided not to make me the steward of his dying. I couldn't blame him.

"I couldn't come with you," he said, his lips near my hair, near my ear. "I wanted to, but I couldn't. Forgive me."

I kissed him a dozen times. A thousand times. I nodded.

"I know. I know it all. I know about Tom."

"The leukemia is back," he said. "That's it in a nutshell. I had tests done before I met you, and the results came back in Paris. Not good. None of it is good."

"Who was the woman?"

He appeared puzzled for a second, then smiled.

"It was my aunt. She came to see what my grandfather had discovered in Batak. She left this morning."

I held him. I kissed him. He was dying. His body had already lost its thickness, its strength and force. Leukemia was taking him. He put his arm around my shoulders. The festival raged at its peak. Tomorrow, I knew, it would begin to wind down. Mr. Roo would shut down some of his rooms and go back to being a humbler innkeeper. The city would sweep up, and Old Man Winter would begin his life high up in the mountains, living his one summer before he grew to maturity and turned white with frost and ice.

We had hardly established the fact of each other's company when a group of dancers surrounded us and demanded we dance with them. You could not be in the common and fail to dance. That was the unspoken rule. The group grabbed us and forced us to spin, to dance, while their bells made a cacophonous racket. For an instant, just an instant, I felt the joy in my heart join with a thousand bells throughout the square. It made me dance harder, and I moved to Jack and put my arms around him, held him, told him I loved him in every part of my soul. He told me he loved me, too. He put his arms around me and kissed me. We danced apart from the world, our foreheads together, our breaths mingled, our bodies finding the charge from each to each. He told me that the people in Batak believed the souls of the dead could live in trees, and if that were true, he promised to live in the Esche, where I could find him when I needed him. He said he would be in Paris always, our Paris. We continued to dance, bracing ourselves against the fate that had offered us so much and removed it so easily, and we killed winter at last. We danced until I could not breathe, until whatever I was had somehow entered the alpine air, had pushed away the cold in my heart and kept my eyes on the mountains where spring waited, where hope started again each season.